THE PHOENIX EGG

By

RICHARD A. BAMBERG

Publisher's Note:
This is a work of fiction. Names, characters, places, and incidents are either the product of the author's imagination or are used fictitiously, and any resemblance to actual persons living or dead, events, mind control technologies, or locales is entirely coincidental.

ISBN: 1-931468-15-X

Cover Design by Kirk Heydt
Cover Photo: "Vie Photography" by A. Bamberg
First Printing

The Invisible College Press, LLC
P.O. Box 209
Woodbridge VA 22194-0209
http://www.invispress.com

Please send question and comments to:
editor@invispress.com

This book is dedicated to those that had a significant impact on its creation: Tom Kappel and Rene' Smeraglia, fellow writers who have helped me immensely and Del Stone Jr. the most terrifying of horror writers when he's not whipping me at billiards. Thanks without limit to my loving wife Joy, who keeps me writing, and to my parents, Buford and Frances, for their support and love.

-Richard A. Bamberg

CHAPTER I

Fog rolled in from the Pacific, deepening the twilight gloom of Darwin Street. Lights came on in the Victorian townhouses and a shadow passed across the curtains of the second floor of 3909.

In the darkness between the globular illumination of street lamps, a white minivan with a PP&G logo idled at the curb. From the rear of the van, John Blalock, a muscular, compact man, could see the front of number 3909 and even the shadows on the second floor. However, John concentrated his attention on a pair of computer screens. On one screen, encrypted data flowed in a gibberish stream of alphanumerics, on the other deciphered text revealed the true purpose of the man in the townhouse.

He manipulated the image, revealing that the text flowed down still another screen. Another man sat at that terminal. Tom M. Blevins, a balding computer programmer who upon turning forty had taken to augmenting his income through the sale of company secrets. The image panned right and took in a cluttered office. Books were stacked on every surface; crumpled fast food bags littered the floors overflowing a little plastic trashcan, and green light from a thirty-gallon aquarium reflected garishly off the walls.

John typed and the screen of encrypted text split on the horizontal and a decrypted version appeared on the lower half. John studied the data for a moment, then smiled as he had seen enough. He took mirrored shades from the desk and slipped them on until they touched the gold contacts on what looked like an antique hearing aid hanging over his left ear. The image from Blevin's townhouse appeared on the left lens.

He opened the side door, snatched his overcoat from the chair, and stepped down to the sidewalk. While scanning the street, he slipped the coat on and rolled the collar up until it touched the brim of his battered Henshel hat. A row of parked cars lined both sides of the street and disappeared into the fog, but he was alone. He left the coat unbuttoned, slid the van's door closed, and triggered the remote locks.

At the front door of the townhouse, John glanced around, seeing no one , he pulled a pair of steel picks from a case and knelt in front of the door. Although he'd worked this lock a couple of days earlier, breaking and entering was never easy when his thick fingers had to manipulate the delicate picks. His teeth clenched as though that would help make the tumblers align. The last one lifted into place and he rotated the lock. The bolt slid back with a soft klack. He exhaled softly.

John stowed the picks and stood. He aimed a small silver case at the LED on the door’s security panel and pressed its only switch. The case transmitted a series of signals and the LED shifted from red to green

He slipped inside and closed the door behind him.

A single low wattage bulb barely illuminated the faded print of tiny blue birds in the wallpaper. A pair of doors led to the left and a narrow set of stairs went up the right hand wall. The air smelled of garlic and spices from Chinese takeout. John listened. The townhouse was quiet save for the soft bubbling of an aquarium pump. He closed the door and climbed the stairs.

The stairs had groaned with his weight on his first visit. This trip John kept his feet close to the wall. At the upper floor, he paused in the hallway. The image in his sunglasses showed Blevins hadn't moved. John stowed the glasses in his shirt pocket.

Moving slower, listening, careful of every step, he crept down the hallway toward the only room with a light on. As he drew near he could hear Blevins typing on a keyboard.

John’s hand went to his belt and detached a foot long metal rod. Holding it behind him in his right hand, he stepped into the doorway.

Blevins hunched over the computer screen. Five steps before John reached him, the man reacted.

Whirling toward John, he reached under his jacket.

"Don't," John said and took another step.

Blevins didn't reply, but metal glinted in his emerging hand.

John snapped the telescoping baton its full length and lunged forward. His hand swept upward and chopped the weighted baton against Blevins' fingers.

Blevins uttered a single a cry of pain, dropped a small revolver to the floor, and yanked his injured hand back. Without hesitating, Blevins stood and jabbed at John's face with a left. John blocked the blow with his raised forearm. When Blevins followed up with a right cross, John slashed downward.

A bleat of pain followed the sharp crack of breaking bone.

Blevins backed away, holding his wrist. "My arm. My arm. You son of a bitch, you broke my arm!"

"I warned you." He followed Blevins step for step at a safe distance.

Blevins backed up until he reached a table with a heavy brass lamp. He turned, grabbed the lamp with his good hand, and swung at John's head.

John ducked as the base of the lamp swung past him and hit with the baton. The first blow caught Blevins' left knee and the second caressed his temple as he fell. The lamp left Blevins' hand and crashed out a front window showering glass onto the sidewalk below.

Blevins lay on the floor, temporarily stunned.

John stood over him for a moment, waiting for another attack. But Blevins had had enough.

John collapsed the baton and jammed it back into his belt.

Turning toward the computer, John hit the switch on the power strip. He removed a pair of snips from a jacket pocket and quickly cut all the cables leading to the computer.

With a wary eye on Blevins, John took a trash bag from another pocket and ransacked the desk for disks. When he had all of them in the bag he tied the end in a knot and set it on top of the computer.

Blevins rolled over and sat up. He made the mistake of trying to use his right hand and let out a little screech.

John turned to face him. "You know who I am?"

Blevins nodded.

"Then you know you're getting off easy this time. If I run into you again, I won't be as forgiving. Either find another line of work or another state to work in."

He paused. Blevins' face gave no indication that he had understood. John pulled out the baton and snapped it into extension.

Blevins eyes widened. He nodded his head slowly.

"That's better." John collapsed the baton and stowed it again. He lifted the trash bag in one hand and the computer in the other.

The hair on his neck tingled. Then he saw what his subconscious had already noticed, a shadowy movement in the aquarium. Not the fish. A reflection, at the door, behind him.

Without turning, John dove over the desk as a gunshot thundered behind him. He scrambled around; groping for the gun Blevins had dropped. Another gunshot and splinters flew from the desk near his head. John flattened.

Where was that damn gun? He could have sworn it fell right here. His hand brushed cold metal. Instantly, his fingers tightened around the barrel. John drew the gun toward him even as his head twisted to find the shooter. Still on the floor, he could see beneath the desk. Past dust bunnies and a discarded candy wrapper, he saw a pair of shoes near the door.

Rotating the revolver in his hand, John aimed and fired in one quick motion.

He missed and the shooter's feet disappeared through the doorway before John could get off a second round.

"What's the matter asshole?" John taunted. "Don't go away mad, the party's just starting."

He held his breath, his gun aimed for the open door, and he waited for the shoes to reappear.

"I've got all night," John said. "But you know someone's called the police by now. Give yourself up before they get here. They don't have to know you were trying to kill me. A little corporate espionage will only get you three to five, attempted murder will get you ten to fifteen."

No reply. John glanced over at Blevins. The geek still held his broken wrist.

The man met his gaze and John smiled at him. "Suit yourself. I'm sure Blevins can work a plea bargain and get off if he turns you in."

Blevins panicked. "No, he's lying. I wouldn't do that. Honest you know me better than that. I'd never—"

The gunshot that opened a hole in Blevins' head stopped his protest.

Blevins sagged back against the wall like a scarecrow without its magic.

John swung back toward the door, too late. He could hear footsteps pounding down the hall.

He lept to his feet and rushed to the door. The hallway was empty. Had the killer run down the stairs or was he waiting for John to step into the open?

His ears still rang from the blast of the gunshots, but he thought he heard the creak of the stairs. John flicked the lights off and stepped into the hall. He crept forward, the revolver pointed at the top of the stairwell. Halfway down the hall he heard the front door slam.

John walked to the top of the stairs and looked around the corner. The killer would want to be long gone before the police arrived and he could already hear sirens in the distance.

John took a deep breath. Lowering his weapon, he returned to the upstairs office.

Blevins hadn't moved. His dead eyes stared accusingly at John. To the right company, the patent for what Blevins stole was a multimillion dollar jackpot, to Blevins it was a one way ticket to the grave.

John set Blevins' revolver on the desk and went outside to wait for the police.

CHAPTER 2

Scott Corning signed out in the Los Alamos visitor's log and passed his temporary security badge to the nearest guard.

"Sir, your briefcase."

Scott glanced up and barely avoided flinching when he caught sight of the disturbingly ugly mole on the guard's thick neck. Covering his reaction with a cough, Scott set his briefcase on the counter. He flicked the latches and swung open the top, the guard briefly inspected the interior.

"Thank you, sir."

Scott mumbled a "you're welcome" to the shorter man, but the guard's attention had wandered off. He closed his briefcase and left by the double glass doors that led to the parking lot.

Outside, the cold afternoon air immediately fogged his glasses. Scott tugged a neatly folded handkerchief from the breast pocket of his wool suit and wiped off the fog as he crossed the parking lot. It'd be dark soon and he wanted to get down the mesa before the roads worsened. He got behind the wheel of the Taurus and set the briefcase on the seat next to him. He backed out of the parking space and turned toward the gate. At the traffic light he turned left across the concrete and steel bridge that spanned the canyon between the laboratory and the town of Los Alamos. Once across the bridge he turned right onto state highway 502 that lead south through town, past the small airfield, and then down the mesa to Santa Fe.

Back in the early days of Los Alamos they carved the road out of the piñon and mesquite covered mesa wall and had never really improved on the original work. The ride gave a beautiful view of the valley and the other mesas, but Scott had seen it many times before and the vista had become mundane. The afternoon rush of people from the lab had passed and the road was nearly deserted. Ice formed on his radio antenna and made inroads onto the windshield even though he had the defroster on full.

Black ice might be forming on the road, but still Scott had to consciously force himself to keep his speed below forty. The deal had taken the better part of two years to arrange, but now that it was finally a go, he had to stay on top of things.

Nearly halfway down the mesa he rounded a curve and had to slow as a delivery truck pulled onto the road from the shoulder, blocking his lane. Belching dense black smoke from its exhaust, the truck slowly accelerated. Scott hung back as they entered a series of curves.

They were doing less than 20 mph. His fingers drummed against the steering wheel. He cursed under his breath and sounded his horn.

There was no response from the truck.

"Damn fool. There's no excuse for this. It never fails. Anytime I'm in a hurry I encounter some moron putzing along."

Scott started around the truck, but pulled back in immediately. They were in a long sloping curve to the right and he couldn't see more than a hundred feet ahead. He was in a hurry, but he wasn't crazy. In about a mile, the road straightened out for a short stretch and he could easily pass the truck there. Might as well relax, he told himself.

The dash clock read after six, Caitlin's meeting with the new clients should be over. He clicked the power button for the cell phone.

"Dial Caitlin," Scott said and waited for the connection.

*　　　*　　　*

The sun was a ball of crimson fire, only half seen above the distant horizon. Its light gleamed off the bridge and bathed the aircraft carrier passing beneath it with a ruddy glow. The bridge dwarfed the carrier, which in turn dwarfed the score of sailboats that flanked its passage through San

Francisco's Golden Gate. Caitlin Maxwell stood at the railing. She held her drink in one hand and clutched her linen jacket together with the other. Although she was nearly a thousand feet above the breakers, the wind bore the distinctive briny odor of the sea.

Dean Koenig touched her elbow and her raven hair fanned out to the side when she turned to him.

"Magnificent view, isn't it?" he asked.

"Magnificent? It's like looking down on the mortals from atop Mount Olympus."

The observation deck at the top of the Pacific Rim Suites, built on what had been the officer's housing complex of Presidio Army Post, enjoyed an immense panoramic view of the coastline, the Bay, and the city. From the northeast corner, Caitlin could see the hills around Napa Valley, the green oasis of distant Muir Woods, and the gray skyline of Oakland. The foreboding walls of inescapable Alcatraz were visible to the left of Coit Tower. To seaward, the windblown cliffs on the western edge of the peninsula held dozens of homes that teetered on the brink of destruction, as if waiting to plummet to the surf during the next winter storm.

"Mount Olympus? You missed your calling, Caitlin. You should have been a poet."

She chuckled, faint and melodious. "No, I tried poetry. I never had the feel for it. Poetry requires a measure of innate talent that I lack."

"I find it hard to believe you lack anything," the voice came from behind her.

She turned to greet Carl Teigue. The meeting with Teigue and Koenig on Caitlin's improved data interface had gone into overtime and they'd moved from the main floor lounge to the hotel's rooftop bar. On the third round of drinks, the men concluded that the packaging Caitlin had offered them two hours earlier was exactly what they needed.

Caitlin felt certain they had made up their minds before coming upstairs. She'd seen the surreptitious glances that passed from Koenig to Teigue as he proposed they adjourn to the bar. The blue-eyed Teigue, at thirty-two, was married, but the forty-four year old Koenig was a perennial bachelor and Caitlin had known since lunch that he was going to try to entice her back up to his apartment.

She wasn't sure what her response would be. Still, the obvious attraction he showed was flattering and reminded her that it'd been six months since her last physical encounter with a man. That had been the start of her separation from Scott. Maybe she had spent too much time worrying about business and not enough enjoying life.

Teigue was saying something Caitlin could scarcely hear over the wind. "It's been a pleasure, Caitlin. I have to run or Sandra will worry about me."

Caitlin let go of her jacket and took his extended hand. The crisp February wind whirled the material out from her thin silk blouse. Goose bumps popped out along her arms. She suppressed a shiver. "That's all right, Carl. It was nice to meet you. I'm looking forward to working with you."

"Yes, on your next trip Sandra and I must have you over for dinner. Keep in touch."

"Sure, I'll call when I get back to Albuquerque."

Carl gave her a warm smile and turned. She watched him cross the deck and go inside the bar.

Dean took her hand. His palm was warm and comfortable. "Well, alone at last."

Where had he gotten that line?

Caitlin started to pull her hand back, but part of her found the contact stimulating. A little male attention was nice.

"Tell me something," he said.

"As long as it isn't my weight or age." Caitlin grinned.

He returned her smile. "Nothing so personal as that. I was wondering about you and your partner. I thought you were married, but I couldn't help noticing that you don't wear a ring."

"We're separated. Divorcing really, it's final next week."

"Ah, that's too bad."

Caitlin noticed his eyes seemed to brighten even as he gave her his regrets.

"I'm sorry to hear it. Will your divorce have any impact on your company?"

"No, not really. It's an amicable divorce. We're still friends. We formed Cutting Edge Technologies seven years ago and neither of us wants to break up the business. In truth, business is so good that we'd be fools to break up the partnership."

"That's good."

An irritating buzz came from her jacket.

She took out her phone, flipped it open, and held it to her ear. "Caitlin Maxwell."

"Hi Caitlin, how'd the meeting go?"

"Scott? We're just wrapping up. Everything looks fine. We'll have the statement of work signed tomorrow and I'll bring the contract back with me. Where are you?"

"I'm just outside Los Alamos, on my way home. Any problems at that end?"

Caitlin smiled toward Dean. "It's my partner, Scott."

Dean nodded. "Tell him everything's in the bag. We're very happy with the proposal."

Caitlin raised the telephone to her mouth. "Dean says everything's fine. They're happy with the deal."

"Good. Look Caitlin there's something I should tell you. Can you get away from him and go secure?"

"I guess so." To Dean she said, "Please excuse me for a moment."

"Oh sure, no problem. I'll get us another drink."

She considered stopping him. She'd had enough to drink, but it did give her a moment of privacy.

"All right, Scott, I'm going secure." Caitlin depressed the secure transmission switch. With the telephone back to her ear, Scott's voice came through sharp and clear.

* * *

"Caitlin, you there?"

"Yes, Scott. What's so important that I had to send a client off?"

"Don't worry about him. His contract is small potatoes."

They were finally coming out of the last curve. Scott noticed the truck had slowly picked up speed. The driver must have been emboldened by the sight of the straightaway. No matter, he'd probably slow again when they reached the next set of curves.

"What are you talking about? This contract is good for a quarter mil' over the next three years."

"Caitlin, I've been working a deal that'll make us rich."

"What kind of deal, Scott? You haven't gone back to investing in startup companies?"

"That's just like you to bring that up again." How was he to know they hadn't owned the patent to their main product?

Scott eased the accelerator down and pulled out. The road ahead was clear. He juiced the engine slowly. A nagging fear of ice on the roadway still bothered him. Abreast of the truck's cab, he could see its dirty orange panels were unadorned and the windows were tinted too dark to make out the driver.

The next curve was coming up fast. Scott took a quick look at his dash and was surprised to see he was doing nearly sixty.

"Tell me," Caitlin said.

"All right, if you'll give me a chance. There's a risk involved, but I've taken care of --"

If he were going to get back in, he'd have to move fast. Scott pressed down on the throttle. The entire car shuddered as if struck.

"What the hell?" For an instant, he thought he'd had a blowout. Then the car rocked violently and he gripped the wheel to keep it on the road. The truck had veered over the centerline and slammed into the side of his car.

"You son-of-a-bitch!"

"Scott? What's the matter Scott?"

Scott lifted his foot from the accelerator and braked, but the truck still pushed, pushed him toward the edge of the road, toward the precipice beyond. He cursed again and cut his own wheel back toward the right, but the truck's greater mass moved him inexorably toward the edge.

This straight away was one of the few spots on the entire road without a guardrail. Scott could see the next curve and the start of the next guardrail. If he could just make it a little farther, he'd be safe.

"Scott? Scott!"

Who drove the truck? Why was he doing this? Scott looked to his left across the wide valley far below. If he didn't get around the truck soon....

"Just a moment Caitlin. Some sonofabitch in a truck is trying to --"

He tightened his grip on the steering wheel and stomped the throttle to the floor. The Taurus started to pull ahead of the truck. Sparks flew and metal screamed piercingly. His bumper edged even with the truck's.

Then his front door.

His back door.

Too late.

His bumper struck the buried end of the guardrail and rode up on the steel. Like a VSTOL jet launching off a carrier the car launched into the sky. His racing engine slowed and then only the howl of the wind accompanied Scott on his long fall.. Through his windshield, Scott could see the thick dark clouds. The front of the car dipped lower and the horizon swam into view. A calm came over him as the piñon covered ground quickly filled his view. For a moment, he wondered if the car's air bag could handle this sort of impact.

"I'm so sorry. There's so much I wanted to say. Good-bye, Caitlin. I love you."

"Scott?"

Pity. They had so much to look forward to.

Then ... nothing.

CHAPTER 3

"Scott?"

Caitlin could hear rushing wind, an engine racing, then there came the briefest sound of rending metal and the line died. "Scott? Oh, God. Scott?"

Caitlin lowered the telephone and stared at it. The display indicated she had lost the signal.

What happened? It sounded like he had an accident, but why had it become so quiet before the crash? The calm lasted for several seconds. Long enough for Scott to say good-bye. My God. He said good-bye. But he wasn't hanging up the telephone. Oh, my God. He was assuming he'd never see her again. Why else would he say he loved her when their divorce would be final in another week? Why else would he say good-bye?

"Oh God. Oh God."

Caitlin felt her pulse racing. Her throat tightened until she couldn't talk. She had to calm down, relax, and get a grip on her emotions.

What to do? She should call someone. The highway patrol. Yes, that's it. Scott might still be alive. If they found him in time. Where was he? Leaving Los Alamos?

Caitlin called information. A computer-generated voice answered. "Your request, please."

"Los Alamos, New Mexico, emergency number."

"One moment, please."

The number came almost immediately and Caitlin auto-dialed it.

The telephone rang twice before a woman's voice answered. "Los Alamos dispatch."

Caitlin tried to control her voice, but it still broke as she said, "This is Caitlin Maxwell in San Francisco. I believe my husband has just had an accident between Los Alamos and Santa Fe."

The woman asked for particulars. What distance was he from Los Alamos? What kind of car he was driving? Did she know the license number?

Caitlin answered each question in turn and finally the woman told her that a patrol car would search the route and look for any sign of an accident. Caitlin gave the woman her telephone number and broke the connection.

Closing the phone, she dropped it into her purse.

"Caitlin? Are you all right?"

She looked up to see Dean standing next to her. He held two glasses of champagne. Some kind of film covered her eyes, blurring her vision, but she could see his concern. She wiped at her eyes with the back of her hands and nodded once.

He set the glasses down on the railing and put an arm about her shoulders.

Caitlin pushed gently away from him. Her gut tightened. She felt sick. Control, she had to get control.

Facing the ocean, Caitlin deeply inhaled the thick air. She took a handkerchief from her purse and wiped her eyes.

"I'm sorry, Dean. I've got to go."

"Wait a minute. What did Scott say to you?"

She shook her head and returned the handkerchief to her purse. "It wasn't what he said. He ... I think Scott is dead."

Dean leaned back and stared at her face. His features reflected his incredulity.

"Scott is dead."

"I ... I don't understand. You were just talking to him."

"I know. He was driving, in the mountains, he had some kind of accident."

"Dear Lord, I'm sorry Caitlin. But how can you be sure he's dead?"

She fought back the rush that hit her as she thought of Scott and the long span of time with just the sound of wind and the racing engine in the telephone. "A car accident. Icy road. He must have skidded off the road. Something like that."

But, that wasn't all of it. He'd said something about a truck and she heard screeching metal before he'd left the road. What had happened?

"But still you can't be sure. Do you know where he called from?"

Caitlin nodded.

"Then call the highway patrol. They ought to be able to locate him."

"I did already, but it won't do any good. I know he's dead. I can feel it. He even said good-bye before the crash."

Dean shook his head slowly. "I'm sorry, Caitlin."

His eyes darkened as he looked away from her toward the setting sun and she realized he wanted to say something else. "What is it?"

"You're going to think me cold, but I have to ask."

"What?"

"Is this going to affect your company's ability to fulfill our contract?"

For a moment, Caitlin just stared at him. How could he? What kind of an asshole would even think......" Our contract? No. We live up to our agreements, no matter what."

He nodded. A moment later he frowned. "Look, I'm sorry, but business is business. I had to know."

"I understand."

"Can I walk you to your room?" He asked as though trying to recover his good manners.

"No. Thank you. Really, I need to be alone. I'll contact you later."

Caitlin slid her purse strap back on her shoulder. Her posture stiff, she stood and walked toward the door. The wind had lost its bite. Her heart held a cold stronger than the ocean air. She opened the door and marched across the crowded bar, hardly conscious of the crush of people watching the sunset. Then, in a rush, the anger left her to be replaced by a deep sadness.

She reached the elevator and summoned it.

Scott was dead. She knew it as well as she knew her own name. My God, to be talking with someone and the next second they're dead.

She felt like her life had just taken a left turn into the twilight zone.

The elevator doors parted with a chime.

"Floor thirty-one," Caitlin said as she stepped in. The elevator doors slid shut and she dropped swiftly.

She had come to terms with not being married to Scott, but a world without Scott was another matter entirely. Alone in the elevator and without the eyes of strangers on her she no longer held back her grief. She sobbed into her handkerchief until the door opened at her floor Then she wiped at her cheeks, removing some of the external marks of Scott's death, but she couldn't begin to touch the ache in her heart.

Half blinded in agony, Caitlin eased along the wide, cheerfully lit, corridor. From the outer pocket of her computer case, she removed a rod-shaped, electronic key. At 3142, she put the tip of the key into the receptacle. The door swung open and Caitlin stepped across the threshold while dropping the key back into her case.

"Lights."

The broad-spectrum, fluorescent lights lit the suite with a warm glow.

She crossed the small sitting room and entered the bedroom.

Two steps into the room Caitlin stopped in surprise. Empty dresser drawers hung open and her clothes were neatly stacked on top of the dresser. The suitcase she'd left in the corner of the closet lay splayed wide on the bed.

For a moment she couldn't understand what had happened, then a fresh chill flooded through her. Somebody had gone through her personal belongings.

She took another step into the room and froze. What if they were still here? Her left hand dipped back into her case, searching for the room key.

The lights dimmed to almost pitch black.

Someone grabbed her shoulder and tried to turn her around.

Caitlin spun away from the grip and stumbled against the bed. She swayed, trying to catch her balance, but fell backward onto the bedspread.

The silhouette of a large man filled the doorway.

"Who the hell are you?" Caitlin asked.

He didn't answer.

Her voice rose. "What do you want?"

He came toward her.

Caitlin rolled to put the bed between them, but a hand closed around her ankle. . She clutched uselessly at the covers while he pulled her toward him. Realizing she had little time to react, she twisted onto her back and cocked her free foot back. Before he could react, she kicked out, catching him in the forehead.

He grunted and staggered, but held tight to her ankle and tried to grab her other leg.

Caitlin kicked at his face again and heard a loud crunch. His grip weakened and she jerked hastily away. She rolled off the far side of the bed and scrambled to her feet.

"Stay away from me, damn you!"

Still silent, he came around the corner of the bed.

Her case had slipped off her shoulder, but she had held onto its strap. When he came at her again, she stepped back and swung the case upward. It passed between his outstretched hands and slammed into his chin.

He staggered back, tripped, and fell into the closet.

Without waiting to see if he would recover, Caitlin dashed past him into the other room. She saw the telephone on the wet bar, but she could already hear movement in the bedroom. No, her cell phone would be safer, but first she had to get out of there. Rushing toward the door, Caitlin pulled her room key from her case and fumbled for the distress button. She put her thumb on the end and pressed. It refused to budge.

She yanked open the door, lurched into an empty hallway, and turned toward the elevators. She considered screaming for help and pounding on doors, but until she put distance between her and her attacker, she didn't dare stop.

Reaching the elevators, she bent over, gasping for air and stabbing at the down button. She turned her head to look back up the hall and saw her attacker coming out of her room. He held something long and slender.

A gun. He had a gun.

A fresh surge of adrenaline coursed through her. She spun away from the elevator and slammed into the stairwell door across the hall.

Leaping down the stairs two at a time, she made two landings before stumbling, swearing frantically as the heel of her right shoe broke. She grabbed the handrail to keep from falling. Her hands slid against the metal. She stumbled, and thought she would fall, but then got her feet under her again.

The shoe was useless; both shoes were useless for running. Kicking off first one shoe and then the other, Caitlin continued her hurried descent in stocking feet.

Footsteps pounded above her.

She descended another floor. The pounding of his steps were closer. Her feet already hurt from running on the hard concrete stairs. If she couldn't outrun him, she had to outthink him.

She glanced upwards as she used the railing to pull her around the next turn.

Good God! He was aiming at her.

She heard a soft coughing sound and a bullet whined off the metal handrail.

Caitlin reflexively ducked. She stumbled to her knees, smashing them painfully into the stairwell before she caught herself and lurched back to her feet.

At the next landing she pulled open the door and slammed it back against the wall. Before it closed, she moved down the stairs again. This time she hugged the wall, moved silently, and didn't breathe as she prayed her trick would work.

One floor below, she heard the door she'd opened, open again. Had she fooled him?

Caitlin kept moving, afraid to stop. She descended another floor before hearing a door open. Heavy male footsteps pounded the stairs.

It hadn't worked.

Caitlin opened the next door. Squeezing through it, she carefully, silently, pulled it shut behind her. She came out in a long hallway as empty her own had been. She ran to the elevator doors and pressed the down button. Panting, she listened, for an indication that the elevator was coming. Nothing. She gave up waiting and ran down the hall toward the exit sign at the far end.

With every step, she could feel the door behind her opening. With every second, she imagined him peering at her over his gun sights.

She slammed into the stairwell door, grabbed its handle, and pushed it open. She cast an expectant look over her shoulder, no sign of him, and ducked inside. Inside the stairwell, she stopped and tried to catch her breath. She felt winded and although the distance she'd run wasn't great, her pulse pounded in her ears as though she had run a marathon.

What now? Had he given up or did he still stalk her?

Just when she had regained her breath, she realized she still held the key in her hand. Why hadn't it worked when she needed it? She looked at it and immediately saw she held the slim key upside down. In her panic, she had been pressing on the bottom, not on the top, of the emergency signal.

Flipping the key over, she pressed, and held it down. An LED began to flash. She sat with her back propped against the door. Safe. In a minute, two at the most, help would arrive.

CHAPTER 4

"Hell no, I don't want to lie down."

Caitlin wasn't sure what frustrated her more, this cold bitch's inability to believe her story or her own inability to keep from imagining her hands around the throat of Captain Patricia Ferguson.

More than an hour had passed since two of the hotel's security personnel had found her crouching in the stairwell. No, that wasn't right. She hadn't been crouching; she'd been cowering. The guards were courteous and exemplary in their behavior and apparent concern, even after escorting her back to her suite where two more guards waited.

She had entered the room slowly; despite assurances they had already searched her rooms and pronounced them clear. Her bedroom was shockingly immaculate. Her suitcase was back in its corner, her clothes were in the dresser, and the bed was neatly made. Things went downhill from there.

The muscular woman sitting across the desk from her was chief of security for the Pacific Rim Suites. Captain Ferguson had tried for more than an hour to convince Caitlin that she shouldn't file a police report. Finally, Ferguson relented and called the police.

A buzzer sounded and Ferguson glanced down at her desk.

"Yes, I'll be right there." Ferguson stood and walked toward the door. "There are some other matters I have to see to. I'll be back before the police arrive. Will you be all right here or should I send someone in?"

"I'll be fine. Could someone get me some ibuprofen and water?"

"Certainly."

Ferguson opened the door and stepped into the outer office. Before the heavy door closed Caitlin heard her relaying her requests to the receptionist.

Caitlin sat still for a few minutes feeling the pulse of her blood, listening to the echo of her heart, then she stood and paced the room. Outlandishly colorful fish swam in a saltwater aquarium mounted in the wall behind Ferguson's desk. A monitor wall on her right, displayed different areas of the hotel. The fish would normally have interested her more, but she found herself drawn to the monitors.

Hotel guests moved across several of the monitors, through the lobby, in one of the two restaurants, and in the each of the three lounges. A crowd still occupied the rooftop lounge. The sun had set and now artificial torches along the railing provided the only light.

The door opened and the male receptionist came in with a bottle of Evian and a small container. "Your water and ibuprofen."

"Thank you." Caitlin took them and noticed each was still sealed.

The receptionist nodded, smiled, and left, closing the door behind him.

Caitlin broke open the bottle, took a small drink, then set it down while she opened the pill container. Caitlin shook three of the pills into her hand, popped them into the back of her mouth, and then drank heavily from the water bottle.

The door opened again and Ferguson came in followed by a man Caitlin hadn't seen before. He was about her height, but maybe a bit younger. His hair was trimmed short above his ears and he wore a neat but unimpressive suit.

"Ms. Maxwell, this is Detective Mark Romax," Ferguson said.

Romax offered his hand. "Good evening, Ma'am. I understand you've had a problem."

The man's accent didn't sound like a native Californian; it was from somewhere back east.

"A problem?" Caitlin couldn't keep her voice from breaking. She held out her left hand, palm toward the detective. He stopped.

She closed the water bottle, took a breath, and let it out slowly. "Yes, I have a problem Detective Romax. Would you like to hear about my problem?"

"Yes, Ma'am." He fished a notepad from an inside pocket of his jacket.

Ferguson pulled one of the chairs from the front of her desk and slid it to him. "Thank you, he said."

He sat down and motioned for Caitlin to sit on the sofa. After a moment, she did.

"Now I understand you're reporting a prowler who attempted to assault you in your room. Is that basically correct?"

She nodded. "As far as it goes."

Romax took out a pen and started jotting notes. "Okay, let's take it from when you entered your room. What did you notice?"

"Well, nothing really. The lights were off. I turned them on and went into the bedroom."

"Did you notice anything out of place?"

"No, but I'm afraid I wasn't very observant. I'd been crying and I guess I was preoccupied."

His hand rose in a disaffecting manner and his head shook briefly. "That's okay. It's not important. Do you mind telling me why you were crying?"

"I believed my husband was just killed in a car accident."

Romax stopped writing and stared at her. "Come again?"

"I was talking with him on the phone. He was in the mountains outside Los Alamos and there was a crash and his phone went dead."

"Have you tried to contact him since then?"

"Yes, his phone doesn't respond. The recording says it's out of range. I did contact the local police and they said they'd send out a car to investigate."

"I'm very sorry, but you can't be sure he's dead. Even if he was in an accident, it might have been minor."

"No, it couldn't have..."

How to describe to him the horrible silence that preceded the crash and Scott almost calmly telling her goodbye? She blinked back tears and shook her head.

Romax waited for her to regain her composure before speaking. "I'm sure everything will turn out all right Ms. Maxwell. Now if you can continue?"

She nodded and picked up where she had left off.

When Caitlin finished, Romax closed his notebook and sat back. He watched her for a few moments before speaking.

"Ms. Maxwell, let me be frank with you. While I'm not dismissing your story, Capt. Ferguson tells me there's no evidence to support your claim of an intruder in your room. And, since nothing was taken, there's no real proof that anyone was there. Now, it's probably just a matter of you having been confused by the shock of your husband's accident. You got off the wrong floor, went into what you thought was your room, and had a scuffle with someone who thought you were an intruder."

"Someone who chased and then shot at me?"

"The imagination does strange things. You being in shock and all, I'm not surprised that you think this person shot at you."

"You sonofabitch." She looked between him and Ferguson who sat calmly watching the proceedings from behind her desk. "The two of you discussed this before you even listened to me. That's why you had to leave the room. You had to make sure he was agreeable to your side of the story before I saw him."

Ferguson leaned forward across her desk. "Look Ms. Maxwell. We've reassigned you to a room on the concierge floor. There's around-the-clock surveillance there. If anyone leaves or enters a room it's recorded and there's a video record of the hallways. I can assure you that you won't be bothered."

Caitlin looked away from Ferguson, met Romax's eyes, and stared into them. There was something there, something that didn't fit. An instant later it was gone and his face had the rehearsed calmness of a disbelieving policeman again.

"Oh? Well assure me that I just happened into someone else's room by mistake and that they couldn't really have fired at me with a silenced pistol."

Ferguson's eyes had the tired look of someone dealing with a troublesome child.

"Never mind, just give me the damn key. I'll be out of here in the morning."

Ferguson slid another of the slender electronic keys across her desk. "Ms. Maxwell, the management wants you to know that we don't doubt your sincerity even if there isn't any evidence to support your claim. Pacific Rim Suite's guarantees its guests' satisfaction and your stay here will be at no charge."

"I would rather have your support."

For once Ferguson appeared embarrassed. "Well, ummh --"

"Then fuck you and your guests' satisfaction, Captain Ferguson." Caitlin stood and picked up the key. There were no markings on it to indicate her new room number.

"Thirty-four thirty-four. Your things have already been transferred."

"Thank you." She paused to eye Romax again. "I'm sorry to have taken up your valuable time, Detective."

Romax's voice stopped her before she reached the door. "Your purse."

She turned. He held her purse at arm's length toward her. Caitlin went back and took it with a muttered, "Thank you."

Opening the door, Caitlin walked quickly past the receptionist in the outer office. Her heels clicked loudly against the tile floor of the gleaming white corridor. She reached the pair of elevator doors, pressed the only button there, and a few seconds later the nearer door opened.

The trip from the subbasement was long and uninterrupted. The doors opened silently and Caitlin stepped hesitantly into the hallway.

A burly man in a dark blue suit bearing a hotel nametag greeted her. "Good evening Ms. Maxwell."

She nodded at him and then eyed him carefully. She didn't remember seeing him before, but he recognized her. He was about six feet tall and looked like a Secret Service agent on a protection detail. His hair was neatly trimmed and his suit tailored into a comfortable fit. Caitlin noticed a slight bulge beneath his left arm as he moved.

She looked for the normal markers on the wall. There were none.

"Your room is this way Ms. Maxwell." The guard motioned to her right.

Caitlin nodded and took a couple of steps past him. Pausing, she turned and looked at the nearest door. There were no numbers on it.

"How --"

"Your key will indicate your room when you get in front of the door. It's about eight doors down on the right."

"Thank you."

She walked slowly down the hall. Although the hall was brightly lit, Caitlin found herself nervously eyeing each door she passed as if one of them would suddenly open and her attacker would step out.

Twice she stopped and turned back to face the guard. Each time she saw him standing in the same position, watching her.

At the seventh door one end of her key began to glow. The closer she got to the door, the brighter it got. Caitlin slipped the key into its slot. Taking a deep breath, Caitlin pushed the door open to reveal a dark room dark. She fumbled for the light switch, missed it, and said, "Lights."

The lights went on immediately. Standing in the doorway she swept the room with her gaze before stepping inside. She left the door open went in and made a quick search of the suite, looking in the closet, under the bed, on the balcony, and even in the spacious shower before she hurried back to shut the door. She threw the privacy bolt and then leaned against the door. A nervous shudder went through her.

Dear God, Scott.

In the excitement of the attack, she'd almost forgotten about Scott. She opened her cell phone and recalled the number for the Los Alamos police department.

The 911 operator answered and Caitlin identified herself.

"Yes, Ms. Maxwell, please hold on the line." The line went silent for a few moments, and then another voice came on. "Ms. Maxwell?"

"Yes. Who is this?"

"This is Sergeant Ortiz of the Los Alamos police department."

"Did you find my husband?"

A brief pause ensued, then, "We think so. There was an accident on the road about fives miles south of town. It was called in shortly after your call. We dispatched a helicopter ambulance to the scene."

"And my husband, is he alive?"

"I'm sorry ma'am, we haven't identified the body, but the vehicle was registered to you and Mr. Scott Corning."

Caitlin choked back a sob. "All right. Thank you, I ... I'll call back tomorrow. I can't talk right now."

"I understand ma'am. Can you give me a number where you can be reached?"

Caitlin quickly gave her cell phone number, thanked him again, and disconnected.

She should call someone, but whom? Connie Dryer, her personal secretary, would probably be home by now. She ought to let her know, maybe they should close the office for a couple of days, hang a big black wreath on the door and stay home.

What about Scott's family?

Caitlin hadn't seen any of them except his father in more than three years. She'd never gotten along with Big Scott, as he liked to be called. The man was nearly a Neanderthal.

Still it wasn't right to let him wait until the police notified him of his son's death.

Caitlin sat down on the couch and picked up the telephone.

She stared at it for a few seconds. She didn't remember his telephone number, and it wasn't stored in her computer.

Caitlin punched in information. While waiting for the operator to come on, Caitlin picked up a pen and pad from beside the hotel's telephone. She gave the electronic operator the town and Big Scott's name, a moment later the electronic voice recited the number. Caitlin auto dialed it and waited.

The telephone rang five times before someone picked up. "Yeah, who is it?"

"It's Caitlin."

"Yeah? Whatta you want?"

"Scott ... I --"

"I already know about my son. If that's what you're trying to say?" His voice was slurred.

"I'm sorry. How did you hear?"

"Some state cop from New Mexico called me a half hour ago."

"Already? Why would Ortiz call you first?"

"Ortiz? Who the hell is Ortiz? Nah, this guy was anglo."

Then who had called him?

"I ... Scott, I'm so sorry," Caitlin said.

"Yeah? Well, shit happens, don't it? Now if you ain't got nothin' else to say, I got some grieving to do."

"I --"

The line went dead. Caitlin stared at it, wanting to throw it against the wall and scream. She wanted to stomp on the telephone until it was nothing but fragments of plastic and wiring.

Why had he heard already? The police weren't even positive the body was Scott and how had they located his father so soon? She closed the telephone and put it back in her case. It was too much to worry about just now.

Caitlin went to the window, wrapped her arms around herself, and stared out at the distant lights. Her sobs were faint, but uncontrolled.

It was nearly twenty minutes later when Caitlin turned away from the night and went into the bath. Her eyes burned after so much crying. Her waterproof mascara hadn't lived up to the name and what hadn't come off on the back of her hand, had found it's way into her eyes. She splashed cold water onto her face until the stinging died, then stared at her reflection. God, she looked ghastly. Her eyes were puffy and red and streaks of makeup marred her face. Normally she used so little that nothing disturbed it, but today she had dressed for the clients.

The hotel staff had dutifully set out her toiletries in the same order she'd left them in her other room. Caitlin picked up the brush and made a few passes through her nape length black hair. Then she shook her head from side to side. Her hair floated out and then fell back into place.

Caitlin dampened a wash cloth and carefully removed the remains of her makeup. She eyed herself in the mirror. Better, but her eyes were still puffy.

A soft sound came from the den and her heart lurched. Her pulse pounding in her temples, she eased the door open and stepped out into the room.

Nothing, it must have come from somewhere else. Then her eyes fell on the dark opening to the bedroom. Had it come from there?

Suddenly unable to bear another moment in the room, she jerked her purse off the sofa, unlatched the door, and left. The concierge stood near the elevators, watching her. She walked toward him, grew self-conscious about her red puffy eyes, and took her sunglasses from her purse and slipped them on. She nodded to him and punched the elevator call button. He smiled and returned her nod.

The doors opened and she stepped in. He was still smiling at her when the doors closed.

Caitlin stepped out on the ground floor and made her way through the crowded lobby to the revolving doors.

Entering the night air, Caitlin felt the cool dampness of a sea breeze.

One of the uniformed doormen eyed her expectantly. She shook her head and turned away from the taxi stand. She felt a need to walk. The fresh air would clear her head. Taxis were always going to and from the hotel. She could flag one down when she got tired of walking.

The sun had long since set and the street was dark except for the small oasis of light beneath regularly spaced lamps. Once she got out of sight of the people around the hotel, Caitlin removed her sunglasses.

The ocean breeze tossed the crest of the trees and they swayed dimly against the yellow gray bellies of scattered clouds. This area of Presidio had been set aside for development when the rest of the old Army post had been converted to a national park. Caitlin didn't know whose pockets had been lined by that exclusion, but it was obvious that someone's had. The view from the top of the hill was just too spectacular not to develop.

The developed area ended abruptly and Caitlin found herself in the park. She walked slowly, paying little attention to where she was going, but she kept to the sidewalk. Trails ran throughout the park, but she was neither dressed for hiking nor in the mood to explore the darker paths that wound between the oleander and beneath the eucalyptus and firs.

Twelve years. Twelve years she and Scott had been married and for two years before that they'd been lovers. They had shared common interests, common goals, and ... much love. She had never expected their love to fade, but it had. The love had gone, vanished somewhere in time, but they were still friends. Good friends. This was the loss that bothered her so. Good friends were even harder to find than mates. And they had been such friends. Scott was a great listener. When she was troubled he would sit with rapt attention until she had unburdened her soul and he understood. Unlike most men, he didn't automatically offer fixes for what bothered her; rather he empathized and allowed her the space to determine her own solutions.

Fog gradually enveloped her. It came in from the seaward side of the peninsula, rolling in, hugging the ground in its embrace until visibility was less than a hundred feet.

Caitlin became aware of the strap on her case digging into her shoulder. She remembered she'd left her notebook computer in it. Its two pounds seemed more like twenty after a long walk. She should have left it in her room.

Caitlin shifted the thick strap to her other shoulder. After dark, parking was banned in the park and the street was deserted. Caitlin continued to walk and listened for the sound of a car engine. She didn't have long to wait.

Turning, she saw the lights of a car coming through the opalescent fog. It moved slowly, cautiously. When it neared, she saw it was a yellow cab. Caitlin stepped to the curve and held up her hand. The taxi slowed and pulled toward her. Wipers dragged noisily against the windshield as they removed the thickening mist. Caitlin shivered. It would be good to be in a warm restaurant.

The cab stopped with its rear door even with her. Caitlin gripped the handle and pulled the door open. The interior light was out. She had one foot inside when she realized the back seat was already occupied.

"Oh, excuse me. I thought this cab was free."

The man's voice was pleasantly soft. "That's all right. I told him to stop for you. I don't mind sharing."

"That's very considerate."

"Where to lady?" the driver asked.

"Alliotto's, please."

Another car appeared in the fog and its headlights lit the interior of the cab for a few seconds before it passed.

Still half in the door, Caitlin froze.

In those brief seconds the headlights played across the stranger's face, Caitlin recognized him. It was the man from her room. The one with the gun, except that now a thin bandage covered his nose. Caitlin pushed herself back out of the taxi as the man lunged across the seat after her. His fingers brushed the edge of her skirt, closed on it, and pulled.

She stumbled and caught herself against the door and roof. He lunged closer, trying for a better grip. Caitlin pushed away from the taxi and slammed the door hard against his wrist.

"Ow! Damn bitch!"

Her skirt slipped free of his grasp and Caitlin caught the edge of the door with both hands and slammed it again. Too late, the man had pulled his hand safely inside.

"Hey! What the hell do you think you're doing?" the driver yelled.

"Mind your own business." The glass muffled the passenger's voice.

Caitlin moved back from the taxi. Her head twisted from side to side looking for an escape route.

"Yeah? Get outta my cab!"

She could see the driver silhouetted against the dashboard lights, a microphone raised to his lips. "Central, I need --"

Over the noise of the taxi's engine, Caitlin heard a soft spitting sound and the driver's head snapped forward against the steering wheel.

Fear burned through her veins like acid. She backed away. Away from the taxi's bright headlights. Away from the man with the gun. Away from certain death.

Her feet reached the edge of the walk. Unprepared for the sharp drop, she stumbled. She flailed wildly as she fell into the thick oleander. The branches clutched at her, keeping her upright, but impeding her retreat. Caitlin turned, lowered her head, raised an arm to protect her face, and pressed into the undergrowth.

Behind her she heard the taxi's door open.

Caitlin didn't look back. Her fate would match the cabby's if she didn't get out of sight soon. She pressed deeper into the brush. The undergrowth clung to her as if it were some vassal of the killer.

Hard-soled shoes pounded the pavement behind her.

The spitting sound came again and the air buzzed near her.

A startled squeal escaped her lips. She forced the branches back and dropped to her knees. For a moment she froze, breathing heavy, and listening.

"Come on now, Ms. Maxwell. It doesn't have to be like this. Just come on out. I don't have to kill you."

What was the killer talking about? He'd already tried to kill her twice. Did he really think she'd turn around and walk into his clutches? Either he wasn't giving her any credit at all or else she was giving him way too much credit. Somehow, Caitlin didn't expect a killer to be that stupid.

"This can go anyway you want it, Ms. Maxwell. You can walk out of here and go with me. I'll guarantee your safety. On the other hand, you can force me to hunt you down in which case I'll just have to kill you."

Her eyes were adjusting to the dim light filtering through the branches. The branches thinned nearer the ground. She'd make better time crawling She eased forward, still moving directly away from the street and the sound of the killer's voice. "My patience is wearing thin, Ms. Maxwell. If you want to live you're going to have to come out in the next thirty seconds."

Caitlin's purse strap caught on a branch and for a moment she considering leaving it, but it held everything, her money, her credit cards, her computer ... all the things she'd need if she escaped this maniac. She pulled it free and slipped its strap tighter against her.

"Twenty seconds." His voice came from slightly to her left now. What was he doing? Looking for a way through the oleander?

Caitlin crawled two, then three more feet, and stopped. Right in front of her a tiny path, a game trail, cut through the brush. She'd seen enough of them in her childhood to recognize it. What kind of animals did they have in the park? She wasn't sure, but it may have been a rabbit path. Regardless, it was big enough to follow.

She turned toward the right, away from the killer's voice. She crawled faster now, but still moved the brush around her as gently as possible.

"Five seconds."

His voice was farther away, but it didn't sound as if he was still on the sidewalk. Had he found a path around the undergrowth? Her breathing came faster. Her pulse quickened. Caitlin knew she was in danger of losing it. That might get her killed. She had to remain calm. She must maintain control. Control was crucial. Panic and you die. Panic and you die.

She drummed the phrase repeatedly into her mind until it obscured all else. Her breathing steadied. Her pulse slowed. Although she continued to crawl as fast as she dared, her breathing and pulse now matched her exertion level, rather than her level of fear.

The last five seconds ticked by, but the killer remained quiet. Caitlin wished he'd keep talking. It gave her his position and improved her chances of not coming out from under the oleander right in front of him.

She paused for a second, listening, straining to hear over the sound of her own breathing. Nothing. Either he had moved farther away or he was standing still waiting for some sound that would reveal her position.

Caitlin moved again. A few feet farther and she pulled free of the brush.

She faced a small walkway. Although it was brighter than the rabbit trail, fog still draped the walk and the nearest light shone vaguely off to her right. She hesitated, looking for motion and listening for sound.

Nothing.

Caitlin eased out onto the path and got her feet under her, but she remained crouched. The last time she'd heard from the killer, he'd been moving downhill, away from her. She turned uphill and moved toward the light.

She wanted to run, but her shoes made a slight sound against the pavement no matter how carefully she walked. Running would surely bring the killer.

Her thoughts turned to the future for the first time since she'd seen the killer in the back seat of the cab. The police would listen to her now. Assuming she lived long enough to reach them. That Ferguson woman would believe her this time too. With the cabby murdered, everything changed. None of them could ignore her. She'd have the police back in her room. They'd do a thorough investigation this time. The killer must have left some evidence of his break-in. The police could track him down. They would. They must. Then she would be on the next plane out of San Francisco, and back to Albuquerque. Home. Where she was safe.

Her thoughts came back to the here and now as she neared the light. Thirty feet from the light she stopped. The curvy rabbit trail had tricked her. She was back on the street near where she had started.

She saw a tiny movement at the point that the path and sidewalk met. She prayed that it was just the wind moving the brush, but the wind, while still moving the treetops, moved nothing beneath the canopy.

Caitlin felt her pulse leap again. She eased carefully to the side of the path and willed herself to vanish into the thick leaves of the oleander, pressing back against them as if they would part to allow her through.

Panic and you die. Panic and you die.

Caitlin watched the spot where the movement had occurred. Was that spot of brush darker than the rest? Maybe it was just a dog. Yeah, it might be just a dog.

She heard the sound of a car engine coming slowly up the hill. Headlights illuminated the fog with a ghostly glow and beams of light danced around the brush until one struck the shadows at the end of the trail.

The killer rose into the light like some creature rising out of the depths. The long barreled handgun was in his right hand.

Caitlin pressed tighter into the brush.

Holstering his gun, the killer stepped to the curb. The car slowed, then stopped beneath the street light.

The driver's window rolled down and a man's face appeared.

Caitlin's breath caught in her throat.

It was Mark Romax.

The detective.

The goddamn detective!

CHAPTER 5

Caitlin froze against the protective shroud of the bush while her attacker approached the car.

"Any luck, Holdren?"

Holdren leaned against the driver's door and shook his head. "No. She disappeared into the damn undergrowth. There's not much chance of locating her in this fog."

"That your work down the street?"

"Yeah, get a crew over to clean up the mess."

"What were you doing in a cab? Didn't you have a car?"

"Yeah, I had a car, but when I found out she'd left the hotel on foot I got the idea that she might hail a cab. There wasn't time to order one up so I grabbed the first one available."

"Jeez, did you have to pop him?"

"He was a witness."

"That's not much of a reason. We could have leaned on him and he wouldn't have talked."

"I know, but he got smart, tried to stop me with some pissant little gun. I didn't have time to reason with him."

"Well, it's your butt if Cronski doesn't like the excuse. We're not suppose to be doing wet work here. This was supposed to be a quick snatch."

Holdren's voice tightened and his posture stiffened. "Yeah? Why don't you tell me about it, Romax? I was cleaning up messes for assholes like Cronski when you were still in diapers. Nobody ever complains about the body count if the mission is successful."

"Look Holdren, I don't care what things were like in the good old days of the cold war. Times have changed; you can't leave bodies lying about, especially in domestic operations. If you can't adapt, then maybe it's time for you to retire."

Holdren leaned down placing his nose nearly in contact with Romax's. His voice came out slow and so low that

Caitlin could barely make out his words. "Anytime one of you young punks think you can retire me, you're welcome to try."

Romax paled and his head moved back, away from the confrontation. He shook his head. "That's not what I meant. Jesus Christ, Holdren, we don't retire people that way."

"Yeah, maybe not now, but don't you ever forget that I've been around a lot longer than you. I've done things that would make you piss your pants. Anytime you want I'll be happy to enlighten you."

Romax shook his head again. "Ah, no, thanks anyway. Look I'm sorry. I was just trying to follow Cronski's orders."

Holdren grinned and straightened, obviously enjoying playing with his partner. "I'll handle Cronski. You just get a cleanup crew in here. Then get some patrol cars around the park's perimeter. She'll try to contact the police again and we might get lucky if she sees a patrol car."

"Yeah, I can see that happening. What are you going to do?"

"Take me back to my room. I have night goggles there. I think I'll do a little hunting," Holdren said.

"Jeez. You know, I think you enjoy this too much," Romax said.

"Hey, the job has to have some perks. You can ask for a reassignment to a desk job anytime you want."

Holdren walked around to the passenger side of Romax's car and got in.

Caitlin watched the killer get in the passenger side of the car. It pulled away from the curb and headed back up the hill toward the Pacific Rim.

She waited until the sound of the engine had vanished into the fog, then stepped out from the bush and hesitated, torn between the trail and the street. She had to get out of the park before Holdren came back. In a few minutes there could be patrol cars wandering the park looking for her. She had to move fast.

Caitlin turned toward the street, her soles made slapping sounds as she ran. She reached the sidewalk and looked downhill. Nothing, just a glow in the fog from the nearest street light.

Fearful that their conversation may have been a ruse for her benefit, Caitlin listened for an approaching engine as she ran.

She almost ran into the taxi's bumper. Its lights were off and the doors were shut.

Caitlin stepped off the curb and went to the driver's door. She opened it. The body lay slumped down on the front seat.

Gritting her teeth, she pushed the body over enough to allow her to slide behind the wheel. The keys were in the ignition. She cranked the engine and turned on the lights.

Bitter bile rose in her throat as her stomach convulsed. The windshield and steering wheel were splattered with blood, pieces of skin and hair, and little bits of gray matter.

She forced down the bile and took a small box of tissues from her purse. There wasn't enough tissue in the box to clean everything. Caitlin swabbed the steering wheel and then carefully cleaned enough of the windshield to see through.

She tossed the tissue aside, put the transmission in gear, and accelerated down the hill.

A few minutes later she reached the park gate and stopped at the intersection with highway 101. Somewhere to her left, invisible in the fog, rose the massive bridge, to her right lay San Francisco. Which way? Away from town and the police she no longer trusted or into the city where she could lose herself among the masses. Neither way offered much.

Still, there was someone, someone she thought she could trust. If she could find him. She turned right.

CHAPTER 6

Romax drove the heavy Buick carefully through the fog. Neither of the men spoke until they were nearly back to the Pacific Rim.

Holdren said, "While I'm retrieving the transmitter, I want you to call in additional help in case she gets by our people in the park."

"The FBI?"

"Oh hell no. Their bureau chief has been looking for ways to get involved in our operations. Call the local NCIX, tell them it's an information espionage case and they'll fall all over themselves to help. Ask them to check out Alliotto's. She asked the cabby to take her there. Dumb bitch will probably show up there and order dinner."

"This the same dumb bitch that's gotten away from you twice tonight?"

"Didn't I ask you to put a transmitter in her purse?"

Romax nodded. "Yeah, you asked."

"And?"

"So I did. It's a short range unit, not good for more than a mile or so, less if she gets downtown among the high rise buildings."

Holdren didn't say anything else until the car stopped. The doorman came toward them. "You want to tell me why you used that unit instead of one of the satellite trackers?"

"There wasn't time to get a bigger transmitter in her purse. I thought it'd be better to have one she wasn't likely to find than to just drop a satellite transmitter into her purse and hope she didn't come across it. After all, you were suppose to keep her under surveillance until we could make the snatch."

Holdren shrugged. "Everyone has to go to the can eventually. It's my bad luck she chose that moment to walk out of the hotel."

Holdren's door opened.

"You have the receiver?" Holdren asked and slid from the car.

"In my room."

Holdren held out his hand. Romax took an electronic key from his pocket and placed it in his partner's palm.

Holdren stepped away from the car, ignored the doorman, and went to the revolving door. He crossed the thinly populated lobby to the elevator bank and took a waiting car to the thirty-third floor.

Romax's room lay across the hall from his. He unlocked the door and went in. A single suitcase sat on the dresser, next to a photo of Romax and his wife, June. Holdren stopped for a moment and starred at the photo. It was an old photo, taken before they had learned that June couldn't have children. He could tell; their marriage hadn't been happy after that. Within six months, June had become first an addict and then deceased. Holdren shrugged mentally. Some people just couldn't handle what life gave them.

He flipped the case open. It appeared empty. Romax always unpacked as soon as they reached a hotel. Sliding back the concealed catches opened the storage compartment. Inside were a couple of spare magazines for Romax's Sig P229, two thousand dollars in cash, a passport and credit card in one of Romax's aliases, a directional receiver and the satellite locator.

Holdren took the receiver and put the suitcase back the way he had found it. He flipped the receiver on and examined its display. Nothing. She was out of range.

Never leave important matters to an underling. He should have placed the transmitter himself.

He pulled the door shut behind him and unlocked his own room. Except for a couple of shirts on hangers, Holdren's clothes were still in his suitcase. He was always ready to leave at a moment's notice.

His equipment case sat on the dresser. There were no photos of ex-wives on Holdren's dresser. He'd never found the time to marry and raise rug-rats. His country always came first and someone had to protect it from those who were always chipping away at its foundations.

Holdren lifted the small gold chain with the inch long cross from under his shirt and slipped it over his head. He inserted the base of the cross into the hole in the front of his case, then dialed in the combination.

Anyone attempting to open his equipment bag without both the cross and the proper combination would be making an unplanned trip to the morgue.

He popped the catches and opened the lid.

Like Romax, he carried cash and a spare passport and spare credit cards, all in a fictitious name, among the other items he considered essential for any field operation.

The night vision goggles were the latest thing and looked more like a pair of fashionable Ray-Bans than the older low light scopes. He took them out, checked the charge, and then slipped them into a jacket pocket.

His answering machine's message light blinked. He wondered what Cronski wanted now. He probably just wanted to keep up with the operation. Cronski always tried to micro-manage Holdren's work, but then again, maybe the crew assigned to Corning had found something.

Flipping open the case, he woke up the main processor, placed his thumb on the pad to verify his identity, and then ordered a replay of messages.

The flat screen came online and he saw Cronski's image appear. His face bore the telltales of daily stress. That wasn't good for a man his age. Deep lines shadowed Cronski's face all the way to his hairline. At least the man maintained a healthy crop of hair. Holdren wondered if he'd had implants or one of the new drug therapies.

Cronski's voice sounded thin and soft.

"Volume up."

"Bitter and Reed screwed up the Los Alamos assignment. They killed Corning without questioning him. We've learned that he had the prototype in his possession for a couple of days before his untimely demise. Unfortunately, he either passed it on to a buyer or stashed it somewhere. We need his partner alive until we recover it. That's an order. No matter what, you must make sure she stays alive until then.

"You should have had time to search her things by now. Why haven't you reported in? I won't stand for your normal methods on this job. You report in with developments or I'll send someone to relieve you. Do I make myself clear?"

Holdren frowned sadly.

Cronski just didn't understand the complexity of fieldwork. These days there were too many players involved. You had to be careful and even then, there were times you were forced to improvise.

Cronski hadn't been with Holdren back in the cold war days and had moved into the agency from the CIA only five years ago. Holdren's sources said Cronski made the lateral transfer to avoid being fired over some screw up in the Balkans.

He shut down the computer without replying to the message and closed his case. Returning the cross to his neck, he went into the bathroom.

The sight of his reflection's bandaged nose made him frown again. "Keep her alive. Well, he didn't say in what condition."

CHAPTER 7

The fog was thicker near the water and she almost missed the turnoff to Fisherman's Wharf. She pulled the taxi onto a side street and parked it in front of a closed business near the mariner's museum.

She killed the engine and sat for a moment watching the street. It wasn't deserted, but the few people she could see were on the next block and facing away from her. Caitlin opened the door. The interior light stayed out. Seeing the cabby's body, she felt a wave of pity for him. She accepted her share of the responsibility for his death. Did he have a wife, children? She should see them and explain that he'd been killed trying to help her, but she had to wait, wait until she was safe.

Caitlin swung her legs from the seat and got out. Then she took a pen light from her purse, flicked it on, and played it around the front seat. On the floor, light glistened off metal. Leaning over, she picked up the small handgun that Holdren had mentioned.

Turning to rise, Caitlin found herself looking into the dead man's open eyes. They were brown, but a third dark eye glistened wet just above the bridge of his nose. Seconds passed before Caitlin could break away from his sightless stare.

She straightened and put the gun into her purse. His name. She should at least know his name. Her light played across the dash and lit a photo ID of Lucas Griffin.

"Thank you, Lucas." She reached down and gently pressed his eyelids closed. When she pulled her fingers away, his eyes remained closed.

She'd better get moving. But first, she grabbed a crumpled hamburger wrapper from the floor and used it to wipe down the steering wheel and everything else she could remember touching.

Except for Lucas' eyes. She stared at the wrapper and at Lucas. Then with her free hand she softly ran her fingertips across his lids, smearing whatever fingerprints she might have left.

Getting out of the cab, Caitlin pushed the door shut, then wiped off the handle.

She looked up and down the street. Seeing no on, she turned toward the wharf, and started walking. At the corner, she dropped the hamburger wrapper into a trashcan before crossing the street.

A few minutes later she reached the wharf. There was a small crowd, but nothing like what she'd seen on more pleasant nights. She stopped under a street lamp and eyed her reflection in a storefront window. Her blouse and jacket looked rumpled and a twig clung to her hair. Both of her knees looked like she had been crawling through grass. She plucked the twig from her hair, took a brush from her purse, and ran it through her hair a few times. As always, it fell back into place with a minimum of fuss.

Her pantyhose proved more difficult. Caitlin walked back up the street to the next corner and went around it. The side street was deserted, for the moment. After making sure no one could see her, Caitlin pulled up her skirt and hooked her thumbs into the waistband of her pantyhose. She stripped them down to her ankles in one clean motion, then stepped out of one shoe at a time and pulled the pantyhose off. Wadding them into a small ball, she wiped them across her knees several times, then stuffed them into her purse before slipping her shoes back on.

She stopped in front of the window again. The marks on her knees were nearly gone. Caitlin brushed the wrinkles out of her skirt with the back of her hand then headed across the street. Her bare feet stuck to the bottom of her shoes then pulled loose with each step. At the entrance to Alliotto's she hesitated, turned to look around once more. No one appeared to be interested in her. Releasing the breath she'd been holding, Caitlin went inside.

The hostess, a strikingly beautiful, fiftyish woman, eyed her softly as she approached. "Good evening. Will you be dining?"

"Yes, but I need to make a stop first. Where's the ladies' room?"

The hostess nodded with her head. "That way, miss."

"Thank you."

In the empty ladies' room she used the first stall, then went to the sink. The mirror's clear reflection revealed more flaws than the storefront window had. She wet a paper towel and washed her face and legs. Then she opened her purse and removed her makeup case. It held the basics, mascara, lipstick, and powder. Caitlin used each sparingly, then eyed her reflection one more time. Much better, not perfect, but much better.

She put everything back in her purse and went out to meet the hostess. The older woman gave her an approving smile.

"Right this way." Carrying a menu, she led Caitlin to a table next to the window and pulled a chair out for her.

"May I send a waitress over with a before dinner drink?" She held out the menu as Caitlin sat.

"Yes, please, a brandy Manhattan, with olives. Ah, make it a double."

Caitlin felt uncomfortable ordering a double, but she need to calm down as much or more than she needed to keep her wits about her.

The hostess nodded and moved away. Caitlin scanned the dining room, quickly taking in each patron. None appeared threatening, or appeared to take any notice of her.

At the near end of the room, above the door to the kitchen, an exit sign glowed dimly. Looking over her shoulder, she could see the hostess's podium near the front door. It felt comfortable to be near an exit, but she got out of her chair and sat down in the opposite chair so she could see anyone entering the dining room from the front.

She looked over the menu and had narrowed her selection to a few things by the time the waitress arrived with her drink. Caitlin made the final cut, ordering calamari for an appetizer and a shark steak for her entree.

As soon as the waitress left, Caitlin picked up the glass and downed a third of the Manhattan in one gulp. Its smooth warmth spread to her stomach.

Now what, Ms. Maxwell? You've shaken the killer for now, but you're a thousand miles from home and don't know who to trust. The first order of business is to get some food in you and that's taken care of. But then what? You can't trust anyone in this town, certainly not the police. Who else is in on this? Is that Romax character a real policeman? Is Patricia Ferguson in with them or did she really call the police? Holdren implied they had patrol cars available and certainly no one but the police had access to patrol cars. And just what the hell do they want with you?

She needed help, but from whom? The only person she knew in San Francisco besides Koenig and Teigue, and she wasn't sure she could trust them, was ... John Blalock. God, she hadn't seen him in twelve years. Only by accident had she even learned he was in San Francisco. She'd come across a reference to him on the Web a few months ago and had tracked it to a home page that indicated he now did business in the Bay Area. She could probably trust him or at least she had been able to once, but she hadn't seen him since before her wedding.

A lot had changed since then.

He'd once saved her life. Would he be as willing to do it again?

The calamari arrived. It had been sautéed in garlic and lemon before being browned in olive oil and tasted delicious. While she munched on it, Caitlin took the notebook computer from her purse. She pushed the appetizer plate to one side, set the notebook down, and powered up. She set her cell phone next to it and connected the short cable between them. Activating her Web browser, Caitlin selected a telephone number in the Bay Area and accessed the Web.

Searching the area directories for John Q. Blalock yielded nothing. She dropped out of the telephone database and called up a search engine. A minute more and she had a list of references to John Blalock.

One was the item she'd noticed last month. The article concerned the return of stolen industrial secrets to a small Bay Area firm by the Blalock Security Service of San Francisco. It provided a brief bio of the owner of the service. When it mentioned the University of Colorado at Colorado Springs, Caitlin realized it had to be John Q. Blalock.

She cross referenced to Blalock Security Service and found its Web page address. Accessing it, she received a list of services offered and a list of references to past employers of the Blalock Security Service. She recognized many of the names on that list.

The page had the usual feedback notation at the bottom, but it also had an emergency response button.

Caitlin clicked on it and her screen went red. A second later an icon, a yellow rose with the electrical symbol for a lightning suppresser, appeared with the subscript.

"Searching --"

Caitlin watched the screen for a minute, growing impatient, but then the subscript changed to: "Found --"

She waited another thirty seconds, then the screen shifted into a chat mode with Blalock Security Service at the top and her screen log-on at the bottom.

"You have an emergency?" appeared in the top box.

Caitlin put down her fork and typed. "Yes, I do. Is this John?"

"Yes. State your problem."

"John, this is Caitlin Maxwell, from Colorado."

There was a noticeable hesitation before the next line appeared. "Hello Caitlin. It's been awhile. What's your emergency?"

"Is this secure?"

"As secure as anything can be on the Web."

"I'm in San Francisco. I'm being hunted by people I don't know. They've broken into my room, tried to kill me."

He responded immediately. "Are you safe where you are?"

"I don't know. I'm in a public place."

"Safe enough for the moment then. Do you want to go into detail?"

"Not over the net. I used a public access number, but they may be able to track it back to me."

"Right, I'll meet you. I'm going to send an encrypted address. The decryption key will be...."

Caitlin leaned back. Security over the web was always a problem. You couldn't encrypt things unless the other party knew the decryption key and you couldn't send it to them through unsecured channels or anyone else could use it to decrypt the same message. How was he going to do this?

Letters appeared on the screen. "The name of the last place I saw you."

Ah, that limited the choices. "All right."

"Sending."

A download symbol appeared briefly and then disappeared.

"File received. How soon?"

"Thirty minutes."

"All right, I'll --"

Caitlin stopped typing as she noticed movement by the entrance. A woman, wearing a dark suit with her blond hair pulled back in a tight knot, had come in and stood talking to the hostess. She appeared to be showing her a photo.

A premonition seized Caitlin. She killed the connection and quickly returned the notebook computer and cell phone to her bag. She stood up.

The hostess shook her head and handed the photo back to the stranger.

Turning away, Caitlin walked slowly toward the nearest exit. When she ducked into the kitchen she spotted her waitress.

"Excuse me," Caitlin said and touched the young woman on the arm.

The woman turned and started as she realized who was talking. "You shouldn't be back here, ma'am."

Caitlin dropped her voice into a conspiratorial tone. "Look, my ex-boyfriend just came in the restaurant looking for me. We broke up a few weeks ago and he's been really pushy trying to get me to come back. I don't want to have a public scene with him. You know how some men are...."

"Do I ever."

As the waitress spoke Caitlin fished a roll of bills from her purse. She peeled off a pair of fifties and held them out. "Do you think you could show me the back way out of here and then forget about me?"

The waitress stared at the money. She nodded. "But there's no need to pay me. I'll take fifty to pay for your food and drink, but I'll be happy to help you duck the bum."

"Please, consider it a tip," Caitlin said, still extending both bills.

"All right then." She took the bills and they disappeared into a pocket in her blouse. "This way."

Caitlin followed her through the kitchen to the rear door. The waitress held the door while Caitlin examined the loading dock. No one was in sight.

"Thanks," she said.

"Anytime."

Caitlin walked quickly past dumpsters that smelled strongly of fish and sour milk and then slowed as she approached the street. Hugging the wall, she peered around the corner. A light green Ford sat at the curb by the front entrance. Another woman, dressed much like the one inside, stood by the driver's door.

Who in hell were these people?

Were they with Romax and Holdren?

Caitlin noticed the license plate. It was a federal government plate. She took a pen and pad from her purse and jotted down the license number. Just as she turned to slip away another car screeched to a halt next to the first.

The front doors opened and Romax and Holdren got out.

CHAPTER 8

Holdren climbed out before Romax could kill the engine and strode purposefully toward the agent stationed at the front of Alliotto's. He took his identity card from a breast pocket and flashed it in the woman's face.

"Agent Bailey?" he asked.

The muscular woman eyed his ID. She studied it as though memorizing its information. "Wesson, Special Agent Bailey's inside."

Wesson was average height for a female NCIX agent, about five feet eight and from the way her muscles stretched the sleeves of her jacket, she had to weigh over one-fifty.

"Inside? I thought I made myself clear that no one was to approach the suspect until I arrived."

"Yeah, well Agent Bailey thought it made more sense to check the place out and see if the suspect had already left. There's not much point in standing around waiting for someone who's not going to show."

Holdren felt a familiar pounding in his temples. He should have known better than expecting the local NCIX agents to take orders from outside their chain of command.

"She did, did she? If she's spooked the suspect, there'll be hell to pay when I talk to the director. I didn't go through months of work to see someone else barge into my case and fuck it up."

Wesson's attitude chilled. "Cool down, Agent Holdren. We haven't fucked anything up. I've been watching the outside since she went in and no one's come out. But come to think of it, we were told you had her and let her get away once tonight already."

"Yeah? Well, don't believe everything you hear."

"What makes you think she's coming here anyway? The assistance request didn't specify."

"She took a cab from the Pacific Rim and gave this destination."

"Did you talk to the driver?"

"No, the driver hasn't reported in and they can't raise him on the radio."

"Then you don't know she came here."

"No I don't, but I suspect she may have been intending to meet someone here. If so, she'll have to show up or call off the meeting. Either way we've prevented her from handing over the material."

He tossed the locator to Romax. "Is she in there or not?"

Romax flicked the tracker on and watched the display. A few seconds later he pointed it toward the front door. "That way."

"All right, she must be in there. Get a couple more units down here. I want to make sure she doesn't get away. As soon as they're here we'll take her."

"How about her contact?" Wesson asked.

"If there's anyone with her we'll take them too, otherwise I'll settle for getting her before she can pass anything on."

* * *

Caitlin saw Romax raise his hand. He held something. Her stomach spasmed as he pointed it directly at her. She couldn’t take anymore. Ducking behind the side of the building, she ran.

A block later, Caitlin stared back over her shoulder as she crossed the street. She expected Holdren and his people to come around the side of Alliotto's at any second. She made it to the next corner without any sign of them and headed west toward Victorian Park. The Powell-Hyde trolley turned around there. She didn't know if they ran this late, but it was the quickest path away from Fisherman's Wharf without calling a taxi. They would be watching for her to summon a taxi.

For the first time tonight, she was in luck. A trolley was turning around as she reached it. Caitlin climbed on with three couples and the trolley began to move almost immediately. Caitlin held onto the brass rail by her seat and stared back down the hill. No one ran after her and gradually, her pulse subsided to near normal levels.

Were the government women working with Romax and Holdren or were they looking for her for some other reason? But what? What had she done that would have government agents and killers after her? She thought back over all the projects she'd worked on in the last year, but could think of nothing with a connection to the government.

How had they tracked her to the restaurant? When she'd flagged down Lucas Griffin's taxi, did she mention Alliotto's? She couldn't recall for sure. But from the argument they'd had, the government women hadn't been with Holdren. Then what had brought them? She knew the technology existed to track her on the Web, but she had scrupulously avoided using her normal log-on site and even if they had found her on the Web they couldn't have located her. Cell phones could be traced. That implied not only scanning frequencies, but also knowing the code for her personal telephone. If that was how they found her then they were certainly going to a lot of effort.

She needed to access John's file and see where he wanted to meet.

The trolley ride would take a little time, but she wanted to be ready to run if Holdren or his people spotted her. Caitlin leaned back against the seat and watched the streets. In five or six minutes, they reached Powell Avenue and she signaled the driver that she wanted to get off.

When the trolley stopped, Caitlin climbed off and walked up Powell until she reached a set of steps up to an old building. She went up into the portico. It smelled of stale urine. Opening her purse, Caitlin set her computer on the top step and booted up.

She called up John's file and activated the decryption program. "All right, John, how tricky were you? Let's try Grand Canyon."

The screen displayed "password accepted" and a few seconds later a single line of text appeared. "The Gleaning Cube, 1242 Battery Street."

"Well, that was easy enough. Now where's Battery Street?"

Caitlin switched over to the main menu and called up the street map of San Francisco she'd downloaded last week. She entered the address and a moment later a small red dot glowed on the southeast side of town, near the waterfront. After reading the address on a building across the street, Caitlin typed it in and clicked on directions.

A faint green line stretched east on Powell, cut over a few blocks, east again, then ran south to stop at the blue dot.

The readout said 2.3 miles.

"Hell."

Her watch indicated she had fifteen minutes before their appointment. She couldn't walk it in time. Three blocks farther down Powell she could see the marquee for a hotel. She shutdown the computer, put it in her purse, and left the telephone booth.

Paranoia overtook over as she neared the hotel. She stepped into the shadows of another doorway and spent a couple of minutes watching the hotel's entrance. A few people came and went. One couple looked like they had just returned from the opera. When the man helped his date from the taxi, he swept her into his arms and kissed her passionately. Caitlin felt a twinge of envy at the sight of their happiness.

No one sat in a parked car like in the movies when the police staked out a scene. In fact, everything appeared normal.

She slipped her hand into her purse and closed her fingers around the small gun she'd taken from the cab. She took one deep breath, then walked the rest of the way. The doorman watched her approach and when she motioned to him he raised a white-gloved hand and summoned a waiting cab. It pulled forward and stopped at the curb. The doorman held the door for her and Caitlin slipped a bill into his hand as she carefully studied the cab. The back seat was empty.

She slipped quickly in and waited until the door shut.

"Where to?"

"No where in particular. How about just letting me look around?"

"It's your money." The cabby flicked the meter down and pulled out into the street.

Caitlin turned to look out the rear window. No other cars pulled out to follow them and the doorman had forgotten her as soon as he'd shut the door.

"Any particular area you want to see?"

Caitlin hesitated, she didn't want to come right out and give the address on the chance that somehow those after her could hear. She realized she was being a little too paranoid, but being shot at did that to her. "Take me through downtown and then maybe we'll turn south and drive along the waterfront."

"Sure thing."

"I guess I sound a little oddball," Caitlin said as she leaned forward to examine the cabby's ID. It appeared genuine and the photo seemed to match what she could see of him.

"Nah, not oddball. I've seen them all. Wackos, dopeheads, homicidal maniacs, you name it. You seem pretty normal compared to them guys."

She relaxed a little and released her grip on the gun. "Really? How could you tell?"

Her gaze met his in the rearview mirror. He raised a finger and touched his eyes.

"Are you kidding? It's in the eyes." He pointed to the mirror.

"Lady, I've seen them looking at me right there. I tell ya, some of the things I've seen would make your blood go cold."

They stopped at a traffic light on Market Street and two young couples sporting facial tattoos and various body piercings crossed in front of them.

"Case in point." He motioned toward them.

"And yet you continue to drive a cab."

"I'm one of them people watchers. I like watching people and listening to them. You know people will talk about stuff in a cab that they wouldn't tell a priest."

The light changed. Caitlin's thoughts wandered as they crossed Market and went a couple of blocks before turning east again. "You can tell a lot by watching people, take you for instance."

"Me?"

"Yes, you. You've got that dark mysterious look that's big in the movies these days, but I can tell right off that you're not in that line of work."

"Oh? What gives it away?"

"Your clothes. Movie people dress one of two ways. They're either dolled up, which usually implies they're going somewhere they want to be recognized or else they dress down in a kind of nouveau trash. You've seen the type. They'll wear old sneakers that they paid two hundred dollars for and maybe some faded jeans that they bought that way. They won't do anything with their face and hair, like brushing their hair or shaving is beneath them unless they're doing a part."

"And you can tell they're not just someone with Salvation Army clothes who can't afford to look any better?"

"Damn straight. You see, no matter how down they dress, they still have a couple of things that sets them apart."

"And that is?" Caitlin asked. She found herself smiling, enjoying their conversation.

"Expensive jewelry, like a necklace or perhaps a twenty thousand dollar Rolex."

"Yes, I imagine that would be a dead give away, but you said two things."

He grinned. "You're sharp. I like that. The other thing is health, like clear skin and perfect teeth. You see someone who's down on their luck, and their skin shows it. If they've been down long enough you can see it in their teeth and gums, but the movie people, well, they have all their teeth straightened or capped and their skin is perfect."

Caitlin nodded. His theory was logical enough.

The cab turned right along the waterfront. "Now take you."

"Uh huh?"

"Yeah, like I said, you've got that dark mysterious look, although since you've smiled some of it is gone. Something's bothering you tonight, can't say what it might be, but it's serious."

"How perceptive. What else can you tell me about myself?" Their conversation had become a game.

"My first impression is that you're in town on business."

"That's good. What gave me away?" Caitlin asked. She looked out the left window as the bay appeared between rows of dockside warehouses.

"You don't have the local accent and you aren't too familiar with the city, so you're from out of town. You're dressed more formally than most tourists, but not like you were out on the town, if you know what I mean?"

Caitlin caught his gaze in the mirror and nodded.

"You also have a notebook computer in that purse."

Surprised, Caitlin checked to see if her purse was open. It wasn't. "Okay, that's good, but how did you know?"

"Lady, I get five or six women a day who have a purse just like that one. Occasionally they take out their computers to do work while I'm taking them to the airport or wherever. It's almost become a uniform for business women."

"I hadn't noticed."

"Now then, second impressions, you're from the southwest or maybe Colorado originally. You've got a parent or grandparent who's a native, Cherokee perhaps. I thought Navajo at first, but that was because your accent threw me off. You don't have the rounded facial features of a Navajo."

Caitlin had to sit back in her seat and stare at his reflected eyes. "I don't get it. How could you possibly know I had Cherokee blood?"

"A combination of things. The straight black hair, the eyes, and the tan."

"Tan? I don't have a tan and my eyes are blue."

"The blue wasn't what I was talking about. It's the way they're set in your face, and the tan, it's not from the sun, I knew that right away. None of you computer carrying businesswomen go in for tanning saloons or even lying out on the beach. That would be as bad as smoking."

"Really?"

"Sure thing, so the tan is hereditary. That puts you either in the Native American group or perhaps the Indian subcontinent, but I ruled them out. Their tan is a more subdued brown."

A sign caught Caitlin's attention. It was a cube outlined in neon with the words, The Gleaning Cube.

"I hate to break off this fascinating conversation, but I need to get out."

Silently for once, the cabby pulled to the curb, just past and across the street from the Cube.

Caitlin looked at the meter, then pulled a bill from her purse. She held it out. The driver turned in his seat and took it.

"Thanks for an interesting ride. Tell me, what did you do before you became a cabby?"

"Me? I've always been a cabby. It gives me a chance to study."

"What are you studying?"

He smiled warmly. "People."

Caitlin got out and then waited in the cold fog until the taxi had turned the corner and disappeared from view. The night air smelled of brine and diesel fuel. She walked north along the street until she faced the bar from the opposite side of the street. It appeared to be a wharf side bar. Faded gray paint over cement block made up the facade. Large windows set to either side of the door. In one window, she could see an illuminated Heineken sign. The few cars parked in front varied from a late model Lexus to a ratty old Ford F150 pickup that would have been more at home in her native Colorado than on the San Francisco waterfront.

Caitlin checked her watch. Thirty-two minutes had passed since John's message to meet him here. She took a deep breath and let it out. The taxi ride and the conversation with the cabby had relaxed her, but not to the point of making her feel safe.

She stepped off the curb and walked across the wide street. When she reached the front door, Caitlin stopped and turned her head quickly to each side hoping to catch anyone watching her. She saw nothing unusual.

Opening the door, she went inside.

*   *   *

Holdren and Romax stood outside Alliotto's as the two NCIX agents drove away.

"I don't understand how it could have happened. The locator placed her in the restaurant." Romax tugged on his ear lobe.

Holdren stared at him and then shook his head. Why did he always have to explain the basics to Romax? "Think about it. The readout tells you what?"

Romax stared at the instrument's display. "Distance and bearing."

"And how accurate is it?"

"I'm not positive. Range, maybe fifty feet, bearing, maybe a couple of degrees."

"That is a model 4D12."

"Yes."

"The 4D12 is accurate to within fifty feet in distance, but for bearing it's only within five degrees. How far from the restaurant were we when you took the reading?" Holdren asked.

"About where we are now, maybe thirty feet from the door."

"And the reading was?"

"Directly toward the restaurant, at a range of eighty feet."

"So, she could have been as much as 130 feet away at up to 5 degrees to either side. That means she could have been behind the restaurant or on either side of it when you checked. By the time we discovered she wasn't in the restaurant she was out of range."

"Yeah, I guess it could have happened that way."

"You guess? Damn you Romax...." The buzz of Holdren's cell phone interrupted what he wanted to say about Romax's competence. He flicked it open and noticed the scrambled signal indicator. The phone automatically went secure when queried by a similar device. He raised it to his ear. "Holdren."

"This is Kirby, we have a blip on the frequency of your locator."

"What's your location?"

"Embarcadero, near the Bay Bridge."

"What direction is the signal coming from?"

"It's hard to tell, but it's somewhere south of here. It appears to be moving, but in the downtown area, it's almost impossible to get a direct feed. There are just too many reflections."

"That's all right, I understand. Contact the other units and sweep the area, sooner or later you'll have to get a straight shot at it."

"Yes, sir."

Holdren closed his cell phone and glowered at Romax. "You heard?"

"Enough."

"Then get the car. I don't want her slipping away again."

* * *

The Gleaning Cube's interior was dimly lit, as most late hour bars seem to be. A dozen or so tables were scattered around a room that could easily hold twice as many. A wide bar blocked most of her view of the rear, but she could see more tables back there. The Gleaning Cube was perhaps a third full. Three people sat on bar stools, none of them next to each other. On the nearest barstool sat an older woman who Caitlin had pegged as a street person until a closer look showed that her clothing, while old, was clean and well maintained. A pair of young couples talked at a nearby table; from their neat hair and expensive attire, Caitlin guessed they belonged to the Lexus.

The bar seemed to have two sets of clientele. The locals who sat either at the bar or away from the door and the young professionals who grouped near the front. Most of them were like the Lexus couples.

Caitlin quickly checked out each of the patrons who were within view of the door. She recognized no one. Trying to appear casual, she went to the bar and motioned to the bartender. He was a younger man, dressed comfortably in loose fitting jeans and a flannel shirt. A gold stud decorated his left ear and a bar towel hung over his shoulder.

"Good evening. What'll you have?"

"I'm looking for a man."

"Anyone in particular or will I do?"

Caitlin gave him a tired stare. "His name is John Blalock."

The bartender's lips pursed and he appeared to think about it. "The name sounds familiar."

He turned part way around and looked over the nearer tables.

Caitlin had already looked over those tables and no one looked anything like John. Yet, when the bartender turned back he nodded. "He's expecting you."

"Really?"

"Yes. You'll find him against the back wall."

Caitlin looked past the bartender and spotted a table where a lone man sat facing her. A weathered hat blocked most of his features.

"Are you sure?"

"Who can ever be sure of anything? I understand that's a name he goes by."

Caitlin gave the man another look, then thanked the bartender. She walked around the bar and moved slowly toward the back.

Three feet from the table she stopped.

Something was wrong here. John had been a computer nerd. They'd only met the one time, in the canyon. He'd been big, as big as this man, she remembered him saying something about wrestling in high school. His skin had been smooth and unblemished and she would have bet that the cabby would have spotted him as a computer nerd immediately. He'd had long hair, tied in a ponytail, and wore shorts over those thick thighs. His height and weight looked about the same as she remembered. His hair was the right color, nearly as dark as hers, but was cut much shorter and trimmed as neatly as his fingernails. His lightweight trench coat hung open to reveal a simple khaki shirt. His face didn't fit what she remembered. For the brief time she'd known him, it had always been cheerful, boyishly cheerful. His lips had always hidden a laugh, one that just waited for an excuse to erupt. A mustache hid most of his upper lip now. His face had lost all signs of boyishness and was now weathered, tight, and scarred.

Well, one scar anyway. A deep cicatricial scar ran from the corner of his left eye to somewhere beneath his mustache. It gave his scowling features a menacing look that she couldn't connect with the man she had known so long ago.

He stood as she reached the table. She met his gaze and knew it immediately that it was John. His eyes had changed; the skin around them had tightened and showed the first signs of crows' feet and the pupils themselves looked sadder, but they were still the pale, almost gray-blue that she remembered each time she thought of him.

"Hello Caitlin."

"My God, John. I hardly recognized you. You've changed."

"It's been a dozen years, Caitlin. Sometimes they slip by without leaving any sign of their passage, much as they've treated you. Other times, they just pile up."

"Is that what they've done to you, pile up?"

"Some have. Won't you sit? Can I order you a drink?"

Caitlin pulled the only other chair out and sat down. "No, thank you. I had one earlier and life has become a little too interesting to dull with more alcohol just now."

"Coffee then?"

She nodded.

John caught the bartender's eye, mouthed coffee, and held up two fingers before sitting down across from her.

The bartender appeared almost immediately and placed two cups on the table. "Cream or sugar?"

"No thanks," Caitlin said.

John waited until the bartender had moved off. "I understand you need some assistance. From your abrupt disconnect, I gather it's rather immediate."

"Right to the point, eh John? You've changed more than in just your appearance. I remember when you could make small talk until sunup."

He didn't reply.

A chair grated across the wood floor and Caitlin's head snapped around. Across the room a man stood up and staggered toward them. She watched him until he passed their table and disappeared down a hall marked with a small sign labeled restrooms.

"Would you care to slide your chair around so you can see the front?"

She nodded, and scooted her chair sideways until she sat elbow to elbow with him. She now had a good view of the rest of the bar and the front door.

John's right hand moved toward her and, for a moment, she thought he was putting his arm around her, then his hand moved toward her purse.

"What?"

He raised a finger to his lips and swept his right hand over her purse.

For the first time, she noticed he wore a bracelet on that wrist. A tiny light blinked on the bracelet.

Without a word, John opened the purse and beginning removing its contents one item at a time. His lack of explanation was irritating and she reached for her purse to yank it away from him, when he paused and held a pearl button over his bracelet. The light stopped blinking and burned steady.

John closed his left fist tightly around the button. "Just a minute."

Pushing his chair silently back, John stood and went to the bar. Caitlin watched him speak to the bartender, who nodded once and then held out his hand. John dropped the button into it and came back.

"What was that all about?"

"Did you recognize that?"

"No. It could have been one of my buttons, but I don't normally have buttons in the bottom of my purse."

"You didn't this time either. That was a transmitter. Someone's been tracking you."

"Tracking me? Are you serious?"

"Of course."

"Then this is some kind of detector?" she said and she reached for his wrist.

He pulled back.

Surprised, she dropped her hand back to her side.

"That's right, an electric field detector."

"Why'd you give the transmitter to the bartender?"

"He has a microwave behind the bar."

"A microwave? What's he going to do? Scramble it or fry it?"

"Neither, for now. If I just wanted to destroy it I could have stepped on it."

"Then why?"

"Microwave ovens have a shield to keep the microwave radiation inside during operation. The same shield will block the transmitter's signal while I decide what to do with it.

"Now, perhaps you should tell me what's going on."

Caitlin took a deep breath and began. "Someone is after me."

She spoke in a rush. She had a need to get it said, as if the telling would make it seem more believable.

When she finished, John's face betrayed no sign of emotion. "Doesn't sound much like a professional job. Are you having troubles with ... Scott wasn't it?"

Caitlin's face darkened. "Scott's dead."

"Oh? Recently?"

"This afternoon."

For the first time, his eyes seemed to shift and soften. "I'm sorry. Did his death have anything to do with the attack on you?"

"I ... I don't know, but I can't see it not having some connection. We were on the telephone when he was killed."

John stared at her until she began to feel uncomfortable, then he looked away, and took a small notepad from an inside pocket. "Give me those names again."

Caitlin recited them and then took out the piece of paper where she'd written the license plate numbers. John copied them and returned the notepad and pen to his jacket pocket.

"You're sure the plates on the one car were government plates?"

"As sure as I am of anything tonight."

John tapped his pen against the table. "Caitlin, how did you happen to find me?"

"I ... I came across your name on the Web a couple of months ago. It didn't take long to find your home page after that."

"I see. Well, I'm not tied up at the moment so I can probably help you. Business is business, but I'll give you the cut rate for my time and whatever expenses I incur while helping you."

"Expenses? Business? I thought, never mind. Do you take American Express?"

He almost smiled. "Caitlin, normally I do, but I wouldn't recommend you use any of your cards just now. If the government is really involved, your cards would lead them right to us."

"I see. Well, I'm not carrying much cash. What are your rates?"

He quoted a figure that made her wince. "But that's the going rate. For you, half that, after all, what are friends for?"

"Yeah, right."

"You sound like you don't think I should be charging you."

"I came to you because we were friends once."

"And?"

"And? And friends are suppose to help friends."

"Tell me something, Caitlin. If I came to you and asked you to design a special computer interface for me, would you do it for free?"

Caitlin shook her head. "No, we run a business, I couldn't very well --"

"Exactly."

"But this isn't in your line of work.

"Is that so? What is it that you think I do?"

"The article mentioned something about recovery of stolen information or something like that."

"Yeah, that's one aspect. I provide security, security for property, ideas, and self. I think you're in need of a little self-protection. Wouldn't you agree?"

Caitlin hesitated, then reluctantly nodded. "Then how can I pay you?"

"We'll work something out, assuming we both live through this. If not, well, satisfaction is guaranteed or your money back."

Caitlin sat back in her chair and stared at him. "Is that your idea of humor?"

"No, not at all. I want to be honest with you. You're in serious trouble and I think I can help you. But until we have some inkling as to who these people are and why they want you dead, it's going to be very hard to protect you."

The front door opened and Caitlin's eyes jerked toward it. It was the Lexus couples leaving. She turned back to John. His steady gaze was questioning.

"Okay," she said. "You're hired. What's our first move?"

"Our? Our first move is to put you somewhere out of sight. Then I'll talk to the hotel security and check with the police, to see if your report was filed, and then I'll run down these license numbers."

CHAPTER 9

John settled his tab and told the bartender to give the transmitter thirty seconds on high. Then he directed Caitlin down a hallway choked with cases of beer, boxes of snack mix, and both full and empty kegs, toward the rear of the bar. They passed the restrooms and reached a steel fire door.

John opened it and looked around, then motioned for her to follow.

His car, a classic 1973 'Cuda was backed into a space on the wharf next to a garbage bin. As they approached it, he remotely triggered the locks.

The drive took them down the two eighty, past Daly City, onto highway 1, and across the last hills to the coastal road. A half-hour later they pulled into the lot of a motel overlooking Half Moon Bay.

"Why here?" Caitlin asked.

He pulled into a parking space out of sight of the lobby and stopped. "I've used it on several occasions, but never under my real name. It's far enough out of San Francisco to skip a check if they're circulating your photo, but close enough to run back into the city."

"I see."

"Besides, you'll like the view of the bay."

Caitlin's eyes narrowed. "I hardly think I'll be admiring the view."

"Relax, no one will bother you. Wait here while I get the key. I'd prefer you be seen as little as possible."

"But you just said...."

"I know what I said, but there's no sense in tempting fate."

He left the motor running, the big V-8 hummed softly as if alive. The fog had turned into a heavy mist as they neared the coast. Odds were slim that anyone would see Caitlin well enough to identify her, but he didn't play the odds, he played the sure thing.

He walked around to the lobby and entered the main door. His trenchcoat dripped water onto the thick vermilion tile. The night clerk, an attractive young woman barely out of her teens, studyied a textbook on oceanography. John figured her to be a student at Palo Alto. That was one of the things he liked about this motel. The night clerks were almost always students and seldom worked more than a semester before deciding the graveyard shift crimped their sex life. The ones who did stay longer only did so because they could study most of their shift. That meant they spent as little time as possible noticing who came and went, a definite plus in John's view.

As he approached her counter, she reluctantly looked up from the book on oceanography. Her dark eyes widened as they focused on his scar. Then she met his gaze and forced a smile. Her teeth were straight and clean, but had a faint stain.

John nodded to her and flipped a credit card onto the counter. "I'd like a room for two people, separate beds, overlooking the bay."

She picked up the card and did a quick scan. He could almost read the computer screen as information scrolled down, she nodded. "Yes sir, Mr. Kurdys. How many nights will that be for?"

"Let's start with a week and see how we like it."

"Yes sir."

She punched information into the terminal and then passed the card back to him. Ducking under the counter for a moment, she came up with a small map and a plastic card. She set them both on the counter and indicated a point on the map. "You're booked into room 187. It's right here."

"Thanks, I can find it."

He checked the map, then picked up the key.

"Have a pleasant stay."

John tucked the credit card and the key into a pocket of his coat and nodded. "Thanks."

He walked back to the car and got in next to Caitlin.

"How'd it go?"

"No problems."

He put the car into reverse, backed down the length of the hotel, and stopped two doors past room 187. There were several cars parked nearby, but no one was in sight. It didn't look like the hotel did a lot of business after midnight.

"Come on, it looks clear," he said.

He killed the engine, opened his door, and then popped the latch on the trunk before getting out. At the rear of the 'Cuda, John reached into the trunk and pulled out a small overnight bag. He slammed the lid shut and saw Caitlin facing him.

"What's that?"

"An overnight bag."

"You always carry one in your car?"

"Most times. You never can tell where the night will find you."

Caitlin followed him to the room. He slid the plastic key into the door and the locked clicked.

"Wait here," John said.

Pushing the door open, John hit the lights and stepped inside. He told himself that he shouldn't have worried about anyone being there ahead of them. He rarely came here and tonight's trip had been decided after he went through an elaborate search for any tails. The final drive along the coast's winding road made it easy to spot someone following. Still, there was no such thing as too much paranoia. He checked the closet, the shower and even under the beds before telling Caitlin it was clear.

Caitlin came in and sat heavily on the bed farthest from the door.

"You'll be all right here," John said. "Since you don't have any more business in town, I'll go in later and see if I can get a lead on who's after you."

"Would it be all right for me to go with you?"

He shook his head. "I'd rather you stay here. You're safe here and if you're with me they'd have the advantage."

"The advantage? What do you mean?"

"They know what you look like. If they see you with me then they'll know me too."

"That's a problem?"

"I can't sneak up on someone if he can see me coming."

She nodded. "I guess you're right. After all, it is your business."

"That's right."

He turned away and went to the window overlooking Half Moon Bay. Drawing back the curtain, he looked out. Below the window, waves broke against rock, sending a thick saltwater spray into the fog. He leaned against the glass, blotting out the reflection of the room. The pounding of the surf cloaked Caitlin's footsteps on the carpet. He flinched when her hand touched his shoulder.

"John, I appreciate what you're doing for me."

He nodded, once. Her words were echoes from the past.

"I never forgot you, John, or what you did for me."

Did she expect a response? Twelve years had passed since the Canyon. A lot of water had passed down that Canyon in the years since. A lot of memories through his life.

"I'd almost forgotten about you," he lied. "Hearing from you tonight was a hell of a shock, but that was then, this is now. I'll get you through this safely and then you can go on with your life. Just like last time."

Her arms went around his chest and he felt her cheek against his shoulder. Part of him wanted to turn and take her in his arms, but he kept his hands firmly at his sides while he continued to stare out at the pounding surf.

"J-John," her voice broke. "I owe you so much from before and now I've shown up on your doorstep, in as much trouble as then."

He kept his eyes on the surf.

"I've been thinking about seeing you ever since I learned you were out here. I ... I could have let Scott make this trip, but I thought it might give me a chance to see you again."

"Then why didn't you contact me before now?"

"You disappeared right after the canyon trip. I thought it was out of bitterness or something. I'm not sure. I was going to contact you tomorrow."

He didn't really believe her. Her answer was too convenient. Back in the Canyon, he hadn't thought she was the lying type, but he'd been naive about many things back then. "Okay, so you were going to contact me. Now you have."

"I wanted to see if you still had feelings for me. Back then I was engaged. I couldn't get involved with you, but there's always been some regret over my decision."

When he spoke he picked his words carefully. "You may not have made the right choice then, but I've changed too much. You don't know me."

She gave him a final squeeze and let go. "I'm sorry. I don't want you to think I only said this to make you help me again. I honestly had intended to look you up even before this trouble."

"That's all right. Either way I'd help you. Business is business and don't think it has anything to do with your choice twelve years ago. It's only a matter of what I am."

"And what are you?"

"I'm your bodyguard for now. Other than that, you don't want to know."

He could feel her stepping back and growing distant in more than space.

When she spoke, frost formed on the back of his neck. "I see."

"No. I don't think you do, but that's all right. You'd better get some sleep. I won't leave until you're up."

He watched her reflection in the window. She turned, took her purse from the bed, and went into the bathroom. Over the sound of the surf, he could hear water running. He left the window and went to the door.

He flicked off the interior lights then opened the door and looked outside. The fog was still thick, but all the cars he could see were there when they arrived. He activated his car's silent alarm, then closed the door, latched it firmly, and threw the night bolt.

John opened his overnight bag and took out a ring and a small plastic box. The face of the box had a microswitch and two LED's, one red and one green. A short loop of wire extruded from one end. He slipped the wire over the doorknob, letting the capacitance alarm hang free, then pushed one of the buttons. The green LED lit.

John slipped the ring over his right pinkie and then touched the doorknob with his left hand. The green LED went out and the red one lit. Simultaneously, the ring gave him a tiny jolt of current. Satisfied it was working properly John reset the alarm.

He went around the room, turning off all the lights except for the one between the beds. Then he turned the covers down on Caitlin's bed before going back to the window.

A few minutes passed and the bathroom door opened. He didn't turn around. Her reflection, dim in the reduced glow of the single light, came out wearing a short slip. She hung her clothes on hangers and came up behind him again.

When she spoke he could feel her soft breath melting the frost on his nape. "Thanks for turning down the covers."

Her lips gently touched his cheek. "Good night, John."

He murmured a good night and watched her reflection walk to the bed.

How many months had it taken him to be able to think about her without feeling the wrenching pain in his gut? How many times had he wanted to look her up and convince her to leave Scott? Even now, the moment she walked into the Gleaning Cube, he had to restrain himself from rushing to meet her. What was it about her that affected him like no other woman in his entire life? He'd had lovers, more than a few, but none had ever made him want to give everything else up, just to be with them.

He stood alone, staring out at the pounding surf, thinking back a dozen years and about all the might have beens.

*   *   *

The thunderous roar of water against rock filled John Blalock with anticipation. His pulse quickened and an uneasy smile creased his stubble-darkened face. Sitting in the bow, he gripped the nylon safety line and watched as their yellow and black Domar raft neared the tongue of Crystal Rapids. At flow rates greater than 40,000 cubic feet per second, the Crystal was the most dangerous rapid on the Colorado.

The pair of rafts drifted between great cliffs along a river whose surface danced from a barrage of raindrops. Like the others, John wore a sturdy life vest over his tee shirt and shorts. His feet were partially covered by well-worn sandals.

Glen Phillips, the leader of their little expedition, adjusted the oars in the locks. This was Glen's third trip down the Canyon, but only he and Steward Phillips, John's roommate who manned the oars in the second raft, had ever traveled the Canyon before.

Leaning back, John stared upwards into the warm rain at steep canyon walls topped by a barely visible strip of rain filled sky. Here and there, pink veins of Zoraster Granite shot through the massive cliffs of gray schist that rose jaggedly from the water. A thousand feet up, the gray altered to ledgy layers of Tapeats Sandstone which in turn was topped by four thousand feet of Paleozoic cliffs. The Canyon was a marvel of nature, a place of almost unimagined beauty.

Even the Canyon's beauty couldn't keep John's thoughts off the Crystal.

A chuckle came from his left.

Caitlin Maxwell's raven hair hung from beneath a Colorado Cellars Winery cap and draped across the back of her orange life vest. She was nearly as tall as John's own five foot ten inches and her skin was tanned two shades darker. Her large blue eyes were cheerful and she showed a wide stretch of perfect teeth as she smiled.

She leaned close so she wouldn't be overheard. "Hey, cheer up. It can't be as bad as Glen's making out. He's been through it before."

"I wouldn't be so sure, at least not under these conditions. Did you ever read Michael Ghiglieri's book `Canyon'?"

She shook her head.

"He's a professional guide. His book describes a run down the Canyon. He put a lot of pages into detailing Crystal's dangers."

John pointed down river toward the rapids. "You see, the only relatively safe path is to hit it hard on the right side. But if we get off the right edge of the tongue, we'll be in trouble because that feeds into New Wave. From there, the tongue cuts left into the Slate Creek diagonal then rollercoasters into Crystal Hole.

"Still, the greatest dangers of Crystal are below the Hole if we get flipped. Besides the hypothermia, there's the chance of getting trapped under the boat and drowned. Beneath the Hole is a submerged island of boulders called the Bone Yard. If you fall in, don't forget, keep your feet up and pointed downstream. Stay high in the water and wait for a calm section to try for shore."

He lowered his arm and Caitlin stared at him for a moment, then she laughed and put her right hand on his bare leg. "Don't worry so much, John. Life's too short, you have to enjoy what you find."

Her touch sent a shiver through him. Why did she have to be engaged? It would have been better had he never met her. Anything would be preferable to watching her marry someone else. Damn, but his timing was bad. Three months. If only he'd met her three months ago. It would have been enough time to convince her she should drop Scott and marry him instead. Three, no two months, perhaps even one month, but there was no way to convince her in so short a time. Now only a week remained before the end of the trip at Diamond Creek, a dozen miles up river from Lake Mead.

Lake Mead.

Where her fiancé waited.

Damn him anyway. If Scott hadn't broken his leg in a rock climbing accident, he would be on this trip and John would be home; warm, dry, and working on his doctoral dissertation.

As they accelerated into the rapids, the cacophony of water clashing with stone grew until it drowned out normal conversation.

In running rapids, entrance is everything. Either you're lined up properly for the safest possible run or you're not. There is no second chance. John glanced back at Glen. Glen was a few years older than most of them and had made the Canyon trip twice before, but always as a passenger, not a guide. John mentally shrugged. You had to trust your oarsman. He held their lives in his grip on the oars and the rest of them could do nothing unless he called for assistance.

The tongue carried them between enormous boulders washed down the Crystal Creek tributary over three decades ago. In the bow, the impact with the first standing diagonal drenched John and Caitlin with frigid water. The raft pivoted off the diagonal as Glen struggled with the oars to keep the bow downstream. They struck the second diagonal before they were straight. It absorbed their momentum and cast them off toward the right shoulder of New Wave.

They were drenched, again and again as Glen struggled to keep the raft to the right of the channel.

The raft shuddered as it collided with a boulder. Chilling water cascaded over the side striking John with tangible force. He held his breath and squeezed his eyes shut to clear the water. The front of the raft rose out of the water for a moment before plunging down into another trough. Frothy water spilled onto John's legs and pooled around his sandals. A boulder loomed to his right. The raft compressed against the rock's smooth side, bounced off, and continued into the next slot.

John held tight to a rigging strap and wondered what he was doing there.

They skirted the edge of New Wave barely avoiding its dangers. The raft surfed sideways into the Slate Creek diagonal. The impact threw Caitlin from her seat; John caught her arm and held her upright until she regained her balance.

"Forward!" Glen yelled.

John and Caitlin scrambled onto the lip of the bow as the raft pivoted. Their weight helped pull the bow off the wave and they swept on.

"Hole!" John shouted and pointed toward the trap.

"I see it. Hold on, this is going to be close."

The raft swept toward the hole. Glen rowed furiously and they inched right, away from danger. John relaxed; they were going to make it past.

Then some variation in the current moved them too far right. A moment later they crashed into a granite outcrop. The jarring collision sent them spinning back left.

Before Glen could straighten the raft, the current forced them sideways into the massive standing wave of Crystal Hole.

The force of the impact nearly threw John off the bow. He clutched at the rigging strap while the raft spun into the hole formed by an enormous boulder hidden just beneath the water's surface. The raft slammed into the wave again and the river sucked the rear end under the surface, only to spit it out moments later.

They bobbed up with teeth-jarring acceleration. For a second John thought they were going to pull free, but the vortex sucked the rear of the raft back down. It was the absolute worst situation on any run. The other raft might be able to toss them a line and pull them free, but there wasn't time. They had to free themselves before the churning water ripped their raft apart.

Everyone hollered at once. Glen shouted instructions, but the two men in the stern had enough trouble just staying in the raft.

John grabbed his paddle and turned to help Glen push away from the hole.

He froze. Caitlin wasn't sitting next to him.

She wasn't anywhere on the raft.

His first thought was that the hole had sucked her into its maw. It happened sometimes. And sometimes the hole would bounce a person in and out for hours before some slight deviation in the current would spit their lifeless body free of the trap. No. Not the hole. She couldn't be there.

He saw a flash of color in the water a hundred feet down river. The bright orange of a life vest rapidly receded through the rapids.

Without thinking John yelled to the others and dove in after her.

He didn't know what compelled him to dive in, she'd been on as many raft trips as he had and she seemed able enough. If he'd stopped to think about it, he probably would have stayed in the raft. That was the logical thing to do. Let the other raft recover any swimmers. But John reacted without thinking.

The force of his leap carried him beneath the surface for a moment before the buoyancy of his life vest popped him up. Being splashed by fifty-degree water is not the same as being immersed in it. It was a numbing cold.

Twenty yards downstream, he could see Caitlin. She had remembered the drill, and had lined up properly, but to catch up with her John would have to swim.

She was already entering the Bone Yard. He couldn't swim in there. He'd have to hurry.

The life vest impeded his movement and he was still far from her when he reached the first rocks of the Bone Yard. The river looked like a liquid version of the moguls on the extreme slopes at Copper Mountain. John stopped swimming and brought his feet around in front of him. His sandaled feet struck something unseen, compressing his knees back against his life vest and spinning him sideways.

The current forced him under and an enormous impact against his chest forced the air from his lungs. Swimming hard, he tried to reach the surface, but the spinning, agitated current disorientated him. Several more impacts left him battered and barely conscious before he finally broke the surface. Oxygen starved, he gasped while swirling into another crest and inhaled almost as much water as air

The rush of air brought a stabbing pain to his chest. He coughed out water and inhaled again.

He floated lower in the water now and bits of his vest's floatation material littered the water around him.

Meteoric stars shot across John's vision as he looked for Caitlin. He swept between two boulders that protruded menacingly from the water and then caught sight of her. She struggled with a length of orange and black cord.

He yelled and she turned in his direction. Drawing back her arm, she cast the line toward him.

It fell far short.

He swam toward it, trying to reach it before the next set of rapids.

Caitlin was already into the run when John managed to get a grip on her line. He looped it around his left hand as they tumbled through the cold muddy water. Although the line was no more than forty feet long, he rarely saw her for the first few minutes.

He lost track of the number of times the current slammed him into boulders, but twice more he hit them so hard that the spasms of pain shooting through his chest caused him to loose his grip on her line. Each time it slipped through his numb fingers until it reached the end he'd looped around his wrist. Each time he had to restart the torturous process of slowly pulling them closer together.

Breathing became difficult. The pain in his chest massed into burning agony with each inhalation and for the first time he realized that he could die. Not tomorrow. Not years from now. But in the next minute. He could feel the panic seize his heart.

But panic could kill him faster than the river. He forced it from his mind and concentrated on closing the distance between them.

After an indeterminable period, his hand brushed something at the end of the rope. It was Caitlin. He pulled her to him. Her eyes were closed and her face was slack. An angry welt blossomed above her right eye. John gripped the back of her vest and looked for an eddy.

In the raft, he could spot eddies without much trouble. But that was with his eyes three or four feet above the water line and, in the raft, he had the power of the oars to push whatever direction he chose. Here, they were under the surface of the river as often as not and had almost no ability to push in any direction.

They must have been miles farther down river before John saw an opportunity to hit an eddy. It was a small eddy and John didn't see it until they were on top of it. He almost let it pass, but he was beyond fatigue and couldn't go on. He'd been knocked into near unconsciousness on several occasions and had swallowed enough water to float the S.S. Minnow. No matter how small the eddy was, he knew it had to be this one or none.

They entered fast, too fast. Their momentum nearly carried them through the eddy, but John got a grip on one jagged edge of a boulder and held tight, as it felt like his shoulder would separate. Every cell in his body screamed at him to rest, but he knew he had to keep moving. With one hand he pulled them along the boulder until they reached the back of the eddy.

His feet found purchase on a sandy bottom. He staggered to the water's edge and then up a small embankment where he collapsed to the dirt. He was desperate to rest. His muscles ached more than he could ever remember, but he had to check Caitlin first.

She was still breathing. He felt her limbs and torso for breaks, nothing seemed broken.

It was late afternoon, but the sun had long since dropped below the rim of the canyon and with the heavy rain there was next to no light. John took the small Mag-Lite from the clip on his belt and twisted it on. In its light, he could see splotches of red on her clothing. As he played the beam over her, he realized the stains were from the lacerations on his hand. Blood flowed freely from the hand he'd used to grip the rock. He shined the light directly on his palm. There were several gashes crisscrossing its surface, but none looked serious.

He sat down beside her and pulled her eyelids back. Her pupils were dilated unevenly.

John shined the light around and found they were at the mouth of a small canyon. He turned upstream hoping for some sign of the rafts, but there was only the river.

Standing there in the rain, John realized how cold he was. Even with all his exertion, the river had sucked the heat from his bones. He was beginning to shiver. He ... They needed dry clothes and a fire, but all he wanted to do was lie down and rest. He couldn't, not yet anyway. If he lay down now, neither of them might live to see the sunrise.

He made sure Caitlin couldn't roll back into the water, then walked up the gorge following the muddy stream that flowed through it. The gorge widened significantly, and he soon found a copse of juniper and piñon with enough dead wood for a good fire, but everything was wet. A little farther on, he found an overhang that provided protection against the driving rain. There he also found a little dry wood. The protected area was small, but it would have to do.

He returned to the river.

When he bent to lift Caitlin, a stabbing pain went through his ribs like an eight-inch butcher's knife. He screamed and dropped to his knees. When the wave of pain receded, John tried again. She weighed no more than one hundred and forty pounds, but even with the thick layers of striated muscles that won him the state heavyweight wrestling championship in high school he couldn't lift her.

John took a firm grip on her vest and dragged her up the canyon. Each step caused him to grimace in pain, but he clenched his teeth together and focused. One more step, just one more step and he could stop. It wasn't a long trip, not more than a hundred yards, but it seemed to take hours.

Staggering forward, he found himself humming the lines to "Radar Love." It was one of those old songs that could swim around in his mind for days without relief.

Finally, they reached the outcropping. John left Caitlin against the cliff side, as far from the rain as possible, and then collected enough dry wood to get a fire started and made a pile near Caitlin. After breaking the smaller pieces to get enough splinters to serve as kindling, John arranged them neatly beneath the larger sticks. Taking his old Zippo lighter from its pocket, he struck it with shivering fingers. His grandfather had carried the brass Zippo through Europe in World War II and had passed it on to him when John had convinced him to give up smoking. John carried it as a lucky charm.

The wood caught and burned well. When the fire burned steadily, John went out into the rain, and dragged more sticks into the lee of the overhang.

When he thought he had enough he checked Caitlin, she was still unconscious. Her skin was cold and she was shivering. Hypothermia was a more immediate threat than the concussion.

Each of them carried a small emergency kit clipped to their belts. Besides the bandages, antiseptics, and a couple of food bars, it held a metallic rescue blanket folded into something the size of a napkin.

His teeth chattered uncontrollably as he tore open the sealed packages and laid the blankets on the dry sand.

As gently as he could, John stripped off Caitlin's clothing. The firelight revealed welts and bruises scattered about her slim body. He wrapped her in both blankets before jamming a few sticks into the ground near the fire. He hung her clothes over them and then stripped out of his own. It turned out to be the hardest thing he'd ever done. The pain in his chest became so severe he had to scream again. Somehow, he still managed to remove his shirt.

He coughed a deep rasping cough that burned like fire. His mouth had the flavor of old nails and he spit blood onto the rocks.

He stared at the foamy red patch of his life.

Hell.

Blood.

He'd punctured a lung.

Dear God, what could he do for a punctured lung?

He didn't know. Well, it'd either stop bleeding or he'd die. Right now, he was too tired to care which. Rest, he must rest. He hung his clothes beside hers, threw a few of the larger sticks onto the fire, and crawled into the blankets with her.

They shivered together under the blankets, his arms wrapped around her for what little warmth they might add to each other. Her soft skin was clammy against his, but he didn't mind. He was past the point of noticing or caring.

At some point, he slept.

He awoke feeling groggy. His backside had come uncovered and the night air was cold. Embers from the dying fire glowed in the dark. Caitlin was still cradled in his arms. Her shivering had stopped and she now breathed easily.

He slid out from under the blankets and dragged a few more branches onto the coals. After rearranging the wood, he blew the fire alit. He knelt with his hands against the flames until it was too hot to bear. Then he slid back between the blankets and pulled Caitlin close. In a moment, he fell asleep.

The next thing John knew it was daylight, at least as close to it as it was likely to get that day. The rain still fell. Caitlin lay with her head on his right shoulder. Her breath was warm against his skin. Only embers remained of the fire, but he no longer felt cold. The fire had warmed the rock wall behind and above them enough to break the chill of the morning air.

For the first time, he was conscious of the curves in the body pressing against him. Yesterday, he'd been too worried about her dying to think of anything else as he'd stripped off her clothes and slid beneath the blankets with her.

That morning was another matter. They had already spent seven days together in the close proximity of the raft. He'd seen her swim in quiet crystal pools and shower under soft waterfalls, heard her laugh at his feeble jokes. He'd eaten numerous meals with her and had slept just a few feet from her each night. He'd been attracted to her since the first day, had a crush on her by day three, and by day six was deeply in love.

Nevertheless, she was engaged to be married when they finished the trip, if they finished the trip.

He wasn't worried, yet. If Glen and the others didn't spot them, Glen would use the radio to call in a rescue helicopter. It might take a day or two to find them, but they could survive that long without food. No, the only real worry was Caitlin's condition.

As if on cue, she stirred. Her right hand slid up along his torso and stopped when it reached his thick chest hair.

Her head jerked up and her eyes popped open.

"John?"

Her right hand moved again, lower this time, until she understood that he was naked beneath the blanket. She jerked her hand away as though she'd been burned.

"Good morning," he said with little humor.

"Where the hell are my clothes?"

John pointed with a tilt of his head.

Her head twisted around as she took in their location. Their clothes still hung next to the remains of the fire. When she turned back to face him, she was much calmer than he imagined she would be.

He had half-expected scorn or derision, but her voice was calm and perhaps even lighthearted.

"I can't believe you. How'd you manage that?" she asked.

"It wasn't easy. Look, we were both chilled. There was no other way to warm you up in a hurry."

"I think I could have warmed up just fine with my panties on."

He wrinkled his eyebrows in what he hoped was a disarming gesture. "In for a penny, in for a pound."

"What?" she asked.

"Dickens."

"What does it have to do -- never mind."

She shifted and those luscious curves moved against him. He diverted his thoughts to an interface control problem he'd been working on for his thesis. She moved again and his thoughts leapt back.

"I -- we have to get dressed. The others could catch up with us at any time and I won't have my fiancé hearing that I was found naked, wrapped in a blanket with another man."

He nodded.

She placed one hand on his chest for leverage and pushed. Fire shot through him and he opened his mouth to scream, but nothing came out.

Dear God, how his ribs hurt.

The weight left his chest as Caitlin jerked her hand back.

"What? What's the matter?"

"My ribs," he gasped. "I cracked a couple…."

Her face reddened. "Oh, I'm sorry. I didn't think."

For a minute, she sat quiet, while he struggled to breathe. "I'm sorry, John. I haven't thanked you for saving my life. I don't remember much after I fell off the raft, but I do remember you in the water with me. You risked your own life to save me and I'm complaining while you lay there with broken ribs. I must sound like a fool."

Her eyes met his. He wanted to drown in those pools to swim away and never come back; to ... She blinked and looked away. Her fingers lightly touched his chest, gently feeling the lumps beneath his skin. Her touch was fire, but this time he enjoyed it.

When she spoke again her voice was deeper, almost sultry.

"I'd better get dressed."

She pulled at the blankets until she found an edge and slipped it off her. In the gray light of the canyon's morning, he watched her stand slowly. She groaned as she discovered her own body hadn't escaped the river unscathed. She swayed for a moment before her head seemed to clear. Walking across the sand, she pulled her panties from the first stick. Keeping her back to him, she stepped into them and pulled them up.

She slipped into her T-shirt and shorts. As she zipped up her shorts, she turned to face him.

She didn't appear to mind that he'd been watching her and she hadn't asked him to look away.

"Are you getting up?"

"In a minute."

Caitlin rolled her shoulders and stretched. She turned around giving John a profile shot, and motioned toward the end of the side canyon and the roaring Colorado.

"Maybe I should see if there's anyone on the river. We wouldn't want to miss them."

"Okay, but take one of these blankets. There's no point in getting soaked again."

Caitlin nodded and took the edge of the blanket he handed her. After a little wriggling on his part, she pulled it free. She wrapped it about her shoulders and wordlessly followed the stream toward the river.

He waited another minute before throwing back the blanket. As quickly as the pain in his chest let him, he stood up and dressed. Bending over was the worse part, but he managed to pull up his shorts without getting too much sand into them.

A cough racked him.

He spit more foamy blood onto the ground.

Perhaps Caitlin's condition wasn't his only worry after all.

Only one of his sandals had made it through the swim, but both of Caitlin's had reached landfall. He picked them up, wrapped the other blanket about his shoulders, and took them with him as he followed her downstream.

She sat on a boulder, looking out over the tumultuous river. When he reached her, he slid soundlessly beside her and offered her the sandals.

She took them from him and slipped them on.

"Thanks. Do you think they've already passed us?"

The river was empty of life as far as he could see in either direction.

"Who can say? There was time for them to get this far I guess, but I have no idea how far downstream we came. The raft would make better speed than we could, but they may have stopped to search all the eddies for us. Then again, they could have left early this morning and passed us today."

"That's what I guessed. I suppose we'll just have to wait."

"There should be other rafters coming by today. We can always hitch a ride out with them."

"Of course," she said.

He didn't reply. After a minute of silence, Caitlin turned to him.

"I'm cold, John. Could put your arm around me?"

"Sure."

They adjusted the blankets to shield them from the steady rain and he slipped his right arm around her waist. She leaned her head against his shoulder.

"Thanks, John."

"Anytime."

It was a lame response and he regretted it immediately.

For a few minutes they sat on that rock, staring up the river without talking, each lost in their own thoughts.

"John?" Her voice was soft, but she spoke with her lips near his ear so that he could hear her over the river.

"Yes?"

"I want you to know how much I appreciate what you did for me yesterday. I know I owe you my life."

His first reaction was to say, "Don't mention it." But that tired expression said nothing that he wanted to say. Instead, he nodded while gathering his thoughts.

Finally he said, "Caitlin, for you, I'd do it all over again."

Her cheek moved against his shoulder, but he didn't trust himself to look into her eyes. He continued to stare up river.

"You really mean that don't you?"

"Yes," he said and added a faint nod.

She was quiet for a few moments. "I've noticed you on this trip. I'm not blind, John. I am attracted to you. You are charming, intelligent, and handsome, but I am engaged. I'm going to be married next Saturday."

He wanted to tell her not to, to tell her to give them a chance to get to know each other better, to give herself time to fall in love with him, just as he had already fallen for her.

Instead, he said, "I understand. You love him and that's all that matters."

"It's not all that matters, John. I'm very fond of you and given a little time, I would probably fall in love with you, but I can't turn my back on someone I love and I don't think you're a person who would want me to."

John wasn't so sure. Right then, he'd have given anything to have her forget Scott and love him.

He looked out over the thundering water and heard her say, "Another time, another place. It could have been us, but it ... I'm so sorry, John."

"Don't be sorry, Caitlin. It's your decision to make and either way, no regrets."

He saw a quick movement up the river. A raft bobbed into view atop a ridge of water. Someone was coming.

"We have company," John said, pointing with his left hand.

Caitlin followed his direction as the raft crested another ridge.

She turned to him and his eyes met hers. He knew he was lost. He'd never find anyone like her again. He'd heard it said that there was a special someone for everyone. Well, if that was so then this was his someone.

Her lips moved. "John, kiss me. I want to know what I'm passing up."

He slowly lowered his mouth to hers and in that moment he knew, the pain in his chest wasn't from cracked ribs.

His heart was breaking.

CHAPTER 10

Sunrise brought a change in the wind. The fog returned to its home in the sea leaving John staring out over the surf at a few fishing boats that plowed toward the deep blue. Gulls cried above them, encouraging their day's work, wishing the fishermen plentiful catches so they would receive their share of the bounty.

He turned away from the bright morning. Caitlin still slept. John had thought about sleeping, but found his mind too troubled with memories of the canyon, and paths not taken. Twelve years had passed since he'd last seen her. He had thought of her often during those years, but had never tried to look for her or to find out what had happened to her. His life went in a different direction after the canyon, and although he occasionally looked in the rearview mirror, he never tried to reverse course.

He went into the bathroom and took the razor and deodorant from his overnighter. When he finished, he found Caitlin still sleeping soundly. He watched her for a moment, then scribbled her a quick note on the motel's stationary, and left it on the telephone.

John pulled on his hat and trenchcoat, deactivated the alarm, and tossed it on the bed. He slipped the latch and then eased the door open. Bright sunlight burst into the room. He stepped outside and silently pulled the door closed behind him. A few people were in the parking lot, but they went about their business and he spent only a moment examining each of them for some sign of danger.

A Waffle House shared the opposite end of the motel's parking lot. The vehicles of early-risers clustered around it like gnu's around a Serengeti water hole.

He had long since postulated a certain clientele for each of the restaurant chains. McDonald's drew mostly from the rushing non-adventurous, Wendy's from more sedate easy-goers, Waffle House from the early-risers and the all-nighters. This time of the morning bought the rare meeting of both groups.

He entered the little building with the scurrying cooks and waitresses and savored the smell of sizzling meat and fresh coffee. There were two vacant stools near the cash register. The nearer stool had an excellent view of the motel. John sat down on cleaned and shiny yellow plastic seat tipped his hat back. A college-aged waitress appeared immediately.

"What'll it be?" she held out a plastic coated menu that deserved retirement.

He didn't offer to take it and she stuck it in back in her apron.

"Give me a couple of steak biscuits and two large coffees, to go."

"You got it, Mister. Anything else?"

John shook his head.

She made a quick notation on her pad and turned away.

Single early-risers took up most of the counter; they had a code that each occupied stool must have at least one empty stool on either side of it. Until the stool supply became tight, they'd never think of sitting next to someone else. The booths were another matter; most of them were occupied by the all-nighters. Couples and threesomes, who had run the gamut of bars and parties, were now forcing down a high-protein breakfast before they returned to their coffins until another sundown.

John appraised the early-risers. These were not the health nuts you could see out jogging at sunrise every morning. Not these boys, they were more the type to suck down a kilo of cholesterol and a liter of coffee before launching their boat for a day of killing fish and swilling beer.

Shortly, his order arrived in a white paper bag. He paid the waitress and left her a decent tip. The walk back to the room was relaxing. Although the morning breeze came across the peninsula, it had a pleasant, fresh smell that belied the dense population farther inland.

He slipped the key in the slot and opened the door. He heard the shower running and saw Caitlin's empty bed.

He removed the lids from the paper cups so they'd cool, and carried them to the small table by the back window. Then he made himself comfortable in the nearest chair and waited.

She wasn't long.

The water turned off and a minute later the door opened. Caitlin's damp hair hung against the back of the towel she'd wrapped around her. He stood when she came out. Not out of some misplaced chivalry, but out of the realization that the hotel's towel, like most hotel towels, barely covered her crotch.

He didn't need the temptation. Not now, not until he had a handle on his own thoughts and emotions.

"Good morning, John." She sniffed the air. "Coffee? Thanks, I could use some."

She stopped in front of him so close that the top of her towel brushed against his coat.

"Good morning to you too. I brought you a biscuit. I hope it's all right."

"You're a darling," she said and briefly kissed him on the cheek before he could respond.

She turned, fished one of the biscuits from the bag, and sat across from him. Demurely she crossed her legs, leaving him with the vivid realization that resisting her would be a lot tougher than he had originally thought.

He took out the other biscuit, unwrapped it, and ate while it was still warm. He washed down each bite with a sip of coffee and tried to keep his attention above Caitlin's neck.

"So, tell me," she said between bites. "What have you been doing for the last twelve years?"

"This and that. Mostly that," he said and took another bite.

She frowned. Most faces wrinkle when they frown, but not Caitlin's. Her's was more of the pouty expression of a smooth faced baby.

"That's not an answer," she said. "I can understand you not wanting to pick up where we left off. That's not what really asking. I just want to get to know you again. I haven't heard anything from or about you until I chanced upon your name on the Web last month. You didn't even come to the wedding."

The comment surprised him. "How could I have come to the wedding? You know I wouldn't have been able to watch you marry him."

"But you disappeared after that. You were already out of the hospital when we finished the trip and you never returned to Colorado Springs to finish your doctorate."

He shrugged. "After the canyon I couldn't see the point. Everyone has a turning point in their life, mine was the canyon."

"Because of me?"

He stared at her for a second. Could she really so vain that she thought he had changed his entire life because he couldn't have her? No, it was probably an innocent question. "No, Caitlin, even if you had been willing to dump what's-his-name for me, I still wouldn't have returned to college."

"So what did happen to you? Where did..." Her gaze wandered away.

He recognized the sudden change in her voice. He'd heard it before in women and even in some men. It had a strange fascination that both attracted and repelled and somehow they were all embarrassed by it. "You mean the scar?"

She nodded and turned back toward him. Mentioning the scar removed her timidity and she took a good long look.

The scar started above his left eye, parted his eyebrow, skipped across his eye, and ran to a point inside his mustache. Even after all the years he'd had it, it still had a tendency to color when his emotions raged. Nothing outlandish, but it would redden as though it was still fresh whenever he grew angry or, for that matter, aroused.

"Haiti."

"Haiti? How? What were you doing in Haiti? I mean, well, if you don't mind telling me."

"Actually, I do. I don't like to go into my past too much."

She colored slightly and turned to stare at the window that faced the street. When she looked back, she said, "Excuse me. I ... damn it, John. I want to find out what's happened to you. We were close once. I know it was for a very short time, but no matter what else, I haven't forgotten that I owe you my life. I know it's an impossible debt to repay, but it's made me care about you. Your disappearing for the last twelve years has just made me more concerned."

He looked at her softly. Her face as beautiful to him as the day they'd parted, her body just as luscious, her blue eyes just as deep. "Can't you just accept that I've changed and leave it at that?"

"No, I don't think I can," she said with a distinct note of sincerity.

"Then I'm sorry, you'll have to get used to disappointment."

For a moment, he thought she would push the issue, but then she abruptly switched subjects. "What are you planning today?"

"I'm heading to the Pacific Rim first to take a look at your room and talk to hotel security. Perhaps I can learn something. Then I'll check in with the police and make a few calls. You know, the usual stuff you see in the movies. If I don't develop any leads, I'll get you a flight back to Albuquerque and escort you home."

She frowned. "I already told you it wouldn't do any good for me to go home. You can't guarantee me they won't follow me there and if the government is after me then they'll be waiting for me."

"That's true."

He didn't particularly want to argue with her, her chances of winning were too good.

For a moment, neither of them spoke, he out of stubbornness, she ... who knew what went through a woman's head, certainly not him.

She said, "You were saying what you intended to do today."

"Yeah, anyway, after I've checked out the hotel and the police, I'll backtrack to the business you've conducted since you arrived. I'll need a list of places you've been and people you've seen."

"Do you have to bother my clients?"

"If you want me to be thorough."

She nodded. "If you must, but remember, I have to work with these people again."

"Certainly."

What did she take him for, some hard-nosed bruiser who wasn't above intimidation to get information out of a suspect? She'd be right, but she wasn't supposed to know the current John Blalock. She should only remember the nice graduate student she'd met all those years ago.

"And what am I suppose to do while you're gone?"

"Sit back, relax." He waved a hand toward the window facing the bay. "Enjoy the view."

"Humph, I have work to do."

"Don't take an attitude, it's for your own good. Can't you use your computer here?"

"For some things, but the rest will require a Web link."

"Don't use your phone ... look, I'll pick up a sat modem while I'm out. You can use it to link up."

"Wouldn't that leave a trace to you?"

"I've done this before, no one will trace your link back to me."

"All right. If you're sure?"

"As sure as I am of anything," he replied, then he stood and walked to the front door. "I'll get your things from the hotel and I'll call back later to check on you."

He opened the door and stepped outside. The parking lot was clear of people except for a couple down the way loading their car.

"John."

He looked over his shoulder. Caitlin stood silhouetted against the ocean. She was everything he remembered and more.

"Be careful," she said.

"That's me, Mr. Careful." He closed the door, blocking her from his sight.

CHAPTER II

On the drive back toward San Francisco, John filed a verbal contract notice with the California Bodyguard License Board. It was a legal requirement and the board's records were open to the public. Anyone looking for Caitlin was sure to monitor the Web for any mention of her name and the contract should draw them out of the woodwork.

The Pacific Rim Suites was one of those new places built with a mind toward the rapidly developing countries of the same name. Its forty stories were packed with the most modern of conveniences and the most obscene of the new electronic gadgets that so fascinated those nations caught up in the rapid rush into this new millennium. The hotel had risen like a Phoenix on the ashes of the old Presidio army post. Its location high on the hill of what had once been officer housing gave it a sweeping 360-degree view of the Bay Area. Caitlin's registering here told him a couple of things about her company. They had money and they were heavy into this new technology.

His instincts told him that the people after Caitlin were actually after some new development of her company. He knew something about industrial espionage. In the Bay Area it had become a thriving business over the last decade. If he could learn what Caitlin's company was working on he could probably find out who sought it. Everyone had their own specialty, except perhaps him. He preferred to diversify his talents wherever possible.

At the entrance to the hotel's underground parking, he stopped beside a simple booth to show Caitlin's room key to a security guard, a man younger and more fit than any parking lot attendant had a right to be. The guard took the key and slipped it into a reader.

A moment later he frowned and turned to John.

"Ms. Maxwell?" he asked.

"Yeah, sure. Why? Do you have a problem with my wardrobe?"

For a moment he took the hook, then his frown deepened. "Excuse me, sir, but you hardly look like the type."

"What type is that?"

The guard started to open his mouth, hesitated, and said, "I'll have to see some ID before I can let you in."

"Sure," John answered and fished out his card.

Whenever he could, he avoided showing it. The less people that could place his face with a name the better. Most service-oriented people in the Bay Area were reluctant to criticize another's quirks, whether it was cross-dressing, or choice of life style. His pretending to be Ms. Maxwell would have usually gotten him passage without having to prove it. He had suspected the hotel's security was better than average and the guard's actions had confirmed it. The guard eyeballed the holograph image on John's card.

"Personal security, eh? What can we do for you, Mr. Brown?"

Of course, he wasn't going to give this clown his real card. "I'm here representing Ms. Maxwell. I need to talk to your supervisor."

The guard nodded suddenly as if remembering something. "That's right. I thought the name sounded familiar. She's the resident who filed an attack charge yesterday. They briefed us when I came on duty. All right. Park over there and I'll direct you to the day watch commander."

The guard pointed toward a couple of empty spaces labeled RESERVED and held out John's card. John took it and nodded.

Their security was tight. He didn't see him call anyone, but by the time John got out of his car another guard was marching toward him. "Mr. Brown, I'll escort you to the watch commander."

He was identical to the guard in the booth. John wondered if someone was cloning them or whether there was a manufacturing center making robots that appeared to be in their mid-twenties with perfect skin and perfect posture.

"Sure, lead on," John said.

Without looking back to see if John was following, the guard turned and marched toward a bank of elevators on the opposite wall. John trailed along, making a mental note of the visible security systems as he went.

Ultra-sonic and passive-infrared detectors covered the underground parking lot and each detector had a mini-camera. There were three elevators, two labeled guests, and one labeled employees only. The guard pressed his hand against a palm-plate and looked straight ahead into another minicam. John assumed they were using facial recognition software to compare the guard's face and palm print. A few moments later the elevator opened. They stepped inside an austere platform and the doors closed. The guard pressed a button and they descended. John guessed they'd dropped a couple of floors judging by the acceleration and duration.

The doors opened and his escort stepped out into a tiled corridor. A minicam faced the open door.

He followed the guard to the left until they reached a door labeled security. As before, the door opened as they approached.

The guard led him past the interior door into an office only marginally less Spartan than the outer hallway. A receptionist, with a shoulder holster hanging from his left armpit, sat behind a black and tan desk. He looked up from a monitor when they entered. John couldn't see the screen from his side of the desk, but he guessed it was slaved to one or all of the cameras they'd passed on the way in.

Three other doors led off this small room, one on each wall. Of the other three, only the door on his right lay open. It revealed an inner office.

"Identification," the receptionist said and held out his left hand. John's escort stepped back against the door they'd entered and assumed a watch position as John fished out his Mr. Brown card again. He placed the card in the outstretched hand and casually moved toward the receptionist's right.

The right side would give him a slight advantage if the receptionist reached for his gun since the man by the door no longer stood behind him. But John didn't anticipate a fight. He was nervous at being in a situation where he wasn't in control. He felt he could take these two and probably whoever occupied the office behind the open door, but the other two doors held unknowns, and getting back out of this sub-basement would be harder than getting in.

No, the best he could hope for in a fight would be to take some of them with him.

He shook it from his mind. He was becoming more paranoid with each case he took. A few more and he'd have to take a sabbatical, or else start seeing a witch doctor with a couch.

The receptionist ran his ID/business card through a reader and studied the screen. John knew what would show up. He regularly scanned his business cards through a similar reader to verify their authenticity.

While his new position still didn't give him a view of the monitor, it did let him see the LED that lit up next to it.

The receptionist passed the card back to John and motioned toward the open door. "Captain Ferguson will see you."

He took the card, slipped it casually into a jacket pocket, and murmured thanks, then crossed the room and went into the inner office.

A muscular woman sat behind an L-shaped desk centered on the far side of the office. Brightly tinted fish swam in a saltwater aquarium behind the desk. A monitor wall was on his right, each unit broadcasting different views of the hotel.

When he entered, she looked up from a small monitor set in the top of her desk. She stood and held out a hand. "Good morning, Mr. Brown, I'm Patricia Ferguson. How can I help the Blalock Agency?"

John took three steps, smiled, and shook her strong, dry hand. "We represent Ms. Caitlin Maxwell, a registered guest of your hotel. As I'm sure the outside guard told you, I'm investigating the assaults on her."

Her face darkened. "Alleged assault. We have no evidence that an assault actually took place."

"Come now Captain Ferguson, you can't expect me to believe our client made up this story."

"I don't mean to imply she's lying. Look, Mr. Brown, it's not that I don't sympathize with her problem, but we have the most sophisticated hotel security system in the state of California. If this assault took place, we would have some evidence. Unfortunately, we have none."

"That's sounds a lot like you're saying our client is lying," John said.

"Now, Mr. Brown. We aren't interested in pointing fingers or getting into name-calling. We are both professionals and as such I'm sure you can see our side of this."

John stroked his mustache to give an air of consideration and slowly turned toward the monitor wall. Two of the monitors showed the hotel's lobby, one showed the central security room, and the rest oscillated between the seemingly hundreds of cameras placed about the hotel.

While he watched the monitor in the upper left corner switched to the interior view of a hotel room. A small number in one corner showed Caitlin's room number, the other corner displayed a date-time group that would match the time Caitlin told him she ran into her attacker the first time.

The room was empty and neat.

He turned to Captain Ferguson.

"If you will keep watching," she said and touched a spot on her desk.

John faced the screen. The time readout sped up until minutes swept past in seconds.

On the replay, the door opened and two security guards with drawn guns entered the room.

"As you can see, the room was empty for a full half hour before Ms. Maxwell reported an assault. There's no way anyone could have been in her room during the time she claims to have been attacked."

That was more than passing strange, but it explained why hotel security and the police would have discounted her claim.

John thought for a moment, then asked, "Where was she when she hit the alarm?"

Captain Ferguson touched another point on her desk and a third monitor lit up. This one showed Caitlin running down the stairs. The readout said the 31st floor, northwest corner. She stopped, sat on a step, and fumbled with a pen-like object.

"That the panic switch she told me about?"

"Yes, it's standard on our keys."

"And why is the camera already following her before she presses the alarm."

"The cameras are always recording, but when she hit the panic button it flashed the alarm to central security and showed them where the alarm's location. I've just replayed the entire time she occupied the stairwell."

"I see."

"This panic button, what's it like?"

"I understand you have Ms. Maxwell's key." She held out her hand.

"Yes." John pulled it from an inner pocket and passed it to her. She flipped it right side up and pointed toward the end.

"This is it," she said and handed it back.

He took it and made a quick appraisal. He hadn't paid any attention to it when Caitlin gave it to him. It still appeared to be little more than a light blue, plastic ink pen, with a pocket clip. Pacific Rim Suites was etched in gold on the barrel. It had a red top, but the key's opposite end drew his attention. Micro channels were etched into the sides. He'd seen them before, but not on this type of device. They were connectors for a data link. The guts of this little pen hid a microchip.

"How does it work?"

"As you know, it's the guest's key. Each is encoded with the guest room number and other pertinent information. At any hotel terminal they use it to call up information on their account or access our many services."

It sounded like a canned statement.

"And the panic button?"

"If the clip and button are both held down it broadcasts a signal to our computer alerting us that the guest is in trouble. The computer automatically pinpoints the guest's location and we can have security or if necessary a medical staff on the site within seconds."

"Impressive."

The technology wasn't what impressed him, although she probably assumed it had and he didn't feel the need to correct her. No, what impressed him was that someone felt like they needed that much protection.

"So that's how you were able to reach her so soon."

"Exactly."

John toyed with the device and then innocently asked, "Does it also write?"

She smiled. "Of course."

John put the marvelous toy in his pocket and turned back to the monitor wall. In one screen he could see the two guards searching Caitlin's room, in another guards were just reaching her in the stairwell.

"Do the guests know there are cameras in their rooms?"

"It's not something we put in our brochures, but I can assure you that the room cameras are not monitored unless something causes the computer to alert security."

Why did the idea of blackmail enter his head? "And the video tapes?"

"The tapes from private rooms are in a sealed area that can only be accessed by both the day manager and the watch commander. There is no way they can be used for anything other than legal purposes. We're a bonded security firm."

John didn't argue the point, but it was a cinch he'd never stay in one of the Rim's suites.

"I guess there's no way for anyone to tamper with the recordings."

Captain Ferguson blinked once and said, "No, there are two guards in security central at all times and cameras recording everything that occurs there. If anyone modified the equipment it would have to show up on the recordings."

John didn't reveal his thoughts, "Unless that recording was modified also." What was the point? Being able to prove the tapes were modified would be next to impossible.

Instead, he said, "Can you give me a copy of Ms. Maxwell's complaint?"

"Certainly, hard or soft?"

"Soft will be fine."

Captain Ferguson tapped a recessed keyboard and a moment later a mini-DVD optical disk popped out of the desk. She picked it up and tossed it to John.

He caught it in his left hand and dropped it into a pocket. "Thanks. I'd also like to see my client's room and pick up her things."

"That won't be a problem. Your contract is registered with the California Bodyguard License Board. As such, we are more than happy to help you in any way we can. Of course, you realize that Ms. Maxwell's well being is our primary concern, but don't forget that we also have a reputation to protect. It wouldn't do for someone to go around making unsubstantiated claims against our hotel." She glazed the threat with a thick sugar coating, but it was still a threat.

"You have nothing to worry about, that is unless I determine my client was attacked in your hotel and your security didn't catch it."

"There's no chance of that."
John didn't answer.

CHAPTER 12

The guard who had escorted John in to see Captain Ferguson waited for him outside her office. They took the same elevator to the thirty-first floor. The thickly carpeted hallway was impressively wide. Evenly spaced doors were set in both sides. The rooms on his left had balconies on the building's central shaft and from the direction they were walking he guessed the other's must have had a view of the Golden Gate.

They stopped in front of Caitlin's original room and the guard inserted one of the chrome keys into the keyhole in the door.

"Does that pen open any of the hotel's rooms?" John asked.

"Any that it's keyed for," he hesitated and then expanded. "The security computer can reprogram it for any lock in the building, but these keys can only access one guest's room at a time.

"Then there are keys that can open any of the rooms?"

He pushed the door opened and motioned for John to enter. "Sure, management has a couple of keys and the watch commander has another one that can access all the rooms. But the computer notes every door they unlock. The gold key holders have free run of the building, but we always know where they are."

He stepped into the room.

"Lights," he said.

John looked around the living room portion of the small suite. On his left, set a modern but comfortable looking sofa. The chrome and glass coffee table and would have fit any room in the last twenty years. A wet bar and a small refrigerator were set in the far wall and the wall to his right held a wide screen monitor.

"Has the staff cleaned the room since the attack?"

"I'd have to check to be sure, but they normally come through each morning." He consulted his wristwatch and shrugged. "They may not have been here yet."

John nodded and walked back toward the bedroom. The curtains were drawn back from the windows, lighting the room nicely. He'd been right about the view. It looked like rain was coming to Napa Valley.

The bedroom was as clean as the den. If there had been any clues to find, they'd been carefully removed long before he'd arrived. He browsed anyway, looking for any signs of a struggle. After five minutes, he'd found nothing more than a little shoe polish against the baseboard across from the bed. It wasn't the same color as the shoes Caitlin had worn, but that neither proved nor disproved anything. The mark could have been there for months, but somehow he doubted that.

He didn't mention the mark as he made one last sweep of the room, identified the disguised mini-camera, and then told the guard he was satisfied.

He wasn't, but once a cleanup crew goes through a room there's little hope of finding anything important.

Caitlin's new room was three floors up, but gave the same basic view. She'd already transferred her clothes from suitcase to dresser. He found a nearly new, hard-side Samsonite in the closet and repacked her clothes neatly, barely conscious of the feel of silk against his skin.

While the guard watched, he went into the bath and returned with the basic toiletries all women carry. It took him a few more minutes, but eventually he got the suitcase packed well enough to close.

"Will that be all, Mr. Brown?" the guard asked as John lifted the case of the bed.

"For now. I'll have to review the incident reports and see if any questions arise."

"Certainly. If you'll follow me I'll take you back to your car."

Less than three minutes later John was standing beside his car. He got in and shoved the suitcase into the back seat.

The engine started and he pulled out of the garage. The guard in the booth nodded as John passed.

John drove down the hill and out to Fort Point beneath the Golden Gate Bridge. The cool air was thick with moisture and fog would probably roll in again as soon as the wind changed direction later in the day.

The business at the Pacific Rim bothered John. He could see three distinct possibilities.

One: someone high up in security at the hotel had helped Caitlin's attackers.

Two: someone, be they government or corporate, broke into a very sophisticated security system to get something Caitlin didn't even know she had.

Three: Caitlin was lying to him.

He didn't like the last choice. Regardless of how much he'd changed over the years, he still had that special pain of unrequited love.

The second choice was almost as troublesome, even if it didn't involve a betrayal of trust. To break into Pacific Rim's security system was one thing, but to remain undetected even after being searched for was another entirely. The technology existed, he was certain of that, but it was almost exclusively in the hands of huge corporations and even larger governments.

However, Caitlin did believe government agencies were involved. That made the second choice the most likely. But getting to one of the higher ups at Pacific Rim would involve significant coercion. It was the simplest solution, but John didn't believe in using Occam's Razor except when absolutely necessary.

He pulled his notebook computer from beneath the front seat, then slipped the optical disk from Captain Ferguson out of his pocket and into the computer. In a few seconds, he was reading the official report.

The report was detailed, well constructed, and totally believable. Guards were in her room within two minutes of her pressing the panic button and yet the room was clean. That indicated more than one person was involved.

There was still the murdered cabby. John had been listening to the radio all morning, but hadn't heard anything about a shooting. Caitlin had given him the name of the cab company and they could tell him whether the guy was still breathing. First, he should verify the police report.

John pulled the 'Cuda out of the overlook and headed down the Golden Gate Promenade into the city. He hadn't gone far before he noticed the green, two-door sedan tailing him. Tails weren't uncommon and occasionally John found them to be useful. This case for instance. The tail knew something, more than John did anyway, and therefore he was going to be helpful, if John could convince him.

He did have a few misgivings about the tail picking him up so soon. He was almost positive that he hadn't been followed away from the hotel, so how had they sniffed him out? Regardless, he wasn't going to pass up an opportunity.

John led him along, without indicating he'd spotted the tail. Now that he had him, the last thing he wanted was to lose him. He went past the marina and turned south into an area he was well acquainted with. John used to laugh at movies when people had trouble shaking a tail. Normally, it was a lot easier than they made it seem. In fact, many times he had trouble holding on to one. This was one of those times.

When the tail first showed up he expected it to be the Feds Caitlin had seen the night before. But the longer they followed him the more certain he became that they were amateurs.

The guy had trouble keeping with him in traffic. He continuously got out of position, allowing John to maneuver without responding. Once John had to go two blocks out of his way because he couldn't have made the turn he wanted without losing the tail.

Finally, John found what he was looking for. He maneuvered in front of a city bus, just as it stopped to pick up a half dozen or more passengers. Between the traffic and the bus, his tail had to wait until the bus pulled away from the curb. By then, John was two blocks away on the side street. He slowed, waiting for the tail to make the corner. Once they had, he took the next left before they could accelerate enough to catch him. John knew this route. He could maintain the speed limit and still keep them from gaining too much ground. Each time he turned, they were just pulling onto the street he'd left. With luck, they wouldn't even suspect he was leading them on.

He made his last turn into a side street and put the gas pedal to the firewall. His tires squealed as the 440, Six-Pack, V-8 shot the 'Cuda across the concrete. A block away he slammed on the brakes, made a quick right, accelerated, braked, and then turned right again. He pulled out onto the main street just in time to see his tail turn down the corner he'd taken. John accelerated after them and reached the side street as they cruised past the first turn he'd made. It was just shy of a hill that hid the rest of the street. The hill would lead a tail to think his quarry had continued on. At the top of the hill, they'd find the narrow street dead-ended at a deserted warehouse.

They were effectively trapped.

John accelerated rapidly and reached the top of the hill about the same time his tail realized they'd missed a turn. They slowed and started a three-point turn in the middle of the street. John burned more rubber off his tires as he slid to a stop behind them.

For the first time, he could see the faces of the men in the car. There were two of them. Both had Asiatic features, Japanese, or maybe Korean, he couldn't always tell. Before they could react, he leapt from his car and ran to the driver's door. When the driver tried to open it, John kicked it shut and bent down so he could watch both of them through the glass.

John motioned to the driver to lower the window and he did. Dark sunglasses hid the driver's eyes.

"Can I help you?" John asked.

"Your car is blocking mine. Please move it."

The driver's answer helped him confirm the Japanese suspicion. He spoke in excellent English, but John still detected the hint of an accent.

"I assumed you wanted to talk, that seems only right since you've gone through so much trouble to follow me. Now I'm here and we can talk. What did you want?"

The driver didn't bat an eye, but his partner twitched toward his door handle. The driver placed a hand on his partner's arm, restraining him.

"Following you? You must be mistaken. We turned down this street by mistake."

"I don't think so, but I'm open to convincing."

The passenger made a quick comment in Japanese. John didn't catch all of it, but he seemed to be offering to do the convincing. The driver snapped back at him in the same language to be patient.

John maintained a straight face as if he hadn't understood the exchange.

"Please," the driver said. "Why would we be following you? We are simple businessmen who are late for a meeting."

The bulge in the armpit of his partner's custom tailored suit belied the simple businessmen remark.

His question was another matter. It could be rhetorical or he could be trying to confirm that John was working for Caitlin. If someone at the Pacific Rim had put them on him, they would already know whom he worked for. How else could they have picked him up? But they hadn't been behind him when he left the hotel. He was sure of that.

John decided to go on a fishing expedition. "Well, if you weren't following me then you must accept my apology. Perhaps I was overly cautious. But when you're in possession of ... Never mind, I'm sorry I disturbed you."

He made a slight bow and turned toward his car.

Three steps later the driver called out. "Excuse me, perhaps I was hasty. I, too, am cautious. We should talk."

John stopped and turned back to the face the driver who now leaned out of his window.

"Perhaps," John said. "What did you have in mind?"

The driver's words were slow and calculated. "As businessmen we are always on the watch for ... lucrative investments. If you have something of value to sell, we could, perhaps, talk."

John waited to give him the impression he was thinking it over. "I don't see where talking could hurt. Perhaps we could meet later, over drinks."

The driver hesitated now. Was he playing the same game?

"Assuredly," he said at last. "Did you have a particular place in mind?"

"Someplace open, you know breezy. I like fresh air. How about Melville's, on Pier 34?"

"I am not familiar with the place."

"That's all right. It's very popular, once you reach the pier you won't be able to miss it. Just follow the crowds."

"Ah, excellent. What time shall we meet?"

"Let's say five this afternoon. I have other errands to run between now and then."

"Very well, I look forward to talking with you at greater length, Mr. --"

"White, John White." John stepped back to the window and put a business card in his hand. "My Web address is on the card. If you find you can't make it I'd appreciate a note to save me the trouble of going down to the pier."

The driver's gaze roved across the card and he nodded, once. "Certainly Mr. White."

He offered John neither a card nor a name.

John returned to his car. This time they didn't call out.

* * *

Caitlin watched the waves crash against the bay's retaining wall and nervously eyed her watch. John had been gone nearly two hours and she hadn't heard from him. She couldn't sit still much longer. As long as she sat there, she thought of Scott and of the cab driver. Scott must have been involved in something that had brought this trouble on her. Unless she could find out what it was she would never know peace.

She turned away from the blue waters, opened her purse, and took out her computer. She set it on the writing desk and woke it up, then called up the schedule program and went over each appointment Scott had kept over the last month. Only three entries made her curious. The three were all with the same man, a Richard Curtis of Curtis Associates in Santa Fe. Scott had never mentioned Curtis Associates to her. That was strange, because they always kept each other informed of prospective clients. She cross referenced the appointments with Scott's log of business meetings and found that he hadn't made any entries regarding Curtis Associates. If he was seeing Curtis professionally then he should have logged the minutes of each meeting.

Caitlin checked the records of company expenses and looked for Scott's expense vouchers for the trips to Santa Fe. There were none. Maybe he just hadn't had a chance to file them, but the first trip was nearly a month ago and her files were up to date. It was out of character for Scott to leave paper work incomplete. They had been audited on more than one occasion and Scott was meticulous in his record keeping.

Was this his illicit business? She needed to get on the Web and find out just what Curtis Associates was involved in.

*　　　　*　　　　*

Alain Dewatre sipped his coffee on his apartment's balcony and watched the morning mist evaporate off the dark waters of the bay. Dewatre was a tall man with overly handsome features that had attracted teasing when he was a boy, but the attention of many women as he matured.

His beeper chirped. He glanced at the display, then rose from his chair, and went inside.

He had occupied this apartment for three years and had spent a small part of his salary and bonuses on decorating it with fine, but inexpensive art. His taste was traditionalist and there wasn't an impressionist or cubist painting anywhere.

Sitting in front of the computer terminal, he ordered up the new message and read it while finishing his coffee.

He was smiling by the end of the message.

They had a hit on the Maxwell search.

The John Blalock Security Agency had filed a personal security contract for Ms. Caitlin Maxwell with the California Bodyguard License Board this morning. That she would seek protection had been anticipated, but that she would seek it from John Blalock was an unexpected plus.

He had come across Blalock several times over the last three years. They had lost five excellent sources thanks to Blalock, including the recent loss of the late Mr. Blevins. Blalock had done more to hurt their operations in the Bay Area than the twenty-person operation that NCIX, the National Counterintelligence Executive, maintained in northern California.

Dewatre spent a few minutes considering his options for acquiring Maxwell or Blalock, then composed a short message, had the computer encrypt it with a one time key and set it for burst transmission on the satellite's next pass.

CHAPTER 13

John pulled away from the Japanese and they didn't follow. He made a couple of turns, just to make sure. There was no sign of them.

The Japanese businessmen were going to be a problem. For one thing, they were carrying weapons. The Japanese didn't carry weapons often, at least not handguns. Firearms were restricted in their country and it wasn't a simple matter for them to get a concealed weapon permit in San Francisco. But money and connections have a way of bending the law.

It was the type of businessmen who carried firearms that concerned John.

So far, he had at least three separate organizations after Caitlin, assuming the killers and the government agents didn't work for the same group.

John was also concerned that the Japanese hadn't known the name he'd used at the hotel, unless they were very good at keeping a straight face. You could never be absolutely positive. It might mean that someone set them on him at the hotel. The person must not have heard his name mentioned, but he was sure that everyone he'd come in contact with had heard it. They could have been listening in with a bug or maybe a parabolic microphone and picked up his mentioning Caitlin, but why wouldn't they have heard his name? And why hadn't they followed him all the way from the hotel. He was willing to bet they hadn't been following him until after he left the overlook.

This was becoming an interesting case. Much more so than he had originally thought.

He continued to work the possibilities around in his head while he drove to the police substation that handled the hotel's call. Once there, he parked behind the three story brick building in the public parking lot.

The station was busy, about the normal for a workday in the Bay Area. He'd been here once before, but he didn't know anyone well enough to be on a first name basis.

A desk sergeant, on the down slope from fifty, looked up from a monitor. "What can I do for you?"

John noticed his nametag read Morris.

"I'm looking for a detective Romax. He was the reporting detective on my client's case." John expanded with a brief description of the events at the Pacific Rim.

"You have identification?" the sergeant asked.

John passed him a business card. The sergeant read it then studied him carefully.

"So, Mr. Black, what kind of security work do you do?"

"Whatever is needed."

John's mother used to say he had an honest face, but somewhere along the way, he had grown out of it.

Morris passed the card back and shook his head. "Sorry buddy, we don't have a detective Romax here. If you can wait a while, I can get you in to see the Captain. He could find out if Romax works in another precinct."

John eyed the few vacant chairs and took in the atmosphere. The foyer had the population and sounds of a Cairo bazaar. It only lacked smoke and the smell of camel dung.

"Sorry, I still have a life. Can't you find out for me?"

"We can't give out information on officers without the Captain's permission."

"I don't need information on him. I just need to know if there is a Detective Romax in the San Francisco Police Department."

Morris frowned, then turned to his computer, and typed in a query. A few seconds later he shook his head. "Looks like you must have gotten the name wrong. There's no one in the computer named Romax."

John nodded. "Okay, thanks anyway, Sergeant Morris."

"Yeah, just doing my job."

John made his way back past the dregs of San Francisco's West Side and back out into the bright morning sunshine. It was nearly noon. He squinted at the sky, slipped on his sunglasses, and pulled the brim of his hat down on his forehead. He was hungry and far from his regular haunts.

There was a sign for a Chinese restaurant just down the street. John decided to leave his car where it was and grab a bite.

The restaurant wasn't packed, but there were only a few booths left vacant. While waiting for the maitre' de John scanned the menu mounted on the wall by the front door. The maitre' de arrived and John asked for, and was taken to a booth at the back of the room. He sat facing the door. The maitre' de disappeared and a waiter arrived a moment later and asked if he wanted the buffet. John "no thanked" him and ordered black tea, fried rice, and General Pao chicken.

The waiter gave a slight bow and vanished into the kitchen.

The tea came in a small porcelain pot with an even smaller handle-less cup. John poured a small amount into the cup and raised it to his lips. It was hot, astringent, and excellent.

As he refilled the cup, the front door opened, and two suits walked in. John felt his gut tighten. They could have been twins. One had her hair pulled back in a tight knot while the other's hair was cropped close around her ears in a style that had been very popular a decade or so ago. Their suits were dark blue, with vertical pin strips, cut loose to conceal the bulges at the right sides of their belts.

More people with guns, this was getting a little too interesting.

As they swept the restaurant with their gaze, John knew they were going to be introducing themselves to him very shortly.

The one with the knot spotted him and her twin turned to him immediately as if there was some mental link between them.

He tried to stay relaxed as they drew near. These suits had the unpleasant aroma of the federal government following them like a cloud. His first instinct was to leave by the back door, but that wouldn't help Caitlin.

John sipped his tea and waited.

They stopped just out of reach, a nice safe distance when confronting an unknown element.

"Black?" The hair knot asked.

John gazed up into her mirrored sunglasses and smiled. "I prefer African-American."

"What?" She didn't return the smile.

"Humor. You know. You ask a question. I make a snappy reply. We all laugh."

The tightening of her lips did nothing for his attitude.

"Are you Mr. John Black?" she demanded.

"Perhaps. Depends on who's asking."

They both reached into inside coat pockets and he remained calm. Their weapons were on their hips. Like animatronics, they pulled out holograph ID cards. They held them out like tiny shields against his question, then simultaneously returned them to their sanctuaries.

"Is your name Mr. John Black, alias Mr. John Blalock, of the Blalock Security Services Agency?" the Knot asked in more detail.

He put down his tea and stared into her mirrored glasses. He had taken a good look at their ID before the holograph images disappeared back into their pockets. He'd seen the National Counterintelligence Executive, the NCIX, emblem on holographs before. He'd pegged these two as Feds the instant they started toward him. No matter which way fashion trends drifted, Feds always wore the same neatly tailored suits. Unless, of course, they were undercover, but these two could hardly be in disguise.

"Yeah, that's me." John motioned toward the opposite side of the booth. The knot sat down, her partner pulled a chair up and reversed it and sat just far enough to the side to force John to turn his head to look at her.

"What can I do for the Executive?" John asked.

"I'm Agent Bailey, this is Agent Wesson. We're looking for a client of yours. A Ms. Caitlin Maxwell," Knot said.

Unknown killers, the Japanese, and now the Feds, San Francisco was starting to feel crowded.

"Any particular reason?" John asked and sipped his tea.

"Nothing too serious. There are some questions we want to ask her," Bailey said.

"Anything you can expand on?" he asked.

She shook her head. "Not at the moment. Can you tell us where to find her?"

"No, not at the moment anyway. I told her to hide herself and call me later today."

Wesson cleared her throat noisily.

He ignored her.

Bailey twisted her head toward her partner for a pair of seconds and then looked back at him.

"Very well, Mr. Blalock ... I can call you Mr. Blalock, can't I?"

He shrugged. "It's still a free country. Call me whatever you want."

"Thank you. Do you think you could bring her into the Executive's San Francisco office later?"

"I'd rather she stay hidden until I can find out why someone's trying to kill her."

Bailey's forehead developed the smallest of betraying wrinkles. "What makes you think someone's trying to kill her?"

"I don't know, it's just always been my assumption that when people start shooting at you they aren't trying to become friends."

"You have proof someone's trying to kill her?"

"You know a Fed with a broken nose?" John asked.

That got more of a response out of her. She started lying. "No ... I can't say that I do."

"Which?" John asked.

"Which what?"

"Which is it? Do you not know one or just can't say that you know one?"

A hand fell on his shoulder. He didn't take his eyes off Bailey.

"Listen Blalock," Wesson said. "If you're going to turn into a smart ass we're going to have to look into your background."

"I do not know any agents that currently have a broken nose," Bailey offered. "If you're worried about Ms. Maxwell safety, we can guarantee it while she's being questioned."

"But I'd have to get her down there and then back to a safe location again. It'd be simpler to have her call you."

"Christ!" Wesson exclaimed.

John finally turned his head slightly so he could see her.

"This clown's just trying to hinder our investigation. We ought to take him down to the office. Maybe he'll be more cooperative there."

John had heard that line before. Hindering investigations was the phrase all authoritative types used when they couldn't get their way. It could be a real nuisance to anyone trying to do his job.

"I don't think that's necessary just yet. Perhaps you could bring Ms. Maxwell down to the office tomorrow morning. What do you say?"

He looked back toward Bailey and shrugged. "I guess that could be arranged. Any particular time?"

"How about nine?"

"That's a little early. I have my beauty sleep to worry about. How 'bout eleven?"

Wesson growled something under her breath, but he ignored her.

"Eleven will be fine," Bailey agreed. Her right hand dipped into a pocket and came out with a card. "Here, the address and room number is on the card. Show this to the receptionist and he'll page me."

John took the card and gave it a polite read. He knew the federal building and NCIX's office, but that was before, and these two agents hadn't been assigned to the northern California office then or at least he hadn't run across them before.

He slipped the card into his own pocket and nodded as Bailey stood.

"Always happy to be able to help the Executive," he lied.

Wesson grunted something again. It sounded like an insult, but he couldn't be sure.

"Thanks citizen," Bailey said. "We'll be expecting you."

As Bailey started to walk away, Wesson leaned down next to him and softly rumbled, "You'd better not be late. You wouldn't want us to have to come find you."

"It's been a pleasure. Come back anytime," John answered and smiled as her frown deepened.

Without another word, she turned and marched after her partner.

*   *   *

Alain Dewatre sat in a late model utility van and watched John Blalock leave the restaurant and make his way back to the vintage car.

As Blalock pulled out of the public parking lot, the color monitor between the van's front seats gave Dewatre a bird's eye view of the car. In the corner of the screen, a digital readout posted the location, direction, and distance of the car from his van's position. A similar readout across the bottom of the screen gave remaining fuel and estimated flight time for the small RPV that currently flew in a tight circle a thousand feet above Dewatre's van.

Blalock's car turned west and the RPV followed, maintaining its position. The RPV was programmed to track the small spot of infrared dye Dewatre had squirted onto the car while it was in the Pacific Rim parking garage. Unless Blalock left town on one of the high-speed freeways, the little RPV could track him for another hour before Dewatre would have to launch its backup from the cradle in the back of his van.

CHAPTER 14

It was nearing noon when John pulled onto highway one and drove south along the rocky coastal crags toward Half Moon Bay.

He'd been on Caitlin's case for less than twelve hours and he was already wishing she'd dropped it on someone else. It wasn't that he didn't enjoy a difficult assignment, in fact, he lived for it. Every since the canyon he'd developed a basic craving, almost an addiction, for the adrenaline rush that comes with risky business. However, it was one thing to put yourself in the line of fire for the joy of living, but it was an entirely different feeling when you were there to protect someone else, someone you cared for. While he hadn't been able to admit to Caitlin that he still had feelings for her, he doubted if he'd ever feel that way about anyone else.

His 'Cuda was old, but it took to the curves of highway one like an adolescent male to a cheerleader. He could have taken one oh one down to Palo Alto and then cut across the peninsular to Half Moon Bay, but more than his car than enjoyed the curves which snaked above the crashing surf of the cold Pacific.

For a while he was trapped behind a slow moving tourist in a rental who spent too much time pointing at the surf, but then they reached an open area and John accelerated past him.

In the clear, his thoughts turned back to the case. There were now at least three parties involved besides Caitlin. There was whoever had attacked her at the hotel, the Japanese businessmen, and now the NCIX. The advent of the NCIX added a threat that he particularly didn't like. He'd done business with them before, anyone involved in information security came across them sooner or later, and it always left a bad taste in his mouth, sort of like the feeling you have when you wake at three A.M. with a full bladder and a beer hangover. These guys didn't leap into simple cases and they normally leapt toward throwing someone into prison. That didn't bode well for Caitlin, and unless he cooperated, there was a small room somewhere with his name on it.

To top it off, the NCIX muscle showed up immediately after he visited the police station. They wouldn't sit outside the station hoping Caitlin would come by, but they might leave a tag in the computer. They had addressed him by the alias he had given the desk sergeant. In this case, it would mean the name of the bogus detective Romax was tagged. It also meant that they were interested in whatever this thing was that everyone else sought. Their involvement came long after the first assault on Caitlin, or they would have visited her at the hotel last night. Caitlin had mentioned seeing two women at Alliotto's in a federal car. Could it have been the same two? How many Amazonian pairs operated in the Bay Area?

Too much was happening too fast. Too many opponents were coming out of the woodwork. He needed more information from Caitlin. There had to be something else she could tell him. Something she or Scott had done out of the ordinary and it must have been recent, perhaps as late as yesterday, but certainly not longer than a week ago. Otherwise, these fast-break artists would have shown up sooner.

He reached the hotel just after one. It was the off season, as tourists go, but the streets were already packed. The hotel's parking lot was nearly empty. It was after checkout, and before check-in, the only cars in the lot would most likely belong to tourists spending the day walking around town.

He parked in front of Caitlin's room and got out. There was no one around who looked suspicious, a rolling cart of dirty laundry waited outside an open door a few rooms away and the sound of Latin music came from the open door.

His knock on Caitlin’s door wasn't answered. He waited a full minute and knocked again, louder. Still no answer.

He took out his key, unlocked the door, and pushed it open. The lights were off, but the curtains overlooking the bay were open. There was plenty of light to see that no one was home.

He went inside and made a quick inspection. There wasn't much to find. The toiletries were still in the bathroom, but otherwise there was nothing to show that Caitlin Maxwell had ever been in here.

Where had she gone? He was almost certain no one could have found her here, but that would mean she left on her own after he specifically told her to lay low and not even leave the room.

Could someone have found her? No, it just wasn't possible. As much as he didn't want to believe it, she had run out on him, again.

No, scratch that.

She hadn't run out on him before. She had simply remained with the man she loved. He couldn't fault her for that. It was the right thing for her to do.

Then why was his gut clenching?

He told himself he was overreacting. There were plenty of reasons she could have left. Maybe she got claustrophobic and went for a walk. Maybe it was that time of the month for her and she'd needed things that he hadn't thought to include in his overnight toiletries. Maybe she'd had a craving for ice cream and went looking for a Baskin-Robins. He wouldn't know until he found her.

He wrote a quick note on the hotel's stationary, telling her to stay put when she got back. He stuck it on the phone and went outside.

He suddenly realized he'd gotten careless and his first clue was the gun in his ribs.

A husky male voice spoke softly at his ear. "Don't close it. We are going back inside."

The voice had a faint accent; French was his first guess, perhaps Belgium, or one of the other Low Countries.

"Whatever you say, pal," John responded and pushed the door fully open. John guessed he wanted him inside before anyone came along and saw him holding a gun on John. The Frenchman was right behind him when he crossed the threshold.

When the door closed, he spoke again, "Where is she?"

"Who?"

The gun dug deeper into his ribs. "Maxwell of course. Don't play with me. I know you have her."

"Au contere mon ami," John answered. "As you can plainly see I do not have her or anyone else for that matter. What makes you think I do?"

"Never mind that, walk toward the back."

He obviously wanted to check the bathroom. It was what John would've done. When he saw she wasn't there, he would be confused, making him vulnerable. That's when John would have his best chance.

"Wait," he ordered halfway across the room.

He'd seen something.

What?

Damn. The note he'd left. So much for convincing him, he had the wrong guy.

John considered jumping him when he tried to read the note. The pressure of the gun eased and he could see him reaching for the note out of the corner of his eye. No, this was too soon; he didn't know who the man was or what his involvement was. He needed to learn more from him and as long as he had the gun, he'd be more apt to give something away.

Besides, jumping a man with a loaded gun is always a last resort maneuver. John didn't like getting shot. He had tried it a couple of times and found it unpleasant at best.

"Nice penmanship. It shows you have an orderly personality. So you don't know her, eh?"

"I didn't say I didn't know a woman. I said I didn't have anyone here," John said.

"And you don't know where she's gone."

"Obviously."

He didn't answer. John could feel him moving closer and the hair on his nape began to tingle. Guns at his back did that.

"What has she done with it?" he asked.

"Look, I'm just an employee here. Ms. Maxwell hired me to find out who was after her and nothing more. I don't know anything about her or her business. That's the truth." Well, a half-truth, anyway.

"Why should I believe you?"

He didn't sound like he particularly wanted to.

"Look, if I was working with her rather than just being a simple employee don't you think she would have told me where she was going? I put her here for her own safety and I just came back to find her gone."

The guy was irritating, but he was also scary. John had no idea whether he'd shoot him just for the hell of it or let him go. Given a choice, he preferred the latter, but the tingling in his nape was getting worse.

"I suppose I could give you the benefit of the doubt. One shouldn't leave too many bodies lying about. It attracts attention."

What the hell was he talking about?

"All right," he said, stepping closer. "I'll let you live, but drop her case. You won't be so lucky the next time I run into you."

"Sure thing, anything you say."

John didn't have any trouble sounding relieved, but he had no intention of dropping the case.

He felt a double pin prick in his back and before he could move fire lanced through him. His muscles locked, snapping his mouth shut and arching his back like a fish floundering on the bottom of a boat. He lost control of his body, but was unable to fall away from the electrodes jabbed into his back.

John didn't know how long the Frenchman held the trigger of his shocker down, but it was too long.

*   *   *

When John came to he was face down with his nose buried in the dingy brown carpet. Everything, absolutely everything hurt. It felt like he'd been exercising until the muscles locked up. He had pain in places he didn't even think he had muscles. He tried to move, but his arms and legs didn't want to respond. Trying again, he finally defeated inertia and pushed away from the floor.

The outside door was closed and he was alone in the room. He staggered to the bathroom and leaned against the sink. The image in the mirror looked almost as bad as he felt. Blood still oozed from a nose that stood at a sharp angle to what he considered normal. The old scar glowed red against his face. Its glow echoed his mood. He gritted his teeth, took a firm grip on his nose, and yanked it straight.

The pain was sharp, but bearable, as fresh blood streamed down across his mustache. He ignored it.

The shocker was a nasty stun weapon. Its high frequency and high voltage shock locks the voluntary muscles in the body, but when the charge is spent, the muscles relax. Normally, they'd hurt for a couple of days, depending on the physical condition of the victim. In his case, he expected a day would be enough, but it was going to be one hell of a day.

His left nostril still seeped crimson. He yanked off a foot of toilet tissue, rolled it into a cylinder, and jammed it into his nostril, inflicting almost as much pain as straightening it had.

He picked up his overnighter from where he'd left it and started for the front door.

The note he'd written lay crumbled on the floor. He bent to retrieve it and then changed his mind. If Caitlin came back, she would have enough evidence that something was wrong when she saw the pool of blood his nose had left in the carpet. That should cause her to leave without stopping to look for a note. She'd get back in touch with him over the Web or back at The Gleaning Cube.

He went to the front door and looked out. There were a few people moving about the lot, but there was no sign of his assailant. Just as well, it'd be a few more hours before he was limber enough to handle a fight. He opened the door and walked stiffly to the rear of his car, unlocked the trunk, and tossed in his overnighter.

John bent and pulled back the carpet. Then he unlatched the hidden compartment in the floor and lifted out a small case. He closed the trunk, went around to the driver's door, and got in.

He set the case on the seat next to him and keyed in the combination. Opening the lid revealed his handgun and holster. He took the gun out, checked that there was a round in the chamber and a full magazine, then set it back down while he strapped on the shoulder holster. It was normally difficult in the front seat of a car, but with his stiff muscles, it took a few minutes. Finally, he got it on and slid the handgun home.

He didn't usually pack the gun. Relying on a gun instead of your wits often gets you into more trouble than it's worth, but once a case starts getting serious, it tends to stay that way. Besides, Frenchy and he had some unfinished business.

While the case had already been interesting, Frenchy had made it something personal. The next time he saw the Frenchman, things would be different.

CHAPTER 15

John pulled onto highway one for the drive back up the coast. He appreciated the usually uncomfortable weight of the handgun. It felt as comforting as a baby's pacifier. He hadn't felt the need to carry it in months and he'd forgotten how safe you feel with a fully loaded Colt ten millimeter strapped to your side.

Regardless of how good the Colt felt, his gut had grown cold.

Caitlin had disappeared without a note. The Frenchman had found the hotel and had known she would be there. Had she done something to tip him off? She could have placed a call, either to someone whose phone was tapped by the Frenchman or she could have logged into the Web and left evidence that an efficient Web rider could trace. But if she had, why had she then left without so much as a note?

Someone else could have traced her signal and gotten to the hotel before the Frenchman. They could have removed her and left no evidence of a struggle, but who? The Japanese? The killer? The Feds? And who was the Frenchman aligned with?

The only other possibility was just as disturbing. Caitlin could have ignored his instructions and left on her own. He had thought she'd be able to handle instructions, but having no contact with her for over twelve years made her temperament a trait he couldn't really judge. However, if she were being honest with him then she would have left a note.

What was her motive?

Could she have set him up?

He didn't want to think about the possibility, but it wouldn't be the first time someone had taken advantage of his trust.

Caitlin was different. Wasn't she?

He still had feelings for her, but they were illogical and made no sense, especially now that she had disappeared on him. He didn't need to be in love with her or anyone else. He didn't need to trust. What he needed was....

He didn't know what he needed, unless it was to find Caitlin and the Frenchman. At that moment, the order didn't matter. But on the chance that someone had taken her, he had to concentrate on finding her first.

He turned off onto Del Mar and headed across the peninsular toward Palo Alto. It was a faster route than highway one. The road wound past new homes where a decade earlier a Christmas tree farm had provided color and coolness to the landscape. Development continued to spoil what had once been a nice place to live. Not that he had been here then. He'd only moved into the Bay Area about five years ago, but he'd heard it was once nice. He came here for the work, not for the unspoiled beauty of the area.

It was nearly four when he pulled up to an apartment he maintained in one of the less desirable areas of San Francisco. He circled the block once, looking for anything out of place. Nothing attracted his attention. He left his car in one of the unmarked spaces behind the building and took the stairs to the third floor. The hallway was empty; at this time of day most people were either still at work or sleeping if they worked the night shifts. He held his keys in his left hand and kept the right free for action.

His lock appeared to be a simple deadbolt, but he'd replaced it without asking the landlord for permission. No one, including the landlord, had any business in John's place. John slipped the key home, twisted it to the left, held it for a full second to disconnect the alarm, and then turned it to the right to unlock the bolt. Anyone picking the lock would usually miss something that simple.

He pushed the door open and stepped inside. Shatter resistant glass covered the curtain-less windows; to his left lay his computer with its associated hardware, books, and software. Next to the computer was the storage vault holding his weapons and a few other high-priced items. A small sofa and entertainment center occupied the middle of the room. The right side of the apartment held a small kitchen, bedroom, and bathroom.

The computer ran constantly, but went into the catnap mode whenever he left the apartment. John walked over to it and tapped the mouse button. The monitor awoke to show his security program.

"Alarm status?" he asked.

"All secure."

"Full security," John ordered.

His apartment's security had three levels, low, normal, and full. He rarely used low. Normal provided for entry control and automatically summoned the police in case of an attempted break-in or the fire department in case the fire alarm activated.

Full didn't call the police. It electrified a series of metal strips bordering the windows and the keyhole on the door with a charge similar to the stunner that had taken him down.

In addition, it booby trapped the computer so that if someone did get in, the computer and certain other quasi-legal things stored there would be melted down with the generous use of thermite. Of course, the system would summon the fire department simultaneously to prevent the fire from spreading, and no one would gain access to anything he wouldn't want them to have.

"Messages?" he asked.

"Two e-mails."

No voice mail and the e-mail could wait.

He stripped down, tossed his clothing in the hamper, and took a shower. He still didn't feel clean from the effects of the stunner. Normal stunners have a preset time they discharge, usually less than a second does. The Frenchman's stunner was either illegally modified or a black-market version. Either of which would explain his severe reaction.

John toweled dry, pulled on fresh clothes, and added a vest beneath his trenchcoat. The heavy vest's multiple layers of Kevlar II were protection from most bullets. It'd also prevent a stunner's electrodes from reaching his skin.

John had never been a Boy Scout, but he was a fast learner when it came to being prepared.

He grabbed a snack out of the fridge and called up the messages on the computer. The monitor displayed a short message concerning some hardware he'd ordered. It was signed simply, T.V.

T.V. was a good friend in the black market world of electronics. If he couldn't purchase it somewhere, he could jury-rig it out of a couple of chips and a battery. The man had a genius for gadgets and only his dislike for established corporations and the world in general kept him from great wealth.

He also happened to be one of the few people in the Bay Area John could count on.

The other message was more confusing. It was encrypted. Generally, messages on the Web were in either simple ASCII or HTML and could be read by anyone with enough sophistication to break into the Web's mail system and read someone else's personal mail. In practice, it rarely happened.

That someone had taken the trouble to encrypt a message implied they either didn't trust his account's integrity or else the Web's integrity. The return address was a public account, one of the anonymous logons that anyone could use, much like pay phones.

Caitlin had used one to send her query to him last night. Could this message be from her?

Encryption meant he had to have a specific password to decrypt the message. Assuming the message was from Caitlin and since they hadn't discussed encryption earlier, the password would have to be something they had in common. There was little chance of anyone else knowing they had met before. So it must be something from their past. He had only known her for that brief period twelve years ago, in the canyon....

He called up a decryption program. He'd used Grand Canyon last night and doubted if she would use the same one, but then.

He typed in Grand Canyon. The message unraveled.

"John, I'm sorry I won't be there when you return, but there was something I had to find out and I couldn't do it from the room. I'll meet you where we met last night at seven tonight. Caitlin."

So, that explained her absence, or did it? He didn't like this. His gut instinct was always one of caution. Was Caitlin being honest with him? Could he walk away from this case if she wasn't?

No. He couldn't. It amazed him that people had the ability to develop attachments in so short a period as they had shared during the rafting trip. It was even more amazing that after all these years he still found himself wanting her.

He checked the clock and did a quick calculation of driving times between the wharf and The Gleaning Cube. He could meet the Japanese businessmen and still make the connection with Caitlin at seven.

John reset the alarms, locked up, and went down the back stairs to his car.

CHAPTER 16

In the City by the Bay, taxis, buses, trolleys, and private cars always compete for right of way with thick crowds of pedestrians, especially at that time of day. Twilight stole over the city like some sinister visitor only to be driven off by the bright halogen glow of flickering streetlights. Humanity had feared the dark since it crouched around campfires and shivered at the sounds of beasts prowling the night. Not too long ago some congressman had even suggested placing gigantic reflectors in orbit over cities to provide illumination throughout the night. The suggestion hadn't shocked John; rather it was the proposal's defeat. Perhaps homosapiens were losing their fear of the dark. Then again, perhaps it sounded too much like big brother in space.

He reached the wharf with a little time to spare. He parked in the multistory parking garage and took the pedestrian walkway across the street. The wharf area never lost its special air. A lot of which came from the fish vendors on the west end of the wharves. Since the breeze usually came from that direction there was always the aroma of dying fish surrounding the wharf. He didn't mind the smell and apparently neither did the tourists who had flocked to the area for more than a century.

He stayed on the elevated wooden walkway of Pier 34 and moved unnoticed through the crowds of tourists examining the myriad shops that hungered for their money.

Melville's wasn't an old bar and had to make up for its newness with artificial atmosphere. The tourists, however, couldn't tell the difference. Images of the great whale hunting days of the nineteenth century abounded. Paraphernalia that looked real, but was actually created in a small town in New Hampshire, hung everywhere around the bar. Reproduced photographs showed the struggle of man against the sea. Nowhere did you see the gallons of blood that washed the decks of the whaling ships.

The bar's owners were not crazy. Japanese tourists particularly loved the bar. Since MacArthur introduced whale meat to their culture back in the forties, they've had a sweet tooth for whale flesh. He asked the Japanese businessmen to meet him here only because it was the first bar that came to mind when he thought of Japan.

John was a little early. He wanted enough time to check the bar's clientele for suspicious persons; namely other Japanese businessmen with arm pit bulges. He ordered and paid for a draft ale, then slowly cruised the bar, trying to give the impression that he was studying the paraphernalia. After ten minutes, he was fairly certain that the Japanese hadn't sent ringers in ahead of them.

He went out onto the deck and took a table by the side railing, away from the main crowd at the railing overlooking the bay, old Alcatraz, and the Gate. There was a drop of nearly fifteen feet to the lower deck. It'd be tough on the ankles, but he'd made worse leaps before.

His schooner of ale was half gone when the gentlemen he'd come to meet stepped onto the deck. For a minute they looked around, then they spotted him.

They approached with the measured tread of hunters following the track of a wounded leopard. Did they know something or where they just being cautious?

They stopped a few feet away and the one he knew only as the driver said, "Mr. White?"

"Yes."

He held up the card that John had given him earlier. "The same Mr. White that works for the Blalock Security Agency?"

He was fishing. John didn't nibble. "The same."

"Curious company, the Blalock Agency. It seems there are several employee's listed in the state register, but they are all named John."

"What a coincidence," he said and took a sip from the schooner.

"There also seems to be no evidence of employees except on the state register. It would seem, to an honest businessman such as myself, that the Blalock Agency has something to hide."

"Nonsense, the agency is strictly a legitimate enterprise. I am merely ... an honest businessman."

The driver stared down at him for a few seconds then made the slightest of bows, nothing more than a tip of his head really. His associate pulled out a chair and sat down.

The driver continued, "Very well. Let me introduce Mr. Ichiro Hosokawa."

Hosokawa's head tilt was more of a lowering of eyebrows than anything approaching a level of courtesy. No one would have seen it except the person he was facing at close range. If the Japanese still used head bows as a symbol of respect, he wasn't awarding John much.

"Please to meet you," John responded automatically and gave him a slightly deeper eyebrow dip. His driver took it as an insult. At least, that was John's impression from the man's low growl. "Have your man sit. He will draw attention if he stands at your side while we talk."

Hosokawa made a simple movement with his left hand. The driver bowed, tilting until John thought he might fall over. Then the driver straightened quickly and walked to a point on the rail where he could watch them while he appeared to be studying the sea lions on the jetty.

"Mr. White," Hosokawa began. "You represent a Ms. Caitlin Maxwell--"

"My agency," John interrupted.

"Pardon?"

"My agency. The Blalock Security Agency has Ms. Maxwell as a client."

"There's a difference?" Hosokawa asked.

"Of course," John answered. "We don't normally give out that kind of information, but since we registered a contract with Ms. Maxwell it would be foolish of me to deny it. However, I make no claims to being the person handling her case."

Hosokawa stewed on that for a few seconds while keeping his face a death mask. His English was excellent, with little of the accent so well publicized in the old movies. "Very well, we'll play the game your way, Mr. White. Your client has something that we would like to purchase."

"I see," he said, not seeing at all. "And what would that be?"

"If she hasn't told you what it is, then I see no reason to tell you myself. Employees do not need to know the business of their employers. You can tell Ms. Maxwell that we are prepared to negotiate a price for the item in question."

John took a sip from his beer and gazed off toward the driver. "I suppose she might be willing to sell it, not that I can guarantee anything."

"Of course," he agreed. "I am just requesting that you relay our offer. I am sure she would be most satisfied with our negotiations."

John nodded slightly. "Really? Well then, I'll definitely let her know what you've said. Do you have an initial bid?"

His mask cracked. "Pardon?"

"An initial bid. You know the drill. She has something you want. She's placing it up for bid. You make an offer; the other interested parties make their offers. She goes with the highest bidder."

Hosokawa frowned. "We have no intention in getting into a bidding war, Mr. White. We are prepared to pay handsomely for what has come into her possession, but there are limits to everything."

"I don't think so," John snapped. "You aren't the only interested party Mr. Hosokawa. As an honest businessman, you know that price is governed by demand. In this case it seems that demand is high, so we expect an equivalently high price."

Hosokawa's mask slid back into place as he thought over John's words. "Mr. White, I can see you are a businessman of some intelligence. This thing in Ms. Maxwell's possession came to her though no fault of her own. She didn't design it, buy it, or steal it. It has simply been left in her care. We have already paid well for the delivery of this item and are not interested in seeing it end up in someone else's hands."

"So you are saying this ... this thing belongs to you. It's something you paid for and are still awaiting delivery."

"Exactly."

"You know the NCIX is interested in this thing?"

Hosokawa's attention sharpened. John might as well have waved a steak in front of pit bull.

"No," Hosokawa said. "What business would they have with it?"

"I can't answer that. I'd like to, really I would, but you can see that with the Feds involved, I, as a legitimate businessman, would have to turn it over to them until they determine proper and legal ownership."

The tension in Hosokawa became a physical force that insinuated itself into his words. "Mr. White, we have worked long and hard for this device. My partners are not tolerant of failure when they have invested so much time and money. As one businessman to another I am sure you can see our position."

John nodded to keep him talking.

"We are willing to go to extraordinary lengths to acquire that which we consider to be ours. If you were able to persuade Ms. Maxwell that the item should be ours then I'm certain we could arrange a worthy finder's fee for yourself."

"Above what you're willing to pay her for the item?"

"Certainly," he said. "We have no reason to deny Ms. Maxwell a profit, even though it is totally unearned. You, however, will be earning your profit."

John nodded again. "Just what size finder's fee are we talking about here?"

"That can be negotiated, but let's start with the equivalent of five years salary."

"You know how much I make in a year?" John asked.

"I know how much the Blalock Agency reported on their taxes last year. It is a respectable figure."

John didn't ask how he'd gotten his information. The IRS computers were about as easy to enter as a nun's dormitory room after midnight, but bribing an official or hiring a code breaker were easily within Mr. Hosokawa's means.

"That sounds like a generous offer, Mr. Hosokawa. I can't make any promises, but I will see what I can do."

"Make no mistake, Mr. White," he said. His voice grew even softer than before. "Our displeasure can be even greater than our pleasure."

John nodded. "Message received and understood. Do you have a number where I can reach you?"

Hosokawa's left hand dipped into a pocket and came up with a business card. He slid it across the table. John palmed the card without reading it.

Hosokawa stood and the driver appeared at his elbow.

"Don't take too long in responding, Mr. Blalock. Events are rushing down time's highway and I fear it is a one way road."

John didn't have an answer to that.

Hosokawa left without even the eyebrow dip.

*　　　*　　　*

Holdren's cell phone buzzed as they were leaving the offices of the NCIX at San Francisco's federal building.

A stiff ocean breeze swept through the crowded streets. It temporarily removed some of the smell of car exhaust, rotting garbage, and human urine. San Francisco was once again going through a period of social permissiveness that allowed bums to fill the streets, defecating in alleys, living on park benches, and clogging the sidewalks with their wasted lives.

Holdren had never had patience with the miscreants that made up the lower rungs of modern civilization. He supposed all ages had suffered the disease-ridden vermin, but in most ages, their very diseases helped thin the herd. In modern America, a permissiveness called social welfare maintained their numbers through feeding, clothing, housing, and caring for the teaming vermin.

He flicked open the phone. "Holdren."

"This is Kirby again, sir. Maxwell is logged onto the Web."

"Do you have a location?" Holdren asked.

"Downtown, near the Trans America building."

"We're close. Do you have anyone closer?"

"Yes, sir. There's a car not two blocks away."

"Excellent. Get them on her. Have them keep her in sight until I arrive, but under no circumstances are they to move in before I get there."

"Yes, sir."

Holdren returned the phone to his pocket.

"This time we have her," he said.

CHAPTER 17

Darkness had swept over the city by the time John reached The Gleaning Cube. Its cool embrace was comfort to many, fear to others, and opportunity to the slime inhabiting the city's more notorious areas. For John it was simply night. That half of the day that provided cover from prying eyes, solace to eyes weary of the world's cruelty, and as always, freedom. However, this night was business and he found no pleasure in its embrace.

He parked near end of the small wharf behind The Gleaning Cube, backing the car in only after his headlights illuminated every niche where someone could hide. The encounter with the Frenchman had reminded him that caution was a lifetime pursuit. When caution lapsed, death soon followed.

John got out and activated the car's alarm. It wasn't one of those noisy things that honked the horn and flashed the lights. No, if someone was trying to get into his car he wanted to know about it before they knew he knew. His alarm system beeped his remote and signaled what caused the alarm, whether it was the motion sensor, the hood or trunk lock, or one of the doors. If the ignition was tampered with, another signal would notify him it was being hot-wired.

John took another careful look around the wharf before he walked to the back door of the bar. It was unlocked. He opened it, slipped inside, and locked it behind him. You could never tell when the door would be locked, but there was a buzzer that usually brought the bartender or the bar-back.

He eased down the hall until he reached the men's room. A quick check told him it was unoccupied. He did the same at the ladies' room and the storeroom, which also served as an office. Both were empty.

The jukebox played not-so-modern jazz.

John checked the bar from the shelter of the hallway. There were a couple of customers he recognized, but for the most part the clientele at this hour were tourists. He entered smoothly and went to the bar, taking note that no one appeared interested or even surprised that he had come out of the back. The bar was small enough that it was possible to keep up with everyone even when crowded, but this crowd was only interested in themselves.

"Evening, Becky," he said to the bartender.

Becky was a student at Stanford. She had a scholarship that paid her books and tuition, but not for her room and board. For nearly two years, she had worked afternoons and early evenings at the Gleaning Cube. They'd talked on several occasions, sometimes at length. Tonight her auburn hair was pulled back in a French braid. John recognized it as the hairstyle she used whenever she was rushed for time.

Becky wiped the bar off in front of a stool when John approached. "Hi John, what'll it be tonight?"

"Molson."

"Right. Working eh?"

"Am I that obvious?"

She grinned. "Damn straight, John. You'll order Black Bush if you're here for a drink, but when you expect to be here a while, as in waiting for a client, you always get beer."

He returned her grin. "Guess I come here too much. I'd better find a bar where no one knows me."

She popped the top on a Molson and poured it into a tall pilsner, letting a half inch of foam develop on the top. She placed a small square napkin on the bar, set the glass on it, and shook her head. "Don't get that way, John. You know all the local bars need their characters to make regular appearances in order to hold onto their tourist clientele."

He took a quick gulp from the Molson. It was cold and sharp. "Is that what I am now, Becky, local color?"

"Please. Color? No, I wouldn't use that term. Local character maybe, but color? Who knows? Perhaps, it's all semantics. In any case, you're a well-known local. People ask about you when they come in."

"Really?"

That was news to him. He had no idea that he came here often enough to have developed a name. It was disconcerting.

"Sure, you have all the requisite attributes. You're distinctive, mysterious, and handsome."

"Handsome?" John ran a finger down the scar on the left side of his face. He hadn't realized Becky was nearsighted.

"Yes, handsome. Don't think the scar makes you less attractive. It's not what you'd call disfiguring. Ladies are intrigued by it. Many want to know how you got it."

"What do you tell them?"

Becky shrugged. "It depends on who's asking, but mostly we just say it's something you picked up in the Marines and don't like to talk about."

He took another swallow of beer. She was right about his not liking to talk about it. It was a prime example of carelessness and of caring too much. Anytime he started feeling philanthropic he'd touch the scar and remember what trying to be helpful could cost you. Becky was nice. Many times she had made the nights pass enjoyably with her wit and charm.

The front door opened.

Caitlin Maxwell stepped in from the dark. She'd lost none of the furtive moves that she'd had displayed so well last night and examined the entire room before moving inside.

Becky noticed John's gaze and glanced toward the door. "Nice lady. Client?"

"Yes, a client."

Caitlin swept around the counter and laid her bag on the bar. Before he could stop her, she wrapped her arms around him and kissed him in a very friendly manner. The taste of her was sweet. The press of her body against his was moving.

John found himself unable to resist either the embrace or the kiss.

When Caitlin finally broke the clutch, Becky cleared her throat. "Can I get your client a drink?"

He eyeballed her with what he hoped was a menacing scowl. From the smile that lit her face, he knew he hadn't succeeded.

He really was going to have to find a new bar.

"White wine, chardonnay, if you have it," Caitlin said without taking her eyes off John. "Miss me?"

Becky had moved down the bar and was decanting a portion of wine into a tall stemmed glass, but he could tell she was still listening.

John's voice came out low and tense. "Miss you? You leave the room after I distinctly told you not to. You left nothing to tell me what happened to you, and now you have the audacity to ask me if I missed you. You've got some nerve lady, you could have been spotted, you could have left a trail back to here, hell you could have been killed."

"Lighten up, John. I'm fine."

"Lighten up?"

That expression usually accomplished the opposite when directed at him. He kept his voice low. "I have neither the disposition nor the time to lighten up. I expect a little professionalism when I'm working. In case you've forgotten, you came to me for help."

"No, I haven't forgotten. But there was something I had to do and I couldn't do it from the hotel room."

"And what...."

Becky's returning with Caitlin's wine interrupted his sentence. As much as he liked Becky, there was a limit to how much he trusted anyone.

"Let's move to a table," John said as he picked up his glass and started toward the back without waiting for a reply.

His usual table was vacant and he sat down before Caitlin caught up.

She sat down next to him. "My, aren't we touchy tonight."

"Touchy my ass. One more stunt like you pulled today and you can forget my help. You either follow my instructions or find yourself another boy," John said and put more emphasis on his growl after seeing his scowl fail with Becky.

For the first time, Caitlin seemed to realize he was serious. She lowered her eyes and looked away. "I'm sorry. I thought I'd be back before you. There was something I needed to do."

"Okay and while we're getting things straight, what was with that kiss?"

"Oh, I thought it'd look better if we were meeting for other than business reasons. You know how they're always doing it in the movies."

"This isn't the movies. You're not fooling anyone."

"I don't know, the bartender seemed convinced."

"She's just a kid, they're easy to fool."

"Sure they are."

"Enough of this. What was so important that you had to leave the hotel?"

"After you left, I got to thinking about the connection between what happened to me and Scott's death." She paused.

When it became obvious she was waiting for him to ask, he did. "And?"

"I checked my Web site and found a message from Scott. It was a huge file, but the kick in the pants is that it was sent after he died."

"After? Well, that's not impossible. He could have had a delayed transmission set up, but then he could have also had it stored somewhere and the news of his death somehow activated the transmission. How large was it?"

"Over a gig."

"Humph, that is large. Did he send you files like that often?"

"Are you kidding? No, of course you're not. The answer is no, normally he didn't send me anything, because I saw him at the office every day.

"What kind of work was he involved in?"

"I'm really not sure what he could have been involved with that would get him killed. It's not like we dealt in classified information."

John nodded. "What did he say about this file?"

"Nothing at all."

"So what's in the file?"

Caitlin opened her bag, took something out, and then placed it on the table between them. John looked around the room. No one had developed an unhealthy interest.

He palmed the disk and lowered it to his side. It looked like an ordinary 3 inch DVD that could hold something like 30 Gigabytes of data.

"Would you mind putting it back in your bag? I'd just as well not attract too much attention."

"Oh, I'm sorry. I should have thought."

Caitlin took the disk from his hand and slipped it back into her bag discreetly.

"What's in the file?" he repeated.

"It's encoded. I don't have the encryption code."

"Damn. Did Scott leave you any clues as to the content of this file?"

She shrugged. "I'm not positive. He made a vague reference to May first."

"Oh? What's significant about that date?"

"It's the day my parents go back to their home in Colorado. I can't think of anything else."

"Your parents still live in Black Forest?"

"Yes, but they've become snowbirds and spend each winter in Florida. There's a couple of other strange messages, besides the one from Scott."

Strange messages? What sort of messages did she get when she wasn't being hunted?

"You want to tell me about the messages?"

"Well, sure. The first was from someone wanting to buy something from me. The message didn't state what or who they were, they wanted my reply sent to a public e-mail drop."

John nodded thoughtfully and wondered about Mr. Hosokawa.

"The other message was a claim to something I have ... and a warning. It warned that if I didn't return it immediately there would be dire consequences."

"Dire consequences?"

"Yeah, that's just what it said. Can you believe it?" She smiled humorously and gave a nervous little laugh. "Sounds like something out of a paperback novel."

He smiled with her. "Yeah, like a paperback ... or perhaps someone who learned English as a second language."

Her head cocked slightly to one side. It was a mannerism he remembered from the Canyon.

"You know something?"

"Yeah, a little." He gave her a brief run down of the day's events. She nodded a few times, drank about half her wine, and allowed him to talk uninterrupted.

When he finished, she didn't say anything for nearly a full minute while she took nervous little sips of her wine.

She licked her lips in a way that distracted him more than it should have.

"It sounds like Mr. Hosokawa sent me the first message and if you're right about the second language then the Frenchman could have sent the second."

John nodded. "That'd be my guess. The Japanese are probably affiliated with JETRO, the Japanese External Trade Organization. They are responsible for most of their country's industrial espionage. The Frenchman probably works for one of the subagencies under the DGRG, the Direction General des Renseignements Gereraux, most likely the Recherche."

"Recherche?"

"Intelligence collection, it's one of the four directions of the DGRG."

"Then what they're after must be the same thing the killer's after. It must be this file Scott sent me."

Again, he nodded. "Yeah, I suppose it must be."

"But what is the NCIX's connection to this?"

John could think of one thing, but he didn't want to go into it until he knew for sure. "They've taken over all aspects of industrial espionage from the FBI and the CIA. I'd be surprised if they hadn't shown an interest."

Caitlin sipped her wine. He could tell she was giving it some thought. "No, not Scott. He's, he wasn't the type."

He didn't have to ask what type she was talking about? It was the same thought that had occurred to him when he heard about the file.

"You knew him that well?"

Her pupils dilated and after a moment, she shook her head violently. "No, it's not possible. For crying out loud we were married for twelve years."

"People change."

She blinked, paused, and blinked again. He could see that her thoughts must have shifted to how much John had changed in the intervening years. Had he really changed that much? Sure he was more cynical, more paranoid, and perhaps colder, but down deep, where it really matter, he still believed in goodness, motherhood, apple pie, and all that rot he grew up with. Didn't he? When was the last time he'd questioned his own values?

Unconsciously, he found himself again stroking the scar.

Yeah, he remembered.

It was right after he'd received this testament to youth's follies. He'd been doing what he thought was right and it nearly got him killed. He was in Haiti, part of the peacekeeper detachment overseeing another attempt at free elections and starting a democracy. The police had become a nonexistent entity and they were filling in wherever they could.

* * *

It had been a calm day and he guess he'd relaxed a little too much at the small bar that they'd adopted as their own. John decided to hoof it back over to the barracks and he left alone, leaving his buds to finish drinking the night away.

He was two blocks from the bar when he heard the woman screaming.

John had always figured there were distinctive levels to screaming. On a scale from one to ten, a one can be compared to that of a two-year-old opening presents at their birthday party. A ten is the scream that comes when the earth opens up beneath your feet and you start that long plunge into hell.

He gave this one at least a seven.

John ran down a side alley, through an open doorway, and up the stairs into one of the many tenements that threatened to collapse into the town square.

The scream came again as he reached the second floor landing. He ran down a hallway that was empty of the riff-raff that normally slept inside when the rainy season was in full force.

The third scream made his skin crawl and he bumped it up to an eight as he slammed into the apartment door without pausing. He busted into the apartment in time to see a dreadlocked-man with a meat cleaver going after a woman who had a kid clinging to each leg.

John's crashing through the door snapped the attacker's attention away from his victims. He was as tall as John, but slender, the kind of slender that you equate with drug use or disease.

Her attacker turned from her and came toward John with the cleaver. He was too close for John to unsnap the strap on his side arm. He should have already unsnapped, but peacekeepers weren't supposed to shoot first.

He swung at John with the cleaver and John sidestepped into the apartment, trying to place himself between the loony and the woman. Mr. Deadlocks anticipated John's move and cut him off. John waited until the cleaver's next swing and stepped inside after the blade passed. Before his hand could start back, John looped an arm over his and immobilized the cleaver. A swift chop of John's free hand broke the man's collarbone and he dropped the cleaver.

Without the cleaver, he wasn't much of a threat. John took the wind out of his sails with a few punches to his belly, then bounced him off the wall until he passed out.

Luck.

What was it that made some people luckily and some just dead?

Luck made him turn in time to see the woman swinging the cleaver down toward his head.

Only fast reflexes got his head off the chopping block.

Almost.

She didn't split his skull, but she creased it from eyebrow to jaw.

John staggered away from her as she drew back for another swing. He dropped low and swept her feet out from under her with his right foot. She fell hard.

Before she recovered from the fall, he had snatched the cleaver out of her hand. He stood over her; the cleaver in his right hand, as blood from his face cascaded onto hers. She blinked, trying to clear her eyes, and raised her hands to ward off what she thought was coming.

John stared at her with his clear eye. She was young, perhaps even younger than he. A roaring filled his ears and for an instance he couldn't place the sound. Then he noticed the screaming children huddled in a corner of the small apartment. They watched terrified as John tried to decide what to do with the cleaver.

It didn't take long him long to realize what a fool he'd been.

He left the cleaver buried in the apartment's doorjamb and went looking for the UN first aid station.

He made it as far as the camp entrance before he started feeling lightheaded. The gate guard took one look at his blood-soaked uniform and radioed for an ambulance. John thanked him and sat down against the side of the guard shack to rest. The guard started asking him questions, and John tried to answer them, but he was getting sleepy. He didn't remember the ambulance arriving.

When he woke up the Gunny was standing over him. John blinked his unbandaged eye and greeted Gunnery Sergeant Zim. "Morning Gunny. What brings you out?"

"Damn it, Lieutenant. Do I have to watch you twenty-four hours a day?"

"Come on, Gunny, it could have happened to anyone."

The short gray hairs on the Gunny's head glistened in the artificial light as his head shook sadly from side to side. "Lieutenant, it couldn't have happened to anyone who followed SOP. It shouldn't have happened to anyone that I've spent so much time training. What have I told you about being a hero?"

"A hero? Gunny I wasn't trying to be a hero, I was--"

"Don't give me that. I saw the gate SP's report."

John tried to remember what he'd told the shore patrolman at the gate, but it wouldn't come.

"You were trying to save some woman and she ended up trying to kill you. If you'd paid any attention to me over the last year you would have called for assistance before you ever entered that building."

"Ah, Gunny, there wasn't time. I'd have called if--"

"Wrong answer, Lieutenant. There's always time if you're not trying to be a hero. The standard operating procedures insist that no one get involved in local fighting without the commander's authorization unless UN forces are under attack."

"Hell, I--"

"Yeah, I know what you're going to say, 'There wasn't time. It was a judgment call. You did what you felt you had to do.'"

"Yeah, that's right. Ah, do you think the Colonel will buy it?"

The Gunny shook his head again. "No, I don't think he'll buy it, but for official purposes he will. Hell, he may even give you a medal, but you aren't fooling anyone."

"I don't want a medal."

"I'll tell him you said that, but the Colonel has to keep the politicos happy. If one of his men gets cut up saving a local his hands are tied, even if both of us know you need your head examined more than you need a medal."

The door opened and a nurse stepped inside. "Your time is up, Sergeant Zim. The Lieutenant needs his rest."

"I was just leaving."

The Gunny turned back to John and for a moment, his face grew sad. "Look Lieutenant, you were lucky this time, but it won't last. You can't save everybody who needs saving."

He hesitated. "John, even heroes die. Remember that anytime you want to rush into a fight. It'll save your life."

*   *   *

Modern antibiotics kept the wound from festering, but soldiers don't always have access to the plastic surgeons who could skillfully remove such a scar. Later, after he'd left the service of both the UN and the US, John found he didn't want the scar removed.

It was a good reminder of what happens when you let emotion overcome caution.

Caitlin was staring at him when he came out of his flashback on ancient history.

"What's the matter? Is something stuck in my mustache?"

She frowned in distaste and shook her head slightly. "No, I was just wondering what you were thinking about."

"Old memories."

"Anything you care to talk about?"

He took a quick gulp of beer and shook his head. "No more than I'd like to suck this beer up my nose with a straw."

Again, she frowned. "Must you be so crude?"

"Life's crude," he replied with a dismissing wave of his hand.

"That may be, but nothing forces you to be the same."

He took another mouthful and let its cool bitterness slide across his tongue. She was right. The memory of Haiti had dragged an old crudeness from him. The scar wasn't her fault. He had only himself to blame for it. Was his crudeness a simple attempt to shock her? Perhaps, but unnecessary crudeness wasn't him. He just wanted her to realize he was no longer the kid who'd fallen so quickly for her in the Canyon.

He set the glass down and gave her a half-hearted smile.

"My apologies, Caitlin. You're right. There's no reason for the crudeness. It was just an old memory stirring forgotten emotions."

"Memory?"

She repeated and he saw her gaze move to encompass the scar. "Of how you got that?"

"How very perceptive. Yeah, it was the scar."

"You could tell me about it," she said.

"I don't think so."

Her hand slide across the table and softly came to rest on the back of his. His eyes rose slowly to meet her gaze.

"All right. Not that there's much to tell, but if you're sure you want to know?"

She nodded.

He gave her a brief playback of the memory. It didn't take long.

When he finished her hand was still upon his. The emotions playing across her face were too easy to read. He pulled free of her hand and downed the rest of his beer.

"I don't need your pity," he said with unnecessary bitterness.

She sat back and looked him in the eye. "It's not pity I'm feeling. It's understanding."

Was it? He wasn't sure. He had been madly in love with her for a time, but so much had changed, at least for him. Could it be that he was afraid the spark still glowed? No, it wasn't possible. Too much time had flowed through life's canyon. But if he were so sure then what would it hurt?

"All right, understanding then. Tell you what, from here on out, I'll be honest with you and you with me."

"Deal. What now?" she asked with the first cheerful smile he'd seen on her face in nearly twelve years.

The front door opened.

"Now? Now we go see someone I know about a file."

A man came through the door. A man with a splint over his nose.

"Oh, where --"

John interrupted her. "Caitlin, I want you to go to the restroom. Stand up slowly and don't turn around."

"What?"

"I think your Mr. Holdren has put in an appearance."

CHAPTER 18

Caitlin's eyes widened and fear shadowed her face. "Here? How did he find me here?"

"This isn't the time to be wondering. Just do what I said. He probably won't notice you leaving the room, if he does he'll hopefully just think you're on the way to the facilities. Go to the back door, but don't open it until I get there."

"All right, but --"

"Look, just do it all right?"

Caitlin frowned, but nodded. John watched Holdren as he walked slowly from table to table at the front on the bar. When he was turned away from them, John nodded. "Now."

Caitlin stood and walked past him to the back hallway.

It was one of those days you can't get a break.. Holdren turned back their way as Caitlin was leaving. He obviously saw something familiar in the way Caitlin walked for a second after she had disappeared through the back hallway, he went after her.

Holdren looked to be in his late thirties, maybe early forties. He was about six feet tall and his fine, graying hair was cut neatly away from his ears in a typical military cut. Not the severe cut of adrenaline pumped grunts, but the classic cut of the officer corps. His face was creased from wrinkles that made John think of worry lines rather than weathering. Thick eyebrows shaded his eyes and his lips were curled in what looked like a permanent frown.

Holdren raised his hand as he moved across the room and spoke into the cuff of his hound's tooth jacket.

John ducked his head so the brim of his hat would cover his face. With any luck at all, Holdren wouldn't stop to wonder which table Caitlin had been occupying.

Why was it that anything involving luck always seemed to be on the other guy's side?

As Holdren neared, John watched the man's hands. When he was ten feet away, Holdren's right hand went inside his jacket. John didn't wait to see what it might emerge with. He scooped up the beer mug and flicked it backhanded at Holdren's face.

Holdren's hand came out of his jacket with the silenced pistol Caitlin had described. Before he could level the gun, the glass mug caught him just above the right eye. It popped his head back and the pistol made a soft coughing sound as it discharged into the ceiling.

Holdren staggered. Blood seeped from the gash in his forehead. He caught his balance and lowered the gun. John was up and closing the distance between them. Holdren brought the gun down and John stepped to the side.

The little gun coughed again and John felt a hot pain in his left shoulder.

He seized Holdren's outstretched wrist with both hands and pivoted.

The gun coughed a third time. John leaned forward. His action pulled Holdren toward him then John slammed his elbow back toward the man's chin.

Holdren twisted away and John's blow glanced against his temple. John shifted one hand against the silencer and bent the gun back toward Holdren's thumb. The rotation against the weakest link popped the weapon from Holdren's hand.

Holdren's left arm snaked around John's neck and he pulled back against him in a chokehold.

John dropped the gun to the floor. He bent his knees, transferring most of his weight to Holdren's grip. Holdren braced himself and leaned in to support the additional weight. With a quick movement, John straightened, jumping backwards against his opponent.

The sudden shift swayed Holdren off balance. Together they fell toward the floor.

John continued his leap. Tucking his legs in, he pivoted against Holdren's grip, going upside down for a moment. John's feet met the floor. In an instant he released Holdren's wrist, wrapped both hands around the man's torso, and lifted him feet first into the air.

John spun him half way around and slung him down.

As Holdren crashed against the wood, John's weight slammed into the man's back, driving the air from his lungs.

Before Holdren could recover, John brought his right elbow down hard against the man's neck.

Holdren sagged into unconsciousness.

John stood up, spotted the Holdren's gun lying a few feet away, and scooped it up. He raised the barrel and sighted down it at Holdren's head, but the man was unconscious.

John hesitated, took a deep breath, and then noticed that the bar was silent. John raised his gaze to scope out the patrons. No one moved. The front door was still closed. Whatever backup Holdren had was still outside.

John lowered the gun. Even if Holdren had killed the cab driver like Caitlin claimed, there was still the chance that he was a federal agent. Shooting a federal agent in front of witnesses would not be prudent.

John retrieved his hat and settled it against his head with his left hand. His shoulder burned as he did. There were times that he just couldn't believe his luck. Holdren's shot had missed his vest. The damn little gun would hardly have left a bruise if it had hit him in the chest. No, the SOB had to plink him just outside the edge of his vest. John could feel a warmth trickling down his biceps.

Becky caught his eye.

John gave her a half grin and touched the brim of his hat with the silencer. He turned quickly and walked into the hallway.

Caitlin waited at the back door.

"What happened?" she asked.

John stopped beside her and looked back toward the bar. "Holdren made me as being with you."

She seemed to notice the gun in his hand for the first time. "Did ... did you kill him?"

"No, just put him down for awhile. Enough time for us to get out of here."

John popped the magazine from the little Ruger .22 caliber and checked it by the light of the exit sign. There were five more rounds. The .22 was an assassin's handgun. It didn't carry enough knockdown power for a serious weapon, but more than enough for putting a round in the back of someone's head. In the hands of an expert, it could deliver a one-shot kill at ranges out to twenty yards, but beyond that luck overtook skill. He snapped the magazine back into place.

He'd hold onto it for now.

"Listen Caitlin, my car is in the same place as last night. I'm going to it. I want you to count to sixty, then follow me, unless I call you sooner. Understand?"

"You think there might be more of them?"

"That's a safe bet. If so, they may or may not have a guard on the back door. We'll see in a second."

Caitlin nodded her understanding.

John listened. The bar sounds had returned to near normal. He opened the door casually. Keeping the Ruger down low and just behind him, he stepped out and put on a bit of a stagger.

His voice came out in a heavily intoxicated slur. "Don't you worry 'bout me."

He weaved a little, spinning about as if he had trouble with the short step-down, while he covered the wharf for signs of a watcher.

There was movement in the shadows at the corner of the building. One, maybe two men waited there.

John held up his keys in his left hand, ignoring the burning in his shoulder, and shook them at the closed door. "I don't need anyone telling me when I'm too in--intoc--drunk to drive. No sir. Not me."

He staggered back away from the door, moving indirectly toward the corner where the watcher waited.

Twice he used the wall to steady himself.

"Damn right. Gotta drive home tonight ... ain't in no condition to walk."

He reached the corner and acted as if he were seeing the watcher for the first time. Swaying back on his feet, John put his hands out, balancing, then shook his keys at the watcher.

"Essuse me, there sonny. How 'bout fetching my Caddy. I seem to have misplaced it."

The watcher, a man of stout build and close-cropped hair, had a bulge under his left arm and a receiver in his ear. He watched John dangle the keys in his face for a second, then spoke into his left cuff. "It's just some damn old drunk."

He moved his left hand away from his face and made a motion over his shoulder. "Go on, get out of here."

"That's no way to talk to me. I...."

John swayed again. He bent at the waist and made what he hoped was a horrible retching sound.

The watcher's tone was disgusted. "Ah, Gees. Don't do that here...."

He stepped forward and put a hand on John's shoulder as if to push him away. John straightened quickly and brought his left fist upward into the man's abdomen.

With an explosive grunt, the man doubled over in much the same position John had just left. While he was still bent, John raised the Ruger and chopped it hard against the back of the man's head. The man sprawled unconscious to the pavement.

John heard the door opening behind him. He turned quickly, the Ruger outstretched.

It was Caitlin.

He lowered the gun.

She caught sight of him, noticed the body at his feet, and then swept the wharf with her gaze.

John motioned toward his car and then unlocked the doors and disarmed the security system with the remote. He bent and quickly patted down the unconscious man's clothing. John found a Sig/Sauer 9 mm strapped in a shoulder holster, and his pockets held a handkerchief, some keys, and a thin leather wallet. John transferred the wallet and keys to his jacket pocket and pulled the Sig from the holster.

It was a good weapon. It was the weapon of choice for the FBI and numerous police agencies around the country. It gave a little more credence to the chance that these were federal agents.

There was also no point in leaving it behind.

Standing, he trotted over to his car. Caitlin waited by the passenger door. Her eyes didn't hold on him, instead they jumped from the building's corner to the rear door and back.

"It's unlocked. Get in," John said.

He climbed behind the driver's seat, fastened his shoulder harness, and cranked the engine. Caitlin put her bag on the floor and sat down.

"Buckle up. This may get interesting."

John put the car in gear and eased around the corner of the bar. He drove slowly, looking for sign of Holdren's accomplices, there were bound to be more. The street looked deserted, but there was a suspicious van a half block toward the right.

The van was facing The Gleaning Cube. John considered, then immediately turned in that direction. He flicked his headlights on bright. As the lights fell fully on the van, John pointed out across the bay toward distant Oakland.

"Would you look at that," he said.

Caitlin reflexively turned her face.

"What is it?" Her voice was edgy.

"Nothing, but keeping looking that way for a few seconds."

John accelerated smoothly until they were past the van. "All right, you can stop looking."

Caitlin turned and stared at him. "What was that about?"

"That van back there. I thought they might be inside, watching for you to show."

Caitlin turned in the seat and looked back.

"No!"

Caitlin jerked back around. "What? What'd I do?"

"They could have been watching."

"They couldn't see my face from here."

"Did you ever hear of night scopes?"

In the rearview mirror, John saw the van's tail lights come on.

"Shit."

He took the next left and punched the accelerator to the floor. "They hadn't gotten a good look at you before because the headlights would have washed out our images. They were bound to keep watching until either they had a good view of you or we were out of sight.

"If I didn't know better I'd swear you were trying to let them see you."

Behind them, the van turned the corner and accelerated. John took the next right, sliding on wet pavement in the curve, before straightening.

"How can you suggest that?" Caitlin asked.

"I can suggest a lot."

"It's me they're trying to kill." Her voice quivered.

"Well, I did say I knew better, but it does seem damn strange that you'd turn around to look at them."

John reached behind him and fumbled through the canvas bag he'd set on the floor. His fingers closed on the goggles and he pulled them out.

"What's that?"

"Haven't you ever seen night vision goggles?"

"Is that what those are? I thought they were big bulky things."

"Used to be, most still are, but these aren't. Isn't technology grand?"

John slipped them over his head with one hand, but didn't pull them down. His fingers found the on switch and he activated them.

The van was just coming around the last corner when John reached the alley he'd been aiming for. He opened the center console and flicked the middle of three toggle switches.

The toggle switch energized a relay disconnecting all of the car's lights, including the brake lights.

"Hold on," John said.

Jamming on the brakes, John slowed quickly in the darkness between two street lamps and took a sharp turn into an alley. The interior of the alley was pitch black.

Caitlin let out a little screech and grabbed the dash as she saw the narrow gap John was aiming for.

John pulled the goggles over his eyes.

The greenish cast, typical of starlight devices, was disorientating if you weren't used to it. John drove through the alley, still accelerating, the big V-8 booming off the brick walls like thunder. In the mirror, he saw the van flash by the alley's entrance without slowing.

At the next street, John slowed and turned back in the direction they'd come. He flicked the toggle switch back and the car's lights came back on. John pulled the goggles off his head and tossed them back in the bag.

He turned to Caitlin. "Now then, where were we?"

She stared at him for a moment. "Have you done that before?"

"A couple of times. It's quite a rush without the goggles."

"Without the goggles?"

"Yeah, but I didn't want to take the chance of them hearing anything. The last time I did it without the goggles I had to have the paint touched up on your side."

John took a left and turned toward one oh one.

* * *

Dewatre munched on a sandwich as he watched Blalock maneuver to elude his pursuers. He admired the man's forethought. Such careful planning explained how Blalock was able to do so much damage to French recherché operations. Perhaps such a formidable antagonist would have to be neutralized even as one of his compatriots was moving to neutralize the competition from the Japanese.

Dewatre had already called in a support team. They would arrive within twenty-four hours. Until then, he'd have to keep Maxwell and Blalock under surveillance to make sure they didn't pass the material to someone else. He might also have to look at having a false trail laid down to lead the men of NCIX away from their mutual quarry.

CHAPTER 19

Caitlin watched the traffic flowing along the north bound lanes of one oh one. It still amazed her that even near midnight the freeway was as crowded and possibly even more crowded than Albuquerque's at rush hour.

She didn't say much to John on the thirty-minute trip down the peninsular. Occasionally she found herself staring at him. Although the scar wasn't visible from this side, he hardly looked like the same John Blalock she'd known. He was too young to have developed crow's feet, but there were the first signs of them around his eyes. He was always squinting, could he need glasses? Somehow, she didn't think so. Something in the way he had changed had given him a perpetual squint. It was as though he was suspicious of everyone and everything.

Strangely enough, she was still attracted to him. It wasn't his physical appearance although he was still handsome, even with the scar and the squint. No, the attraction was on a deeper level. Could it be just because he had saved her life once and was doing a good job of repeating the deed?

Stop trying to analyze your feelings. You're not some kid on an adventure. You're a grown woman whose husband was just killed and if you don't keep your mind clear, you may follow him down that path sooner than you want.

Caitlin felt the car slow and noticed John taking the exit. "Who are we going to see?"

"Louie Grayson."

"And you think he can decipher the encoding on this disk?"

"If anyone can."

They went over a couple of streets, then turned south on Camino Real. A few blocks later they turned into a neighborhood of older apartments and few houses. The few houses there looked much older than even the apartments.

"Not exactly the cutting edge of development," Caitlin said.

"No, Louie's grandparents left him the house they bought when they moved out to the Bay Area after the Second World War. These apartments were built in the seventies. Students at Stanford take up most of them."

"Really."

"Yeah, you ought to see this neighborhood on the weekends. Drunken parties everywhere."

He slowed and turned into a driveway. As he killed the lights and the engine, Caitlin looked around.

"Not exactly pretentious," she said.

The yard was nearly dark and the nearest street light was a half block away. Even in the dim light, she could tell the yard needed mowing and she could see the darker shadows of various sized clumps of leaves. The trees and shrubbery hadn't been pruned in years. From all appearances, the house may have been vacant for months.

"Louie has never been one to care much for appearances," John said.

They got out of the car and John walked toward the rear.

"Where are you going?"

"I've got to get something from the trunk." He unlocked it, reached in, and pulled out his overnight bag.

"We're staying here tonight?"

"No, I just need some of my things."

They left the car and walked toward the porch and stopped beneath the single yellow light that glowed above the front door.

"You think he can help us?"

John rang the bell. She could hear its distant chime.

"Yeah, he can help us. Smile at the camera."

Caitlin followed his gaze and saw a security monitor mounted in the corner of the ceiling.

"Louie, it's John with a friend."

A few seconds later she could hear footsteps. The door opened and a man stepped into view. Louie was a balding, middle-aged man with the physical stature of a fourth grader. His large nose and long beard gave him the appearance of a Tolkien dwarf, but his garish Hawaiian shirt, knee-length purple shorts, and orange and blue sneakers spoiled the illusion making him look more like a David Dorman rendition of a Tolkien dwarf.

Caitlin had to suppress a chuckle. He did dress like a software nerd.

"Hi, John. Who's the lady?" he asked.

"Louie, let me introduce Caitlin Maxwell, a friend from way back. Caitlin, this is Louie Grayson, the best computer man in the Bay Area."

"Pleased to meet you."

"Charmed," said Louie with perfunctory bow.

"Mind if we come in? We have some business to discuss."

"My door is always open to you or your friends, John," Louie replied and stepped back from the door.

John motioned for her to go ahead. She took a brief look around the street, more out of nervousness than because she thought they might have actually been followed, and then walked past Louie.

Louie closed the door after them and reset the locks. "Can I get you anything? Drinks? Have you eaten?"

"Not just now, Louie," John said. "This is a business call."

Louie seemed almost disappointed. "Uh huh."

He looked John over for a moment and then shook his head sadly. "Are you going to need help with that?"

John lifted his bag and passed it to him. "Yeah, I think so."

"Very well, come on."

Louie led them into the kitchen.

"Take your coat off," Louie said as he set John's bag on the counter and opened it.

What was going on?

John?" Caitlin asked.

As he shrugged out of his trenchcoat, she saw the fresh blood stain that ran down his shirt.

"My God, were you shot?"

"Yeah. It's not much."

"Not much? You've been shot."

"Yeah, I think we've determined that."

He loosened the Velcro closures on his vest.

Caitlin stepped close to him and pushed his hands away. "Let me do that."

She lifted the vest from his shoulders and was surprised by its weight. While he watched, she unbuttoned each button on his shirt and pulled its tail from his pants. She lifted it carefully off his shoulders and felt her stomach get queasy as the puckered wound was revealed.

It was a tiny thing, red and raw around the edges and surrounded by the darkening circle of a bruise. Blood still seeped from it and trickled down the outside of his arm.

Caitlin stepped behind him and gingerly pulled the shirt down his arms.

John examined the wound as she draped his shirt over the back of a chair.

"Not too bad," Louie said.

Caitlin saw he was carrying a dark bottle and a gauze bandage.

"You should sit down if you want me to work on it."

Caitlin pulled another chair from the table and held it for John.

"Thanks," he said as he sat.

Louie soaked the bandage in something from the bottle that resembled iodine, and used it to clean around the edges of the wound. He went back to John's bag and returned with a small aerosol bottle and a sealed plastic bag that contained forceps. After shaking the bottle for a few seconds, he sprayed a fine stream of liquid into the center of the wound.

"What's that?" she asked.

"Topical anesthetic. It'll cut some of the pain."

He set the bottle to one side and raised the forceps.

Caitlin found herself staring at the floor.

"Hey."

She looked up and met John's gaze. "Yes?"

"You had better watch this."

"Why?"

"Because you may have to do it yourself," Louie said.

"What?" Caitlin asked.

"If you're one of John's clients then there's always the possibility that something like this is going to come up again. You never can tell when you may have to learn a new skill."

"You can't be serious."

"He's serious, Caitlin. Now please watch, I don't like doing this sort of thing either, but the ability comes in handy."

Caitlin stepped closer. John raised his right hand and she took it in both of hers.

Louie probed the interior of the wound and the forceps sunk more than two inches into John's shoulder. Caitlin's hands tightened around John's.

He seemed so calm, so relaxed. He even smiled and gave her hands a light squeeze, but Caitlin could see a line of sweat beading up along his forehead. The anesthetic wasn't blocking all the pain.

Caitlin tried to return his smile, but she didn't feel much like smiling. It was her fault he'd been shot. She shouldn't have involved him. She should have found someone else to help her.

"Caitlin, it's what you're paying me to do, protect you. I knew the risks before I agreed to help you."

"That doesn't make me feel any better. I didn't have to bring this to you."

"You wanted someone you could trust. You can trust me." He grimaced as Louie expanded the forceps.

Caitlin stared into John's eyes. They had softened. Earlier they had seemed so cold, so distant. Now they were soft and warm just as she remembered them. It brought a real smile to her face.

Another grimace went across his features and the warmth fell away from his eyes.

Louie slowly drew the forceps from the wound. As he did, a small bloody, copper covered bullet appeared.

"Well, that wasn't so bad. Must have been a short. A higher power bullet would have passed on through," Louie said as he held the bullet up for them to see.

"You want it?" he asked John.

"No thanks, I don't need a reminder."

"How 'bout you?"

Caitlin stared at it for a second, then slowly shook her head.

"Oh well." He carried it to a trashcan that stood in the corner. He dropped the bullet into it and went back to John's bag.

When he returned he was opening a small package that Caitlin saw contained a fishhook-like needle and sutures.

She forced herself to watch as Louie put three stitches into the wound to close it. He cleaned the outside of the wound one more time, then covered it with a small bandage.

He took one more package from John's bag. It contained a syringe and a two-cell bottle.

"What's that?" Caitlin asked.

He opened the package and held up the bottle. It had a powder in one side and a clear liquid in the other. He pressed the end of the bottle and the liquid flowed into the powder.

He shook it, mixing the liquid and powder. "Antibiotics. They're freeze dried and have to be moistened before injection."

After a minute, he filled the syringe and injected the contents into an already cleaned area of John's upper arm.

"There, you'll be as good as new in a week."

"Yeah, good as new," John agreed.

Caitlin got the impression that there was some private joke passing between them.

"Caitlin, there's a clean shirt in my bag."

"What? Oh, I'll get it."

Reluctantly, she released his hand and went for his shirt. She helped him into it and then buttoned it up for him. When she started to tuck the tail into his pants, he stopped her.

"I can do that myself. Let's show Louie why we came here."

"Yes, I'm very curious."

"We'll need your computer," John said.

"Well, you know where it is," Louie said, then led them from his kitchen.

They followed him to his office, which like the rest of his house appeared cluttered and unattended. On every surface, magazines and books lay open, held that way mostly by computer printouts and here and there by a few open containers of cookies. Louie apparently had a sweet tooth.

"What do you have for me?" Louie asked as he sat in the worn swivel chair in front of his monitor.

John motioned to her and Caitlin popped open her bag and took out the disk.

Louie held out his hand and Caitlin laid it on his palm.

He held it up between his fingers and watched the light reflect off its surface. "All right. Do you want to tell me what I'm looking for?"

Caitlin said, "There's an encrypted file in it."

"And you've forgotten the encryption code?" Louie asked.

"No. I never had it. It was sent to me as is, with no other data."

Behind his beard, Louie frowned. "Okay, let's see what we're dealing with."

He swiveled the chair around and set the disk into a reader in the top of his computer. He slipped a wand over his index finger and pointed at his screen. The 21-inch monitor gave a brief view of what he'd been working on before the interruption. A second later the screen shifted in three quick displays as he called up another program. A red LED lit on the reader and the monitor displayed the general contents of the disk.

Caitlin moved to Louie's left shoulder while John looked over his right.

"One file," Louie said. "It's a large file all right. The last modification on it was three days ago."

He touched the wand again. The screen shifted to show the hex code for the disk's FAT tables.

"This appears to be a self extracting file." He eyed Caitlin. "Have you tried running it?"

"Yes. It wants a password before it will decompress."

"Really." Louie pointed and the screen shifted, went black, and then a single line appeared with a group of eight asterisks above it. Louie's fingers went to the keyboard and he typed in something Caitlin couldn't read. Each time his fingers hit a key one of the asterisks disappeared. When they were all gone he hit the enter key.

The asterisks reappeared.

"Not even a comment. Usually these are done with a few statements to tell the user that you screwed the password up. That would seem to indicate that the file was not meant for general consumption."

"Oh?" John asked.

"Sure, if it was meant for others to use the programmers would have added bells and whistles. Since they didn't it stands to reason that they never intended anyone but themselves to call it up."

Caitlin nodded. She knew what he was talking about.

"What else can you tell me about the file?" Louie asked.

Caitlin gave him a brief run down on how she received it and who sent it to her. Louie listened carefully without interruption.

When she finished Louie said, "You say he was leaving Los Alamos when he was killed?"

"That's right."

"As in Los Alamos National Laboratory?"

"I'd guess. He could have been in town to see someone who didn't work out at the Lab, but I can't imagine whom. It's practically a one industry town."

"Yes, I know. Los Alamos is operated by the University of California for the Department of Energy. That's big money and the best encryption programs available. I'll look into it, but I can't make any guarantees. If your husband didn't want anyone else to get into this then no one will."

"He must have wanted me to be able to open the file or why else would he have bothered to send it to me?" Caitlin asked.

Louie shrugged his shoulders and turned back to the monitor. Moving the wand around too fast for her to keep up with his selections, Louie called up first one and then another program.

“Well at least he didn’t use one of the 256 bit encryption schemes like Rijndael or Twofish. Either of those would have made this practically impossible.”

“We used Serpent at the office, but I’ve already tried our office passwords. None of them worked,” Caitlin said.

“I don’t think he’s used Serpent either. I thought it might have been RC6, but that program isn’t used often since Charlie Levins broke its mathematical structure a few years ago. Give me a little time.”

A few minutes passed in silence as they watched him work. Then he turned around in his chair. He stood, walked across the room to another computer, and powered it up. A minute later he popped the disk out of the reader and handed it back to Caitlin. She stared at it for a second.

"All right. That's all I can do for now," Louie said.

"What? That's it?" Caitlin asked. "You're giving up."

"Giving up?" Louie repeated. "No, no. Of course not. I've started my decryption programs, now we have to wait."

Caitlin watched the monitor's display for a second.

"It's counting up," she said.

"Right," Louie responded.

"You're not going to just try every possible password are you?" she asked.

"Just?" Louie repeated. "My dear, lady. Nothing I do is just anything."

"Then what?" she asked, her tone exasperated.

Louie's grin split his face nearly in two. She noticed a trace of a smile on John's face also. "I've isolated the section of the code that reads the password and copied it. You can't do that with fully encrypted files, but when the password decryption sequence is in the file it leaves it vulnerable. While this computer," he indicated the first one, "goes in one direction, the other is running backwards. That way I've halved the time it'll take to try all the combinations."

"But the possible combinations are in the millions," Caitlin said.

"Quite," Louie agreed.

"What is it? Something like ten to the twenty-sixth?" John asked.

"Modern passwords also use the extended ASCII character set. It's more like ten to the one hundred and twenty-sixth."

"Good God, that could take months," Caitlin moaned.

"Probably not. I've set a mini-program to try the basic alphanumerics. If those don't fit then it will farm out portions of the task to some of my contacts on the Web. If we don't have immediate success then we'll have at least twenty computers working on the task by midnight. I'd say we'll have the password by early tomorrow afternoon at the latest."

"And no one else will realize what the password is for?" John asked.

Louie nodded. "Right. By separating off the password identifying portion of the code no one will have any idea what the program itself does."

"We'd better be going now. You know how to reach me when you learn something," John said.

"Sure thing," Louie responded.

He led them out and followed them to their car.

"Be careful with this one Louie," John said as he opened the car door. "There are too many parties involved and I have a bad feeling in my gut."

"Anything you say. I'll play it tight."

"Goodbye and thanks, Louie," Caitlin said.

"Glad I could help. You take care of her, John," Louie added with a nod of his head.

John returned the nod and got in the car.

Louie waited until they pulled out of the drive, then gave a final wave, and turned back toward his house.

As they accelerated toward highway 101, Caitlin looked at him. "What now?"

"Now we find another motel and hole up for the night. By tomorrow we should have something on this disk and you can decide what you want to do with it."

"What I want to do with it?"

John nodded. "Yeah, are you going to turn it over to the Feds, sell it to the Japanese, or what?"

Caitlin turned toward the windshield and for a moment watched the headlights on southbound one oh one flash by. "You know, I haven't really thought about it. I mean, what do I do with it? Do you think giving it to the NCIX will stop this killer?"

"It could. Unless it's one of those situations where they want everyone dead who's seen the information. In that case we're both going to need to disappear."

Caitlin looked at him. After a couple of seconds, he turned to face her. In the constant glare of oncoming headlights, she could see his face was nearly expressionless.

"Tell me you're joking," she said.

"I wish I could."

"But that's so --"

"Cold hearted?"

"I was going to say Oliver Stone-ish. I never thought you'd be an Ollie. The government doesn't really bump people off just because they accidentally learn something."

"Oh? And your belief is based on what?"

"Everything. I mean, look around you. This country is built on openness and freedom of information. Sure there are secrets, but those are military or commercial secrets. There are legal methods to silence anyone who has access to them. There are no secret agendas, no gunman on the grassy knoll, no X-Files cover-up."

"Yeah?"

"What's that look for?" she asked.

"What look?"

"That superior look that says 'Oh you poor naive young thing. You're just a woman who's been protected from the evils of the world. There's no way you'd really know just what people are capable of.'"

"Really? You got all that from one look?"

"Yes."

"Well, maybe you're right. Maybe I was thinking of how naive you sounded. I can't help it. You sound almost like I remembered you."

That was a surprise. It was the first indication he had remembered anything about her.

Caitlin felt the car moving and noticed John exiting the freeway. She was silent for a minute. "You remember me that well?"

"Sometimes, it depends on what you're saying. It's like little flashbacks, little bits keep surfacing."

"After a dozen years I'm surprised you remember anything about me. I know it sounds trite, but it seems like it was a lifetime ago. I look at the college kids now and I can't believe I've changed. I still feel the same now as I did twelve years ago. Sure, my taste in some things have changed, but they're just incidentals. My id, ego, or whatever is the same now as it was then."

They turned right onto Del Mar. The car accelerated smoothly and joined the flow of traffic.

"How can everything feel the same and yet feel like a lifetime ago?" John asked.

"Are you making fun of me?"

"No. I'm just curious."

"I don't know if I have an answer to that. I just know it seems so very long ago."

"Yeah."

A moment passed. "John, I need to contact my parents."

"Out of the question."

"Why?"

"If the government is involved in this then they have the manpower to cover all eventualities. They're sure to have a wire tap on your parent's phone and any calls to them would be traced back."

"But I wouldn't have to stay on long enough for a trace."

John gave her a sideways smile.

"What?"

"You really think you can hang up before they can trace the call?"

"Well, sure, they do it all the time."

"Yeah, in the movies. Caitlin, do you have caller ID?"

"Sure, everyone has it now days. What's that got to do with anything?"

"How long does it take to identify the caller?"

"One ring ... oh."

"Right, the information is automatically transferred between the first and second ring. Anyone tapping the phone can receive the same information and cross-check the phone number location anywhere in the country within seconds."

"But it'll still take them time to send someone to intercept us. We can move again before they can reach us."

"That's taking chances. I have a better idea."

Caitlin waited.

When it became obvious that he wasn't going to finish she asked, "And that is?"

"They still go to a church regularly, Lutheran wasn't it?"

"Yes."

"You can give their pastor a call. Let him call your parents."

The car slowed and Caitlin caught sight of the Best Western sign as they pulled up to the entrance.

John killed the engine. "Wait here. I don't want anyone seeing your face."

"Why? What's wrong with it?"

"Now who's making fun? Just wait here. I'll be back in a minute."

It was more like five.

They drove around to the backside of the motel and John backed in next to the building. Caitlin got out and stretched. The night was cool and pleasant with just a touch of the moisture, which would probably turn to fog by sunrise. John popped the trunk and pulled out his overnight bag and her suitcase.

He grunted softly as he did.

"Let me help you with that," she said and took the one from his left hand. "Thanks for getting them, I'd forgotten to ask."

He nodded and grunted something. He shut the trunk and walked to the door marked 108. Unlocking the door, he pushed it open, flicked on the lights, and went inside.

Caitlin took one last look around the quiet parking lot and followed him in.

The room was plain but clean and had a newness that suggested a recent carpeting and painting. John laid her suitcase on the far bed and then dropped his smaller bag onto the nearer bed.

John took the alarm from his bag, hung it over the door handle, and activated it.

"You can have the bathroom first," he said.

Caitlin nodded, removed some things from her bags, and went in to shower.

When she came out, she saw John napping in the easy chair, facing the door. His arms hung loosely to either side of the chair. She went over to him, wondering if she should wake him.

His face had relaxed some of its hard lines in sleep and his appearance was considerably closer to what she remembered. Asleep, he looked almost innocent. On an impulse, she bent to kiss his forehead. He jerked awake and before she could step back, Caitlin found herself staring down the wide bore of a handgun.

"For Christ's sakes, John," she said without moving.

He lowered the gun immediately. "Sorry, I guess I fell asleep. You through in the bath?"

"Yes, I...."

He stood up and holstered the gun beneath his left shoulder. Without another word he picked up his bag, went into the bath, and pulled the door shut behind him.

Caitlin moved her suitcase, then pulled down the covers on the bed nearest the bathroom. The small alarm clock on the nightstand read just after two. It felt more like five. God, but she was tired. She crawled between the sheets and was asleep when her head hit the pillow.

* * *

Holdren was sipping Darjeeling when his cell phone vibrated against his chest. He set the cup in the saucer and took out the phone. Across the table, Romax's eyes followed him over a cup of decaf Kona blend.

"Holdren here."

It was the watch officer back at the barn. "Mr. Holdren, we have a hit on one of your inquiries."

It was about time.

"Which inquiry?" he asked.

"The Web monitors have spotted a portion of the file you expressed interest in."

"Just a portion?"

"Yes. Max has determined that it's the encryption code portion of the file. It appears someone has broken out that section and is seeking help in breaking the cipher."

Max was the nickname of the big multiprocessor Cray back at the barn. "Interesting. What do we have on the transmission site?"

"It originated in the San Jose area. We're having trouble spotting the exact location. The URL site doesn't match any recorded listings. Max thinks it's a CHAOS location."

"CHAOS? What the hell is that?" Holdren asked.

"Computer Hackers Alliance for Open Speech."

"Shouldn't that be CHAFOS?"

"Yeah, you'd think."

"And what is CHAOS's interest in our file?" Holdren asked.

"Max thinks they had a hand in its theft. Personally, I think they're nothing more than a bunch of computer nerds who have gotten together to increase their own sense of self-worth."

"You came up with that all by yourself?"

There was a pause on the line before the watch officer replied. "Not really. That comes out of the Internal Threat Office. They think Max is giving these guys too much credit."

"So they're just a bunch of computer hackers who just happened to stumble into the most closely guarded secret since Kennedy and Monroe? It sounds like Max may be earning the billions it cost to create it."

"Well, yeah, if they are involved, it'll mean stepping up the surveillance of their activities."

"See to it. We can't wait for the next committee meeting to make a decision. How long before Max can trace that transmission point?"

"He's going back through public utility records for the last decade and comparing them with all changes in --"

Holdren interrupt with an impatient snap. "I don't need to know what he's doing. I just need to know when I'll get the information."

"Yes, one, maybe two hours at the most."

"All right. We'll move our operations to San Jose and be ready to move when you have the address. How long before Max will have the file decrypted?"

"He finished it nearly an hour ago."

"Really? I was told that it would take all of the night and probably most of tomorrow."

"Yes, normally it would have, but Max doesn't work the normal way."

"Oh and how did it find the password so fast."

"Max assumed that since it was sent from Scott Corning to Caitlin Maxwell it had to have a password connected with the two of them."

"Interesting, and how did it isolate the password?"

"He went through everything we know about them and eventually found that the password was the name of a small town near Cancun, Mexico."

"What was its significance?"

"It's where they spent the first night of their honeymoon."

"Max knew that?" Holdren asked.

"Obviously."

"And the contents of the file?"

"Only partial success there. It appears to be the plans for the encoder, but not the plans for the actual devices."

Holdren raised a hand to cover his face. He slowly shook his head. "All right, if that's all there was congratulations on getting at least that much. One more thing...."

"Yes?"

"Put someone on the addresses the file segment was sent to. We'll need to investigate each one thoroughly."

"Max is already working on it."

Holdren closed the phone and picked up his tea. It was cold. He motioned for the waiter over to bring a fresh cup. While waiting, he considered the conversation. The barn's computer seemed to be getting a little too smart.

Holdren waited in the car with Romax while the armed response team cleared the house. It had taken them longer than Max's two-hour estimate to find this house. It took nearly three. Was that an indication of how good these CHAOS people were, or was it more an indication that Max wasn't as good as his programmers thought? Neither answer appealed to Holdren. Perhaps when this operation was under control he should spend some time personally looking into CHAOS.

When the office-in-charge came to the car, his hood was pulled back from his face and his gun slung over his shoulder. Holdren let down his window and smoke billowed out into the night air.

"Mr. Holdren. There was only one occupant. He is being restrained. We found no sign of weapons or explosives."

Holdren tossed his cigarette to the curb and opened his door. "Thank you. You may take us to him now."

"Yes sir, this way."

Romax joined Holdren by the time they reached the edge of the brown lawn. The front door lay back against the side-wall, its hinges and multiple bolts were shattered by the force of the battering ram the response team had used. Holdren and Romax followed the officer to the rear of the house to a room filled with computer hardware.

For a moment, Holdren thought their suspect was a child. Then he focused his attention on the person and realized he was a dwarf, a little person, a damn midget.

He turned to Romax.

"This, this is what gave us so much trouble?" he asked Romax.

Romax met his gaze and shrugged.

Holdren turned to the officer who had led them in. "Take your men and search the rest of the house. Don't interrupt us, but if you find anything noteworthy I want to hear about it when we finish questioning this person."

"Yes sir. All right, everybody out."

The officer and his two men left quickly and Holdren closed the door behind them. He took a chair from one corner and pulled it to a comfortable talking distance from the suspect. Sitting down, he took a pack of cigarettes from an inner pocket and lit it. Taking a deep drag, he exhaled in the dwarf's face.

"Louis Russell?"

The dwarf blinked as if the smoke was burning his eyes, then said, "Yes?"

"Mr. Russell, you have been in contact with a Caitlin Maxwell. She gave you something tonight, something that didn't belong to her. I want you to give it to me and tell me everything you've learned about it."

The dwarf held Romax's stare for several seconds, and then met Holdren's gaze. "Sorry, I don't know what you're talking about."

"That's the wrong attitude to take," Romax counseled.

"Louie, you don't mind if I call you Louie, do you?"

Without waiting for a reply, Holdren continued.

"Louie, this is a matter of national security. We don't want to have to bring charges against you. We feel like you don't really know what Maxwell was getting you involved in and we're willing to give you the benefit of doubt. If you'll answer our questions truthfully, to the best of your knowledge, then I'm sure the special prosecutor will take your behavior into account."

Holdren paused to take another drag on the cigarette.

"I don't know a Caitlin Maxwell."

"See, that's just what I mean. She probably didn't even use her real name, now that shows she wasn't honest with you. If she lied about her name, then she probably lied about everything she told you tonight.

"I'll bet she told you she came by this computer file by accident, that someone sent it to her without explaining how they came by it, even that she doesn't know what's in the file. Am I close?"

Holdren could see the indecision in the dwarf's eyes as he lowered his head. The little guy was unsure of himself. Either he really hadn't known Caitlin Maxwell before tonight or he didn't know her well enough to trust her. They would soon have everything they needed from him.

Something changed in the dwarf's eyes as he raised his head to meet Holdren's gaze. His hesitancy, his indecision was gone.

"No, John wouldn't do me that way. I trust him."

"John? Are you perhaps referring to John Q. Blalock? You should know that the two of them are in this together. They've arranged the theft and sale of technologies critical to national security."

The dwarf frowned. "I think I need to talk to a lawyer before I say anything else."

Holdren's gaze met Romax's and they shared a subtle smile. "Lawyer, Louie? You don't need a lawyer. You aren't under arrest. You're just being questioned about your connection to someone who has violated national security. What would you need a lawyer for?"

"I know my rights. I don't have to answer any questions unless I speak to a lawyer first."

"Ordinarily that would be true, but you see Louie, this isn't an ordinary case. Have you ever heard the term carte blanche? Look it up, if you ever get the chance. You see, Louie, I have authority to deal with this problem anyway I see fit. I can transfer you to a maximum security prison in the Aleutians, which by the way isn't on any map, or I can release you and forget your little mistake. It's all up to me."

"You can't do that. That's not legal."

Holdren dropped his cigarette to the floor and stomped it out. "True, it is one of those gray areas in the Constitution, but regardless, I am the final authority in your case."

The dwarf's eyes hesitated again. He glanced up at Romax as if wanting someone to correct Holdren, to say that he was bound by constitutional constraints, to the rule of law, to morality.

"You see, Louie. This is between just you and me. You will either provide me with everything I need to know or you won't. One way you leave this room free to come and go as you please, an honest law abiding citizen, the other way you disappear, never to be seen again. Which will it be, Louie?"

The dwarf couldn't meet his gaze.

CHAPTER 20

Caitlin awoke to find the room dimly lit by the glow of the morning sun around the thick curtains that shaded the windows. For a second, a heartbeat, she wondered. Full consciousness brought memory. She raised her head and looked about the room. The other bed was unmade, but empty.

"Good morning."

John's voice came out of the gloom, but then she made out the deeper shadows in the chair.

"What time is it?" Caitlin asked.

"About nine."

"Goodness. You shouldn't have let me sleep so late."

"It's not late. Louie wasn't expecting to have anything for several more hours. Besides, you should catch up on your sleep whenever you can. You never can tell when you'll get an opportunity again."

"Gees. You sound cheerful."

"Optimistic."

"Optimistic?"

"Yeah, I always think I'll get another chance to sleep, sooner or later."

That didn't sound optimistic. It sounded fatalistic. "What's first?"

"Get dressed while I check on Louie's progress, then we can get some breakfast."

"Fine by me."

Caitlin slipped out from under the covers. She unzipped her suitcase and removed a folded pair of gray slacks, a light cotton sweater and a pair of charcoal socks. She carried them with her into the bath.

She was zipping up her pants when John knocked.

"Yes?"

"Let's go. We have to leave, now!"

Caitlin opened the door. John was throwing her toiletries into her suitcase and zipping it shut.

"What? What is it?"

He tossed her Rockports toward her and lifted the case from the bed. Caitlin caught them without dropping her socks.

"Something's happened to Louie."

A chill went through her. "What?"

"I don't know, yet. We have to relocate fast. They may have been able to trace my call."

He opened the door a crack and glanced out. "It looks safe. Let's go."

She followed him to his car. He tossed their bags in the back seat and climbed in. As soon as her door closed, he cranked the engine and shifted the transmission into gear. In a few seconds they were at the side street. He turned away from Del Mar and drove up the back street into a residential area.

"Wouldn't we make better time on the main street?"

"Sure, but they got a good look at my car last night. They're sure to be watching for it. In the dark it's one thing, but in broad daylight it's too easy to spot."

In a few blocks the houses became newer and the neighborhood cleaner.

Caitlin brushed a light layer of grit from her soles and pulled on her socks. "What do you think happened to Louie?"

"I don't know."

"Then what are you concerned about?"

His condescending tone made her feel like he felt he was dealing with a slow-witted child. "Caitlin, he didn't answer the phone and when his computer picked up it didn't give the correct recording for his voice mail."

"His voice mail?"

"Yes. His computer is tied into his security system. I helped him upgrade it last year. If there's an intrusion, the computer is programmed to use any of several different pre-recordings until it's reset. It was setup to let him know if an intruder was still in the house and whether or not his computer files had been tampered with and even whether or not his phone line and Web line had been tapped."

He paused as they stopped at an intersection. He glanced both ways and then turned east.

"And which was it?" Caitlin asked as she laced up the Rockports.

"All."

"All?"

"Yeah, his computer had been tampered with, the lines bugged, and someone unauthorized was still on the premises."

"But if the computer was tampered with how could it--"

"How could it still identify that it had been tampered with?"

"Must you do that?" Caitlin asked.

He gave her a curious glance. "Do what?"

"Finish my sentences for me."

He hesitated then smiled. "Sorry, was I doing that again? It's an old habit that I thought I'd kicked."

"It's all right, but it does get annoying."

"Yeah, so I've been told."

"Now, as to how the computer could still tell you the security had been breached?"

"There's a secure chip inside it, an old e-prom that contains the instructions for answering the phone. The only way to modify it is to take it out and first erase its memory with an ultraviolet light. But once it's erased you can't reprogram it unless you know what the original instruction set contained. He kept the old e-prom for just that reason. Hardly anyone uses them these days and don't have the proper equipment for screwing up an e-prom without leaving traces."

"What did his recording say?"

"It said 'You have reached Louie's place. Please leave a message and I will get back to you as soon as possible.'"

"You're kidding."

"No, anyone who knows Louie knows that he'd never leave such a message. It's just not his style."

"I see. And what made you think they were tracing your call. Surely you didn't use the hotel's phone."

"Correct. I used my cellular."

"Then --"

"How did I know they were tracing the call?"

"You did it again."

"Did what?"

"Finished my sentence."

"Oh."

"Well, how did you?" Caitlin resisted a sudden urge to pinch his arm. She didn't remember him being this exasperating.

"If they're tapping his line, then it's no leap of imagination that they're tracing any calls to his number."

"But you can't track a cellular phone's location that easily."

"Who says?"

"Well ... all right it's possible, but you'd have to have receivers to triangulate the transmission. That would mean you'd have to expect the signal to come from a particular area and set your receiver's up before hand."

"You're partially right, but even under those circumstances they could have gotten our location. They would just have to assume that we were still in the Bay Area and be ready to triangulate all calls out of this region."

"But that would take time."

"Right, but that's not how they do it."

"Okay, obviously you know something I don't. Give. What else can they do?"

"For several years now all of the cellular phone chips have been encoded to allow their tracking using the GPS network. Like a GPS receiver, the cellular gets the signal from the GPS satellites. When queried by the proper signal your cellular phone will broadcast that data and bingo, you're located."

"You've got to be joking."

"I wish I were."

"But, how can that be legal?"

"Who knows from legal. How was it legal to install V-chips in all the televisions?"

"But that's different. It just lets the user lock out all the signals that exceed a preset level of violence or sexuality."

"Sure that's what the proponents claimed it would be used for. The V-chip's construction allows it to be reprogrammed remotely. Even people who don't use it can have programs blocked out."

"I don't understand. What would that accomplish?"

"Don't you see? It gives them the power to control what you watch."

"Yes, but it would just control sex and violence. There can't be anything sinister about that. So what if someone doesn't get to watch Playboy After Dark or some such trite?"

John's head shook slowly.

"What?" she asked.

He slowed the car for a traffic light, then turned east again onto the access road for the Mid-Bay Bridge. In a minute, they were driving a few yards above the choppy water.

"Who do you think puts the rating encoding onto the program's signal?"

"I don't know. I guess the networks," she said.

"The V-chip signal can be added remotely, just like the V-chip itself can be encoded remotely."

"You mean someone, the government, can modify the coding on any program they want?"

"That's right. There was a brief mention a couple of years ago about the city of Boise, Idaho missing the CNN news for ten minutes. It was later reported to be a problem with a satellite down link, but it turned out that all of the older televisions, the ones without the V-chips, received CNN."

"Someone blocked the news?"

"That's right. The stories being covered were about a pregnant panda, a minor oil spill off the coast of Chile, and a follow-up story on an ex-figure-skater's saving some woman's life by performing CPR."

"It was a test. My God. Someone was testing their system. That's ... that's un-American."

"Exactly."

"But how can that be? How can anyone get funding to create such a program? How can they hide it? How can...."

Caitlin let her voice trail off. Just now, it didn't matter how it had been done. What mattered was how they were going to get around it?

"What can we do?" she asked.

"What can anyone do? It's the government. It's what happens when we allow more and more of our liberties to be confiscated in the name of public well-being."

"No. I mean, what can we do right now? We need to hide, but yet we have to find out what's behind all this."

"Oh. Well, I have the solution for the telephone problem. That's no problem at all. But we do need to hold up for awhile. In fact, we need to get completely out of town and that message Scott left you has intrigued me."

"What do you mean?" she asked.

"The remark about the first of May. If that's the day your parents are returning to Colorado then it seems to me that Scott wanted to indicate their home in Black Forest. How about we visit here your parents house?"

"Are you serious? They'd obviously be looking for me to contact them. You said so yourself."

"What I said was that they'd have the capability to monitor all the calls over your parents' lines. I don't think they'll actually put a watch on their house unless they lose track of you."

"You've lost me."

"That's all right. It's not an obvious ploy. That's why it should work."

"Why what'll work?"

"All in good time."

They were approaching the eastern shore of the Mid-Bay Bridge. They kept moving east for awhile, then turned north toward Oakland.

"Well? What are you waiting for?" Caitlin finally asked.

"Nothing in particular, but I need to pull off and get something out of the trunk."

"What is it?"

"Patience, patience Caitlin. You'll be more impressed if I show you rather than just blurting it out. Didn't you ever hear the expression of showing rather than telling?"

"Huh? No, I don't think I have."

"Creative writing 101. An old college lecture. Never give away too much by simply telling, you have to show the reader what's going on."

"John, have you ever had a nervous breakdown?"

"No," he answered with a shake of his head.

"Well I am just about to have my first!" Caitlin said, adding emphasis and strength to each word.

John turned to face her and grinned. "All right. Just keep you pants on."

He turned off on the next exit and pulled into a McDonald's parking lot at the first intersection. He parked, got out, and went to the rear of the car. In a minute, he returned with a small plastic toolbox.

"What's in there?" Caitlin asked.

"Tools of the trade."

He set the box on the console and opened it. There was a complete set of miniature tools and a few electronic chips. John selected one of the screwdrivers, took out his cell phone, and in another minute had the back off. He then took what Caitlin recognized as a chip extraction tool and deftly pulled a square chip from the phone. He set it aside, took a similar chip from inside the toolbox, and placed it in the vacant slot.

Caitlin watched as he replaced the back.

"Is that what I think it is?" she asked.

"That depends. Do you think it's the encoding chip?"

"Yes."

"In that case you'd be right," he said.

"Is it stolen?"

His expression was one of feigned pain. "Do I look like a thief?"

"Last week I would've said no, now I think you're capable of just about anything."

John grinned broadly. "Good answer. In answer to your question, no. It isn't stolen. However, its code was lifted from its legitimate owner."

"How'd you do it?"

"You are noisy aren't you?"

Before she could answer, he continued. "I didn't lift it. I purchased the code from some people who do that sort of thing. They move around, but spend a lot of time in apartments that overlook the Bay Bridge. People are always using their cell phones on the bridge. They use a scanner and decoder to pick up the chip codes from passing motorist. Then they transfer the codes to new chips and sell them on the black market."

"I thought the FCC and FBI had shut down that type of operation. Didn't I see that the phone chips are hardware encoded now so that only the original chip can use a particular number?"

"My, you do keep up don't you? The new phones do have hardware-encoded chips. But they currently only make up about sixty percent of the market. This scam will work for a couple more years."

"How do you know the chips still good? What if the original owner has already noticed the increased usage and reported it?"

"Good point. I'm glad to see you're thinking. I paid top dollar for this chip. My supplier assures me it's virgin."

"And you trust him?"

John laughed. It was the first time she had heard him laugh since the canyon. It was the strong laugh of a man comfortable with showing his amusement.

"No, Caitlin. I don't trust him."

"Then?"

"I tapped the phone records for this chip and keep a check on it. So far it hasn't had abnormally high bills."

"Devious aren't you?" she asked.

"I try."

"Now, are you going to tell me your plans?"

"All in good time."

John flicked on the phone and punched in a series of numbers.

Caitlin waited. She was trying to remember what it was she had liked about him before. He'd seemed more open before, more likable.

"Squeeze? It's John ... Yeah, long time. Look, I have a job for you. Can we meet? ... Yeah, I remember the place. Thirty minutes? ... Fine, see you."

John lowered the phone and turned it off.

"Did I hear you right? Did you call him Squeeze?" Caitlin asked.

"Her," John answered.

"Oh."

"We don't have a lot of time. You want a biscuit and some coffee?"

"Ah, yea, that'll be fine." John cranked the car and pulled into the drive-through lane. They got a couple of steak biscuits and large coffees and in a few minutes were back on the freeway heading north.

"Care to tell me where we're going?"

"Oakland."

"What are we going to do there?"

"Among other things, we're going to stash this car and borrow another one. Then we're leaving town."

In less than twenty minutes they pulled into the lot of a small Mexican restaurant in downtown Oakland. John parked the car in the very back of the lot, out of sight of the street.

They walked to the corner of the building and stepped out onto the sidewalk. Miguel's was a small restaurant, not much more than a hole in the wall. A neon light advertising Corona and another for Dos Eques lit one wall. The other wall was a vivid mural of a mararachi band at a garden wedding.

"It's kind of early for lunch isn't it?" Caitlin asked.

"Depends on what time you got up, but yes it is early."

There wasn't much of a crowd, a couple of people sat near the window, and there was someone else along the back wall. John waved at the waiter and then led Caitlin toward the back.

As they approached the lone figure, the woman stood. She was a short, middle-aged woman of dark skin and kinky black hair. Her dress was a dark fabric; Caitlin guessed cotton, with multi-colored flowers. It was the size of a small army tent.

Squeeze stood and met John with open arms. Her head came to the center of his chest as she wrapped her arms around him and squeezed. John returned her hug with enthusiasm as Squeeze began to laugh.

They separated and John raised a hand toward Caitlin.

"Caitlin, let me introduce Lori Turnis. Lori, this is an old friend, Caitlin Maxwell."

"Pleased to meet you, Lori," Caitlin said extending her hand.

The older woman ignored her hand; she stepped close, and gave Caitlin a brief crushing hug without patting her on the back. When Lori stepped back, Caitlin involuntarily inhaled audibly.

"Sakes child, any friend of John's is a friend o'mine. Come, sit. Tell me what you been up to, John."

"Mostly no good, Squeeze. Have you heard from Ronnie?"

"Sure have. He was hoping to come home for Christmas, but his outfit is back over there. Don't know why we have to play policeman to all these countries. Our boys oughtta be home for Christmas."

They joined Squeeze at her table.

"Ronnie and I were in the Marines together," John said.

"Yeah, but he didn't get out. I don't know why he stays in. It's not like his father doesn't try to talk him into leaving. You'd think he'd listen to his father."

"Yeah, like he's such a good example," John said, amusement in his voice.

"It wasn't the same when Bill was in. Things were better, besides, the Navy ain't the Marines."

"Right." John laughed and in a moment, Squeeze joined him.

"Look Squeeze, I'm sorry to be short, but we're in a hurry today. Caitlin's in a lot of trouble and I need to get her out of town for awhile."

Squeeze gave Caitlin a good long look. "Do tell?"

"Yes. I need you to set up a smoke screen for her."

"I see. You want the standard treatment?"

"No, I'm afraid we'll need the luxury accommodations this time," John said.

She observed Caitlin with a new awareness. "My, word. You are in trouble, Child."

"All right, John. Do you have a recent picture?"

"No, there hasn't been time for that."

"That's all right. I brought a camera. It seems like you don't ever come prepared."

While Squeeze dipped into an enormous purse, John gave Caitlin a sideways smile.

Squeeze removed a digital camera from the purse and powered it up. "Give me a big smile, Child."

Caitlin smiled widely. The camera flashed and made a soft hum.

"Would someone mind telling me what this is all about?"

"John, you been keeping this poor young thing in the dark? What have I told you about your manners? I told you that you weren't getting enough home cookin'. You can't be expected to know what the proper manners are without proper eating."

"It's not like that, Squeeze. There hasn't been time."

"Humph, yeah right, didn't I ask you on the way here?"

John laughed lightly. "Squeeze will explain much better than I."

"Sure thing, Child. John never was much of a talker. Look, what I'm going to do is simple. Occasionally, John has a client that needs to disappear for a few days and I provide the cover, the smoke screen."

In mid sentence Squeeze's voice went from a heavy Southern accent to a more sophisticated, Californian tone. "Sometimes, the smoke screen is simple. I check John's client into a hotel, make a few calls from the room, order room service, and even buy them tickets to a concert or some such event. Everything goes on the client's credit card. It gives the appearance that the client is in town and moving around. Meanwhile, John and his client are free to slip out for whatever it is they need to do."

"Oh, I see, and you do this often?" Caitlin asked.

"No, not often, at least not for John. I do have other customers though."

"And this is what you're going to do for me?"

Squeeze laughed and for just a moment her accent returned. "Lands sakes, Child. John said you need the luxury accommodations. No, we're going to have to do something special for you."

"Like what?"

"Well, I don't like to give away secrets, but seeing that you're an old friend of John's, I guess I can make an exception. I'll take this photo." She indicated the camera that now showed a full color view of Caitlin. "Then I'll hire a part-timer and fix them up like you. Hairstyle, body type, dress, you know what I mean. Then anyone being shown a picture of you and asked to identify it would say that was who they saw. Next, your doppelganger will check in to a local motel, nothing flashy, just something simple. She'll use a fake name, but then she'll make a long distance call on your card. That's sure to bring attention, but the call will be brief and your doppelganger will be gone before anyone can arrive. For the next week or until John tells me the service is no longer needed, you will be seen around town several times a day. Waiters will remember you tipping nicely, bartender's will remember what you ordered and how you were dressed. To anyone looking for you it will seem that they are hot on your trail."

Caitlin sat back and stared at the older woman. "I, I don't know what to say. It's amazing. This actually works?"

"Child, I could have given O.J. an iron tight alibi for less effort, but then he apparently didn't need one."

"We'll need the paraphernalia," Squeeze said.

"The what?" Caitlin asked.

"Your credit cards, pin numbers, e-mail account and password. You know, everything that could be used by you and only you."

Caitlin looked at John. He nodded. "Go ahead, it's the only way they be able to pull this off."

"But, then I won't have anything. I--"

"Don't worry about it. I'll pick up the tab for everything until this is over. It'll all be in my bill."

"John, you're charging an old friend?"

He shrugged. "It's business, Squeeze."

"All right, but as soon as this is over I'll be expecting you for dinner. We're going to have to feed you proper for awhile."

Caitlin removed her credit cards from her purse and then wrote their pin numbers along with her e-mail account and password on a napkin and passed the lot to Squeeze.

The older woman put them inside her own purse. She stood. "I guess I'd better get started. You children be careful now. John, I'll see you later."

He stood and gave her a brief hug. "Sure thing, Squeeze. You be careful, too, these aren't nice people we're hiding from and I think they have big ears and very long arms."

"You just let ol' Squeeze worry about herself, you hear?"

"Yes, ma'am."

"Nice meeting you, Caitlin. You trust John here and he'll take care of you."

"Thank you, Lori."

"Sakes child, if you're a friend of John you can call me Squeeze."

"All right, Squeeze."

John sat back down after Squeeze left by the front door.

"Interesting woman," Caitlin said.

"Yes and nice too. Let me have your computer."

Caitlin opened her purse and took out the notebook computer. She flicked it on and then entered her password after the system booted up. When she slid it to John, he connected a short cable between it's serial port and his cell phone.

"What are you doing now?"

"I'm making reservations for a flight from Oakland to Colorado Springs."

"How are you going to arrange it? I thought they'd be on to you too."

"I'm sure they are. I may have tripped a flag when I registered our contract or they may have gotten my plates last night."

"Then what are you going to do?"

"I keep a few aliases set up in the computer files. You know how credit card companies will open accounts for bad risks or people with no credit by letting them deposit money into an account as collateral."

"Yes."

"It's similar. I've opened a couple of accounts under different names by depositing money. The bills go to a couple of mail drops around town so that there's no common address."

"What do you do about the social security numbers?"

"Trash."

"Trash? What do you mean?"

"I went through a few apartment complex's trash a couple years ago and got enough social security numbers to last me. I just draw on one of those when I need another one. By not touching them until I have to, there's no record of my having acquired them."

"Fascinating. Then you do stuff like this all the time?"

"All the time? Hardly, but it has come in useful on occasion."

"I'll bet."

John logged into the West Pac Airlines reservation page, and then did a quick search for flights from Oakland to Colorado Springs. There were several direct flights, the last one late in the afternoon. He reserved two seats in first class, then took a small notepad from his jacket pocket and flipped over a few pages.

"Here we go. Robert and Charlotte Owens." He typed in the credit card number and a moment later the confirmation number appeared.

"But how are we going to get the tickets? They check photo IDs at the ticket counters now."

"I know Caitlin, I have it covered. That's why I took a later flight, that and to give Squeeze a chance to have you make an appearance in the city."

"Oh."

"Do you have a blank disk in your bag?" he asked.

"Sure."

She fished out a small hard case and flipped it open. Taking the top disk out she passed it to him.

John loaded it into the drive and downloaded some information onto it. Then he removed the disk, put it in his jacket pocket, logged off the Web, and powered down the computer.

"Let's go. We have a few stops to make," he said and put the phone back in his pocket.

Caitlin returned the computer to its case and stood.

As they left the restaurant, the lunch crowd was just beginning to appear.

Five minutes later they were heading into west Oakland. John flipped open his phone again and dialed another number from memory.

"Felipe? This is John. ... Yeah, I'm great. You? ... Fine, look Felipe, I need a loaner and storage. ... No, probably long term, a couple of weeks anyway. ... Yeah, I'm on my way. ... Good, see you soon."

He folded the phone and Caitlin looked at him.

"A loaner?"

"Yeah, wheels. I need to get this car off the road. It's only a matter of time before it's spotted."

"You're assuming they have full police cooperation?"

"That's the safe assumption. Even if the police don't know what or whom they're cooperating with. I doubt if they've been told much, probably just a line about national security."

They turned south past a line of waterfront cranes that towered above the docks like something from War of the Worlds. A few blocks down, John turned off the street in front of a warehouse. He stopped at the entrance and hit the horn briefly. The garage door retracted and they pulled inside.

A young, dark skinned man stood next to the door. As they passed, he hit the close button and the door shut behind them.

Another man came out of an office door. He smiled at John as they got out of the car. "John, long time, mi amigo. Carl, take his car and exchange everything with the green Taurus, then park him on level three and bring the Taurus here."

"Shore, Felipe."

John and Felipe shook hands briefly. As Caitlin reached them Felipe gave her a warm smile.

"Nice. You going to introduce me, John?" Felipe asked.

"I don't think so. You're not likely to meet her again and it's better that you not have to lie about meeting her."

Felipe grinned again. "Ignore what he's saying, Ms. Maxwell. I don't mind lying when it involves such a beautiful woman."

John groaned softly.

Caitlin took Felipe's hand and shook it briefly. "You have the advantage on me Felipe. I don't know you and I can't think of how you know me."

"I can," John said with a note of irritability in his voice.

"It's Felipe McDowell, Ms. Maxwell. Come into my office. I'll explain everything."

She glanced questioningly at John, but he merely frowned and shook his head once.

Felipe turned and led the way through the door. His office was more spacious than Caitlin expected. The warehouse floor showed through the windows on the near wall, but the far wall was more than twenty feet away. Along the left side of the room, there was an elaborate audio-visual bank of electronics.

Felipe took a seat in front of the instruments. "John, I'm disappointed. I thought you were more careful then this."

He tapped a key and John's image appeared on the screen. Under the photo, not a recent one but recent enough to show his scar, was a brief description and a list of charges.

"John, someone's really after you. They have you guilty of everything except the Oklahoma City bombing."

Caitlin leaned over Felipe's shoulder and read some of the charges.

Assault on a federal officer, attempted murder, kidnapping, unlawful flight to avoid arrest, theft of classified documents, espionage, and in bold face letters, treason.

John was frowning.

"My God, John. I'm sorry," Caitlin said as she placed a hand on his elbow.

"It's just bullshit. It's so damn typical of the government to use overkill when they don't have any evidence. Don't let it bother you," John said.

"But she should be bothered, John, there's more," Felipe said and touched another key.

Caitlin's driver's license photo appeared and under it was a similar list of charges. Only in her case, the kidnapping charge was replaced by murder charges.

A cold shudder shook her body for a moment, then it was gone.

"What's this on? The news or just interdepartmental?" John asked.

Felipe shrugged. "Just interdepartmental for now. You can't ever tell if they'll go open or not. If they go open there may be uncomfortable questions asked."

"When did you find it?" John asked.

"Earlier this morning when I was doing a little browsing."

"You have access to the police computer lines?" Caitlin asked.

"Some of them. I purchased a subscription a couple of years ago."

"A subscription? What do you mean? Is it something like a software subscription?"

"Yeah, something like that. A disgruntled city employee didn't like the way he was treated, something about an insurance claim that was refused. Anyway, he modified the operating system of one of the city's computers to record any new passwords and their logons. He now taps various city records and provides, shall we say unauthorized access to these records for a fee. I'm one of his subscribers to the police department computer."

"Oh, my God. How can he get away with this? Even the cheaper virus checkers should identify any modifications to the operating system."

Felipe gave her a respectful stare. "Hey, I didn't know I was talking with someone in the club."

John chuckled. "Felipe, she's a software expert. The only difference between the two of you is that she's strictly on the legal end of encoding."

"Really, well I guess that's changed now."

"And why is that?" Caitlin asked.

"You're on the run, lady. The government's after you and you're going to need all the help you can get to stay out of jail. You ought to know that, why else would you have hired John Blalock?"

"What's he talking about?" Caitlin asked looking at John.

"The majority of my clients that Felipe has met have been on the run from the authorities. But that doesn't mean that I only handle people fleeing justice."

Felipe nodded emphatically. "Yeah, I didn't mean to imply any such thing. I'm sure that most of John's clients are unjustly accused or at least the ones that he needs my help on."

"But I have been unjustly accused. I didn't do any of those things," Caitlin protested.

"See," Felipe said.

"This can't be happening. I'm a law-abiding citizen. I don't even speed. I ... I can't take much more of this." Her knees felt weak and her head light. A moment later she felt John's hand on her elbow. He helped her to a chair and sat her down.

She heard Felipe clicking his tongue. "Yeah, that's how all the strictly law-abiding types take it. Man, John, when are the people going to wake up and smell the cappuccino? It amazes me that these people can go through their lives without ever realizing just how much power is wielded by those in control of our government. Nixon, Hoover, Clinton, hell, these people control you, lady. They and thousands of minor disciples of --"

"Give it a rest, Felipe," John ordered.

"I ... sure John, no point in scaring the customers. Eh, Caitlin?"

"Felipe, we're going to need some photo ID's made," John said.

"Sure, no problem, man. You got the players or do you need new ones?"

"I've got valid players. I just need the ID's made."

"Whatever you need. I'll get the camera ready, you come on back when Caitlin's feeling better."

"We'll need a few modifications," John said.

"Okay, wigs all right or do you want the full treatment?"

"Wigs should do, but maybe we could add a mole or something to Caitlin's face, something prominent enough to draw attention."

"Eww. You're not serious."

"Of course I am. If your photo has been circulated then someone's going to recognize you. I'm sorry, but you're too damn pretty to disguise with just a wig."

"Ah, thanks. I think," she said.

"You got it. Two wigs and a beauty mark, extra large."

Felipe went out the door and turned toward the rear of the warehouse.

Caitlin watched him go then looked up at John. She half expected him to be grinning in amusement at her naiveté. To her surprise his face showed understanding even sympathy for what she was feeling.

He's turned out odd, cold and tough on the outside, but still able to sympathize with someone in trouble.

"Are you going to be all right?" he asked.

"Do I have a choice?"

"You always have a choice. You can let it overwhelm you, drive you into a shell until you're helpless to react with the outside world. Oh the other hand, you can get angry at the people who are doing this to you. Nothing beats back depression and anxiety like hate."

"I already hate them. They've killed Scott, murdered an unfortunate cabby, and wrecked my life. I want to get even."

"Good, that's a healthy emotion. But even the worse general knows there are times when you have to run away in order to fight another day. This is one of those times. There's more involved here than just the government. There's always the possibility of being able to play one group against the other."

"Against the government, John? I don't see how that's possible."

"Everyone wants something. If you control what they want, then you can force a trade for what you want."

"I don't know."

"Trust me," he said.

"Did you hear that in a movie? No one trusts someone who says 'trust me.'"

"Yeah, I know. It was meant to be funny."

"Oh, an ice breaker. You're out of practice."

He shrugged. "Come on, let's see if Felipe is ready for us."

John offered her a hand. She took it and he pulled her to her feet. For a moment, they stood still, their faces less than 6 inches apart. She stared into his eyes, and then reluctantly she dropped his hand.

He led the way farther into the warehouse and through another door. There they found Felipe working with a pre-positioned camera like those at the DMV.

"It's ready." Felipe said.

With a wave of his hand, he called their attention to a counter, sink, mirror, and makeup lights.

"Is there anything you don't have?" Caitlin asked.

"I don't have a stylist or a manicurist, yet. Give me a while, I'm thinking of expanding."

"Yeah, he's also thinking of expanding and competing with the DMV on a legitimate basis. You know they're privatizing everything in government these days," John said, his voice serious.

Caitlin studied him for a second, decided he wasn't serious after all, and went to examine the wigs.

They looked real. Someone had sold their hair to make this wig. It depressed Caitlin to think there were people who needed money bad enough to sell their own hair. She picked up a short, black wig and slipped it over her head. In the mirror, her own black hair hung out from under the shorter black strains.

"That's the Demi Moore."

She turned Felipe watching her.

"On you it works. You got the right skin tones and all, but you really could just cut your own hair to get the same look."

Caitlin turned to John. "What do you think?"

"I think it won't change your appearance enough. They're already looking for someone with long black hair, it doesn't take a leap of imagination to identify the same person with short black hair."

She pulled the wig off and dropped it to the counter. "All right then, you choose for me."

John came beside her, glanced over the display, and then selected a long, red wig with enough body to stand on it's own.

"Lord, you don't really see me like that do you?" Caitlin asked.

"Just try it on," he said as he held it out.

Caitlin took it and turned it until she had it aligned. Peering into the mirror she whipped it over her head and pulled it tight.

"Yeah, the Reba McIntire, good choice John."

Caitlin ignored him and studied her reflection. "I don't think I can pull it off. My skin is too dark."

"Felipe will handle that. Won't you Felipe?"

"Sure John. Have a seat Caitlin, I'll be right with you."

Caitlin sat on a stool in front of the makeup lights and mirror and sat down. In a minute, Felipe joined her and stared at her reflection.

He nodded to himself a couple of times, then opened a makeup case.

Twenty minutes later he stepped back and pronounced his work complete. Caitlin took a good look in the mirror. Her normally olive skin was lightened to the point of pinkness. Her dark eyebrows had been bleached out and Felipe had even given her a few freckles across the bridge of her noise.

"Freckles?" John asked coming up behind her.

"I thought it gave her a look of innocence," Felipe replied.

Caitlin saw that John had been busy also. He was now wearing a full beard that was frosted with gray.

She suppressed a grin and said, "My, don't you look distinguished. Is that what you're going to look like in twenty years?"

"Perhaps, assuming I live that long."

Caitlin felt her smile slipping away.

"Let me help you with the wig," Felipe said.

Caitlin turned back to the mirror as he removed the wig and proceeded to pin her own hair up above her neck. That done, he pulled the wig down on her head and carefully arranged it.

"There. How's that?"

Caitlin's reflection was now complete. She eyed it approvingly and turned from side to side to check it out. "You're in the wrong business, Felipe."

"Everyone has to have a hobby. Come on, time to pose."

"Give me a second to brush this wig out," Caitlin said while she looked through her purse for a brush.

"No. It's gotta look like a photo ID. A really nice photo would be a dead giveaway."

"All right, I guess it doesn't matter anyway. It's only temporary."

"We hope," John said.

"What's that mean?"

"You never know...."

Felipe pointed toward the light colored backdrop.

"Just stand over there, this won't take but a second."

Caitlin stepped to where he had a small mark on the concrete floor, then looked up at the camera. Without warning the flash went off.

"Hey, I wasn't ready."

"He told you it was suppose to look like a real DMV photo," John said.

"All right. John, your turn."

Caitlin stepped to the side and John took her place.

"Hey, lose the hat," Felipe said.

"Sorry, forgot I was wearing it."

"Yeah, you always got that hat on. But not for the photo, eh?"

John removed it and held it below his waist.

The flash lit up his face and for just a moment, the bright light reminded Caitlin of how he had looked in the canyon with the Arizona sun beating down on him.

"You say you already have players?"

"Yeah." John took the disk from his jacket and passed it to Felipe.

"This will take a few minutes," Felipe said.

"Do you mind if I watch?" Caitlin asked.

"Of course not. Come on."

She followed him to one of the desks where he loaded the disk into the computer. With a few clicks of the mouse, he changed programs and called up the stored information. He divided the information between the male and female players and then copied it into another file.

"Hey John, you want passports while you're here?"

"No, if we end up having to leave the country we'll need completely new identities. Keep the photos on file, I'll let you know if we need more material."

"Sure, John. I'm going to need your signatures for the licenses. Here." He handed Caitlin a pen. "Practice writing your new name a couple of times on this paper then write it once on a clean sheet. You too, John."

Caitlin wrote out Charlotte S. Owens, until she was comfortable with the appearance, then signed the clean paper. She passed the pen to John and he wrote out Robert A. Owens once then signed it below her signature on the other paper.

Felipe took their signatures and fed them into a scanner. With the mouse, he selected another screen and Caitlin saw her image appear above the name and address information. Another mouse stroke and the laser imager purred. Felipe took the photographic paper from the imager, cut it to shape, and then dropped it into a laminator. A minute later he examined the license, nodded approvingly, then passed it to Caitlin. Felipe reset the equipment and a minute later, John's license came out.

"How good is this?" she asked.

"As good as any you'll get from the DMV. John provided the players, so as long as their address and license numbers are correct then the license is perfect."

"Unless someone gets nosy enough to have the file photo transmitted to them," John said.

"That's right. Do you want me to insert your new photos into the computer records?"

"No, not for this set, but thanks for the offer."

"It's just part of the deluxe package."

"You can really change the file photos in the state's computer?" Caitlin asked.

"Lady, if you want to start drawing an old age pension, I can arrange it for you. But it doesn't come cheap. The more you tamper with the system, the greater the chance someone's watchdog program will notice the unauthorized access. Then I'd have to change my entry method."

"I see. What's all this going to cost me?"

"There's no point in worrying about that now. Once we get things settled I'll give you a bill that itemizes everything."

"Really? Can I use in on a tax return?"

"Sure, why not? Think of it as the cost of doing business. It's just one more business expense."

John checked his watch. "We'd better get moving. We'll want to get to the airport early enough to check it out."

"You got what you need?" Felipe asked.

"Most everything. If I need something else I'll give you a call."

"Anything. Anytime. Anywhere."

They followed Felipe back to the warehouse to a dark green late model Taurus. "Your bags and equipment are in the trunk. The keys are in the ignition."

"Thanks again, Felipe. I'll be seeing you," John said.

"You know it. You be careful. Caitlin, it was nice meeting you. Don't worry, John is as good as they come."

"Really? Thank you, that's good to hear."

Felipe slapped John on the back. "Don't make me out a liar, John."

"Wouldn't think of it."

Caitlin climbed into the passenger side of the front seat. John got in, cranked the car, and pulled out of the warehouse without a backward glance.

CHAPTER 21

The Oakland airport was shrouded in a light mist from low clouds when they reached the short-term parking lot. A chill breeze flowed in from the bay bringing the scent of salt with it. Caitlin shivered and pulled on her coat when she stepped out into the mist.

John already had the trunk open when she reached the rear of the car. She watched as he moved some things from one bag to another, then he bent low over the trunk and pulled a handgun from beneath his coat. As she watched he popped the magazine out, ejected a round from the chamber, and then stored the gun in what looked like a metal tool chest. A couple more magazines appeared in his hands from various pockets and they were pushed down into the case too. He covered the gun and magazines with a padding of dense foam.

Then he lifted his right pants leg and drew an enormous knife from the top of his boot.

"What, no brass knuckles?"

He looked at her, his brows raised in curiosity.

"Thanks for the reminder," he said and dipped his right hand into a coat pocket. It emerged a second later with a thick set of matte finished brass knuckles. He added them to the case, locked it, and lifted the bags from the trunk.

Caitlin picked up her bag. "Can you carry a gun on the plane?"

John tossed the car keys into the trunk and slammed it shut. "No, not into the passenger compartment, but you can carry one in your checked luggage."

They walked toward the terminal. Caitlin noticed John was looking for something. Did he really think that someone might have gotten there before them?

"It used to be that you could just check your weapons and not worry about them. Nowadays they run a random percentage of all bags through a bomb detector and some can even detect the chemicals in the bullets. There's a civil penalty for not notifying the airlines of any weapons you're checking."

"Really? It's that simple?"

"Simple? When you tell them you have weapons in you checked luggage they mark the bag. Anyone in baggage handling can spot those bags. Guns bring a good price on the streets."

"Gees, then why mark the bags? Isn't that just asking for them to be stolen?"

"Yeah, but they'll tell you they need the bags marked so fireman or rescue personnel can spot dangerous items. This is at the same time they tell you that flying is the safest way to travel. That there are less accidents in flying than any other form of transportation."

"Then it doesn't make a lot of sense to say that they have to know where hazardous materials are."

"Exactly. If I were more paranoid I'd think it's some form of organized effort to identify people who carry weapons. It wasn't a big deal when they didn't ask for ID to board a plane, but now you can't just buy a cash ticket and get on a flight. You have to provide identification. It wouldn't take much for the government to identify everyone in the country who had carried firearms on a flight and where they had gone. Once you are identified a computer program could just as easily track all of your movement from then on."

"But what would be the purpose?"

"Purpose? Hell, who can ever follow the government's purpose in anything? Besides, I'm not saying they do track honest citizen's movements. I'm just saying that it's possible and if I was more paranoid, then I'd think they were doing it."

"Are you trying to give me the impression that you're understandably paranoid?" Caitlin asked.

They reached the main terminal and crossed into the building.

"Yeah, I guess so. Look, while we're in here I want you to try to ignore what's been happening. Relax, make cheerful noises, tell me a few old jokes, and above all don't give the impression that you're looking around as if searching for cops."

"Don't look for them or don't give that impression?"

"Don't give the impression. If you want to look around look at the building, the advertisements, the strange people. Act like a tourist, but maintain the patter, the smiles, the chuckles."

"What's that get me?"

"If you were looking for someone on the run would you expect them to be carrying on as if they're on vacation?"

Caitlin gave his question a moment's thought and shook her head. "No, I don't guess I would."

"Right, and neither would anyone else. Most fugitives look the part. That's what a watcher will be looking for."

John indicated a row of chairs near the overhead monitors that announced arrivals and departures. "Here, let's sit down over here for a minute."

They set the bags down and John took some folded papers from a jacket pocket. He looked at them for a moment, then handed them to Caitlin, and pointed at a line.

Confused, she looked at where he was pointing. It was the menu from the restaurant where they'd met Squeeze.

"It just gives us something to look at and look like tourists. There's our flight number. It's on time. We've got about an hour. I haven't spotted any obvious watchers, but that doesn't mean anything. They could have passed photos out to all the ticket counters."

"But didn't Felipe say the warrants were only on the police lines?" Caitlin asked.

"Yeah, but that wouldn't stop them from passing out photos at all the airports and bus terminals and such. They aren't as likely to have their own agents out here. There are just too many airports and too many travelers for anything less than a small army to cover. They'd have to stake out the

San Francisco, San Jose, and even Sacramento airports too. They're all easy to reach from the Bay Area."

"I guess it's not something I'd ever given any thought."

"There was no reason to. That's one of the reasons most criminals get caught. They never give it any thought either. Come on, let's check these bags, and move past security. We can wait in one of the lounges."

They carried their bags to the West Pac desk, waited a few minutes in line and then John stepped to the desk and identified them. Caitlin stood behind John and placed her left hand lightly against his shoulder, while the attendant checked their reservations. Caitlin noticed that the short hairs at the back of John's neck formed silver dollar sized whorls. She tickled the short hairs lightly.

The attendant asked for their identification and they each produced their new driver's license and handed them across the counter. The man took a careful look at each picture and went back to his computer screen. As he printed out the tickets, Caitlin returned the license to her bag and then wrapped both her arms around John's right arm and rested her cheek against his shoulder.

"Are these your only bags?"

"Yes, that's all," John said.

He gave them the normal routine of questioning that determined they hadn't allowed some stranger in a turban and carrying a bomb to help pack their bags, then finished the check-in and passed John the tickets. Caitlin thanked him politely, and continued to hold John's arm as they walked toward the security check in.

As they stepped onto the escalator, Caitlin dropped her hand down to hold his. "I thought you were going to declare that you had a firearm."

"What gave you that idea?"

"Why, your speech about how they can track people carrying firearms and all that. What happens if they have one of the newer model detectors in the luggage area?"

"The case I put the gun in is special. It has dense pockets that disguise its true contents from x-rays and it is hermetically sealed. Odors can't escape it and don't cling to its exterior."

She chuckled lightly and said, "Is there anything you haven't planned for?"

"Well, the wings could still fall off the plane."

"That's not funny." Caitlin said.

"By the way, that was good back there."

"What was?"

"The way you played with my hair."

"Really? You liked it?"

"Yeah, that added a good touch of authenticity. It gave us credibility as a married couple."

With some effort, Caitlin kept the irritability she felt from showing in her voice. "Oh? I'm glad you approve."

They reached security and qued up behind the other flyers.

“Caitlin, just to be safe,, try to keep your eyes on the ground except when the guard checks your ticket, then only look directly at him.”

“Why? What’s wrong now?”

“This airport has installed face recognition software and if we’re programed into the system the computer will spot us a second after it sees our faces.”

“I thought that was what the wigs and stuff were for.”

“It’ll help against the guards, but not against the computer. We didn’t have a choice about coming here and I’m thinking that they haven’t had time to load our images into the local system.”

“You think? That’s not encouraging. I thought you had this all worked out.”

“I know it’s a risk, but what isn’t. They’ve only been looking for you for a couple of days and unless they were really on the ball, they won’t have programed in our faces.”

They reached the front of the line, showed their tickets, and were allowed through. A light breeze fluffed her wig as they passed through the detectors. They failed to activate the sensors.

As they made their way down the corridor to the gate, John took her hand and gave it a little squeeze. "That should do. If the computer had our faces, we would already be under arrest."

"Does that mean that I can stop acting like we're married?"

"Huh? Well, no, I wouldn't go so far as that. Can't be too careful."

“Since you seem to know everything about their security, why is there a breeze when you go through the metal detectors?”

“Breeze? Oh, I barely noticed it. It’s the air samplers. The newer detectors draw air across your body and sample it for chemical or biological agents.”

“Oh, I guess that’s a good thing.”

“Certainly, it keeps anyone from smuggling explosives or darn near anything onto a plane.”

John led her to seats near an emergency exit and they watched the gate until their flight was announced. When Caitlin started to rise, John took her wrist and pulled her back down. "There's no rush. We'll wait until the final boarding call."

"What now?" she asked.

"It'll give us a better opportunity to notice anything that happens. Once on the plane we'd have a difficult time escaping."

"Escaping what? You said no one spotted us and you've gone to a lot of trouble not to leave any traceable path."

"No path is untraceable. It's just a matter of making it a difficult path to follow. Something could still have gone wrong, a check of travelers, for all we know the real Robert and Charlotte Owens could be boarding a flight today also. Then a computer check of travelers would show that one of those couples is bogus and the next thing we'd know your friend Holdren would be pulling us off the plane."

"That's not ... all right. It's possible, but what are the odds of that happening? There has to be a lot of people with that name in the Bay Area. Just because two couples with similar names happen to book flights on the same day shouldn't flag anyone's search program."

John shook his head. "You're forgetting that this isn't a case of the same name. It's the exact name and we're traveling as a couple. I should have planned better and used unrelated names. As long as the airlines are confirming identities then they can also be confirming addresses with DMV on each person traveling. It wouldn't take much to cross reference all the travelers with DMV records."

"But the attendant didn't look at our licenses long enough to copy down an address."

"No, but what if he'd already called up all the Robert and Charlotte Owens in the files. It would only take a second to confirm an address."

Caitlin stared at him for a few seconds and then shook her head. "John, you are just too paranoid."

"Maybe, but we'll still wait 'til final boarding is announced."

There wasn't any point in arguing with him. His mind was made up and besides, she had gone to him for help. She needed to let him do things the way he thought they should be done. He was the one with the experience, not she. It made her wonder. Just what kind of experiences had he encountered? He talked of security and he mentioned serving in the military, but what else had he been doing over the last decade or so. Felipe had implied that he helped people escape the law. Did he work for organized crime, the Mafia or whatever they called it these days? And were they true felons or just someone like herself who was caught up in events beyond her control? She needed to find out what was in the file Scott had sent her. Since it didn't look like Louie was going to be able to decrypt the file, assuming he was still alive, then she would have to deduce the password Scott may have used.

What common item would he have used? Something from their past? Perhaps he'd used a location or a friend's name? But where? Who?

Caitlin was still thinking over possible passwords when John nudged her elbow and broke her train of thought. "Come on, that's the final boarding call."

They walked casually toward the gate. Caitlin looped an arm around John's again and made chattering noises about the weather and the skiing in Colorado.

At the gate, an attendant scanned their boarding passes and identification, then wished them a pleasant flight.

The plane was a Boeing, either a 767 or 777, Caitlin thought. It appeared to be only about two thirds full and they were lucky enough to get two seats alone in a bulkhead row just ahead of the port wing. John stepped past the seats, waited for her to slide in, and then took the middle seat.

She slipped her bag under the seat in front of her and gazed out the window at the rain swept tarmac. There was no sign of flashing blue lights, no unmarked cars sliding to a stop next to the plane, no sign of anything out of the ordinary. But what was ordinary? Should two men still be unloading baggage? What was the man with the funny looking flashlights doing? For once Caitlin wished she'd paid more attention at all the other flight preparations she'd ignored over the years. Normally she'd be engrossed in a novel or working on proposal by this stage of a flight.

She heard a sound near the front of the plane and looked up, half expecting to see Holdren.

John placed a hand on hers and his voice was soft, "That's the door closing. I guess we made it."

Her skin was warm where his lay against hers. She turned her head and his lips were scant inches from hers. While his face was rough and scarred, his lips looked as firm and tender as they had been that time she had kissed them all those years ago. Without conscious volition, she leaned toward him. To her surprise, he turned away, as if he hadn't noticed her movement.

For a moment embarrassment locked her throat. Then she cleared it and spoke as softly as he had, "John, I want to thank you again. I don't know what I would have done if you hadn't helped."

"Don't worry about it."

Caitlin hesitated, unsure of how to phrase the question. She leaned closer to John and lowered her voice to a whisper. "Felipe mentioned something about the type of people you've helped before. Just what is it that you do?"

With a half nod, he said, "I do a fair impression of Abraham Lincoln imitating George Washington."

"No, seriously."

He grinned boyishly. "Another time. Some things shouldn't discussed in public."

"All right, but I'm going to hold you to that."

In a few minutes they were airborne and Caitlin watched the rain shrouded bay disappear below the low clouds. They broke out into late afternoon sunlight. The plane banked to the right and the sun disappeared aft. For a short time, Caitlin watched the under cast that stretched as far as her eye could see, then gave it up, and closed her eyes.

* * *

John got a Samuel Adams from the flight attendant, waved off the offered glass, and sipped from the bottle. Beside him Caitlin dozed. He studied her and wondered about the feelings he'd once felt for her. What had it been that attracted him to her back then? Her looks? She was attractive, even with the skin lightening makeup and the red wig; her natural beauty was still visible. So many years. She'd been the last great love of his life. He'd had a few crushes before her, but none after and none of the others had drawn him with the inescapable pull that she had. For less than two weeks, so long ago, he had spiraled around her. Growing closer and closer until, like a meteor caught in a gravity well, he had burned himself out against her love for Scott.

Now Scott was gone and she was back in his life. Was there anyway he could find that love again?

He took another sip from the bottle and leaned his head back. There were more important things to consider. Mama Squeeze would keep the Feds off them for a week or so, but then they'll realize their prey was no longer in the Bay Area and by then John would have to be ready. Ready for the NCIX, the other Feds, the Japanese businessmen, and this Frenchman. What was on that disk? It held the key. They would have to decrypt it if they were to have a chance.

That brought up Louie. He had to do something about Louie, perhaps drop a line to his contacts in CHAOS. If it was the NCIX that had him Louie could handle it, but if it was Holdren's group. Well, in that case it might already be too late to help Louie.

* * *

Caitlin awoke with a start. John was lightly shaking her elbow. She rubbed the sleep from her eyes with the heels of her thumbs and looked out the window. The sky was dark, but there was a faint trace of sunset on the horizon. In the foreground, the Front Range was pitch black except for an occasional light.

She turned to John. "We're on final?"

"Yeah, please place your seat in its full up tight position."

"Up tight?"

"Yeah, makes more sense, don't you think?"

"How many beers did you have?"

He grinned a half smile that only curled up the right corner of his mouth. It gave him a roguish look. "Not that many. Why? Do I need a breath mint?"

"No, just don't breathe on any policemen."

The plane shook and Caitlin's stomach tightened. "Seems like there's always turbulence coming into the Springs."

"You fly home often?"

"A couple times a year. Sometimes we used to fly in for a ski weekend, when we were coming to visit the folks we'd usually drive up."

"I'd have figured you'd take the Denver airport."

Caitlin shook her head. "Denver's airport is just too damn big. It's great for connections, but it's crowded and too far east of the mountains. It's more relaxing to fly into the Springs."

"Oh. I don't guess I've flown into Denver more than once or twice and I haven't flown into the Springs since college."

"I thought your parents lived near here."

"Not anymore. When Dad retired from the Air Force, they moved home to Alabama. He's working in Huntsville these days."

Outside, the lights of the Springs were now within a thousand feet.

"Do you see them often?"

"No, not really. I went back for Christmas the year before last, but it's hardly like home. Besides, Dad and I haven't gotten along too well since I left the Marines. He thought I was quitting, running away like I had run away from college without finishing my doctorate. 'I didn't raise no damn quitters.'" he chuckled mirthlessly.

"John I'm sorry. I had no idea. Do you want to talk about it?"

"No, I'm not even sure why I mentioned it. Forget I said anything."

There was if a jolt as the wheels touched down. The plane slowed rapidly then turned off the active runway toward the terminal. It was another five minutes before the door was unlatched and the passengers pushed toward the exit.

John and Caitlin sat still until the most of the other passengers were gone, then rose and followed them out.

As they entered the terminal, Caitlin noticed the obvious search John was making of the waiting crowd. Most had already greeted arriving passengers and the few others didn't appear to notice them.

"Do you think they might be looking for us here?"

"No, it's just the smart thing to watch for."

"Tell me if you spot someone," she said.

"Sure, you'll be the first to know."

They tagged along behind the rest of the disembarking passengers as they moved toward the main terminal. They took their time at the top of the escalators and chatted briefly about the weather and skiing conditions until John tilted his head toward the lower floor. They road the escalator down and then went to the baggage carousels.

It was easy to spot their bags. Most of their fellow passengers had already retrieved luggage and moved toward the exits. John lifted each of their bags from the moving conveyor and stacked them until the last one came by. Taking the bags, they went to the car rental agencies, where John motioned her toward the less crowded one.

Ten minutes later they were loading their luggage into the back of Jeep Grand Cherokee. John took a moment to check their surroundings for watchers, then unlocked his bag, and removed his handgun. He loaded it and then it disappeared beneath his coat.

"Get in," he said.

Caitlin went to the driver's door.

"What do you think you're doing?"

"You haven't been to my parents house. I thought you'd want me to drive. Unless you're one of those macho male drivers that can't ride with a woman driver."

"If these were ordinary circumstances, I would be happy for you to drive me, but I'm suppose to be protecting you. Unless you can convince me that you've had a VIP chauffeurs' driving course, I'll drive."

Caitlin put her hands on her hips and cocked her head. "And I suppose you're going to tell me you have one."

"Certainly. There's a good one near San Francisco. I recommend it if you get the chance."

Caitlin surrendered and got in the passenger side. John got behind the wheel, cranked the car, and pulled out of the parking space. At the entrance to the lot a guard checked their paperwork and then motioned them on.

"Which way do we go? Isn't their house out in Black Forest?"

"Yes, turn right on Powers Boulevard. It'll take us out there."

Powers wasn't far. John followed her instructions, turned north, and accelerated up the wide avenue. In a few minutes, they crossed state highway 24. A few miles farther they reached Templeton Gap and Caitlin pointed east away from the city lights.

"It's changed. The city never used to come out so far," John commented.

"Really? I guess that's because you've been gone a couple of years. It's not as noticeable when you come back more often. Just over this hill, you'll want to turn to the left."

John nodded and then slowed as he crested the hill. He stopped, waited for a couple of cars to pass, then turned left onto Black Forest Road. The road left the plains and climbed into the thick pines that gave the area its name.

"How far?"

"Not far, turn right at the stop sign."

In a minute, they reached the small country store, post office, and the few other buildings that marked the community center of Black Forest. Black Forest was a rural community on the outskirts of urban Colorado Springs. The main reason it had remained rural was the foresightedness of a few people in the early 70's. That was when developers were beginning to buy up sections of Black Forest. Their intent was to turn it into one more planned community, but the citizens got together and changed the zoning codes to restrict the sale of any land parcel smaller than 2.5 acres. The result was that more thirty years later you could still build a house out of sight of your neighbors.

At Caitlin's direction, John turned to the east. They traveled a few minutes more and turned off the main road onto a cross street.

"How much farther?"

"About a mile."

John slowed the Jeep and pulled onto the shoulder. Snow filled the drainage ditch and he was careful not to drop the tires into it.

"What are you doing?" Caitlin asked.

"There's something I need from my bags. It'll only take a minute."

He left the motor running and got out. A few seconds later he opened the rear hatch. The cold mountain air mingled with the unpleasant scent of the car's exhaust and swirled into the interior. He opened the hard-sided suitcase and popped out a small plastic case. Then he shut the hatch and returned to the driver's seat.

When he opened the case Caitlin could see a small plastic box with display screen, a couple of switches, and a micro jack. John took out the box and a telescoping antenna she hadn't noticed before. He screwed the antenna into the top of the box and drew it out to about two feet in length.

Next he took an earplug from the case and plugged its jack into the box. He put the earplug in his right ear and flicked one of the switches. The display lit and numbers scrolled across the screen at a pace that was too fast to follow.

"You mind telling me what you're up to?"

"Not at all. If there's a watch on your parent's house whoever is watching will report in regularly and definitely will call in if they receive a late night visit. This scanner will cover the standard bands up to three gigahertz. If they transmit in the clear I'll be able to listen in."

"And if they don't?"

"If they're using the latest digital radios, and I expect they will be, then their broadcast will be encoded."

"Then what good will this do?"

"If anyone starts transmitting there will be a significant increase in background power levels. This will detect those changes and warn us."

Caitlin shrugged, it made sense, and if John thought it'd work then it probably would.

"Here, you hold it. Try to keep it upright. It's not critical, but it'll help reception."

Caitlin took it and watched the numbers scroll for a moment then looked at John as he put the car in gear. "Couldn't we just cruise past their place and see if there's a stakeout?"

He grinned at her.

"Did I say something stupid?" she asked.

"Do you mean look for a panel van with black windows and antennas on the roof that's parked across the road from their driveway?"

"Well, yes, sure. What else would they be in?"

"It depends on how bright they think you are. A dark van might work in the city, but how many people out here would go by one without calling the police to investigate it?"

"All right. I'll give you that. If it stayed for long then someone would probably check it out. But couldn't they just show the police their credentials and maintain the stakeout?"

"Sure they could. But the purpose of a stakeout is to watch without being noticed. If the local police were going to stakeout your parent's place they might just use a van and not worry about being spotted, but I think these guys are more devious than that."

"Then what will they do?"

"I'm not certain. It could be set up in several ways. The simplest is to move into a neighbor's house and watch from there, but I'd bet that wouldn't work out here. The houses are too isolated and people tend to know each other too well."

"You're right there. Mom and Dad have lived here for over twenty years. They know everyone out here."

"Then it's not likely that someone could be using a neighbors house without the neighbors learning of it. They could also have a blind set up in the woods." He paused to gaze out the side windows at the tall pines shrouded with snow. "But I don't think the forest is thick enough to hide them."

"What's that leave?"

"The simplest thing would be a remote surveillance with a radio link. If it was my case, I'd disguise a camera and transmitter in a box of some type, a telephone junction box, cable TV, or even on a power pole. The camera would only activate whenever a vehicle turned into or out of your drive and would then transmit a picture back to wherever these guys are operating."

"How can we get past something like that?"

"It's not impossible. We'll cruise by their driveway and see if the receiver picks up anything. If we don't pickup any transmissions, or spot anything suspicious, we'll try the driveway."

A half-mile up the road, they passed the mailbox and driveway to her parent's house. Caitlin remembered his scolding her about facing a possible camera back in San Francisco and kept her face partially shielded with her hands as she watched the receiver. They passed the house without any indication that the receiver had registered a hidden transmitter.

"Well?" John asked.

"It all looks normal to me."

"Yeah, that's what it should look like if they're doing their job properly."

A quarter mile farther, John turned into another driveway. He backed out onto the road and accelerated back the way they'd come.

"We'll try the driveway. If the receiver picks up something, we can leave before anything happens. They probably aren't watching out here yet and with any luck, Mama Squeeze will have convinced them that you're still in the Bay Area. Keep your face down though, there's no sense taking unnecessary chances."

"All right."

"Didn't you say that your parents didn't have anyone watching the house?"

"Yeah, but Abe Jackson drops by if there's an extremely heavy snowfall or anything like that. You know, in case the snow needs to be cleared from the roof."

"There are fresh tire tracks to their house."

He was right. "I didn't give it any thought, maybe Abe was out here."

"Maybe, or maybe someone else."

John shifted gears again and pulled into the driveway. The drive curved in a gentle sweep to the left around ponderosa pines whose branches drooped under the load of nearly eight inches of snow.

Caitlin stared out the windshield as the headlight illuminated the front of her parent's home through the trees.

"God, maybe we shouldn't have come here," Caitlin said.

"It's your choice. It's not too late to turn back."

"No, we're here now. We'll do what you suggested."

John coasted to a stop at the foot of wide steps that led up to the raised front porch. He killed the engine, left the headlights on, and opened his door.

"Why didn't you back in? What if we have to leave in a hurry?" she asked.

"If there's someone here waiting for us then they'll probably have the road blocked before we can get there. We'd have to find another way out and I don't want to try that in the dark. I'll scout around for an emergency exit tomorrow."

Caitlin opened her own door and stepped down. The snow crunch loudly beneath her feet. That and the sharp metallic ping of the cooling engine were the only noises that reached her. The air felt cold, colder than it had at the airport. She zipped up her jacket and wished she'd thought to buy gloves.

The house, a large two-story log home with hand-hewn, Swedish cope logs and thick chinking, was dark except for a tiny glow that marked the doorbell.

"Caitlin, look here," John said from the other side of the Jeep.

She walked in front of it and found him pointing at a single pair of tracks that led around to the side of the house and returned close by.

"What do you think?" he asked.

"I don't know. It could just be the meter reader from the power company."

"Don't they have the remote reading meters?"

"They didn't as of last summer. I was here when the meter man came by. The meter is around on that side of the house."

"All right, whoever it was left anyway."

Caitlin led the way up the steps to the front porch. Some snow had blown onto the porch and formed a mound a couple of inches deep in front of the glass storm door. Jill opened the outer door, then fished in her case for the keys.

She unlocked the door and stepped into the darken foyer. The house was cold.

Caitlin hit the light switch, stomped the snow from her shoes, and then walked quickly to the front closet. Inside the closet, she pushed a few coats to one side, to reveal a gray, metal security panel. She keyed in her parent's code, a red light winked out, and a green one lit.

"Okay, the security system is disarmed."

"All right, I'll get the bags from the car, you reactivate it after I'm back."

Caitlin went across the great room to the lower floor's thermostat and switched on the furnace. She heard sparking of the automatic igniter and the whoosh of gas as it caught.

She met John at the door and took her bags from him.

He followed her in, shut the door behind him, and threw the bolt. "It's kinda cold in here. How do they keep the pipes from freezing?"

"The water is shut off in the basement. The valve area is heated by a dedicated electric heater to keep it safe."

"That makes sense, no point in heating the whole house just to keep water from freezing."

"It has its drawbacks. We'll have to close the faucets and the valve on the hot water heater before we can turn the water on."

She switched on more lights, illuminating the great room and the dining area on the opposite side of the entry.

"Nice place," John said.

Caitlin gazed at the immense stone chimney that rose twenty feet above the hearth, the elk antler chandelier suspended above the hardwood floor, at the many intricate sculptures that graced bookshelves and end tables. The sculptures were her mothers. She'd begun working in ceramics before Caitlin was born and had branched out into clay when she was still a child. Her mother could have made a decent living off the sale of her art, but she'd never wanted to work for others. Caitlin had once thought that she sounded too much like an artist, unwilling to sacrifice her art for money. As she grew older, Caitlin began to suspect that it was more a fear of rejection than anything else. No matter who told her that her work was outstanding, her mother was always self effacing, never willing to admit to herself that she was actually very talented.

"Thanks, I like it too."

"Does that fireplace work?"

"Of course, there's wood to the left of it. It has a gas igniter. The control is on the right. If you want to start it, I'll fix us a drink. What'll you have?"

"Anything. Whiskey if you have it. Preferably Irish, but on a night like this I'll take whatever is available."

"All right, I'll see what's stocked. Make sure you open the flue."

"I've done this before," John said as he walked toward the fireplace.

Caitlin went to the wall farthest from the door. A maple armoire stood against the wall. She punched a three-digit code into the small keypad on the right door and was rewarded by the click of an electric solenoid. The doors opened and revealed a well-stocked liquor cabinet. She selected a bottle of Black Bush for John and poured two inches into a wide tumbler. For herself, she chose a fine armagnac and splashed a similar amount into a snifter. The top of the armoire held a small microwave oven and she gave her glass a ten-second dose to break the chill.

She left the armoire open and carried both glasses with her. Passing by the light switch, Caitlin dimmed the lights until the room was murky. Then she went to the fireplace, where John was setting a last piece of split wood into the hearth. He turned the small brass key and gas flames ignited under the logs.

"The flue?"

"I was just getting to that."

"I didn't think you'd forget," Caitlin replied, surprised at the lightness in her tone.

John reached into the back of the fireplace and pulled the brass handle, shaped like a duck on the wing, forward.

"It slips through a hole. If you leave it in there it'll blacken."

John reached in and pulled the duck free. He hung it on the set of matching fireplace tools. When he turned, Caitlin held out the tumbler.

"Thanks."

"I didn't ask if you wanted ice."

He chuckled lightly and she found herself smiling.

"I think this will be cold enough. Don't they worry about their stuff freezing?" He said and sipped the whiskey.

"Not this, too much alcohol. The wine is kept in a climate controlled room in the basement."

The seasoned wood caught and she could feel the increased warmth. She motioned toward the thickly padded couch that faced the fire and John nodded.

Caitlin sat at one end and watched John take the opposite end without hesitation. She sniffed the heavy fumes of the armagnac. It burned her sinuses, but the aroma was heavenly. She sipped it. It was already cool, but it burned a path down her throat.

John was watching the flames, his drink balanced on one knee.

"Is that all right?" she asked.

"What? Oh, yeah, I'm surprised your parents keep Black Bush around."

"You surprise me. I wouldn't have thought you could tell the difference."

"I can't tell that many whiskeys by the taste, but I've always been fond of this one."

"I'm glad you like it."

Caitlin unzipped her coat as the fire warmed her front. She watched John as he continued to stare into the flames. His left side was toward her and the scar looked pink in the firelight.

"John."

"Yes?"

She was quiet for awhile and eventually he turned to face her.

"What is it?" he asked.

"These last twelve years, did you ever think about me?"

His eyes were dark lenses except where the sparkle of the fire reflected. His reply was slow in coming. "Is this where we're honest with one another?"

"Yes, please."

"Then, yes. I did think of you. Often at first, but less so as time went on. I wondered how you were. Where you were living. If you were happy."

He paused and, after a moment, she realized he was waiting for something from her.

She took a second to sip her drink and gathered her courage. "I used to look for you in crowds, at airports, crowded restaurants, that sort of thing."

"Oh?"

"Over the years, it became something of a hobby. I even thought I saw you once. I was changing planes at DFW. I saw a man with dark hair, shorter than yours is now, but similar in texture. I didn't get a good look at his face before the crowd separated us, but it could have been you ... before the scar anyway. I almost called after him, but the airport was very crowded and I don't think he would have heard. I caught one more glimpse of him from farther away. The walk, the build, they were familiar."

The firelight danced in his eyes and she could feel the indecision in the way he sat, perfectly still, as if any movement would upset the balance.

She sighed. "It's foolish. I shouldn't have mentioned it."

"Not so foolish. It could have been me. I used to go through DFW often."

His voice was warm, without the harsh edge that it had developed since the canyon.

Caitlin felt something, a connection that hadn't been there earlier. Could they be recovering some of what they'd had in the Canyon? What would it be like to fall in love again? The attraction she'd felt toward John in the Canyon hadn't reached the point of love and she could scarcely remember when she and Scott had first fallen for each other. She did recall that it had been a frantic, needing emotion. Neither of them had been able to get enough of the other. Their days and nights had been filled with sweet promises of the future and intense burning passion of the present. Would it be like that again or was that something that only came around once? Was that sort of intensity reserved for adolescents?

"What are you thinking?" he asked.

She realized she was still staring into his face and as a blush warmed her face she turned away to stare into the fire.

"Nothing really," she lied.

"I thought we were being honest."

"Okay, I was wondering if it would be possible to rediscover what we started in the Canyon."

He shrugged, one of those irritating male traits they used anytime they were avoiding the truth. "Anything is possible. Things will develop naturally if we let them."

When he didn't press his question further, she hesitantly changed the subject. "Do you think we'll be able to contact Louie?"

He accepted the shift in conversation. "I don't know. I'd sure like to find out what happened to him and I think we need to know how they got on to him. It could be important."

"You don't think they tailed us?"

"No. It's possible given enough resources to trail someone without their knowledge, but I would bet anything that we lost whoever might have been on us when we went through that alley."

"What's that leave? Could one of the people he asked to help break the encryption have turned him in?" she asked.

"I doubt it. They're a clannish group and none of them trusts the government. Besides, I really don't think they know where each other live. Still it's a possibility we'll have to consider."

"How about the file? Is there anyway they could have tracked him just because he was accessing the file? Perhaps he got the code. It could have transmitted some kind of signal when he activated it."

John nodded his head and then sipped his drink before replying. "That's possible, but not the most likely option. Louie is bright enough not to allow the program to use his Web link to transmit a signal when he opened it. No, if we weren't followed then Louie must have done something to bring the Feds attention, perhaps it wasn't even related to you or that file."

"You really think so?"

His head shook. "No, I'm afraid that's just wishful thinking."

His head tilted back and he downed the last of the whiskey.

"Would you like another?" she asked.

"No thanks. I think we're safe here, but I better not be impaired, just in case."

The combination of the fire and the furnace had finally brought the room temperature to the point where Caitlin wanted to remove her coat. She held out her glass to John. He took it and then she shrugged out of the heavy coat.

He returned the glass and she downed the remainder of the armagnac and stood up. "Well, I'm going to have another one. I'm too wired to sleep without some kind of aid. One more should mellow me out."

She turned off the gas to the fire and then went to the liquor cabinet. She fixed her another drink, nuked it for fifteen seconds, and returned to the couch.

John's head was back and for a moment, she thought he was staring at something on the ceiling. Then she realized his eyes were closed. Over the soft crackle of the fire, she could hear his deep, even breathing.

Sitting on the hearth, the fire warmed her back while she drank in the aroma of the armagnac and watched him sleep. He looked peaceful and calm for the first time since they'd come back together. What was his life like that he was so guarded with his feelings, so paranoid in his relationships, so dark and foreboding in his outlook on life?

She wanted to explore his feelings for her, but before she could realistically do that, she'd have to determine her own feelings. She had a strong attraction toward him, that much was clear. Was the attraction merely the result of depending on him to protect her, to rescue her again? Or was it something stronger?

A quarter of an hour passed before she finished her drink and set the glass aside. Caitlin closed the doors on the fireplace and gently shook John awake.

He awoke with a start and his hand jerked toward his shoulder holster.

"That won't be necessary. We're all friends here."

His eyes blinked twice in rapid succession and his lips drew back in a wide smile. "Did I fall asleep on you?"

"Understandably. Come on, I can give you a better place to sleep."

John took her outstretched hand. She tugged him up and then led him to the foyer. They paused to pick up their bags and went upstairs. At the upper floor she pointed out the bathroom and then indicated the bedroom on the left as the guestroom. As she released his hand, she stepped close and kissed him lightly on the lips.

"Goodnight, John. Sleep well."

"Sure, uh, you too."

Caitlin carried her bags into her bedroom and closed the door behind her.

CHAPTER 22

John jerked awake when the alarm sent an electric shock into his finger. His right hand reached for the gun he'd left on the nightstand and closed about its checkered grip. As the door opened, he brought the barrel up and applied pressure to the trigger.

Caitlin, wearing faded jeans, a green sweater, and bunny slippers stood in the doorway. Her left hand was still on the doorknob.

"Christ, you're fast," her voice was calm, calmer than John felt.

He lowered the gun and set it back on the nightstand.

"Did you forget how to knock?" he asked.

Her response began with a fast exhalation through her nostrils. "For your information I did knock. I guess I'll have to pound on the door next time."

"No, no that's all right. I'm sorry. I'm just not wide awake yet."

Her voice softened as fast as her features. "Forgiven. I've got coffee made. How do you like your burritos?"

"Burritos? How late did I sleep?"

"There's not a lot of food in the pantry. I found a few breakfast burritos in the freezer. We'll have to go shopping before lunch."

"Okay, did you find any salsa or cheese?"

"Sorry, I was kidding when I asked how you want them. We have a choice of dry goods or frozen food. Anything canned or refrigerated will have to come from the store."

"It looks like your parents could keep a few things down in the wine vault."

"They could, but they're gone for four months usually. Cheese and things like that might spoil even in the refrigerated room. Anyway, come on downstairs when you're ready, unless you want me to bring breakfast up to you?"

"No, that's not necessary. I'll be right down."

She smiled, and closed the door behind her.

John checked his watch. It was nearly ten, California time. He flipped the covers back and reached for the pants he'd left on the bedpost.

Five minutes later he walked into a country kitchen that teemed with the rich aroma of fresh coffee and spicy Mexican food. Caitlin was setting two plates on the table.

"Perfect timing," she said.

"I try."

"Sit down, I'll pour coffee. Is orange juice all right?"

He noticed the tall glass pitcher for the first time.

"Sure," he said and slid out the nearest chair.

Sunlight streamed into the windows that looked out on a small clearing and on thirty-foot ponderosas, everything was laden with thick snow. The light reflected off the snow in a million tiny rays, as if someone had sprinkled diamonds across the Maxwell's property.

John poured orange juice into the flowered glasses by each of their plates. Caitlin returned carrying two earthen mugs, steam rose in thick clouds from the coffee.

They chatted about inconsequential events and the beauty of the morning landscape as they ate. The burritos were spicy; a mixture of eggs, peppers, tomatoes, cilantro, and sausage. The orange juice, not fresh squeezed, had a thick pulp and a strong natural flavor. The coffee wasn't Gevalia, but was a rich roast.

By the time he'd finished two cups of coffee, he was ready to greet the day properly.

He helped Caitlin load the dishes in the dishwasher, then refilled both their cups. "I want to check out the perimeter. I need to know where everything is in case there's trouble."

"All right, I'll show you around. What size do you wear?"

"What size?"

"Dad's snow boots might fit you."

"That's all right. These will do," he said and indicated his own boots. The slip-on boots had eight-inch uppers and he regularly treated them with waterproofing.

"Aren't those cowboy boots? You'll fall on your butt with slick bottoms," Caitlin said with a laugh.

"The bottoms aren't slick, they're Neoprene. I won't have any trouble."

She shrugged. "Okay by me. Give me a minute to get my boots on."

John followed her back to the foyer, where she dug through the shoes in the front closet until she found a pair of leather, work boots toward the back. She sat on the steps and exchanged the bunny slippers for the boots.

His coat hung next to hers in the closet. John took them both down and held Caitlin's out for her.

"Thank you," she said as she slipped her arms into it.

He started pulling his on and grunted as the tight muscles in his left arm sent a spasm of pain through his shoulder.

"Is that arm stiff?"

"Yeah, but it'll pass in a couple of days," John answered as he moved his arm through a wide circle to limber it up.

"We should change the bandage," Caitlin said as she helped him into the sleeve.

"Later."

"Okay, tough guy."

Caitlin safed the alarm system and then opened the front door.

As John stepped out onto the porch, he had to stop and admire the view. The white crest of Pike's Peak soared above the nearest trees. Dark clouds approached the peak from the west, a sure indication of more snow on the way.

"I'd almost forgotten how beautiful it was up here."

Caitlin had stopped at the top step and was also taking in the view. "I never forget, but then I never get tired of it either."

"Why do your parents go to Florida in the winter? That's always been my favorite time in Colorado."

"Dad's arthritis started bothering him more over the last few years. Sometimes the cold exacerbates it."

"I thought the dry air would help."

"It does, but not enough to offset the cold. They don't like to miss the winter either. That's why they're only gone from December to May."

Caitlin led the way down the steps and around the side of the house. She followed the path left through the snow by whoever had been there last. They reached the power meter on the side of the house, but the tracks continued past it.

They stopped by the meter and John felt an uncomfortable sensation between his shoulder blades. He turned and examined the line of trees that were not more than fifty feet away. Nothing moved. "I guess that answers the question of who it wasn't. Now let's see if we can't find out where they did go."

The tracks led to a small shed near the tree line. There was a clear arc where the snow had been pressed back by the opening door. A large Master padlock was closed in the hasp.

"What's in there?" He asked.

"Garden tools, lawnmower, the usual stuff."

"Would your neighbor have a reason to go in there?"

"Who, Abe? I don't know. Dad probably told him where the key is, but I wouldn't think he'd have to bother with any of that stuff. Besides, the footprints only come to here. If Abe came by he'd check all the way around the house and inside too."

"You have the key?" he asked.

"Sure, it's right over the door."

John ran his fingers along the top of the doorjamb. Sure enough, there was a small brass key on the ledge. He took it down and inserted it in the lock. The key turned smoothly and the padlock clicked open.

Caitlin crowded his elbow. He put a hand on her arm and stopped her.

"I'd like you to stand behind that tree," he said and pointed to a nearby pine.

"What for?"

"Caitlin, we don't know who was in here and someone has tried to kill you already. I think it'd be better if you weren't too close to the door when I open it."

Her eyes widened. "You don't think there's a bomb?"

"No, I don't, but I'd rather play it safe.

"What about you?"

"I'll be careful, but we need to know why someone has been in here."

Her voice was tight and filled with emotion. "No, we don't. We can walk back to the house and forget it, act like we never saw the tracks. There's no point in risking your life unnecessarily."

"Caitlin, it could be important. I've handled booby traps before, I'm just being careful."

She crossed her arms in front of her and pursed her lips. "No. I'm not moving. If it's safe enough for you then it's safe enough for me."

"Be reasonable, there's no sense in both of us being here to open the door. It's just not necessary."

"John, I'm not leaving."

He stared at her for a minute. He was half tempted to pick her up and carry her back in the house. But it was her life, she'd hired him to protect her, but not from herself.

"All right then, you're the boss. Stand to my right, at least an arm's length away."

She moved to where he directed. Her arms unfolded and she stretched her fingers out to touch him.

"How's this?"

Although he felt like chuckling, his voice was stern as he replied, "You needn't be so literal."

She grinned at him and he shook his head as if disgusted with her.

He checked the hasp for wires, then pulled it back. He couldn't see any wiring. He eased the door slowly open, listening for the ominous click of a pressure switch. When it was barely open, he took out his pocketknife and extended the longest blade. Moving it backwards, in the space between door and jamb, he determined there was nothing attached to the back of the door.

He closed the knife and pulled the door open. Just inside the entrance, on the seat of a riding lawn mower, was a box with UPS Red markings.

"It's all right," he said.

Caitlin pushed against him to peer inside.

"Were you expecting a package?"

"No, I wasn't planning to come up here again until Mom and Dad got home."

"Well then, let's see who it's from."

The yellow copy of the invoice was folded and shoved under the edge of the box. He slipped it out and passed it to Caitlin.

She unfolded the paper and read it silently for a moment. "It's from Scott."

"Oh? To you?"

"Yes."

"If he sent it UPS Red, then he must have sent it recently. What's the date on it?"

"Four days ago. The day I left for San Francisco."

"Uh oh," He said.

"What? What do you mean?"

"He sent it to you here, the day before he was killed. I'd say that what's in this box is the little item that got him killed."

"Of course, what else could it be? Open it."

John looked from the box to Caitlin. "Are you sure you want to do that? Sometimes it's better to remain ignorant. We could give it back and convince them that you never saw the contents."

"Screw that! They've already tried to kill me and they did kill Scott. I want to know what's so damn important that they're willing to kill for it."

"All right, but you probably ought to wait until we're back in the house." John picked the box up, it wasn't very heavy, maybe ten pounds, and held it out to Caitlin.

She took it from him, hefted it a couple of times like she was estimating its weight, then stuck in under her left arm. "Okay, let's go."

"First things first. I still want to look around the property. Did you say there was another path out of here besides the driveway?"

"Not much of a path, it's for people on foot not for cars. Although, I suppose the Jeep could make it."

"Show me."

She led him toward the southeast corner of the property. The trees thinned in that direction and John watched carefully to judge whether the Jeep would be able to get between them. A hundred yards into the forest, the land dropped sharply for about twenty feet. It descended about the same distance giving a nearly smooth forty-five degree slope, then the path opened onto a clearing that continued down slope for at least a quarter mile. A four-strand, barbed wired fence bisected the field.

"That's Abe Jackson's property. You can just make out his stable at the far end of the clearing."

"Yes, I see it."

"There's a drive leading away from it that will take you down to the road."

"Which road is it?"

"The last one we passed before turning onto ours. You can either turn left there and come out on highway 24 near Falcon or you can turn right and you'll meet back up with Black Forest Road in a couple of miles."

"All right, this looks good. The Jeep shouldn't have any problems fitting between these trees and this slope certainly won't bother it."

"Well, there is something else. You see those lumps in the snow?"

John gazed out across the white expanse. It was difficult to see any contrast in the bright sunlight.

"Yeah, I think I see what you're talking about. What are they?"

"Rocks, the field's littered with them. Some are big enough to rip the oil pan out from under the Jeep."

"That wouldn't be good. Maybe I had better brush the snow away from them."

"That would take hours," Caitlin said.

"Yeah, but it beats having a busted oil pan."

"Later then, if you really want to I'll come out and help you later."

"You in a hurry to get back to the house?"

She held up the box. "What do you think?"

"I think you need to learn patience," he said and then broke into a grin.

"Patience my Aunt Betsy. Let's go."

They walked side by side through the deep snow back to the house.

Caitlin set the package on a table beneath a tall mirror in the foyer while she shrugged out of her coat.

John eased out of his, removing the coat didn't hurt his shoulder as much as putting it on. He hung both of their coats in the closet while she picked up the package and carried it into the great room.

When he caught up with her, she was sitting on the sofa, the torn wrapping of the package at her feet, the box to one side of her, and a letter in her hands.

He sat down on the other side of the box and watched her face as she read. After a few seconds, he grew uncomfortable watching the emotion that darkened her eyes and looked away. Whatever she was reading was personal and she deserved her privacy.

John lifted the box from between them and set it in his lap. Foam had been sprayed into the box to form a custom fitted, shock-absorbing package. He worked the top of the foam out and stared inside. There were four objects in the box. One was another DVD and two of the objects appeared identical. They were oblong like pointy eggs, about the size of hen eggs, and gold in color. His memory drew up a Disney movie from his childhood about a goose and golden eggs and he almost laughed at the connection. Rather than shiny like the goose's eggs, these had a mat finish. Clear jewels (diamonds?) encrusted the surface and a small eyehook protruded from the blunt end. A gold chain ran through the hook. It was a necklace.

The fourth object looked like a bicycle helmet. It was head sized and vented like most bicycle helmets, but it was made of metal. There was a hole in one side of the helmet, that appeared to be the size of the little gold eggs.

John eased one of the eggs from the foam. It was heavy, but not as heavy as solid gold would be. He held it up and watched the light reflect off the gems.

Pretty, but certainly not diamonds. Diamonds wouldn't reflect rainbow patterns that way.

"Scott calls it the Phoenix Egg. It's a telephone."

John looked at Caitlin. Her eyes were misty like she'd been near the point of crying.

"A telephone?" he asked and raised the Egg to his ear.

"What are you doing?"

"Listening for a dial tone."

"Don't be ridiculous."

"You're the one who said it was a telephone."

"It's not that kind of phone," she said.

"So I gather. So, the Phoenix Egg? Interesting name. You realize there's no such thing as a Phoenix Egg, don't you?"

She wiped her eyes with the back of her wrist and nodded. "I remember. The Phoenix is a mythical bird that dies every five hundred years and is reborn in fire. It's immortal, but never has off-spring. Therefore, no egg."

"I wonder if they christened with that named for a reason, or if it was just made in Arizona."

“He doesn’t say.”

“You want to tell me what's in the letter?"

"It's from Scott. He gives a very brief description of this thing and talks about what it does."

"Did he say anything about how he got involved or who these people are who want it?"

She shook her head. Reaching in to the box, she took out the other oval, and turned it over in her hand.

"He says the file he sent me contains a full schematic and manufacturing details necessary to build the helmet. The disk in the box contains the details on the eggs themselves."

"So it is a helmet. If the eggs are telephones, then what's the helmet, a switchboard?"

Caitlin lifted the helmet out of the box and turned it over. The underside had a smooth transparent layer covering an intricate circuit layout.

"It's the encoder," she said.

"You're going to have to expand on that. What does it encode?"

"He didn't go into much detail. He expected me to get everything from the files, but he said that you just load one of the eggs into the helmet." She turned it over and indicated the slot John had noticed. "Then you put the helmet over your head. It encodes the Egg to your particular brain waves."

"Brain waves? What does that have to do with a telephone?"

"It's a more than a telephone, that's just the way he describes it. In fact, he refers to it as an cyberphone."

"Cyberphone?"

"He said the inventor came up with the name. It's a translating interneural transceiver."

"That's a mouthful, but wouldn't that be a tit-phone?"

She almost smiled, then nodded, and wiped at her eyes. "We are not calling it a titphone. The Egg can translate brain waves into intelligent signals, then a source inside the Egg transmits those signals to another unit."

"What? Are you kidding me? This thing can transmit thoughts?"

"Something like that. Scott says it transmits thoughts from the speech center, not just anything you happen to be thinking. It only picks up thoughts that would become verbal after being processed and sent to the vocal cords. It really is more like a telephone than a thought transmitter."

John stared at the Egg in his hand. "Caitlin, is this some kind of flimflam?"

"What? I don't understand."

"You know, flimflam, as in deception, a ruse. Could this be some kind of scheme to rip off investors."

Her voice was both angry and hurt. "How could you say something like that? Scott may have had faults, but he wasn't a crook."

"I'm sorry, but I find it hard to believe that they could put that sort of technology into this small a package. Hell, it's hard enough to believe that anyone has come up with the technology at all. They've been studying brain waves for generations and I've never seen any reports that they might be able to translate brain waves into speech without using the brain to do it."

"So? Just because you haven't read about it doesn't mean that it isn't possible. A lot of research goes on without the intermediate results winding up in open literature."

"Granted, but this ... It hardly seems likely that someone could develop both the technology and the packaging simultaneously. Usually the technology is around for years before the package is ready to market. Hell, look at HDTV. That technology was around forever before they finally settled on a standard and started manufacturing the things."

"Every company had their own standard they wanted used until the government got them together to decide on a particular one. Maybe this time someone wanted to avoid letting other companies have access to the standard. This way they can bring the product to market without any competitors. By the time someone else can develop the technology, they'll have the patent and have a lock on the system."

Her eyes widened, as she seemed to realize the importance of something. "My God, it'll be just like the telephone system in the early days. One company will control the entire market. This could make telephones obsolete, the market value of this product is beyond comprehension."

He put a hand on her arm. "Whoa now. Don't you think you're being a little over reactive? So it could replace phones, there will still be the need for the infrastructure that's already set up. Even if they work, you'll still need switchboards, satellite relays, and even operators. It'll be like when cellular phones were introduced. Sure there was a tremendous market, but it didn't affect the existing market."

"But this time there won't be a hundred different companies trying to set up local service. There'll only be one with the patent, with the technology."

"All right, I can see that. But I can't see why you make it sound like the company that brings it out will have some kind of ultimate power. It's still just a phone system."

Her face was so pallid, so ashen that he thought she might faint.

"I don't think you're seeing the whole picture, John. I think this will obsolete every phone on the planet almost over night."

"Come on, aren't you being melodramatic?"

"No. Scott's letter mentioned one other item about this thing."

"And that was?"

"Because of where it interacts with the brain, it bypasses the language center. When you talk with someone else, it doesn't matter whether they're speaking English or Russian or Swahili. That's where the ultra part comes in. It stands for universal language translator."

Shit, when she was right she was right. It was more than just a telephone. What would something like that be worth to the company or government that had initial control of it? Billions certainly, trillions? Whatever the final value, there was no doubt that people would kill to acquire it. No doubt whatsoever.

John felt a sudden wave of apprehension. He'd been underestimating the value of what Scott had acquired. He hadn't taken all possible precautions. They'd already reached Louie, were Squeeze and Felipe in danger too? He had to warn them, and then they'd better get on the move. If the device could actually do what Caitlin said no place would be safe for them until they disposed of it. No, not disposed, they had to get it to someone with enough power to defend themselves against the others who wanted it. Who? The Japanese gentlemen from JETRO, the NCIX, somehow he didn't think the group Holdren represented would allow either of them to keep it.

Without warning, Caitlin popped the Egg she held into the helmet's slot and set the helmet over her head.

"Hey!" He said, too late to stop her. "My God, Caitlin, what do you think you're doing?"

She fastened the thin chinstrap and met his gaze. "I'm going to try it out. They killed Scott for this, I'm going to see if it really works."

"How do you know it's ready to use? It may have to be prepped or something? What if it's dangerous?"

"More dangerous than not knowing? They've killed for this. I have to know if it's real."

"Did Scott say anything about how to set it up? Where's the on button?"

"The rest of it was personal, something about our honeymoon. He just said that you put the Egg in the helmet and put it on. That's all there is to it."

"Then how will you know when it's finished?"

Her face showed her uncertainty and she shrugged. "Christ, Caitlin. Wait, you said he talked about your honeymoon. Was there something in particular about it?"

"That's personal."

"I don't mean that. I mean did he mention any places, things you saw, you know something that could be used as the password for the file."

"Yes, the town we went to in Mexico. That could be the password."

"Where's your computer?"

"In my case, upstairs in my room."

She started to get up, but John put a hand on her arm. "No, let me get it. You shouldn't be walking around with that thing on your head. We don't know what it's doing. It might suddenly make you fall asleep or make you dizzy. Christ, they're screwing around with your thoughts. Who knows what this thing could do to you?"

"I don't think it's dangerous. Scott would have warned me if it were."

"Yeah? Well maybe the warning is in the computer file."

"You really are the most paranoid person in the world."

He shrugged. "Just because you're paranoid--"

"Yeah, I know, it doesn't mean they're not out to get you. Really John, don't you think that sounds contrived?"

Again, he shrugged. "I'll be right back."

Her purse was on top of the dresser in her room. He took it and hurried back to her. She watched him walk down the stairs without comment. Stopping in front of her, he held out the case.

"I'm not dead yet. I...."

She convulsed and flopped limply back on the sofa.

"Ah shit!" He said and sat down beside her. He checked her throat for a pulse then pried back one eyelid.

Her eye stared back at him.

"Jesus H. Christ. What the hell's wrong with you?" He snapped and jerked his hand back from her face.

She sat upright, the grin on her face irritatingly coy. "Lighten up John. It was just a joke."

"How can you joke about it? A minute ago you were ... never mind."

"What? I was upset about Scott? Damned right and I still am, but you can't run on just remorse. You have to have humor or you might as well be dead too."

He wanted to argue, but what was the use? He passed the computer case to her and waited for her to boot up the system.

She loaded in the DVD and called up the protected program. When it asked for the password, Caitlin typed in something too quick for him to follow.

The screen went from black to blue, then text appeared.

"All right, we're in." She paged down to the contents. There was an executive summary, a list of construction drawings, and chapters broken into different aspects of the techniques of design and theoretical operation of the device.

"Well, that's about everything you'd need to build it."

"See who the author is."

Caitlin paged back to the cover sheet, but instead of the usual document page that detailed the writer, inventor, and document reviewers, there was a single line of text that said R.E. Curtis.

"I suppose that could be the inventor," she said.

"Then why doesn't it say so, besides anything with this level of sophistication will normally have an entire team of researchers. Where's the background on the development? Did one man invent and then put his invention into these cute packages?" He asked as he rolled the other Egg around in his hand."

"I don't know? Perhaps the executive overview will go into it."

"All right, you read it. I'm going to set a few things up in case we get unexpected visitors."

"All right."

John set the Egg back in it's foam shell and went to the stairs. He turned back to look at Caitlin. She was leaning forward over the computer. Her gaze was intent, but the bicycle helmet spoiled the air of concentration. He shook his head. What the hell had Scott gotten her mixed up in? His gut told him to get rid of the devices and the disk and then have Felipe make them up permanent identities so they could disappear for awhile, like twenty or thirty years.

He climbed the stairs and went into the guestroom. Taking his case from the corner, he opened it and started removing things.

When he went back downstairs, Caitlin was still hunched over the computer. He slipped his coat on and went outside. It was just over a hundred yards to the road. He hiked through the snow, staying in the ruts as much as possible until he reached the last trees.

He moved off the road and squatted next to a large pine. Using a length of monofilament line, he fastened a CCD camera to the trunk, just above the snow. He slipped his glasses on and powered up the camera, then he adjusted the camera until the image covered the entrance to the drive and the road beyond. Setting the camera's controls to the auto detect position, John stood up. He broke a small branch from the tree and backed to the driveway, smearing out his tracks as he went. There, they would have a warning if anyone came to the house, but it wasn't enough. It'd only give them a few seconds at best. He needed something else; a land mine would be nice.

Unfortunately, he didn't have one, but something could be arranged.

He walked back to the house and went around back to the shed where they'd found the package. He opened the door and looked around inside. There was a small stack of lumber stored on the rafters. He took a couple of used 2x4 studs down and searched the workbench until he found a box of eight inch nails. Ten minutes later, every nail was embedded in the studs.

John carried the spiked studs out, closed the door behind him, and went back down the driveway. Fifty feet from the road, he laid the studs diagonally across the drive and brushed snow across them.

The Colorado sun had warmed the day and John unzipped his coat as he walked back to the house. He reached the porch and turned to gaze across the thirty odd miles to Pikes Peak. Dark clouds enveloped the crest and everything west of the Front Range, but on this side it was sunny and the incredibly bright blue, which John always thought of as Colorado blue, lit the heavens with an intensity he'd forgotten. He leaned against one of the bark-less tree trunks that held up the porch and a smile grew bright on his face.

Why did he move to the Bay Area? The sky there, when you could see it at all, was never more than a bluish white that paled beneath the glorious skies of God's country. Perhaps it was time he moved back. He had a nice nest egg put away. He could afford to buy a piece of land back in the mountains somewhere, maybe out near Durango. There were places out there that hadn't been Californicated like the Aspen and Vail regions. Perhaps it was time he settled down. Perhaps even with Caitlin. Yes, she needed to disappear anyway. He would have Felipe generate new identities for them and they could squirrel themselves away where the government, Frenchmen, and Japanese businessmen would never look for them. There were reservation schools in the Four Corners region that needed teachers. They could do volunteer work on the reservation, make a difference in some kid's life.

John straightened and his face darkened into a frown. Sure, they could do that. If they lived long enough. He turned away from the approaching storm clouds and went inside.

*　　　*　　　*

Felipe never opened his warehouse office until noon. Most of his business was done during the hours of darkness and afternoon drop-ins such as John and Caitlin's were the exception rather than the rule. Usually he spent the afternoons in the never-ending quest to keep his old database up to date and to acquire new ones. Felipe always tried to have at least one spare entry into the government's computer files. You could never predict when some over-eager programmer working for barely more than minimum wage would detect his illegal access.

He opened the small outside door next to the main garage doors and locked it behind him. He didn't turn on the overhead lamps because the high windows cast enough light onto the warehouse floor to see by. Unlocking his office door, Felipe reached for the light switch as he stepped inside.

As the fluorescents lit a voice said, "It's about time. I was about to give up on you."

Felipe reached for the revolver beneath his jacket, but stopped as he saw the large bore automatic pointed at his gut from ten feet away.

"What do you want?" he asked.

Dewatre rose from Felipe's chair and stepped out from behind his desk. "You provided services for a John Blalock and Caitlin Maxwell less than 24 hours ago. I need the names you gave them and their destination."

Felipe stared at the man's eyes and wished he'd taken that vacation he'd been promising himself.

CHAPTER 23

Caitlin had a fire going in the fireplace when John came in. He shrugged out of his coat, stifling a moan as he did, and laid it across the newel post at the foot of the stairs.

"You finish reading the file already?"

"Sort of."

She was smiling like the little girl who had a secret that he didn't know. He walked to the fire and stood with his back to it. "Sort of? What's that smile mean?"

She gazed up at him from the couch, but didn't answer.

After a few seconds John noticed the gold Egg hanging on it's chain, just above her breasts. "Hey, you took the bicycle helmet off. Was it through doing whatever it does?"

"Yes. It took about five minutes. Now it's your turn."

John couldn't help taking a single involuntary step backwards. "Whoa, I never said anything about trying it."

"You have too. How can I tell if it really does what the file says unless there's someone else to communicate with."

The helmet rested on the cushion next to her. The other Egg was already in its slot.

"How come I'm getting flashbacks to The Puppet Masters? You're going to have to convince me that it hasn't done anything to your mind before I try the thing on."

"John, don't be silly. It's perfectly harmless. There's one thing I found that it can do which already makes it the most valuable invention since the computer."

He hadn't thought her smile could get any wider, but then it did. "Okay, start talking."

"Come on, put the helmet on. It'll take more than five minutes to tell you and once the communicator is keyed into your brain waves it'll go much faster and you'll understand without doubting."

She held out the helmet.

John looked at it, then stared into her eyes. "It's safe? It didn't mess you up?"

"Perfectly safe. You have my word."

He took the helmet from her. It was a lot heavier than a bicycle helmet. Adjusting the strap, he pulled it over his head and clinched the strap down.

"I feel foolish," he said.

"You won't regret it. Here, let me show you what I've found."

Caitlin picked up her notebook computer and he noticed that she'd attached the radio modem to it.

"You haven't been making phone calls, have you?"

"No. You see the Phoenix Egg communicates with other units on one of the frequencies currently reserved for cell phone communications. By selecting the right band on the modem you can link the communicator's signal to a cell phone and therefore anything else that the phone can link to."

"Okay, that's interesting, but what good is it? Oh, I see, you can use the cell phone system to talk from one communicator to another, but wouldn't you need an access chip."

"The communicator is programmable. I used my computer to download the chip code on my phone and then transmitted it to the Egg."

"Wait, until you had this Egg..." he stopped and shook his head.

"What's the matter?" she asked.

"You're going to have to come up with a better name for this thing. The 'Egg' just doesn't sound good and communicator is too awkward. You need something snazzy like 'cell phone'."

"You're right, how about what the inventor called it, cyberphone?" she asked.

"I don't know. It seems like everything has cyber tacked onto it these days. Since it works like telepathy, I'd say tele phone, but that's been done."

Caitlin chuckled. "Cute. See, you don't have to be serious all the time."

"Who says I wasn't being serious? I know, we'll call it an egg phone."

Caitlin's faced twisted into a pained expression. "Sounds too much like a Chinese dish."

"I like Chinese."

"So do I, but let's be serious, or at least not stoogeish."

"Hey! Don't knock the Stooges."

"Look, when you come up with a better name, let me know. Now stop interrupting," Caitlin said.

"All right already." He held his hands in front of him as if fending her off.

"I was telling you that I linked the Egg, ah how about neuralphone, to my computer."

"Neural phone, yeah, that sounds better. You were going to explain how you loaded the chip code into this neuralphone so you could access the computer."

"You're interrupting again."

"Sorry."

"I loaded the chip code by telling the neuralphone to record it."

"Huh?"

"Once it's linked to your brain waves you can modify its programming for things like that by just telling it, well thinking at it anyway," Caitlin said.

"So you just thought at it. Yeah, that makes sense." John struggled to keep his face calm, even though he wanted to laugh out loud. The whole thing was bordering the absurd.

"That's right. Then came the really neat part. Here," she turned the computer so he could see the screen, "watch the monitor."

The communications screen was open. Without Caitlin touching the computer, the active screen shrunk into the background and Scott's file opened up. It flashed to the contents, then begin to page down at about a page a second.

"Whoa, how'd you do that?"

"I told you, the neuralphone can link into anything that can receive its signal. I'm telling the computer what to do over the neuralphone."

"Direct access. Fan-fucking-tastic. I'm impressed, but why are you paging down so fast, you can't read anything like that."

"What makes you think so?"

The flash of passing pages doubled in speed.

John stared at the screen for a second, then he met Caitlin's gaze. "You've got to be kidding me!"

She laughed and shook her head gleefully. "Not at all. It is fantastic, John. I can access anything on my computer one hundred, maybe two hundred, times faster than I can read it."

"How can that be? I mean ... hell, I don't know what I mean, but I just don't see how it's possible," he said.

"I don't either. I read the entire file. With the proper tools and a good manufacturing facility I could reproduce these communicators without ever looking at the blueprints again."

"What? How can you remember that much?"

"I don't know that either. Somehow, when it transmits the information into your head, you can concentrate on it and it will be remembered. I could no more forget the contents of that file now than I could forget my mother's name. Using a computer analogy, it's as if you can tell the neuralphone to load the information into nonvolatile memory or regular memory."

"Nonvolatile? Wait a minute, then couldn't you load in too much? Isn't there a danger of over filling your brain with information? What happens then? Will you be walking around remembering things that you can't ever forget, but be unable to learn anything new, like what time you're suppose to meet someone for lunch?"

"I don't think that's likely to happen. They say we never use more than ten percent of our brains, there should be plenty of storage space, but even if there isn't, I get the impression that you could overwrite memories if you want to."

It took a second for what Caitlin had said to sink in, but when it did John felt a rush of nausea. Sweat broke out on his forehead as his paranoia flared into a feverish state.

"Overwrite memories? Good God, Caitlin. You mean someone could use this to erase your memory? We've got to destroy this."

"No, not overwriting memories like that. You couldn't ... well, maybe you could. I don't know John, but I know it's too valuable to destroy."

"Yeah? Well so was the first nuclear weapon. Caitlin, just because it's a technological breakthrough doesn't mean it's something we're ready for."

A male voice said, "Adaptation complete."

John jerked his head toward the door. His hand automatically went to his gun. There was no one there. He turned toward the windows, but still couldn't see where the voice had come from.

He slipped the Colt from its holster and motioned for Caitlin to stay where she was. "John? What's the matter?"

"Someone's here. Stay low. It may be trouble."

"You heard a voice say adaptation complete?"

"Of course I did. Didn't you?" His gaze darted from window to door and back again.

"John, that was the neuralphone. It was just telling you that it had finished its programming."

"No, I heard someone's voice."

"I know John. That's what I heard when mine finished. Look at me."

He turned to face her.

"You can put the gun away John. There's no one here but us." Her words were clear, but her lips hadn't moved when she spoke.

"Well I'll be hanged." He holstered his gun. "The damn thing really works."

"Take the helmet off. Then let's figure out what these things can do together."

John unfastened the helmet. The oval phone slipped easily from its slot. He passed the helmet to Caitlin and dropped the necklace over his head.

"Okay now what?" he thought toward her.

She grinned and responded the same way. "Isn't it easy?"

"Yeah, but we could just as easily talk."

Now that he was paying attention, he could detect the difference between what he heard her say and what she sent over the communicator. It didn't really sound like sound at all, but almost like memory of something she'd said. At first, he thought the words were set apart because he couldn't hear the feeling that he did in her voice. It was almost as if she were speaking in a monotone. As he listened, he began to detect subtle differences in her words. There was emotional content there, but he was having trouble deciphering it. It was like he had to learn to interpret words all over again.

"What kind of range does it have?" he asked.

"A mile or so, it's just like any radio in that concern. With good conditions like over the water it'd have a greater range."

"A mile is good. If it's working off radio frequencies then it'd be simple to rig up a repeater to extend the range."

"Or, you can use it like I did with the cell phone. If you have the code for a phone it'd be simple to place a call," she said.

"I don't know about that part. Linking to your computer is something I still don't understand. There are protocols for digital communications. How does it convert voice to a computer signal?"

"It's not really a voice signal, but the protocol is simple enough. The Eggs were programmed with the basic IEEE protocol format when they were manufactured. The cell phone format was done at the same time."

John hefted the neuralphone in his hand. "That seems like a lot of computing capability for something this small."

"Yeah, that does puzzle me. I'd have thought that the designer would have built ungainly looking prototypes rather than these neat little things."

"That's what I meant earlier. These look too much like a marketable device. Where are the real prototypes?"

A wave of information washed over him. He staggered under the sudden reception of hundreds of pages of information.

"Whoa, slow down! What the hell are you doing?"

"I thought it'd be easier to just give it all to you rather than trying to explain bits and pieces."

"I don't know if I want all that."

"What's the matter?"

"I'm just uncomfortable with the idea of things being written into my memory."

"Really John. That doesn't sound like you at all. You were a doctoral student in computer science twelve years ago. Don't you still have the desire to learn?"

As much as he hated to admit it, she had a point. He did keep up with everything in the business. This was just a faster and more efficient way of learning. "Yes, imagine what it'll do to schools. Why, you could learn a semester's worth of information in a week!"

"Yeah, but you know as well as I do that remembering information is not the same as understanding. I guess there are fields where memorization is enough. Ha. I remember one professor that always poked fun at the biology majors. He'd say that if you could just memorize by rote then you could get a degree in biology, but if you wanted an engineering degree you had to understand the information."

"Yes, but think of history and English, basic math, and foreign languages. All the basic classes could be learned through memorization," Caitlin said.

"Hey, I'm not arguing the point. I agree with you. Much of my early education was taken up with hours and hours of memorization. I never was very good at languages. I tried

Spanish in high school and college and I managed to get by, but I've forgotten most of what I learned."

"But you won't need to learn foreign languages any more. These communicators give anyone instant access to any language. If you only spoke Swahili and I only spoke Hindi, we could still carry on this conversation as if we were both speaking the same language," Caitlin said.

The heat of the fire was making John's backside warm. He stepped away from the fire and sat down on the opposite end of the couch. "That's a part of this thing's capability that I still don't comprehend."

He found that they had begun to carry on the conversation by both audible and inaudible methods.

Caitlin nodded. "I don't either. The file doesn't go into enough detail on how it operates, just on what its capabilities are."

"Okay, go ahead and send me the rest of the file. I've gone this far. I might as well go the rest of the way."

He leaned back and closed his eyes. The images of the file swept over him sequentially until the index flashed by.

"Won't be needing that."

"What's that?"

"The index and contents. Like you said, I can remember all of it, just as though I'd written it myself. This is damned spooky. How was someone able to keep this level of technology hidden away while it was being developed?"

"I guess the same way the government classifies everything in the interest of national security," Caitlin said.

"Somehow, I don't think it worked that way. There are too many players in this game." John paused, then continued, "You know, I've been thinking."

"Oh?"

"Yeah, I'm concerned about your safety."

She reached out and put a hand on his. "I know. You're such a dear."

Her words came through both the air and the device and while he'd begun to connect emotions with words, this time it was pronounced. Her speech had feelings attached, but her unspoken words were saturated with emotional content. The intensity of her emotion surprised him and he felt an inward rush of feelings that matched hers.

Caitlin jerked her hand back from his as if she'd been burned. The emotion he'd been receiving disappeared instantly.

Her eyes met and held his. "My God. I had no idea."

"Neither did I."

Slowly, as if he were afraid of frightening her, he stretched out his hand and cupped hers.

With the first contact of her skin, he felt her emotions flowing back over him. There was a warmth, a caring, to them that he'd never felt from anyone. It was nearly as intense as the emotion he'd felt toward her all those years ago in the Canyon. But there was also a fear in her emotions.

"What's wrong? What are you afraid of?"

Her face mirrored her emotions and for a moment, the fear overwhelmed the other feelings. "This is wrong. It shouldn't be able to do this. Nothing was mentioned about this capability in the file."

She was right. The detailed capabilities of the device made no mention of emotional transfers. "Whoever tried these out before apparently never touched."

"But the theory of operation didn't predict anything other than a straight flow of communication. This is too much like reading your thoughts."

"I know. Do you want to stop?" he asked.

"No, I...."

She suddenly laughed and her fear disappeared.

"What is it?"

"I was the one who wanted to explore its capabilities and yet as soon as we discover something we didn't know about it, I freeze up."

"It's understandable."

"But how does it work?" she asked.

"Well, we know it uses the necklace as an antenna for both brain and radio waves. Perhaps by actually touching we're getting a more direct coupling between the circuits."

"Then would more contact intensify the connection?"

"Shall we see?" he asked.

Caitlin raised her other hand and held it out. John raised his and their fingers intertwined. The intensity did grow, not geometrically, but not linearly either.

He could feel how she felt, feel her warmth toward him, feel her concern for his safety, her love. It was like nothing he'd ever imagined. It was like being a child again, when your mother was taking care of you. When no matter what else the world might do to you, the love of this one person would always be there. It was the feelings you have when your dog sits by your side and places his head in your hand. It was like sitting on the beach and watching a golden harvest moon rise over the surf. It was all that and more. Her emotion swept over him like the tide, it enveloped him in a warm embrace, and for the first time in years, John felt like there was hope for the world, that not everything was cynical and cold. There was a bond between people that could be good; a bond that could bring friendship and caring and love.

At first he tried to deny his feelings toward her, but found them impossible to hide or disguise. He accepted her feelings, feeling them warm and thaw his own emotions until he was able to return everything she gave him with equal intensity.

John watched her face soften and blush with a warmth that brought tears to her eyes.

There was so much he wanted to tell her. But words were unnecessary. Even as he had the thoughts, his emotions flowed outward at a pace words could not maintain. His fingers loosened in hers, but didn't break the connection as they traveled up her arms. He swept her into his arms and they held each other in a loving embrace.

Her breath was hot against his neck. It tickled tiny hairs and caused an erotic sensation to work its way across his skin. He turned his face toward hers and exhaled softly. A moment later he felt her response to his breath send a similar sensation through his mind. His lips brushed the surface of her skin and they marveled at the intimate touch. Her lips touched his ear lobe and they shivered.

Simultaneously, their faces turned and their lips met, softly, gently, as if neither could withstand a sudden burst of new sensation.

They undressed each other, hurriedly, but careful to never break the intimate connection between them. Their love play was soft, gentle, but with an intensity neither had ever experienced before. As their skin to skin contact grew, the more intimate their link became, until when he entered her body their sensations merged and there were no longer separate feelings only mutual combined emotions.

Much later, they lay together on the sofa. Her body was stretched out atop his. Sweat dampened her hair and formed tiny rivulets that ran down her cheek and dripped onto his. She kissed him on each eye, her touch a gossamer mist.

She placed another kiss on his lips and stretched backwards. The hard surface of her neuralphone pulled from between them and hung between the tight flesh of her breasts.

He didn't have to open his eyes to see all this, but then he did open them. His locked on hers and for a moment he was looking at himself staring up at him. He blinked and the double awareness slipped away.

"You needn't speak." Her lips didn't move from their lazy smile.

"I know," he replied. Then he finished his thoughts in wordless communications. "I could lay here forever."

"As could I," her touch said.

"You were so right. This is too precious a thing to destroy."

"I didn't know how precious."

"We have to make sure it gets released properly. The government would fuck it up and a company would try to monopolize it," John said.

"What else is there?"

"We can transmit the information freely. Give it to everyone, every country, every person. Then there'll be no point in their hunting you and no way for them to misuse its powers."

"Yes, the Web. We can transmit the file over the Web to everyone. Once it becomes public knowledge no one will be able to patent the technology or copyright the information."

She moved against him and he smiled as he felt her discomfort. "I know. I don't want to break the connection either, but we'll have to sooner or later."

She laughed. "Yes, won't we? I'll be right back."

Caitlin disengaged and rolled off him. As she stood, she trailed her fingers across his chest, twisting a clump of chest hair as she did. Her emotions fell away from his senses as she drew back until finally, she broke the contact.

She gasped and swayed on her feet with that sudden lightheadedness from standing too soon and he felt an almost nauseous wave pass over him.

He reached toward her.

"Oh my God," she said aloud.

Her fingers dropped back to brace herself against his chest. Instantly, their emotions melded again.

"This is going to be tougher than I thought," she said.

"Yes, try again. We can't go through life joined at the hip."

They laughed simultaneously.

One finger at a time, Caitlin eased off his chest. The sensations thinned gradually and when her index finger finally broke the connection, she wavered again, but this time she smiled down at him. "Goodness, this could become addictive."

"But such a sweet addiction," he answered, his voice low and filled with unaccustomed emotion.

"Yes. I'll be right back."

She padded naked out of the living room. He watched her until she disappeared down the hallway.

He stood and moved to the dying fire. An emptiness hit him as if he was no longer a complete person without Caitlin's touch on his mind. He threw a couple logs on the fire, then looked around for his clothes.

A minute later he heard the sound of the toilet. He pulled his shirt on and was amazed at how limber his injured shoulder felt. The heat of their passion had melted away its stiffness.

Caitlin walked casually back into the room. Her smooth easy walk expressed how comfortable she was being naked in front of him.

He held out both hands as she approached and they joined hands, linked emotions, and kissed tenderly.

"I love you," he said.

"As if I didn't know."

"I just thought I'd put the emotion in words."

"I love you," she said.

They dropped their hands, separating in the smooth fluid manner of couples who had been lovers for years. Their emotions separated again, but each time the pain of decoupling was less, as though their bodies had finally realized that the separation wouldn't be permanent.

She picked up her garments that were strewn about. After stepping into her panties, she slipped on her bra and reached behind to fasten it.

"Let me," John said and let his fingers brush her back.

She shuddered with the contact. "I never thought getting dressed could be so sexy."

"Neither did I."

They dressed slowly, each helping the other with various items until they stood facing each other fully dressed, but filled with a desire to start over.

"There'll be time later," she said without speaking.

"Plenty."

"Are you hungry?"

"For you? Famished."

She smiled and kissed the air in front of his face. "You're sweet, but aren't you hungry for food?"

"Grizzlies and crocodiles."

"What?"

"Lions and tigers."

Her face grew puzzled, and then she caught his mood. "Something wild, eh? Well, I may be able to arrange it. We need a few groceries, too. I'll take you for lunch and we'll pick up some things while we're out."

"Someplace close?"

"Why close?"

"So we'll get back quicker."

Her eyes almost glowed with her agreement, but she said, "Nonsense, we need to rest and we should talk."

"We can talk here."

"You know I won't be able to talk business while touching you. No, there's a restaurant I want to take you to. It's not far. We can be there in ten or fifteen minutes."

"Okay. Come to think of it, there are a few things I should get."

"What kind of things?"

"Oh, you'll see."

Caitlin took her purse off the table and loaded the notebook back in it. John pulled on his shoulder holster and got his coat from the newel post. He removed Caitlin's coat from the closet and held it for her. She slipped her arms in; her fingers touched his and sent another shiver through them both.

"Man, this is going to change everything. I'm not sure I'll ever get used to these intense feelings every time we touch," he said.

"Nonsense, you'll get used to it, but you're right about it changing everything. There's a new world coming."

*　　　*　　　*

"Holdren here."

Holdren was tired of the phone calls. For two days, they had contained nothing but electronic surveillance hits on the Maxwell woman or that Blalock character. Every time they deployed a quick response team, it was only to discover that once again their quarry had eluded them. It was beginning to seem like a big game, but one where only the quarry knew the rules.

"Mr. Holdren?"

It was the barn.

"That's what I said. What do you have for me this time? Did they purchase theater tickets? I know, they bought a pair of cruise tickets on a charge card and will be spending the day touring the bay."

"It's nothing like that, sir. I'm not sure it's even reportable."

"Get on with it then."

"You wanted to hear of any transmissions on a particular frequency."

Holdren was immediately alert. "You have a transmission?"

"Yes sir, but it's not in the area we were expecting to find it. In fact, we wouldn't have noticed it at all except that we had ordered VORTEX 13 to search for it and forgot to tell it to stop looking after it left the target zone."

"Vortex 13? The SIGINT satellite?"

"Yes sir. That's the one."

"Where did the signal originate?"

"Colorado, near Falcon Air Force Base. It could be just a test transmission by the research boys out there. They're always playing around in C band."

"Just how close to Falcon was the signal?" Holdren asked.

"Ten miles, give or take a mile. We can't be more accurate until VORTEX makes another pass. The signal occurred at the limits of its detection range, but it'll be back in view in about an hour."

"Don't you have any other satellites that can cover the area?"

"Not that can pick up signals as weak as this one. It was a very low power transmission," the watch officer said.

"Look, Maxwell's parents have a home in that area. I need to know whether the signal came from there or not."

"Well, there is something else we could try."

"What?" Holdren asked.

"The house was unoccupied at last report, in fact we did a close look at it a few days ago. There was no sign of activity and the house was only a few degrees warmer than its surroundings."

"You have a satellite that can get me a thermal image?"

"One moment ... yes sir, GEO 3, is coming into view now."

"Link it to my computer. I want to see this for myself," Holdren said.

"Yes sir."

Holdren hung up the phone and opened his notebook computer. It woke itself up.

"Link up," Holdren ordered and placed his left thumb on the ID pad.

The watch officer was on the ball for a change. As soon as the link was made the thermal image of a house nestled in trees appeared on the screen. It was immediately obvious that it was much warmer than its surroundings.

"Close up," he ordered.

The image enlarged until it filled the screen. The quality of GEO 3's imager, designed to locate schools of fish at sea, was such that while he couldn't see sharp shapes, he could make out individual heat sources within the structure.

As he watched, two of the images moved.

"Got you."

CHAPTER 24

The electric tingle of John's ring woke him to a room filled with an intense darkness. He lived in the city for so long he'd forgotten how dark the country could be. His hand automatically reached for the gun on the nightstand. Wrapping his fingers around it, he raised it to point at where he suspected the door to be.

The door didn't open.

The house was silent, although occasionally he'd hear wind whistling around the eaves. He lay still, waiting for his eyes to pick out shadows. Nothing, just a hint of light from the windows and a dim, blue-green glow from his left. In a moment, he recognized it being from the alarm clock on Caitlin's side of the bed.

He fumbled for the glasses and earpiece he'd left next to his gun. They clattered against the wood and slipped out of reach. Mumbling to himself, he stretched and gripped the frames. He set the earpiece against his right ear and pulled the frames over his eyes.

The image flickered in the right lens immediately. For a second he wasn't sure what he was looking at, then his eye adjusted to the low light levels and he made out the two Chevy Suburbans parked in the driveway.

Doors opened, interior lights flooded the snow swept scene. Men stepped from the vehicles. Men carrying assault rifles and wearing flak vests over black uniforms.

"Damn!"

Caitlin moved beneath the covers. Her bare skin touched his side. The connection was made and her emotions swept into him. She was afraid. Her dreams were troubling, dark and foreboding. He wanted to wake her gently, to hold her tight until the fear subsided.

But there wasn't time for anything.

He flipped the covers back and shook her roughly.

"What?"

"Time to go. We've got company. You have about thirty seconds to dress. We have to leave now!"

John switched on the nightstand lamp, hit the floor, and grabbed for his clothing. There wasn't time, he ignored his briefs, but pulled on his pants, stepped barefoot into his boots, tugged them on, and pulled a tee shirt over his head without releasing his handgun.

"They're here?"

"You bet, lots of them. They'll be at the front door in less than a minute."

Caitlin got out of bed and John tossed clothing toward her. "Dress fast. Let's go, no other lights, we'll have to feel our way downstairs. We'll wait for them in the hall."

She pulled her pants over her bare buttocks and slipped into a wool cardigan. As her head popped out, John tossed her boots toward her. She caught them, sat on the edge of the bed, and pulled them smoothly on.

John tugged on his shoulder holster with its spare magazines and went to the door. When he touched the door handle, the alarm sent another jolt through his finger. He took it off the door, safed it, and jammed it into his pants. Opening the door, he waved for Caitlin to hurry up, then moved to the top of the stairs.

Caitlin took the Mossberg pump from beside the bed and hurried after him.

In his shades, John could see the rear Suburban pulling to the side of the driveway and slowly moving past the lead vehicle that had run across his makeshift road barricade.

"Hurry. They're going around the barrier. We don't have much longer."

Wordlessly, she followed him down the stairs.

John opened the closet in the foyer, removed both their coats, and passed them to Caitlin as she went around him into the hall.

"They're wearing flak vests, you'll have to aim for their legs or head, preferably their legs."

"Why? I don't mind killing a couple of them. They didn't mind killing Scott or the cabby."

"That's not the point. Wounded men scream, usually a lot, it'll add to the general confusion and make the others more wary. It's demoralizing to listen to the screams of wounded comrades. They'll start to wonder if they'll be next. They'll hesitate, fear will make them cautious and they won't be in such a hurry to rush after us."

Outside there was the sound of an engine. It died as soon as they heard it.

John took the Remington autoloading shotgun and shell bag from the closet. "They'll flank the house, wanting to cover all the exits, and then they'll hit the doors simultaneously. They'll probably lead off with stun grenades. Get your sunglasses and ear protectors on."

He entered the hall and could just make out Caitlin's form as she set the Mossberg down and tipped the mattress over the lower half of the kitchen doorway. John pulled his sunglasses back on, then removed the ear protectors from the ammo bag and adjusted them over his ears. He crouched next to her, his hand moved to touch her, joining their emotions. She was nervous, scared, but almost eager for the confrontation. He tried to relax her, to take away some of the nervousness that could make her hesitate, make mistakes, and spoil her aim.

"You really do get a thrill from this," she transmitted.

"No, I ... Well, all right, I guess I do."

She gathered his emotions and reflected them. He was surprised at the intensity of his own feelings. He'd enjoyed adrenaline rushes every since the Canyon. It was an addiction, but he'd never realized how strong its hold on him was. His anticipation of the coming fight was frightening for he held no fear of death or maiming in his emotions. Rather there was an unhealthy pleasure filling him. For once, he could see his addiction for what it was. He'd heard drug addictions referred to as a monkey on your back, if that was so, there was a five hundred-pound gorilla riding him.

"Scary isn't it? How do you live like this?"

"I didn't realize."

"You need counseling. It's not healthy to need this sensation, this danger."

"Yeah? Well, talk to me later about it, right now we've got things to do."

She didn't reply and he let his hand drop from her shoulder. The connection broke. He'd accomplished what he'd intended, she was no longer nervous about the fight, but he was afraid that if they'd stayed connected much longer he wouldn't have been prepared. This wasn't the time to be thinking of counseling, of career changes, of addictions.

He shook himself and felt the gorilla reach down and take a firm grip on his gut. Adrenaline coursed through him. He took a deep breath and let it out slowly, reveling in the rush. That was more like it. Let them come; it'd been too long since he'd been in a firefight.

Glass shattered throughout the house.

It rained onto hardwood floors and ceramic tile with a musical chime. The heavy thud of metal accompanied it.

"Party time," he transmitted.

The house rocked with the nearly simultaneous detonation of a half dozen stun grenades. Even crouched behind the mattress with his eyes firmly closed he could see the bright flash against his retinas. The booming was nearly deafening, like a volley of Smerch rockets going off. Then there was more glass shattering against the floor as the rubber pellets peppered everything in the house.

John raised the shotgun and flipped off the safety. With his left hand he pulled both the shades and ear protectors from his head and dropped them into the ammo bag.

Dual shotgun blasts came from both the front and back doors as the intruders blew away the hinges.

"The Feds are so predictable," he transmitted.

Caitlin had pushed the mattress to one side and was aiming at the rear door. John faced the front door just as the first man kicked it off its shattered hinges and stood silhouetted against the swirling snow.

As he stepped to one side of the door the second agent appeared. The shotgun bucked in his hands as John shot the second man in the knees. The Remington smoothly chambered another round and John popped the first man the same way even as he turned toward his position.

Both men collapsed. The second man fell outside the house while the first fell face down in the foyer.

The night was suddenly filled with screaming, bleeding bodies, the deep-throated boom of another shotgun, and automatic fire from a dozen weapons.

"Got one of mine," Caitlin transmitted. "The other ducked back outside as soon as he heard your shots."

"All right, give them a second to empty their magazines into the house. Ha, damn nice to have these thick logs. When there's a pause they'll probably try to get us to surrender, that's when we'll pop the charges and hit the back door."

"Ready when you are."

He backed down the hall, keeping his gun sighted on the front door, until he bumped into her. A few seconds later the gunfire suddenly ceased.

The tinny shout of a bullhorn broke the silence. "You in the house. John Blalock. We are Federal Agents. You are surrounded. Surrender now. You won't be offered another chance."

"That's our cue," John transmitted.

He picked up the end of the orange power cord and plugged it into the wall outlet.

Shattering explosions filled the night with one thousand, one inch long, steel brads. Suddenly there was confusion and screaming and more gunfire.

"That's our cue to skidoo," John transmitted.

He ran through the kitchen and onto the back porch. The man Caitlin had shot was still sprawled on the porch, clutching at the mangled mess of his legs, and screaming.

The other man was slumped beside the steps. He had the misfortune to hide not five feet from the Pryrodex powder charge. His flak vest bristled with scores of the small nails, but the ones that reached his head and limbs had sunk in.

John had an unexpected memory flash of the Nails character in Wes Craven's Hellbound.

He scanned both sides of the house, but he could not see any movement through the thick snow.

"Come on," he transmitted. "Allie allie all in free."

Caitlin came through the door and ran past him without giving either of the fallen men more than a moment's inspection.

He gave her a three-second head start, and when there was no sign of pursuit, ran after her.

The wind against his face was cold. He could feel his nose starting to run and his eyes watered. It reminded him of learning to ski at Copper Mountain, nearly twenty years before.

It amazed him what the memory dragged up at the oddest times.

Ahead of him, Caitlin was climbing into the Jeep. He yanked opened the driver's door as Caitlin closed her door. Taking the key from beneath the floor mat, John inserted it in the ignition.

Caitlin was staring back toward the house.

John turned the key and the engine fired to life.

Automatic fire pinged through the Jeep's sheet metal.

Caitlin ducked beneath the windows.

"Damn, I didn't think anyone saw us leave. Get on the floor," John said, slamming the transmission into gear, and goosing the accelerator.

The Jeep shot forward as a second automatic opened up from the opposite side of the house.

"Son of a bitch!"

The Jeep was already aimed at the narrow path he'd picked through the woods and he left the lights off as they rushed toward the trees.

Glass shattered as bullets whined through the interior.

He crouched low in the seat and tried to estimate how long he had before they reached the tree line.

John leaned over Caitlin's head and flipped open the glove box. He fumbled his night goggles out of their case and slipped them over his eyes just in time to avoid the thick pine they'd been about to skewer. The goggles didn't function as well in the snowy landscape as on a clear night, but there was enough light to make out the darker shadows of the trees.

The window next to John's head shattered in a burst of flying glass. Shards of the safety glass peppered the side of his face like the spray from a shotgun.

Then they were into the trees and swerving to avoid the nearer pines. Out of sight of the house, the gunfire died.

"You can get up now. You should get your safety harness on," John said aloud as he pulled his own harness across his body and clicked it into the buckle.

Caitlin climbed onto the seat and struggled to pull out the belt.

They reached the down slope, tipped over the edge, and picked up speed. The lumps of rock he'd spotted during the daylight were invisible in his goggles. He flicked on the parking lights. The added light provided more contrast, but he still couldn't overdrive the lights. He was forced to stay below thirty.

The tires struck something beneath the snow and the Jeep bounced roughly to the side. Caitlin grunted. John turned his head far enough to see that she had bounced off the ceiling and into the side door.

"Damn," she said and tugged on the harness again. For a moment, it wouldn't release as the rough surface kept the belt's locking system frozen. Then it was free and she stretched it across and fastened it.

Lights appeared behind them as the second of the Suburbans reached the top of the slope.

"They made a quick recovery. Let's hope they don't realize what the snow is hiding," John said.

"Or the back seat."

John jumped at the voice behind his head. It sounded familiar.

The cold metal of a gun barrel pressed against the back of his neck.

Caitlin whirled toward the sound and tried to bring her shotgun around.

"No," John transmitted. "Don't do anything yet."

John dogged another hidden rock and then plowed through the barbed wire fence.

"What do you want?" he asked.

"The same thing we all want. A long and peaceful life, but alas, we can't always get what we want."

"But we get what we need. Yeah, I know that song," John said.

"Song?" Dewatre asked.

"Never mind."

"Who are you? Which group do you work for?" Caitlin asked.

"My name is Alain Dewatre. As for who I work for, does it really matter?"

"No, I guess not."

"Good, careful here, Mr. Blalock. I want you to slow down as you enter the trees."

They reached the far side of the clearing and John slowed as he turned onto the drive that led toward the neighbor's house.

"Why? If we slow down the Feds will catch up."

"I just want to be able to watch the fireworks," Dewatre responded.

"What fireworks?" Caitlin asked.

"I thought you might need a little assistance with your getaway. Ah, there. They're entering the woods."

In the rearview mirror, John could see the Suburban pulling onto the drive. Dewatre raised a small transmitter and John's goggles automatically dimmed as the night erupted with thunder and lightning.

John swore under his breath and flicked on the headlights. Behind them, the Suburban swerved off the drive and crashed through the trees until it reached one that was too large to knock over.

"What was that?" Caitlin asked.

"Something like the stun grenades they used on you. I thought they would appreciate the irony."

"Now what?" John asked.

"Now we switch vehicles. They may have gotten a good look at this one. Turn left at the road."

"Okay, but do you think you could move that barrel away from my neck? The road is still rough and I wouldn't want you to accidentally do anything drastic."

"No, I don't think that would be a good idea. You'll just have to avoid the worst bumps. You, Ms. Maxwell, can set the safety on your weapon and pass it back to me."

"John?" she transmitted.

"Go ahead, our chance will come later. Just stay ready to move when I give the signal."

She gave him her silent agreement and passed her shotgun across the seat. Dewatre took it and laid it on the floor.

They turned onto the road and a half-mile later Dewatre had John pull into another driveway. A green Explorer was parked just off the road.

"Stop here," Dewatre ordered.

John stopped the Cherokee along side the Explorer and put the transmission in park.

"Now what?" he asked.

"You remain just where you are. Keep both hands on the top of the steering wheel."

John eased his hands to the eleven and one o'clock positions and waited.

From the corner of his eye, he could see Dewatre slide across the seat until he was behind Caitlin.

"Now, Ms. Maxwell. I want you to get out and shut the door behind you."

Caitlin followed his instructions and stood waiting.

Dewatre opened his door and motioned her to back up. Then he stepped out while keeping his gun on her.

"Turn around and back toward me. That's close enough," he added when she was an arm's length away.

"Now you, Blalock. Remember any wrong move and I will kill your employer. It's hard to collect from a dead woman."

John killed the engine and pocketed the key as he got out.

Dewatre took a grip on Caitlin's coat and pulled her slowly toward the rear of the vehicles. John followed.

"Now open the back of your vehicle," Dewatre ordered.

John complied silently.

"What's he going to do with us?" Caitlin transmitted.

"I don't know. He didn't kill me when he had the chance before, but he may have more motive now. He probably wants the neuralphone's technology. Don't let on to anything we've learned, sooner or later we'll get our chance."

John opened the rear of the Cherokee and waited.

"Where is it?" Dewatre asked.

"Where's what?"

"Don't be smart. You know what I'm after, the disk and the prototype."

"Oh that." John leaned into the back of the Cherokee and slid out the case containing the helmet.

"Open it."

He flipped the latches and opened it slowly. In the dim glow of the dome light, he could just make out the helmet's outline.

"All right, now the disk. Where is it?" Dewatre asked.

"Right here," John replied and took the disk from inside the case. He held it up for Dewatre to see.

The man frowned. "That had better be the right disk, otherwise Ms. Maxwell will die."

"I have no reason to lie about it, Dewatre. It's not worth my life or Ms. Maxwell's."

"That is a good attitude to have. Now set it on the back seat of my car and move away."

John put the disk inside the case and closed it. He crunched through the snow and opened Dewatre's rear car door. He set the case on the seat, stepped back, and closed the door.

"Now turn around and walk to the front of your car. If you look back this way I will have to shoot you."

John turned slowly. Snow swirled in the dim light. He took one step.

"Caitlin, tell me what he's doing," John transmitted.

"He still has the gun at my head. He's forcing me toward his car. John, I'm afraid."

"I won't let anything happen to you. When he tries to force you into the car, he'll have to release you for a moment. You give me the sign and I'll make my move then."

"All right. Please be careful, I don't want you hurt," Caitlin transmitted.

"Damn straight."

Dewatre and Caitlin reached the Ford's front door.

"Open it," he said.

She did and the dim light doubled. Even with the extra light she could barely see John at the front of the Jeep.

"On ne meurt, qu'une fois, et c'est pour si longtemps."

"What was that Frenchy? You forget your English?" John asked.

"John, it's a quote from Molière. `One dies only once, and it's for such a long time.'" Caitlin transmitted.

Although they weren't in physical contact, John could feel her fear.

"He's shifting the gun. Look out!"

John dove for the front of the Jeep even as the shot cracked the calm. He felt a strong blow against his right shoulder blade. The force of the blow spun him half way around. For a fraction of a second, he could see Caitlin struggling to prevent Dewatre from shooting. Then a muzzle flash seared his eyes and a hot lance of pain exploded against his head.

CHAPTER 25

Caitlin watched, frozen in horror as the first bullet hit John. Before he could fire again, she grabbed Dewatre's arm and pulled it out of line as a second shot broke the stillness.

"John!" She screamed.

There was no answer. She broadcast another shout over the Egg, but again there was nothing.

She raised one hand to claw at Dewatre's eyes, but missed and left four deep cuts in his cheek instead.

He cursed and swung the gun's barrel at her. Caitlin ducked under it and ran toward where John had fallen at the front of the Jeep.

Just as she rounded the bumper, a hand closed on her coat and Dewatre jerked her to a halt.

He shoved the gun barrel under her chin until it forced her head back against him. "You bitch, one more stupid move like that and I'll kill you."

The snow was matted down where John had fallen, but there was no sign of him. The compressed area went about five feet to the edge of an embankment and from there the brown dirt was scraped clean of snow.

A red speckling stained the snow around them.

Caitlin felt her knees go weak.

Not John. Not John too.

She tried transmitting to him again, but there was no reply.

The swirling snow parted and, for a moment, she thought she could see the dark shape of a body at the foot of the embankment. It wasn't moving.

Although the bank was only ten or so feet high, it was steep and obviously slippery.

"Damn, life is just one damned thing after another," Dewatre said. "There's no time to be positive. If he was lucky enough to survive, then, c'est le guerre. Come on, give me any more trouble and I'll kill you and take the chance that you don't know anything critical."

She let him pull her toward the Ford. He forced her into the front seat, then got behind the wheel. He cranked the engine, turned around, and pulled onto the road heading toward the Springs.

The Ford was cold, but the shiver that came over her had nothing to do with the temperature. "Why'd you have to kill him?"

His eyes met hers for just a second, then returned to study a road that was barely visible through the snow. "John Blalock impressed me as the unforgiving kind. If I hadn't killed him, then someday he would have come across me again and then I might not have the upper hand."

"John wasn't like that. If you'd let us go he'd wouldn't have ever bothered you again."

"Truly? Well, perhaps, but I think not. He was a hard man with a reputation in the business of being both ruthless and determined. He was not a man to cross."

"No, he wasn't like that. He wasn't a monster like the rest of you," Caitlin said. "I ... he was kind, sacrificing, he wasn't the vendetta type."

"And you base that opinion on what?"

"I knew him once, a long time ago."

"Ah, so he couldn't have changed so much, eh?"

"No, not that much." Caitlin said.

"Did you ever read Nietzsche?"

"A little. A very little, his writings seemed to contain the touch of base paranoia."

"Truly? I suppose that could be one interpretation. But he had a saying that fit this man you once knew."

"I hardly think so."

"'He who fights with monsters might take care lest he thereby become a monster.'"

She stared at him for a moment, then she asked, "Is that what happened to you or were you born this way?"

"Ah, touché. Perhaps the saying may apply to me also. Who knows?"

They reached Powers Boulevard and turned south. "What are you planning? Are you going to kill me too?"

"Only if you make it necessary. You will have a questioning, a debriefing, and if you are honest with us we will give you the choice of returning home or accepting our protection."

"Your protection? Are you crazy?"

"No, Ms. Maxwell, I am not crazy. Surely you realize that those in your government who are after this artifact are willing to kill you to get it."

"And you're not?"

"Ah, well if you insist on a strict interpretation of my orders, then yes, we are also willing to kill for it."

"I think I'll take my chances at home," Caitlin said.

"That is your choice and I do not care."

She stared at him for a moment. "You called it an artifact, why?"

"What else could it be?"

There was a tone in his voice that Caitlin had not expected. His voice held the almost innocent note of a child when confronted with something beyond his keen.

"It's just an advanced telephone system. A technological breakthrough, but artifact certainly doesn't apply. Perhaps your English isn't as good as you think."

For a second he silently drove down the wide deserted boulevard, then his lips pursed and he nodded slowly. "Ah, then you think someone invented this device, this advanced telephone."

"Of course."

"That's not what your government thinks."

"How would you know what they think?"

"We have our sources. When I received this project, I was fully briefed. I know everything Holdren and his crew know."

"And that is?"

"Are you sure you want to know? It may be dangerous information."

Caitlin exhaled an unbelieving grunt of surprise. "Dangerous? Like dangerous in that someone may try to kill me for it? Get real, Dewatre. Someone killed my husband, you've killed John, and I've seen Holdren kill a totally innocent man who just happened to get in the way. I'm already living under a threat of death. What could make it worse?"

"What if I told you that your government doesn't believe anyone here invented this device, that it came from somewhere else?"

"Who else has that capability, the Brits, the Japanese? The French certainly don't."

He didn't respond.

"There aren't any other countries with the basic research needed to achieve this sort of breakthrough," she said.

"I concur."

"I don't understand what you mean. If it wasn't some other country then it must have been here, perhaps in a private lab such as those AT&T funds."

"No, not there either. They are just as anxious to get their hands on it. No, you have to expand your thinking, to think out of the box that your naiveté keeps around you."

"I suppose you intend to convince me it has extraterrestrial origins."

He didn't react.

"You can't be serious," Caitlin said as her hand rose to cover the hard lump beneath her coat.

"I am quite serious. That is exactly where Holdren believes it came from."

"Yeah, but just because that murdering bastard believes it doesn't make it so."

"I didn't say it was so, I just said that your government believes it to be so."

"And your government?"

He shrugged. "Ah, who can say what one's own government believes?"

They turned off Powers and pulled into the old terminal area of the airport.

* * *

John's head pounded so loud that he thought he was stuck in some fantastical kettledrum during a drum solo. Pain assailed him from a multitude of injuries, the least of which seemed to be the place he'd been shot a few days earlier. What the hell had happened? He was foggy on everything since meeting the Frenchman. Dewatre, yes, his name was Dewatre. John opened his eyes.

It was dark, but a faint glow shown from somewhere above. He lay at the bottom of a snow-covered embankment.

Caitlin! Where the hell was Caitlin? He broadcast over the Egg, but there was no reply. Damn, she had to be out of range. She had to be. He didn't want to think of the alternative.

He sat up and received a new set of pain signals from various parts of his anatomy. His right shoulder blade felt like someone had busted it with a sledgehammer. The side of his head screamed its pain as he moved. John raised his left hand and felt blood and something missing. At least half of his left ear was missing.

"Son of a bitch bastard. Rotten no good ... you're going to die when I find you Dewatre!"

The light grew brighter and John realized headlights were approaching. He rolled over onto his knees and struggled erect. If it wasn't Dewatre and Caitlin coming back, then it must be Holdren's men. He had to get moving.

One step, sway a moment, then another step. Stop, sway again, he wanted to shake it off, but as dizzy as he felt, he was certain that shaking his head would compound the problem.

He tried climbing the frozen embankment, but slid back down before he'd gone half way. The road was off to his right. He followed the ditch for forty feet or so until he reached the road. The headlights of a car were already turning into the drive where Dewatre had made him stop.

John waited until the lights were pointed away from him then climbed the short bank onto the road. As he ran after the vehicle, he drew his gun from its holster.

The Suburban parked twenty feet behind John's rented Cherokee. The big Chevy's multiple headlights blanketing the scene through the swirling snow. All four doors of the Chevy opened. Two men got out and advanced toward the Jeep. The other two covered them with drawn weapons.

John slowed and moved silently closer.

"There's blood here," one of the lead men shouted.

"Any bodies?" one by the passenger side of the Suburban asked.

"No, wait. There's a ditch up here and it looks like someone may have fallen into it."

"You check it out. Bennings, check the Jeep," the second man ordered.

John reached the rear of the Suburban and put out his left hand to steady himself. He was in danger of puking up his guts. Bitter bile burned his throat. He swallowed, steeled himself against the buck and sway of the earth, and moved forward again.

Raising his gun, he chopped it down into the temple of the man who had given the orders. The man grunted and sagged to his knees.

John shoved him to the side and fired through the open door at the driver who was trying to bring his weapon to bear. John fired twice in rapid succession.

The first bullet took the driver in the throat; the second opened up his sinuses.

One of the forward men was still standing at the front of the Jeep. He turned at the sound of the shots, his Uzi came up, his finger already on the trigger. A line of shots walked the distance between them then cut off abruptly when John's next shot took him in the chest and shoved him backwards toward the ditch. John took his time and placed another round in his face just before the man pitched backwards out of sight.

He saw no sign of the fourth man. Unless he was a lot more agile than John was, he'd have to hoof it out to the road in order to get back. That gace John a moment of freedom.

The man he'd clubbed tried to rise. John clubbed him again and he decided to sleep instead.

John rolled him over and patted him down. He had a wallet and a badge holder in an inner coat pocket. John shoved both items in one of his pockets, then was suddenly unable to control himself any longer.

He emptied his guts over the prone man. He couldn't stop until there was nothing left but dry heaves. John wiped his mouth on the back of his sleeve, coughed once, and spit out a foul taste.

His minute was almost up. Time to get moving or he'd have another killer to handle. He took an Uzi carbine from the front seat of the Suburban and a satchel of 30 round magazines. John stopped long enough to take the driver's Uzi from his corpse.

It didn't make sense, but the puking seemed to help. John reached the Jeep without needing to stop to catch himself. He slammed the rear hatch closed and climbed into the driver's seat. The engine roared to life. John threw the transmission into reverse, backed around the Suburban, shifted into drive, and accelerated toward the road.

When he turned toward town his headlights lit a figure climbing onto the pavement. John aimed the Cherokee at the man as the man raised his gun. For an instant John thought he'd try to shoot, then the man dove back off the road, and disappeared into the night as the Jeep thundered pass.

John turned his head as the man disappeared from the road. He caught sight of his reflection in the mirror and turned it toward him as he accelerated. Blood matted the hair on the left side of his head. Some of it had begun to dry, but it was renewed by a continual seep from the remains of his ear and from a tear in the side of his scalp. For the first time since he'd been shot, he noticed that sounds reached him oddly. The bullet that had taken off part of his ear must have done something to the inner ear also, unless the ear canal was just full of blood. There wasn't time to clean up the mess and find out just now. He had to locate Caitlin before Dewatre shot her too.

He slowed and turned toward town onto Black Forest road. His guess was that Dewatre would either take her to a safe house for questioning or to the airport so he could get her out of the country. There was a French consulate in Denver, but he didn't think the French government would want to be too obvious about their involvement. It was one thing to have DGRG spies working in an ally's country, but quite another to kidnap one of their citizens and take them onto consulate property.

John turned and spotted the canvas bag he'd left on the floor of the back seat. He stretched back to get it and was rewarded with a fresh stab of pain from his upper back.

"Damn sonofabitch!"

Refusing to let the pain stop him, John clutched the bag and dragged it into the front seat. The movement gave him a sticky feeling beneath his shirt. That wasn't good. He'd thought his back was just tender from taking a round in the Kevlar vest, but sticky meant blood. What had Dewatre been using? Teflon bullets? Maybe even those solid copper bullets the French had produced back in the eighties. He didn't think they were still available, but government agents would have them if anyone did.

Reaching Powers Boulevard, John slowed and turned toward the airport as he opened the bag. The transceiver was in its own leather case. He pulled it out, flipped back the cover to expose the controls, and turned it on.

"Caitlin. Caitlin can you hear me?" he transmitted.

*　　　*　　　*

Caitlin was being dragged by the arm across the tarmac toward a hanger when John's voice sounded inside her head. She stumbled and nearly fell, but Dewatre jerked her to her feet.

"None of that now, Ms. Maxwell, I thought we had an understanding."

"I slipped, damn you. If you weren't pulling so hard I might be able to keep my feet."

Dewatre had holstered his weapon when they parked the Explorer. He'd warned her that as long as she cooperated he wouldn't hurt her.

"John, thank God. I was afraid he'd killed you."

"He came close. Where are you now?"

"We're at the airport. Take the old terminal exit off Powers. We're going into an older hanger. There's a big sign that says Rocky Air Freight over the doors."

"All right, I'm crossing Constitution now. I'll be there in five minutes. Keep me informed on what's happening."

"Okay, I'll try to repeat everything. Are you all right?"

"I'll live, which is more than I can say for our friend Dewatre when I catch up with him."

They reached the hanger and went in a small door set in the large hanger doors. "John, that's what he said you'd do. He said it was why he had to shoot you."

"Really? I wish I knew how he knows me so well. If I get the chance I'll ask him before I kill him."

Caitlin received no emotion in his transmission. Strange that when they shared so much while touching they only shared words when apart. His words were enough though. How could this man who had been so tender with her, who had shared feelings and sensations that no other man or woman had ever shared seem so cold and vengeful now?

Neither man nor woman. Could it be that Dewatre was correct? That aliens had delivered these devices to whomever Scott had gotten them from? But why would they? What would they have to gain? It just didn't make any sense.

The bright light of sodium lights flooded the inside of the hanger. In its shadow-less glare, Caitlin saw at least three planes. One looked like a DC-3 or maybe it was a converted C-47. One was a Brasilia turboprop, and one was a sleek new Learjet. The jet faced the closed doors.

A man sat on the steps of the Learjet reading a paper. When the wind banged the door shut behind them he looked up, then set his paper aside.

In French, he said, "Alain, you have her. Good, did you have any trouble?"

"A little, but we should get moving. Trouble seems to follow this assignment. How long before we can get airborne?"

"It will take a couple of minutes to do the final preflight on the airplane. You call for takeoff clearance, while Carl and I start the engines. How's the weather? Has it gotten any better?"

"No, worse if anything."

"No bother, we're fully equipped."

"Get the engines started. I'll join you after I find Ms. Maxwell a seat. Have Carl get the doors now, I don't want to waste anytime."

"Right. I'll wake Carl."

"Did you get all that John? You don't have much time," Jill transmitted.

"I'm turning off Powers now. I should be there in a minute or so."

"Please be careful, John. You know I don't want anything to happen to you."

"I'll be careful. Aren't I always?"

Dewatre pushed her toward the stairs as the pilot disappeared inside the cabin.

Caitlin turned toward Dewatre. "Look, isn't there some other way we can do this. I get acrophobia real bad."

"Yes, there is another way. I can give you an injection that will knock you out until we land outside Paris. Which would you prefer?"

"Neither really, I don't like needles either."

"Ms. Maxwell, your little stalling tactics are getting tiresome. Either march that cute derrière of yours up those steps or I will knock you down, give you the injection and throw you in the cargo hold for the trip."

Caitlin gave him a little pout for effect and then turned and walked unhurriedly up the steps.

"I'm entering the hanger area now, Caitlin. Where are you?" John broadcast.

"In the third hanger, we're just going into the airplane. It's the big Learjet parked just inside the main doors."

Caitlin stepped into the cabin and bumped into a young man who rubbed his eyes sleepily. He muttered an apology and moved to one side to let her pass.

Dewatre gave the man a disapproving stare and then joined Caitlin. The cabin was about twenty feet long and five wide. There weren't many seats, perhaps enough for ten people.

Dewatre motioned her toward two seats that faced each other across a small table near the cabin door.

"Sit there, facing forward."

Caitlin moved to the chair, she had to stoop to walk, sat down, and waited. Dewatre set the case with the helmet onto the table and flipped the latches. Lifting the lid, he smiled down at the foam-encased helmet, but only for a second. His features puzzled, then grimaced as he turned toward her. "There are two empty positions here. What was in them?"

"I don't know, that's the way it was when we got it."

He stared at her, his pupils wide, his lips curled back off his teeth as if he were going to snarl. His gaze dropped to her chest. He blinked once then suddenly lunged at her. Before she could move, his fingers closed on the neck of her sweater and yanked, popping the top two buttons off as he exposed the swell of her breasts and the gold Egg nestled there.

"*Mon deus*! You lying little bitch."

She slapped his hand away and moved to close her blouse even as his hand returned to slap against the side of her head.

Stars swam before her gaze.

She tried to rise and his fist slammed into her jaw.

* * *

John heard the brief exchange as Dewatre discovered the missing Eggs, but then the connection was broken and no amount of shouting over the link brought any response from Caitlin. He was almost to the hanger. Its great doors were already rolling back, exposing a sleek Learjet 45 to the snowy night.

John took his Colt from its holster and aimed the Jeep at the front of the jet. He waited until the last minute to brake, then cut the wheel sharply to the side putting the Jeep into a sideways slide that narrowly missed the hanger doors before the Jeep bumped up against the jet's nose gear.

He threw the transmission into park. A bullet starred the windshield as he opened the door. He dropped to the pavement and hit the concrete in a jarring impact that sent waves of pain through his back. Rolling sideways, he went under the Jeep while looking for the shooter.

John spotted a man running toward him from the corner of the hanger. It wasn't Dewatre, but he held a weapon aimed at the Jeep.

Still rolling, John fired twice and saw the man go down with a splash of red high on his right thigh. John came to a stop against the jet's nose wheels and then scrambled on his belly toward the right side of the plane.

A shot pinged off the side of the Jeep and passed close by him. John turned to find the man he'd already shot was sitting up and drawing a bead on him. John fired twice more and the man stayed down.

Dewatre's face appeared in the cockpit window.

John snapped off a shot at him and the window starred, but Dewatre had already ducked back out of sight.

John maneuvered toward the wings, ducked under the fuselage, and used the left main landing gear for cover as he waited for Dewatre to come down the stairs. Dewatre couldn't wait too long; for once time was John's ally. The plane couldn't be moved until someone moved the Jeep and the gunfire was sure to bring airport security and the local police in a hurry. But then, perhaps Dewatre had a diplomatic passport. If so, he would be immune to prosecution in the US. John didn't want to have to deal with police. He could probably make bail, but sooner or later Holdren would show up and then there wouldn't be any hope of bail. No, if Dewatre didn't come down those stairs soon, then John would have to go in after him.

He raised his head above the edge of the wing and tried to see in the small ports. He saw no one, but saw an emergency exit over the wing.

Placing his hands on the top of the wing, John lifted himself. His right shoulder burned with pain, but he pressed on until he could swing his legs onto the wing. He rolled over and faced the main door, still no sign of movement. Why in the hell wasn't Dewatre coming out?

John got to his knees and peered into the nearest window.

There was Caitlin, just six feet away. She looked unconscious.

Dewatre had to be in the cockpit. If John had to shoot out a window Dewatre would be on him before he could get inside, there was nothing that could be done for it. John studied the emergency exit. As he had expected, there was a release from the outside.

He holstered his gun, then popped the latches and lifted the hatch upwards and inwards until it cleared the lip of the opening. John pivoted the hatch and pulled it back through the opening.

He saw movement out of the corner of his eye. Dewatre had finally emerged from the plane.

Spinning, he hurled the hatch toward Dewatre. The hatch struck him just as he fired and his shot went wild. He tumbled down the stairs. John dove into the plane's cabin and drew his own weapon.

Another man was coming out of the cockpit, carrying a Beretta. He raised it to fire, but John put three rounds into his chest, driving the man backward out of sight.

Keeping one eye on the main door, John moved alongside Caitlin and shook her. She didn't respond.

On the table in front of her was the open case of the helmet and a syringe. A single drop of blood was visible on the left side of her neck.

"Damn bastards!"

John felt for a pulse. It was strong, but slow. Whatever Dewatre gave her had put her under, but hadn't killed her. They still wanted her alive. John thought he saw movement by the door and snapped off two more shots to keep Dewatre from being too daring.

John gripped Caitlin's coat in both his hands and lifted, but there was unexpected resistance. He looked closely and for the first time noticed the handcuffs that fastened her left wrist to the arm of the seat.

From somewhere outside came the sound of sirens.

"Enough is enough," John growled to himself.

He set his weapon on the table and gripped the seat arm with both hands. Bracing his feet, he pulled up and back. The metal resisted for a moment, then with a screech, ripped free from the seat.

Keeping an eye out for Dewatre, John dragged her closer to the cabin door. He retrieved his weapon, closed the case on the helmet, and set the case next to Caitlin.

He peered out the main door, but saw no sign of Dewatre. Had he decided to cut his losses when the sirens started, or was he hiding somewhere, waiting for another shot at him?

There was only one way to be sure. John leapt down the stairs onto the pavement. He executed a painful tuck and roll, checked his six, dropped quickly and rolled twice to his right until he was beside the Jeep. With his back against the fender, he rose into a crouch and searched for Dewatre.

There was no sign of him in the bright hanger.

The fender moved against his back. Not much, but enough to indicate someone's weight compressing the Jeep's springs. John turned, raising his weapon, expecting to see Dewatre aiming at him.

He saw Dewatre, but not aiming at him. He was in the driver's seat. John fired at the same time the Jeep lunged forward. Dewatre ducked down. The Jeep cut hard and went straight out of the hanger as John emptied the magazine at the fleeing vehicle.

John ejected the magazine and loaded a fresh one, but the Jeep had disappeared into the snow.

Had he hit Dewatre? There wasn't time to find out. The sirens were louder.

Running for the jet, John holstered his weapon. He stopped on the top step, pulled Caitlin to him, and lifted her onto his left shoulder. Grabbing the case in his right hand, he turned, took the three steps to the pavement, and turned toward the hanger doors.

Dewatre walked toward him, not thirty feet away, a Glock 19 raised in his right hand.

"Surprised to see me?" Dewatre asked and moved closer.

John backed away, keeping the distance between them. "Somewhat. I thought you'd shown sense by escaping while you could. I guess I was giving you too much credit."

Dewatre laughed. "No, I believe you have underestimated me. You see, I have known about you for several years now. Ever since you first interfered with an operation I was shepherding. I made a point of looking up your background. You are quite good at what you do."

John ducked under the edge of the wing and continued to back away. "The compliment would mean more if you hadn't tried to kill me earlier."

"Oh, that little thing. It was business, not personal. I admire your capabilities, but studying you convinced me you would never let me walk off with Ms. Maxwell without making an attempt to get her back."

"You studied well," John said and backed out from under the wing.

The whine of the port engine was loud and he could feel its intake drawing air across his head.

Dewatre raised his voice above the roar of the engine. "That's far enough, John. If you don't stand still I'm afraid I'll just have to shoot you again."

"I figured you're planning to do that anyway."

Dewatre shrugged. "Ten minutes ago I would have."

"Oh? And what's changed?"

"I saw that you and Ms. Maxwell have used the prototype. You've configured the communicators to your brain waves."

"So?"

Dewatre stopped at the wing and rested his gun hand on its surface. "Well, I hate to give anything away, but my information is that each device can only be configured once. Like the old CD-ROMs, they can be written, but not erased and then rewritten. Therefore, if we want to study their operation before we build our own we will have to study you and Ms. Maxwell here."

"Really? That's interesting, then I suppose I can draw my gun and shoot you instead."

Dewatre actually smiled at him. "I hardly think so. In that case, I would have to shoot you. The scientists would just have to wait until they get one built. It shouldn't take but a year or two."

John stared at the dark opening in the Glock's barrel. At fifteen feet, John had no doubt that Dewatre had the sights centered between his eyes.

The sirens had drawn close enough for John to be able to hear them above the jet engine that was four feet from his head. "But even if I go with you, how are you going to get away? The police will be here in a moment."

"The police aren't a problem. My diplomatic passport will keep them from interfering with our take off."

"Just as long as we're off the ground before Holdren gets here, eh?"

"Oui. Holdren can be a problem."

John held up the heavy metal case. "All for this. You really want it bad don't you?"

"My government does. Me, I just obey orders."

"All right then. Take it."

John lofted the case upwards, not toward Dewatre, but into the throat of the TFE731-20 turbofan engine.

"No-o-o!" Dewatre screamed, too late.

John ducked under the tail of the Learjet as the heavy case slammed into the intake with the slap of metal on metal.

Then, nothing.

Dewatre's response turned from dismay to anger and bullets whizzed by John's feet, ricocheting off the cement floor and whining away into anything that happened to be in their path.

John had his own weapon out and was firing back, not taking the time to aim, just trying to keep Dewatre's head down while he found cover for himself and Caitlin.

Flashing blue and red lights reflected off the overhead glass panels as the first of the police cars slid to a stop in the open hanger doorway.

John ducked behind a full size toolbox as the police loud speaker blared at them.

"This is the police. Drop your weapons!"

Two rounds hit the toolbox as Dewatre made another attempt at finishing what he'd started.

He peered around the edge of the toolbox and saw that Dewatre was at the foot of the Learjet's stairs and was going inside. He gauged the opening between the hanger doors.

The police car only blocked a small portion of the gap. Dewatre might be able to get away, if he hurried.

John scanned the wall behind him. An emergency exit was just twenty feet away. Staying low he made for the exit, reached it, and pushed through.

Outside the hanger, the snow still fell, but there was a faint glow to the east.

He could hear more sirens approaching, but they couldn't do anything to Dewatre even if they arrived in time. Once he was free, he'd track them down and it would start again. No, John couldn't let that happen. It had to end with Dewatre here and now.

A luggage carrier sat outside the next hanger. He trotted to it as the whine of the Learjet's engines increased in pitch. Pulling back the canvas side, John laid Caitlin inside and then dropped the cover back into place.

She'd be as safe there as anywhere.

He ran full out toward the tarmac and reached the corner of the hanger as the nose of the plane turned toward him. The dual landing lights mounted on its nose gear illuminated the snow with a blinding glare. The police weren't even firing at him. They were letting him get away.

John waited until the cockpit was even with him, Dewatre would be in the left seat, facing the other way, and then made his move. He holstered his gun as he ran for the starboard wing. He leaped and gripped the leading edge with both hands, then pulled himself up.

One of the policemen yelled something, but the roar of the jet's engines drowned his words. Peering through the portal, he could see Dewatre hadn't taken the time to reinstall the emergency escape hatch. The plane accelerated down the taxiway. Snow stung his face and the cold air billowed his jacket. He grabbed one of the small UHF antennas on the top of the cabin and used it to pull himself up.

On top of the cabin, he rested for a moment. The blood loss was starting to tell. Normally this much activity wouldn't have bothered him, but now he felt like he'd already completed a marathon. Three police cars were now chasing them down the tarmac. Their lights gave the falling snow an enchanted glow. Ahead, John could see another car trying to beat them to the turn at the end of the taxiway.

John took another deep breath and let the crisp bite of the dry mountain air chill his lungs. He changed his grip on the antenna and slid down the port side. With his feet on the wing root, he transferred his grip to the open hatch and stepped inside.

The dark interior of the cabin was no warmer, but at least he was out of the wind. John drew his gun and started forward.

As he reached the forward wall, the plane leaned sharply to one side. They were turning from the taxiway onto the active runway. John's foot came down on something soft and yielding and he put his hand out to steady himself, misjudged, lost his balance, and fell atop the dead pilot.

A gunshot barked and a bullet split the space he'd just occupied.

"Well, Mr. Blalock, what a pleasant surprise. I thought you'd be running with Ms. Maxwell before Holdren arrived. I guess it was my turn to underestimate your tenacity."

John caught his breath again as waves of pain burned through his head and back.

The plane accelerated down the active.

"What's the matter, John? Are you getting too weak for repartee'? I noticed my earlier shots didn't entirely miss. Could it be that you're more seriously wounded than I thought?"

John wanted to give a snappy comeback, something you'd hear in the movies, but not often in real life. But he just didn't have it in him. John felt around for the gun the pilot had carried, found it and transferred his own weapon to his left hand.

He braced against the cabin wall, then leapt for the opposite side.

Two shots rang through the cabin. John slammed into the cabin door with a grunt and half fell into the front seat. He raised the pilot's gun. He was directly behind the pilot's seat now. If the pilot's ammo was the same armor piercing rounds that Dewatre carried this was about to be over.

Him aimed for the center of the wall and squeezed off six quick rounds.

Suddenly, Dewatre lunged at him from the cockpit door.

John dropped the pilot's gun and seized Dewatre's right wrist, but not before the man's knife pierced his body armor and plowed a track along his side.

The low cabin ceiling and crowded floor gave no room for fancy maneuvers and once they joined the fight became one of brute strength. John should have easily won a wrestling match with the smaller man, but the loss of blood had already weakened him.

Still, he forced Dewatre's knife hand back while trying to line up the barrel of his gun with Dewatre's torso. Runway lights flashed through the portholes lighting the cabin interior like paparazzi strobes. Even in the cold, Dewatre's face was beaded with sweat.

John bent his wrist until the slender blade of the knife was pointed at his opponent's throat.

"Alas, one dies but once, and it's for such a long time," John said.

Dewatre's eyes grew wide.

The plane lurched, throwing both men off their feet. John fell against something hard and a bolt of agony shot out from his shoulder. Before he could recover, Dewatre had pulled loose and climbed over him, heading toward the rear of the cabin. The aircraft bounced crazily for another moment while John tried to get to his feet.

Then as suddenly as it had started, the bouncing stopped.

John hurried to the emergency exit Dewatre took.

Dewatre crawled out the wing and was standing, holding on to the winglet. John looked around. They were off the runway and back on one of the taxiways and still doing at least fifty knots.

But not for long.

One of the old hangers was dead ahead. Its main doors were open, but the interior was filled with small private planes.

He looked back at Dewatre as the nose of the Learjet reached the hanger. The French agent had seen what was coming and turned to face it.

The end of the Learjet's wing went over the wing of a Piper without touching it. Then it passed between the upper and lower wings of an old biplane.

The upper wing took Dewatre in the chest and he disappeared from John's sight in a spray of blood.

Resigned to the inevitable, John dropped to the floor and awaited the impact.

He didn't have long.

The Learjet shuddered as its wings tore through two airplanes. A moment later there was an explosion of avgas and jet fuel. The exterior lit up with the orange glow of a fireball. The plane bucked. Its nose bisected a vintage P-51, transfixed an OV-1, disintegrated a Bell Ranger, and then crashed into the closed rear hanger doors.

John was hurled forward. He struck the pilot's body and lodged there for a moment. As the nose gear collapsed, the plane tilted crazily throwing John against the ceiling and then back onto the floor.

The cabin broke open just ahead of the wings and the back half of plane began to flip end over end. Fuel sprayed from ruptured tanks, sending long ribbons of flame in every direction. In seconds, flames englobed the wings and tail section in a great blast of heat and light.

John sat still, staring back, transfixed as the hurtling ball of flames expanded toward him.

CHAPTER 26

A sleek black Suburban slid to a stop near the burning hanger. Doors opened. Holdren and Romax emerged from the back seat. Their driver and another man joined them at the front of the vehicle where they surveyed the scene. Both Holdren and Romax wore overcoats that were open to expose their black Kevlar vests.

In the still dark gray of dawn, fire trucks sprayed foam into the hanger's interior in an effort to save the rest of the parked aircraft. An enormous column of fire towered above the hanger, its source somewhere on the opposite side of the hanger. Police cars, blue and red lights flashing, were parked along the tarmac at a safe distance from the fire. Other police cars cruised around the tarmac, playing spotlights into the dark recesses between the buildings. Farther down the line of hangers, other emergency vehicles including two ambulances were parked outside another hanger.

"What a shit storm," Holdren said.

"Think they got out alive?" Romax asked.

"How the hell should I know?" Holdren took the badly chewed cigar from his mouth and tossed it onto the snow. "With the way their luck has been going, I'd guess they're already out of here. I don't understand how anyone can stay one jump ahead of us. I thought for sure we had them at the house, but they responded as if they knew we were coming."

Romax shook his head slowly. He admired the tenacity of Blalock. The man was acting alone and yet staying ahead of them. Why had Blalock ever left the government? "I suspect its Blalock. We know his military background, and although the CIA won't talk about him, we know he must have worked for them for at least three years."

"Yeah, but I worked for them for ten years and I don't think I could have been as lucky as this guy. Well, there's nothing to be done until we find out what happened here. If it was Blalock and Maxwell, then who were they fighting?"

"I've been wondering about that myself. You know, there was a report that two bodies were found in San Francisco," Romax said.

"So?"

"The NCIX report stated they were suspected Japanese External Trade Organization agents."

Holdren's eyes narrowed. "JETRO is on to this? Christ, who else is involved? This is getting way out of hand. Do they think Blalock killed them?"

"They apparently didn't make the connection, or at least they hadn't as of yesterday. It didn't sound like his style."

"Oh, why is that?"

"They were garroted."

Holdren cursed under his breath and turned to the driver. "Morgan, round up whoever is in charge and get them over here, then get our personnel to check the area. I want to know who belongs to that plane and I want IDs on each and every body. ASAP! Look for witnesses and any sign of them. With this much excitement, someone must have seen something."

"Yes sir," Morgan said. He trotted off toward the nearest fire crew.

"Romax, get on the radio and see if we have a location on their transmissions."

"Sure, what are you going to be doing?"

Holdren studied the billowing flames. "Me? I'm going to find some marshmallows."

* * *

John lay on his back, staring up at a tall column of orange and black flames that stank of jet fuel and burning insulation. He watched the flames and marveled at their intensity, until he realized his face was nearly parboiled. He rolled over and lifted himself to his hands and knees. He could no longer feel the localized pain of his destroyed ear, injured shoulder, or cut side. Those pains were lost in the myriad pains of bruised and torn flesh.

Forcing himself to his feet, John swayed in the waves of heat. A few hundred yards away, past the flaming portion of jet, the hanger burned with a lesser intensity. All around him was bare earth, still damp from melted snow. He checked himself, found nothing broken, and found that his handgun was still holstered beneath his armpit. He turned toward the eight-foot high, chain-link fence. There was no way he was going to climb it, he had enough trouble standing. To his right, the night was filled with approaching rescue and fire vehicles, to his left were the bright lights of the distant main terminal. He was still disoriented from events, but he thought that the hanger where he'd left Caitlin was somewhere down that way.

He turned left.

John walked about fifty feet and was just starting to get some kind of stability in his stride when he saw the metal case. He stopped next to it and stared down.

"Well, looky looky. What have we here?"

It was the helmet case. The one he'd thrown into the throat of the jet's port engine. It was beat up, singed along one side, but still intact, and still latched. The intake guards had kept it from being shattered among the spinning turbine blades and, apparently, it had been thrown clear when the rear section of the Learjet broke up.

John bent and fell. The air whooshed out of his lungs. He lay still for a moment, then used both hands to push himself back to his feet. When he bent to pickup the case again, he found himself sprawled beside it on the slushy earth once more.

“Son of a …”

He gripped the case’s handle in his left hand and lurched erect.

It took him a few seconds to reorient his position, then started forward. He reached pavement, an access road. It ran between a row of warehouses and the fence. In the distance, he thought he recognized the Rocky Air Freight hanger.

Caitlin was still unconscious, or he would have been able to reach her over the Egg. She should be safe, but eventually Holdren's men or the police would search every nook and cranny. Then they'd find her.

John moved into a trot.

A hundred yards later he braked to a halt. For a moment, he couldn't believe his eyes. Resting against the fence, in a shallow ditch between two warehouses, was his rented Cherokee.

He walked toward it, suspicious that it was some kind of bizarre trap. The headlights pointed down into the snow filled ditch and were hardly visible. Closer, he saw the driver's door was open and the engine was still running. He peered in the back. His gear was there. Walking around to the driver's side, he saw that the transmission was engaged.

He'd thought Dewatre had driven it away from the Learjet and then circled back to park next to the hanger, but apparently, he'd been in such a hurry that he hadn't bothered to stop.

John tossed the dented metal case into the back seat and climbed in behind the wheel. He shifted into reverse and backed out of the shallow ditch. Now he had transportation. All he had to do was pick up Caitlin and get the hell out of there.

A half-mile farther he pulled to a stop behind the Rocky Air Freight hanger. Police cars were all over the place, but most were on the runway side of the hanger. The few in the back appeared to be empty. John killed the lights and cruised to the side of the hanger.

He saw where the officers from the empty patrol cars were.

They were helping paramedics load Caitlin onto a stretcher.

John watched helplessly as they were joined by two men in dark, unmarked uniforms and Kevlar vests.

Holdren he recognized and the second man matched Caitlin's description of Romax. "Son of a bitch!"

John backed the Jeep up until he was almost out of sight of the cluster of people. After a few minutes, the paramedics wheeled Caitlin around the far side of the hanger. Holdren and Romax talked to the police for a moment more, then followed the paramedics.

John put the Jeep in gear and moved toward the airport exit. Holdren would take Caitlin away from the paramedics. But when? They might let them carry her to a hospital and determine if she was seriously injured before taking her, or Holdren might insist on taking her before they left the airport.

If he had to bet on one or the other, he would choose the hospital. There'd be a damn slim chance of getting her away from them at the hospital. He could try to stop the ambulance in route. He'd have to try.

He located a side street where he could watch the airport entrance without being observed and waited.

Less than two minutes later the ambulance appeared. It was flanked fore and aft by a pair of black Suburbans.

John cursed under his breath as the vehicles passed his position. He waited until they were a block away, then pulled out, and followed. The ambulance wasn't speeding and now that the snow had finally stopped falling, its flashing red and white lights were easy to spot.

They turned north onto Powers and a couple miles later turned west onto Platt. John held back, giving them a little more distance, and letting a couple of other cars get between them. Traffic on Platt was almost nonexistent. In an hour, it would be another story.

John remember there were a couple of hospitals off Platt that might be their destination. Neither would take long to reach.

The ambulance lights crossed Circle Avenue a minute later while John was cresting the hill. A few blocks farther, the ambulance veered off to the right on Boulder. That settled it. They were heading for Memorial Hospital.

John followed their turns until the ambulance backed up to the emergency room doors. He parked across the street, crouched low in the seat, and watched. Several men climbed out of the Suburbans before the ambulance doors opened. Each man carried a compact Uzi carbine and watched the street rather than the ambulance. Did they really think he'd go up against them in the open? They were giving him more credit than he deserved. Maybe if he'd had a sniper rifle ... how good was the 30-06 rifle he'd taken from Caitlin's parent's house? No, it'd be stupid, he wasn't in any condition to try, and by the time he could set up, they'd already have Caitlin inside and out of reach.

He'd wait. Once she was awake she'd contact him and they could coordinate a rescue. John put the car in drive and pulled away from the curb. He needed time to rest, to think.

Hell, what he needed was a small army.

He drove north a ways, then turned east. It was a weekday, there was nearly four inches of snow on the streets, and people wouldn't be moving around any more than necessary. Colorado Springs was not known for it's rapid snow removal. The main streets would be clear soon, but the side streets would wait for the next sunny day.

In a few minutes he found a side street with snow covered alleys leading away in either direction. John found one that looked a little seedier than the others and pulled down it until he found a large Dumpster to park behind. He turned the engine off, killed the lights, and leaned back against the headrest. His body hurt. He would swear that even his hair hurt.

Caitlin shouldn't be out too long, and then he could move again. Right now, he'd rest, then he'd be ready when she woke. Maybe an hour or so. It didn't matter. Any rest was welcome. He closed his eyes. Just a little rest.

*   *   *

Romax and Holdren followed the gurney into the elevator. The other agents tried to follow, but the doctor held up a hand to restrain them. They looked to Holdren for orders.

"Put a man on each entrance and I want two upstairs outside her room."

They nodded as the doors closed.

"Doctor, how soon will the blood test be back?" Holdren asked.

"If it's a common drug, we'll know within the hour. Otherwise, well, there are drugs that don't show up in the bloodstream at all once they combine in the system. If that's the case, then we'd have to look for cell byproducts for identification. In truth, we might never know."

"That's not what I wanted to hear."

"I'm sorry, but her vital signs are normal enough. She shouldn't be in any danger."

"What I want to know is how soon she will be conscious?"

"Oh, well, I can't tell you that until the blood test is done and even then it's questionable. If I had to guess I'd say she will probably be awake within twenty-four hours."

"Twenty-four hours, all right. We can work with that."

The elevator stopped. Romax and Holdren stepped out first, then motioned for the doctor and attendant to come out. They moved the gurney down to a private room and transferred Caitlin to a bed. The doctor adjusted the drip on the IV and left.

Holdren closed the door behind her and turned to Romax, who was staring at the jewel-encrusted, Phoenix Egg he held in his left hand.

"So what are we going to do until she wakes up?" Romax asked.

"I've been thinking about that. We're going to arrange a little trap for Blalock. The profilers said he's a dedicated person. He won't abandon his client, so I think we can get him to attempt a rescue."

"Here? That's a little public, isn't it?"

"No, we'll move her to the Los Alamos facility just as soon as she's awake. We'll need her to be awake to lure him in. You get things arranged. I'm going to sit with our pretty Ms. Maxwell for awhile."

"Sure thing."

Romax closed the door behind him and walked down the hall to the stairwell. Sunlight streamed in through a narrow window in the far wall. Pulling out his cell phone, Romax autodialed the barn.

"Yes?"

"Cronski, please, Mark Romax calling."

A few seconds later his boss picked up the phone. "Romax? How are things?"

"We've made some progress. We have Ms. Maxwell in custody and we have recovered one of the Phoenix Eggs."

"Excellent, that's the best news I've heard all week. Have you recovered the blueprints."

"Just for the encoder. We still haven't found the prints for the Eggs."

"Damn, you know we have to have those prints. That damn Curtis destroyed all the copies except for the one he passed on to Corning. It'll take years to reproduce his work."

"I know, sir. We're working on it, but another problem has surfaced."

The voice on the other end of the call tightened. "What now?"

"It appears that Ms. Maxwell has keyed the Phoenix Egg to herself."

"Damn!" Cronski paused, then said, "Look Romax, make damn sure she stays alive. We can't reprogram the phone and without the blueprints...."

"I know, sir. I suspect that Mr. Blalock has the other Egg keyed into his mind. If so, we'll have to have them both until we can manufacture new ones."

"I agree. You see to it."

"Yes, sir. And if I may add one more thing."

"Yes?"

Romax hesitated while he stared out over the snowy rooftops. "Sir, I am uncomfortable with some of Holdren's actions. It seems to me that he may be losing control."

"That's too bad. He's been a good man. All right, keep an eye on him. If he steps too far out of line, well, I'll back whatever play you determine is necessary. Just get those plans back!"

"Yes, sir."

* * *

The patrol car slowed, stopped, and backed up. Sure enough, there was a brand new Jeep Grand Cherokee parked halfway down the alley. Officer Carl Weber turned into the alley and drove close to the Jeep. The call had come from some lady who was taking out the garbage. She'd reported a body in a car behind her house. Her statement was that the man appeared to be dead from a gunshot or something. She hadn't gotten too close to the body, but there were bullet holes in the vehicle and blood covered the driver's head.

There was someone in the driver's seat. Weber stepped out of his patrol car and paused to report the license plate and his status. Dispatch informed him that the vehicle was a rental, rented two days ago at the airport. It hadn't been reported stolen. Weber adjusted his dark sunglasses and still had to squint against the glare of the noon sun off fresh snow. He unsnapped the clasp on his holster and moved cautiously toward the driver's side.

The Jeep had a couple of windows missing and bullet holes pockmarked the near side. Since no one had reported gunshots in the area, Weber guessed that the driver had been fired on somewhere else and had made it this far before he collapsed.

Weber reached the driver's door and peered in.

The driver's head was slumped back against the headrest. His eyes were closed. Congealed blood covered the left side of his head and it looked like at least half his ear was missing. An old scar ran down the side of his face giving the man a sinister, menacing appearance. Weber stared at him for a minute, looking for some sign of life, but there was none.

Weber tried the door. It wasn't locked. He pulled it open and paused to see if the driver would react. Again, no response. The driver was wearing a heavy coat, torn and scraped; it looked like it had been expensive once. The man's hair and eyebrows were singed and the smell of burnt hair was mingled with a smell similar to diesel fuel, but Weber couldn't identify the odor. He smiled. This was going to be interesting, something to break the monopoly of minor crimes and traffic arrest.

Careful to avoid the blood, Weber reached over and felt the driver's neck. It was still warm. If he was dead, he hadn't been dead long. Weber moved his fingers over the carotid arteries and squeezed in his search for a pulse.

The driver jerked awake.

Before Weber could move the man's left hand shot out and closed on his neck. The strength in his grip was enormous and it tightened against his windpipe. Weber tried to pull away, but was held fast. His right hand tugged at his Sig/Sauer handgun, but he froze when he heard the click of a hammer being pulled back. Something cold and hard was pressed against the underside of his chin.

Oh, God. It wasn't fair. He'd only been on the force for three years and he'd been married less than a year. His wife, Gail, was expecting their first child in April. It just wasn't fair that he wouldn't get to see their child born.

"Please," he said. His voice was hoarse over the grip that compressed his larynx.

The driver's brown eyes were bloodshot and intense. He blinked and seemed to see Weber for the first time. "You a cop?"

The man's voice was as hoarse as Weber's. "Yeah. Look man, you don't want to do this. I can get you a doctor. You're hurt bad."

"Shut up for a second. You alone?" The man's eyes shifted toward Weber's patrol car.

"Yes, but I've checked in and reported your plates. If I don't call back in soon they'll come looking."

"Give it a rest, all right? No one's going to check on you for hours. What are you doing here?"

"Someone reported a body. I thought you were dead."

"Well, they probably were closer than you know."

The pressure on his neck eased, but the gun barrel didn't move. "Come on, man. Put the gun down. I'm not here to hurt you. Let me call you a doctor."

"Thanks, but I'll have to decline. Look, I'm not going to shoot you or anything, but you know if I put my gun down you're going to try to arrest me."

"No, I...."

"Please, cut the bullshit. I'll give you a chance. I don't want to hurt you at all and I haven't done anything that the police are after me for."

"Then put the gun...."

"Shut up already, you're getting boring. Look, there's someone else's life in jeopardy and I can't take the time to explain. If you give me any grief, I'll cripple you and then go on about my business. Do you believe me?"

Weber met his gaze. His eyes were cold. Icy death lurked there. This was not a man to fuck with.

"I understand," Weber said.

"Good. Raise your hands to where I can see them, then back up."

Weber raised his arms horizontal to the ground and took three slow steps backwards. The door to the Jeep opened and the man stepped out. The sights of the Colt never left

Weber's middle. His pants were as tattered as his coat and in places raw flesh gleamed wetly through tears in the material.

"Mister, you ought to let me get you to a doctor." It was fucking amazing that this guy was ambulatory.

"Are you an Ollie, officer?"

"What? No, my name's Weber. Carl Weber."

"I meant as in Stone, Oliver Stone."

"I don't follow you."

"Never mind. Look, I want you to take off your gun belt and radio. Then slide it under your vehicle."

Moving slowly, Weber complied. He unclipped his microphone and shoved it with his gun and utility belt about halfway under his cruiser.

"Good, now step to the back of your vehicle."

Weber backed up, relaxing his arms to his side now that he was weaponless. Without taking the gun sights off him, the man opened the door to his cruiser, killed the motor, and removed the keys. He leaned in farther, gripped the microphone, and yanked it out of the radio.

Standing, he tossed the broken microphone to Weber and jingled the keys. "As long as you don't go for your gun while I'm still in sight, I'll drop these at the other end of the alley. Don't worry about calling in the report. It's your job, but by the time you do, I'll have changed vehicles and will be moving on. I don't anticipate being here any longer than I have to and I won't be breaking any laws."

Not knowing what else to say and still half afraid the man was going to shoot him, Weber nodded.

The man's features grew suddenly tired and lost all sign of menace. He returned the heavy Colt to a shoulder holster, turned, and walked back to his vehicle.

Weber watched him until he reached the end of the alley. There he stopped and dropped the keys in the snow, turned left, and was gone.

* * *

John drove east as soon as he was away from the cop. There was still no contact from Caitlin. He checked his watch and found it was nearly noon. As much as it burned to have her in Holdren's power, he was going to have to be patient.

He turned into Citadel and cruised the mall's open-air parking lot until he spotted another Jeep Cherokee that was the same model and color as his rental. He parked as close as he could and got out.

He took a screwdriver from the bag in the back of the Jeep and quickly removed his license plates from both the front and rear of the Jeep. He took another moment to ensure no one was watching, then removed the plates from an old Ford Taurus that was parked next to him, and replaced them with his plates. Then he went to the other Jeep and exchanged the Taurus's plates for the Jeep's plates.

Ten minutes from the time he'd entered the parking lot, he left with new plates that would show up on any police check as belonging to a local citizen who, hopefully, wasn't wanted for any crimes. With luck, neither of the other drivers would notice the switch for a couple of days since they hadn't had personalized plates. Since the police would look for a Jeep Cherokee first and then at the plates, they probably wouldn't notice his plates on the Taurus. The only glitch would be if a cop ran the plates on the other Cherokee, found they belonged to the Taurus and then stopped the Jeep to see if it was John. There was always the possibility of a mistake, but he'd done the best he could do until he could change cars.

Back on Platt, John headed east again until he passed the Peterson Air Force Base exit. Then he took the next exit onto highway 94, passing the small green sign advertising Falcon Air Force Base and continued east.

About ten minutes later, he turned off 94 onto a side road that skirted the edge of the small town of Falcon. Trees out there were sparse and few grew as high as ten feet. After a mile, he came to a driveway that led along an escarpment.

Forty-year old pines bordered the east side of the drive; none were more than twenty feet tall.

The drive ended at a small fenced-in yard. A weathered split rail fence made of lichen covered cedar ran into the trees on the right. On the left, it paralleled the top of the drop for a least a hundred yards before turning east again. The house was a log home blackened from decades of sun. Its long front porch faced distant Pikes Peak. A thin column of gray smoke rose from the rock chimney.

John parked beside a Dodge 1500 that had seen better days, killed his engine, and got out. Although less snow had fallen out here than back in the Springs, there was still a solid, untouched blanket covering the yard.

He was halfway to the aged drooping steps when the front door opened. A large man with a full, graying beard and shoulder length, gray hair stood behind the screen door and called out, "What's your business?"

John stared up at him; the man's right hand was out of sight behind the doorjamb. "Gunny, it's John Blalock."

Instantly the screen door pushed back and the big man stepped out onto the porch. Although it'd been years since the knee replacement, he still walked with a limp. His right hand was in view now, and the Berretta 9 mm looked small in its grasp.

"Well, Captain Blalock, as I live and breathe. What are you doing up this way, John? Come all this way just to pay respects to your ol' Gunny?"

John noticed that the Gunny hadn't commented on John's obvious injuries. "No, Gunny, although I wish that were the case. I've run into a little trouble."

"I can see that. Well, don't stand out here being a target. Come on inside."

John climbed the snow-covered steps, holding onto the railing as he went, and joined the Gunny on the porch.

The Gunny took his arm and John let him put it over his shoulder and help support John's weight. They went inside where a log fire burned in a massive stone hearth. The great room was filled with old furniture and copies of Renaissance art. An elk antler chandelier hung over a massive polar bear rug.

"Well, Captain. What do you need more, a drink, ministering, or sleep?"

"That order sounds good."

"Then that order it'll be."

Gunnery Sergeant Albert T. Zim, U.S.M.C., Retired, helped him to the sofa, and disappeared in the direction of the kitchen. To the tune of ice clinking against glass, John struggled out of his coat. He tossed it to one side and then found that he couldn't get the shoulder harness rig off no matter how he tried.

He'd given up getting it off when the Gunny returned with two drinks.

"It appears that you've had more than a little trouble. Have you been playing hero again?" Gunny asked as he passed John a tumbler filled with Scotch and a single ice cube.

"No, Gunny, I've just been trying to survive."

"I certainly hope so. You know what I always say."

"Even heroes die," they said in unison.

"The Corps," John said, raising his glass.

"The Corps."

They each drained about half of their drinks. John lowered his glass to the coffee table, taking care to use a recent issue of Guns and Ammo for a coaster.

"Gunny, could you help me out of this rig? I can't seem to get my arm back far enough."

"Sure, John."

Gunny set his glass on the table, directly on the wood. He stood and helped John pull the shoulder holster first off his left arm and then the right.

"Doesn't look like that vest did you too much good."

"I'm not dead."

"You finish your drink. I'll fetch the first aid kit and we'll see what can be done for you."

"Aye, aye, Gunny," John said and retrieved his glass.

This time he sipped and enjoyed the flavor of the single malt while the massive first sip continued to spread fire throughout his chest.

Gunny returned a couple of minutes later with a first aid kit, a bowl of water, and a white towel in one hand. His other hand held a bottle of Glenfiddich and two ice cubes. He dropped one ice cube into each of their glasses, refilled John's glass, and topped his own off.

"Where do you want me to start?" Gunny asked.

"I think the back."

"All right, off with the vest and shirt then."

With Gunny's help, John was able to shuck both items.

"When did you start wearing jewelry?"

"What? Oh, this. It's not jewelry, but it's a long story."

"Well then, save it for when I'm done. Now let's see that back.

As John leaned forward on his knees, Gunny examined the wound.

"How's the lung?" he asked.

"I don't think the bullet got that far. If it weren't for the blood, I'd think the vest stopped it and my shoulder was just bruised."

"Well, it's not just a bruise. Let's clean it and see what we see."

Gunny dipped one end of the towel into the water and softly rubbed. The water was warm, but the touch was pain. John tightened his jaw and waited.

After a minute, Gunny stopped. "There's discoloration and swelling. I believe the bullet is lodged against your shoulder blade."

Gunny set back and picked up his first aid kit. "I've got topicals and the heavy stuff. Which shall it be?"

"You'd better make do with the topicals. We need to talk and I don't think I could stay awake if I have the heavy stuff. Besides, I may have to leave again."

"The Captain is always right."

John coughed. "Please Gunny, I don't think I could laugh just now. It'd hurt too much. Besides, since when have you ever thought the Captain was always right?"

"Most of the time, Captain. I just didn't want it to go to your head. Too many officers go bad when they start to think they know better than their senior noncoms."

John stared at the older man in amazement. He couldn't remember the Gunny giving out many compliments.

"Now, lean forward again and let me numb that wound."

John obeyed and a second later felt the cold spray against his flesh. It stung at first, then the feeling faded.

Gunny pulled out a pair of narrow forceps and clicked them together, twice. "Well, I haven't done this in some time, so if it hurts, keep it to yourself. I don't like to be critiqued while I'm working."

"Aye, aye, Gunny."

"You can start your story anytime you like," Gunny said and leaned over John's back.

While Gunny worked, John retold the events of the last few days, leaving out only what he considered too personal to relate. His dialogue was interrupted several times by pain, but he recovered and continued.

Gunny dropped a bloody piece of copper on the table in front of John. It was sharply conical. "Haven't seen one of those in years. I thought only the French had them now."

"Yes, the French," John agreed and went on with his story.

Gunny dressed his wound and then cleaned and examined the cut along John's ribs. He numbed it and took sutures from the kit.

By the time he had finished stitching up the wound, John had his story up to date.

"Now let's have a look at that ear."

John was having trouble hearing on that side, but he was hoping that it was because the ear canal was filled with blood rather than actual damage to his inner ear.

The Gunny cleaned the area, which hurt almost as much as pulling the bullet out of John's back and then shook his head. "This is going to take plastic surgery to really fix. I don't think it'll do any real good to stitch it up. You've lost nearly half the ear, but there's no wound to sew together."

"Great, just slap some antiseptic and a bandage over it."

"How about this other bandage on your shoulder? Do you want me to change it?"

"I think it's all right. Is it seeping?"

"No, but some of the blood from your gunshot soaked the edges."

"All right, go ahead."

Between the warmth of the fire and the scotch, John's aches and pains had faded to a dull roar, but when he blinked his eyelids kept refusing to open.

Gunny finished with his shoulder and then examined the various cuts and burns that showed through tears in John's clothes.

After a minute, he shook his head. "These don't look too bad, but they will need to be cleaned properly before I bandage them. You might as well take a shower."

"All right, in a minute."

"This bauble you're wearing. You say it's like a radio connected to your head?"

"Essentially."

"And you know the frequency it's broadcasting on?"

"Yes, it's in the C-band."

"Then you have to assume this Holdren fellow knows the frequency too. If you try contacting Caitlin he's going to triangulate your location."

"Yes, of course. I won't use it while I'm here."

"Unless she wakes up and calls you."

"Ah, well I guess I could wait until I move away from your house to respond."

"No, that won't be necessary. You have a repeater in the Jeep?"

It was part of the equipment he'd purchased the previous day. "Yes."

"I'll take it down the road a ways and hide it in the trees. Then if they spot your signal, it'll be the repeater they home in on. I'm sure it puts out more power than that little bauble."

"Ten watts for it, less than a half-watt for this," John said.

"All right. Let's get you in bed and I'll take care of that."

John let the Gunny help him to his feet. "I'm going to need a few more things."

"Yes sir, I imagine you will. Heroes always have needs. Let me worry about logistics."

"Thanks Gunny."

* * *

"John. Oh, John, I feel so groggy. What's happened?"

John snapped from dream to full awareness. "Caitlin? Where are you?"

"I don't know. Everything is dark. I feel ... I don't feel good. John! John, are you all right?"

"I'm safe. It's you I'm worried about. Holdren is near you. They took you from the airport to a hospital, Memorial, over on Union. I'm sorry, I had to let you go. There was just no way for me to get to you."

"The airport. Yes, I was there with Dewatre. I remember now, he gave me something to knock me out. I guess it worked."

John rolled over and looked at the clock next to the bed. It was nearly seven. The clock indicated A.M. but the room was pitch black. "If you're just coming out of it, then you've been down for more then twenty-four hours."

"Lord, no wonder I feel groggy. John, what happened to Dewatre? The last thing I remember he had me on a plane ready to leave the country."

"Dewatre's dead. I wish I could say the same for Holdren."

John threw back the covers and sat up. His body was stiff. Every muscle ached. He was a little groggy himself. Perhaps he shouldn't have taken Gunny up on the drinks. He needed to be alert more than he needed relief from the pain.

"Good riddance. Did you do it?"

"I guess I can take some of the credit, but only indirectly."

For three or four seconds he sent her his impression of the fight. It was one of the marvelous aspects of the Egg. Words weren't necessary, merely recalling a vivid memory would transmit it to whomever you were connected to.

"Oh my God, John. You're injured."

"Ah, well, yes. It's nothing serious though."

He hadn't really expected her to pick up on that part of his memory.

"John, I hear voices. One of them sounds like Holdren."

"Pretend you're still unconscious. If they think you have a serious injury, they probably won't move you until you're awake."

"All right, but don't leave me. Please."

"Caitlin, I swear I won't leave you. If they move you out of range, I'll find you. I will come for Caitlin. You have my word."

* * *

"You can drop the ruse, Ms. Maxwell. I know you're awake." He stood over her and waited. After a few seconds she still hadn't responded. Holdren placed one hand over her mouth and then pinched her nostrils shut with his thumb and index finger.

A half-minute passed without movement, and then she grasped at his hand and bent his thumb backwards.

He laughed. When she continued to bend his thumb back, Holdren slapped her, hard.

She let go of his thumb then and opened her eyes. "You murdering bastard. I hope you rot."

"Now, now, you've got to learn to control your temper if we're going to get along."

"Tell you what. Let me go now and I'll try to keep John from killing you."

Holdren had to laugh again. "Ms. Maxwell, you are just too much. You really think this bodyguard you hired is good enough to get to me?"

"Everyone can be gotten, Holdren. It's just a matter of motivation and patience." Christ, had she really said that? She was beginning to sound like John.

"I won't argue with that, but you must realize that means Blalock can also be gotten."

Holdren stopped.

What had she said? She'd called him by name. Where had she learned his name? Could Blalock have a contact inside the agency? Maybe they should take him alive. Questioning him might prove to be useful. "You're going to be coming with me, Ms. Maxwell. You can either come peacefully on we can drug you and take you out on a stretcher."

She glared at him for a moment and he realized she was more attractive than he had first thought. Perhaps it was the anger. It gave her a healthy glow.

"I'll go peacefully."

He looked at her carefully. He had no doubt that she'd only be as peaceful as necessary. As long as she thought Blalock would try to rescue her, then she would be predictable. "That's better. I'll leave you alone to dress. You have five minutes."

"Where are you taking me?"

"On a little trip," Holdren responded without turning.

* * *

John threw open the door to the bedroom and stormed into the kitchen. Bright light from a rising sun poured in through the windows to his left. To his right, the sun reflected off the snow covered western mountains and the rolling plains of the foothills.

The Gunny sat at the dinette table, working on a piece of electronic equipment. "Well, Captain. It's good to see you're up. I was afraid I'd have to call for the coroner."

"Not likely. They're starting to move her, Gunny. I need to get after them."

"Don't go rushing around too fast. Do you know where they're taking her?"

"Not yet, but I need to be ready."

"Come, sit here. I'll fix you something while we work out what you can do, breakfast okay?"

"I don't have...."

"Don't be giving me that, Captain. There's nothing you can do until you get some food in you. Never go off half cocked, you know what that got you the last time."

John fingered the scar that ran down the left side of his face and nodded.

The Gunny stood and went to the cupboards. "That's better. Eggs, bacon, biscuits, and jelly will get you going. The coffee isn't too fresh, but I put some of it in the Thermos in case you wanted some when you woke."

John sat down and examined the equipment Gunny had been working on. It was another repeater like the one John had used to increase the range on the Egg.

A minute later the Gunny set a large mug of steaming coffee in front of John.

"What's this, Gunny?" John asked as he indicated the equipment.

"Just what it looks like," the Gunny answered as he clattered pans around.

"A dual frequency repeater?"

"That's right. I picked up a couple of them yesterday along with some other things you may find a use for."

"Why a dual frequency repeater?"

"Where's your sense at, Captain? You know they can trace the signal to you. But they'll only be looking for the frequency that keys into these Egg things of yours. Right?"

"Yeah, of course. I must have been shot in the head or something. You've placed a repeater somewhere else. It picks up Caitlin's broadcast and frequency shifts it to this repeater. This repeater shifts the frequency back and transmits the signal to me."

"That's right. You should have thought of this already. I know I taught you better. How would you like your eggs?"

"Over easy, please. What's this other equipment you have for me?"

"You want to be able to rescue the fair damsel, right? Well, if you're going to play hero you'll need some field leveling hardware."

The Gunny cooked while going over a shopping list that would have made the day of any professional thief, or maybe a terrorist. Many of the items could only have been procured illegally, but John didn't ask where or how he had acquired them. He had also driven John's rental back to the airport and rented a Mercury Navigator using one of John's alternate ID's.

Another broadcast from Caitlin interrupted their conversation. "John, we're going up in the elevator. I think they're moving me by helicopter."

"All right, Caitlin. Keep me informed. I'm too far away to get there before you leave, but I should be able to track you. Keep me informed."

"They're putting her in a helicopter. What places around here might they move her to?" John asked.

"By helicopter? Well, they could take her to Fort Carson, it's pretty secure, but Falcon is the most secure area around here other than the mountain."

"Falcon, that'd be difficult. I was hoping they'd pick someplace a little less secure than that."

"That's the problem with world class villains, they like to make things difficult."

John didn't reply. The Gunny was always trying to get his goat, but usually, like now, John just didn't feel like being amused.

The Gunny set a plate filled with crisp bacon, three eggs, and enormous biscuits in front of John. "There's no point in worrying about how bad it could be until you actually know where they're taking her. It might not be Falcon at all."

"Uh huh," John mumbled through a mouthful of biscuit.

"So what are your plans? Are you going to storm the castle with fire and brimstone, kill all your enemies, and carry the maiden away on your white charger?"

John felt his face warm. "I don't expect it to be easy. I'm not totally stupid."

"No, but neither are your opponents. From what you've told me you must know that they're still after you. You have the helmet and the disk. They'll want both. Besides, didn't you say that the Frenchman also wanted you alive for testing the translators."

"Yeah, but that was the French. I figure our government must have more of these things, so what do they need me for?"

Zim looked at him curiously. "Are you expecting an answer?"

"No."

"Good, because you aren't going to get one from me," Zim added. "Look, Johnny, you know I want to go with you, but let's be realistic. From what the doctors tell me my heart wouldn't make it through ten minutes of that much excitement. Hell, I can't even watch a Broncos' game anymore, but I'll still go with you if you think I can help."

"I know Gunny and I understand. You've already helped me more than I could ask from any man, but there is something else you can do for me."

"Anything, Johnny. Absolutely anything."

"I want you to keep the helmet and the disk. There's a group of computer hackers that call themselves CHAOS. They'll know what to do with the file."

"CHAOS? Sounds like something from 'Get Smart'."

"Yeah, doesn't it? It stands Computer Hackers Alliance for Open Speech, but their actions are a little broader than just supporting free speech on the Web. They seem to think that all information should be freely available to the public. Like the old Green Peace organization, peaceful demonstrations are too Ghandi-like for them. They'd rather hack into a government computer and wipe every file they find."

"How do I get in touch with them?"

"My best link to them has been compromised, but I have another one. I'll leave you everything you need to reach them."

"And what do I do with the helmet?"

"Bury it. Literally, that's what I'd do with it. Find an isolated spot and cover it with dirt. Then act like you've never heard of it or me. If I make it through this, I'll eventually try to recover it, but otherwise...."

Gunny nodded once. "And what about your lady friend, assuming you don't make it back?"

"You'd be better off to act like you'd never met me, but if you insist on helping...."

"I do."

"Then find a good lawyer and try getting her out through official channels. It may take a few years, but I've got enough money stashed away to afford a good one. I'll give you the transfer codes and if you haven't heard from me in a couple of days it's yours to do as you see fit."

"I understand, Johnny."

*　　　*　　　*

It was afternoon before John had the Navigator loaded and was on the road. The storm had passed heading south into New Mexico and the air was a crisp blue. He needed to get up on the Web, but couldn't chance logging on at Gunny's place.

The last report from Caitlin had them flying southwest and Romax had even remarked something about going to Los Alamos. That gave John a direction, but he wanted to make sure. South of Pueblo he pulled into a rest area and used his cellular to dial up a public link to the Web.

It didn't take him long to locate Forester.

After a brief introduction, with a password Louie had given him for emergencies, John explained what he needed. Forester agreed to research the problem and pass the information along at John's next call.

John caught up with the storm front at Trinidad. The road crews were keeping the interstate open, but conditions grew steadily worse as he crossed the pass and descended into Raton. At Raton, he left the interstate and 64 toward Taos and Los Alamos.

It was dark before he reached Taos. He picked up a burger and fries at a Blake's Lotta Burger and logged back onto the Web while he ate.

Forester had come through for him. There was only one place in the Los Alamos area that was isolated, secure, and completely off all maps and the records of government installations.

John didn't ask where or how Forester had acquired the information, but thanked him politely and then downloaded everything Forester had.

The facility map had the location of the outer fence, buildings, and its relation to the main Los Alamos complex. As the translator fed the information into John's memory, he selected the optimal entry location and logged off the Web.

As he drove south on 68 out of Taos, he wished the information had contained security details.

CHAPTER 27

The storm had dumped six inches of wet snow in the Jemez Mountains by the time John backed the Navigator off the highway onto the service road.

He killed the engine and doused the lights, then sat quietly in the vehicle. The big V-8 engine pinged as it cooled. The research facility was hidden both by ponderosa and lodgepole pines that hung heavy with snow and by the swirling clouds of snow that limited visibility to a few yards.

There was only one entrance to the isolated facility and it was at the north end. There the narrow arm of the mesa joined the rest of the plateau at the edge of the Jemez Mountains. In better weather, if he had been uninjured, John would have preferred to infiltrate the facility by climbing the rock face of the mesa. It would have been the less obvious route and his rock climbing skills were adequate.

But since that was no longer an option, he'd picked the shallow arroyo that he'd passed a hundred yards back up the road as the most likely point of penetration. He'd come prepared to defeat electronic surveillance and the storm would make that part of his task easier.

He removed the key from the ignition and slipped it under the floor mat. There wasn't much chance of a car thief coming along in the next hour, but you could never tell. He opened the door and the strong wind billowed out his jacket. He ran the zipper up to his neck wind and then trudged through the snow to the rear of the Navigator. At the rear hatch, John slipped night goggles over his eyes and adjusted them. In the greenish cast of the vision, his equipment bags were dark shapes.

John opened the first, removed the tracker, and activated it. In a few seconds its LCD screen illuminated and pointed the direction of Caitlin's signal. As agreed, she was keeping up a continuous chatter over the translator without expecting a reply from John. If he replied, Holdren's men would quickly locate him. After he was inside the complex, it would be another story. Their triangulation equipment might pick him up miles away, but at close range the signals would merge together into a single source. Unless they were being clever. If they were expecting him then they could run the signals through a computer to separate out the encoding and decipher which was which. But that was one of the chances he'd have to take. One of many.

First, he had to get inside.

John draped a bag over each shoulder. Then he took out the poncho he'd sprayed with an inch thick layer of open cell foam and pulled it over his head and shoulders. He closed the rear hatch, then followed his tire tracks back to the pavement.

John didn't see the arroyo until he was almost on it. He paused at the steel guardrail and caught his breath. His exertion was low level, so far, but already he felt tired, drained. He fished in his pocket for a Hershey's chocolate bar, ate it ravenously as he descended the steep bank, and then crammed the wrapper back into the pocket. Fifty yards up the arroyo he saw the fence. It was a typical chain link fence, but it was ten feet high and topped by a single helix of concertina razor wire, just what you'd expect to find at the edge of a national forest.

John crouched beside a boulder and studied the fence. It ran horizontally across the top of the arroyo. Spanning the walls of the arroyo, between the bottom of the fence and the snow covered floor, was six feet of steel grating. The bars were spaced wide enough to let normal water flows pass unhindered and yet narrow enough to keep even a child from sliding between them. But the narrow bars would act as a damn on the rare occasions when a summer storm would send an avalanche of water screaming down the arroyo. For those times the massive grating had been hinged to fold back away from the torrent and allow whatever flotsam the water carried to pass beneath the fence without tearing it away.

Microwave motion detectors would provide the outer perimeter security for the fence. Here at the arroyo, John could see one aimed to cover the base of the fence between the banks. The next detector would be located to cover this one so no one could sneak up and disable one of the sensors without triggering another. Somewhere, there would also be a camera. Security cameras were usually monitored at random intervals and a human guard's attention would wander, particularly at three in the morning when the cameras all showed a swirling mass of snow blowing across the lenses.

However, if anything triggered one of the microwave sensors the adjacent cameras would activate and focus on the trouble spot. That always warranted the guard's full attention.

In order to get past the fence John would have to transverse the microwave field without triggering an alarm. The fence was probably motion sensitive, so any movement would trigger another alarm. But with any luck, the guards would have disabled the fence motion detector because of the wind. Fence detectors were notorious for giving false alarms during a strong wind. Debris, paper, bits of plastic, even tumbleweeds would strike the fence and each successive gust would cause the fence to alarm.

There. A camera was mounted opposite the microwave detector. Its focus was the center of the arroyo and the opposite bank. By staying close to the near wall, he might be able to remain either clear of its field of view or at the periphery where slow movements would be less likely to be noticed by human eyes.

John removed a field strength meter from one of the bags and activated it. The microwave energy levels were less than a microvolt per meter. The energy levels would max out in the millivolt range unless whoever ran security here had disregarded the OSHA safety standards and cranked up the outputs.

Rising out of his crouch, John adjusted the balance of his burdens beneath the poncho. Then stooping once more, John dropped lower until his butt was on his heels, then he duck-walked along the shadow of the near bank. He moved slowly, for motion detectors were more sensitive to a rapid change of field patterns than to a gradual change.

He kept the field strength detector close to his face so it would be readable and to keep its metal parts beneath the cover of his poncho hood.

The field strength rose rapidly as he neared the fence.

Someone had disregarded safety standards. When he stopped at the base of the grate, the energy levels had peaked at nearly a volt per meter, far above normal safety levels. Someone wanted to make sure any movement was detected. If it hadn't been for his makeshift cloak, John wouldn't have been able to get within ten feet of the fence.

Moving the detector along the grating, John was thankful to find that the metal itself was uncharged. That meant no electrification and no capacitance sensors. He could touch the grating without setting off an alarm.

John pulled a large rock next to the grating and braced his feet in the snow. He pushed against the grating. It moved, but only a fraction of an inch.

Well, he hadn't expected it to be easy.

Bracing his back against the grating, John clasped both hands around bars and shoved against the snow-covered sand. As he strained, the heavy grating began to move.

His gaze fell on something he hadn't noticed in the deep shadows at the edge of the grating. He froze and then slowly let the grating return to its original position.

Moving toward the object, he quickly saw it was a tiny position indicator, a limit switch that closed when the grating moved past a set point. If he had opened the grate another inch the switch would have triggered.

The switch was mounted on a metal plate set against the unmoving bars at the grating's edge and its tiny roller was compressed by another plate mounted on the grate itself. A pair of light gauge wires, covered with thick insulation, ran from the back of the switch to a nearby junction box.

Which was it? Normally open or normally closed? He guessed that it was closed as long as the grating was closed. Then opening the grating would interrupt a circuit and close a relay back at security's command post.

John rummaged through his bags until he found the small Fluke multimeter. He activated it and pressed its leads against the tiny wires. The readout showed no voltage. That was one indication that the switch was closed. He changed the setting to microvolts and looped one of the leads several times around one of the wires. This time there he detected a slight electric field, indicating a current flow in the wire.

He had guessed right. The switch was closed and a relay somewhere was sending a signal down the wires and through the switch.

That was easily handled. John returned the multimeter to his bag and took out a short piece of wire with an alligator clip at each end. He attached the clips to each of the tiny wires, pressing them in to make sure they penetrated the insulation.

Moving back into position, he strained against the grating until it slowly moved back and away from him. The pressure brought the fire back to his shoulder. It burned with every inch the grating moved until his eyes involuntarily teared.

He stopped and held the grating about eighteen inches off the ground. Using his left foot, he maneuvered the rock into position and then slowly released the bars. The heavy grate pressed the rock into the arroyo bed about three inches before coming to a stop.

It didn't leave much room, but John didn't think he had the energy to lift the grating again. It would have to do.

He rested for a moment, both to keep from sweating and to restore his energy. There was going to be plenty to sap his reserves without letting them get prematurely low. John pushed his bags under the grating then slid under, stopping only once to free the edge of his poncho. John rose slowly on the other side, then picked up the bags again, and took out his meter.

The field strength was still too high. There must be another detector. It took him nearly a minute to find it mounted on a pole twenty yards farther down the arroyo. Still duck walking, John went another fifty feet before the energy levels were down to the point that he thought he was totally clear of the motion detectors.

Standing was nearly as painful as the long walk. Muscles protested and tried to cramp. He had to stretch them before continuing.

Continuing cautiously down the arroyo, he kept a close watch on the meter. There was always the possibility of multiple layers of protection.

He guessed right.

Twenty yards later the meter picked up another source. John slowed and looked for the transmitter. After a few minutes of fruitless searching he gave up and started forward again. The field strength continued to rise.

He moved the meter, sniffing out the source, until he determined that it was coming from something buried in the sandy floor of the arroyo. It didn't appear to be part of the alarm system. Perhaps it was a buried power cable for some remote equipment. Moving cautiously, he crossed the cable. The meter made no sudden jumps and after a moment of tense anticipation, he relaxed slightly. He paused to set down his burdens. Unzipping one of his bags, John took out the Uzi. He slung it around his neck, picked up his bags, and went on.

A minute later he froze, as something moved farther down the arroyo.

Something dark and low to the ground was moving toward him. It didn't move like a man.

He unslung the Uzi, but knew he couldn't afford to be detected until he reached Caitlin. Dropping his bags to the ground, John drew the long blade of the "Ashley Hunter" from the top of his boot and waited.

The dark shape drew more distinct and separated into two shapes that redefined their appearance and became Rottweilers as they rushed silently toward him.

The lead animal left the ground ten feet from John in a leap that took it straight at his throat. John stepped to the side and jammed the stock of the Uzi in its mouth as it passed. He let the dog rip the gun from his hand as he waited for the second dog's leap.

The other dog didn't leap. It came in low and sank its jaws into the flesh of his calf. In a second, it had pulled John off balance and he dropped heavily to the ground.

He swung the knife hilt at the dog as it dragged him backward through the snow. The heavy hilt made a loud crack as it struck the dog between the eyes. The animal dropped to the ground, but its teeth remained firmly attached to John's leg.

The first dog crashed into him before he could turn to meet it. Its massive jaws closed around the back of John's necked and squeezed down. For once John was glad he wore the thick coat beneath the poncho. The Rottweiler's teeth couldn't reach his flesh, yet. John twisted half around, gripped the dog's collar, and yanked the beast off the ground. In a single heave, John hurled it into the walls of the arroyo.

John bent hurried and pried the unconscious dog's teeth from his leg. As he rose, the massive weight of the first dog struck him as it went for his throat again. He raised his left arm just in time and the wide jaws closed on his forearm as the beast bore John to the ground.

Its jaws tightened, grinding the bones together.

Rolling, he tugged his right arm out from under him and then slammed the point of his knife into the dog's ribs. He twisted the blade violently from side to side.

The pressure on his arm relaxed as the dog made its first sound since the attack started. It yelped once and tried to back away from John. But the strength had gone out of its legs. It sat down, swayed for a moment, and then collapsed across John's legs. Its dark eyes stared up at him and a pitiful whine came from its throat.

John met its gaze and a wave of sorrow swept over him.

What only seconds before had been a menacing killer now lay across him like a family pet. John stroked its face with his gloved hand. "I'm sorry, boy. I know it wasn't personal. It was just your damn training."

But the dog was no longer listening.

He rolled the body gently off his legs which were now soaked with a mixture of the dog's and his own blood. Blood seeped from the deep puncture wounds in his calf. John took a sterile bandage from one of his bags and wrapped it tightly about his wounds.

The second dog was still unconscious. Both dogs wore a receiver/shocker on their collars. That explained the buried wire. It was part of a containment fence for the animals. John cut a few feet from his rope and tied the animal's feet together. It could chew through them after it woke up, but it would take it some time.

Retrieving the Uzi and taking up his burden, John limped up the arroyo.

A couple hundred yards later he saw the glow of lights ahead. He climbed out of the arroyo, only once sliding back down the snow covered bank, and moved toward the lights. In a minute, he was crouching beneath the snow-covered branches of a juniper. Staring across a small parking lot toward the security shack at the gate to the complex, he could see a single guard inside the shack. The woman appeared to be reading a book.

John watched the tracker's screen. Through the snow he could barely make out the building it was pointing toward. Opening one of his bags, John took out a couple of one pound packages. One he tossed near the guard station. The snow muffled its fall.

Well, he was close enough.

"Caitlin," he transmitted.

"John. God, John, am I glad to hear from you."

"I'm glad you were able to stay awake. Otherwise, I'd have never found this place."

"You're nearby then?"

"I'm just inside the gate. Can you give me directions?"

"Yes. We went past a water tower, then turned onto the first street to the right. It can't be more than a hundred yards from the gate. It's a large building. There was a placard near the entrance that mentioned DARPA. Do you know what that is?"

John moved out from under the branches and toward the street. "Yes, Defense Advance Research Projects Agency. It's the agency responsible for all black research programs."

"But that doesn't make sense. What would their connection to neuralphones be?"

John reached the street. There was only one set of recent tracks in the snow. From the tread pattern and the wide placement of the tires, he guessed it came from a Humvee. He paused to set the other package in the gutter next to the curb and to take a couple more from his bags.

"Someone must have come up with a national security justification. They must think it has espionage capabilities. Maybe they think it'll read minds."

He studied the landscape. There was no sign of movement. He rose and trotted to the intersection beneath the yellow glow of a metal halide bulb. The water tower had interesting possibilities.

"That doesn't make sense. There was nothing like that in the documentation."

He went to the base of the tower and placed one more package there, then he tossed a couple more in the snow down each of the intersecting streets. Going back to the corner, he hung a right. A large snow covered rock lay next to the curb. John set another package against the cement curb and covered it with the rock.

He jogged down the sidewalk. "I know, but what else would warrant their funding this research? I can't see DARPA being involved in modernizing the phone system."

John slowed as he neared the building Caitlin had described. It was a large complex with a glass entryway and few other windows.

"I didn't tell you what Dewatre said about it?"

"Oh? What did our friendly Frenchman know?"

"He claimed it was alien technology."

That made John stop. He ducked behind a lodgepole pine and caught his breath. "Was he serious?"

"I thought he was, but that doesn't mean he was right."

"No, but it does add an interesting set of possibilities and might even explain a few things that have been bothering me."

"Oh, like what?"

"Like how did your husband get involved in this mess in the first place? If he received the devices from someone up here then what was his connection with them? For that matter, why was the original research done here, near the Los Alamos lab, when they're more interested in weapons and nuclear power?"

"I've been giving it some thought too. You know I never liked that the helmet and eggs looked like a product run while everyone refers to them as prototypes. What if they are from off world? If someone brought them here for trade or even as a gift it would explain why it looks like it came off a product line rather than out of a lab."

"Yes and that makes sense in one other way."

"What's that?" he asked.

"The documentation said they're independent of language. What if they are meant to be nothing more than a translator? If you're postulating alien races then they need to be able to talk to people they meet. What better way to do it then with a device like this?"

"Yes. I hadn't thought of that. It does make sense."

"Maybe that's why everyone wants it so bad. Whatever government controls it controls all communications with these aliens."

"But still, we're supposing aliens have contacted someone here. That's a pretty far reach for my imagination."

"Oh? Who was it that said you should imagine one impossible thing before breakfast?"

"I don't remember. Let's see about getting you the hell out of there. I'm at the front door. Were there any guards there?"

"Yes, there was a uniformed receptionist. He checked Holdren's ID before letting us pass."

"Damn, human guards are a pain in the butt. Is there any other way in?"

"I don't know. I didn't see any the way we came."

"How about windows? Is there one in your room?"

"Yes, there's one, but it's barred."

"I can handle the bars, but it would be noisy. All right, how do I find you?"

"Take the elevator, turn left and go to the first corridor, turn right and I'm in the third door on the left."

"Okay, lovely lady, prepare to be rescued. If you need to pack, get started."

"I'll be ready, but, John, be careful."

"I'm always careful. Now be quiet for awhile, I need to concentrate on what I'm doing."

"Sure, John."

John moved to the edge of the building. He set both his bags behind a bush and transferred a few items to his coat pockets. Removing his poncho, he covered the bags with it. Then, with another pair of alligator clips and wire, he suspended his driver's license from around his neck. He unzipped his coat, hung the Uzi's strap around his neck, and zipped up.

His pants were dark enough that the blood shouldn't be noticed unless someone really paid too much attention to them.

Turning on the field strength indicator, John walked to the front door. He pushed the door open and walked into the lobby. A few plants were in the corners. A small sofa sat against the left wall, on the coffee table in front of it were several magazines and a telephone. The guard, a young man in a rent-a-cop uniform looked up from a magazine as John walked in.

John raised the power meter to eye level, studied it carefully, then moved it about as though he went trying to find the source of a signal.

"Can I help you?" the guard asked.

"Just trying to find our leak. Some of the experiments release a little radiation and the boss is concerned it may have gotten into the ductwork. Hell, it'll be harder to get out than asbestos."

"You have a radiation leak?" the guard asked. Concern shadowed his voice as he set down the magazine and stood up.

"It's nothing major, a few hundred rads worth at the most. Well, in all probability it wasn't more than a few hundred, a thousand at the outside."

"Why wasn't I told? We're supposed to be notified of any hazardous conditions. It's in our contract."

John moved the meter closer to the fluorescent lights and the readings strengthened.

The guard moved closer for a better look at the meter.

"You think I didn't warn the boss about letting you guys know? I told him, 'Boss, if the union ever finds out we didn't notify them of a class three release, there'll be grievances filed from now to doomsday.'"

The young man's face ashened. "A class three release? My God, that ... that's ... that's bad isn't it?"

"Well, it can be. Say, these readings are higher than I thought we'd get. Maybe we should evacuate the building. How many people are in here?"

"Another guard on the second level and a couple of guests."

"All right. You let them know we may have to evacuate and I'll contact the boss to get a decon team over here ASAP."

The guard turned his back on John to reach for the telephone.

John slipped his handgun from its holster and cold cocked the young man behind his right ear. He went limp and crashed to the floor.

John froze, listening for a sound to indicate he'd been heard. The building was quiet.

A door in the right wall was labeled restrooms. John gripped the guard under his arms and dragged him toward the door. He didn't waste time tying the man up, either he would have Caitlin out of there before the guard woke up or it'd be too late for either of them.

He stopped to read the guard's nametag. Bill Roberts.

It struck him that overcoming the guard had been too easy, but with the perimeter security as good as it was, the inside guards usually got a little lax.

"Caitlin, I'm inside. Are there any other guards?"

"I didn't see any, but there could be."

"All right, be ready. I should be there in a couple of minutes."

John found a pair of elevators just down the hall from the lobby. One set of doors was open. He stepped inside and scanned the controls. There were apparently three floors above ground and two below. He pushed the button for the second floor. The elevator moved silently, but a bell sounded as the doors opened. John pressed the hold button and raised his gun to cover the doorway. No one appeared in the opening. He listened for the sound of footsteps in the hall and waited. In a few seconds, he heard the sound of heavy feet coming toward the elevator.

"That you, Bill?" a voice called.

Judging by the sound the speaker was another young man and not more than ten feet away. John let him get a little closer, then stepped into the hallway. His gun leveled at the speaker.

The man's eyes grew wide, but he made no attempt to reach for his holstered weapon.

"Just remain calm and you won't be hurt."

"What did you do with Bill?"

"He's resting comfortably. Turn around and walk."

The guard nodded slowly, then turned, and moved slowly back the way he had come.

When he reached the first corridor, John stopped him again. "Just hold it there."

There was a desk and telephone there and an open paperback mystery novel lay cover up on the desk.

The book was entitled "S is for Suicide."

Down the right corridor, about seventy feet away, an exit sign glowed red above a door.

John moved close, unsnapped the man's holster, and removed his weapon.

"Turn down that way," John ordered as he shoved the gun into his belt.

At the third door, John again ordered him to stop. "Unlock that door."

"I can't do that."

"Sure you can. Did you forget I have the gun?"

"No, it's just that I don't have the key."

"A jailer without a key? Then what use are you to me?

John clubbed him behind the ear and he went down.

He knelt and removed two spare magazines from a leather pouch on the man's belt. Rising, he stepped over the man's body and knocked lightly on the door. "Hello? Anyone home?"

"John, is that you?"

"Don't you recognize my voice?"

"It's difficult. I can barely hear you."

"Uh-oh."

John tapped the door again with his knuckles.

"What uh-oh?" she asked.

"The door is steel and I don't have a key. I don't guess there's anyway to open it from that side?"

"No, it's a bare knob over here and I've already tried it."

"Just a minute then."

John holstered his weapon and took his lock picks from a coat pocket. He tried to work fast, but his fingers weren't as coordinated as usual. It took him nearly two minutes to pick the lock.

The door swung open and Caitlin stepped into his arms.

Her emotions swept over him as they touched. For a moment he could do nothing but hold her and share the touch, the warmth, the love.

Then she looked up into his eyes. "I told you I'd come for you, Caitlin. I'll never let them separate us again."

"John, you're exhausted. You didn't tell me how bad your wounds were."

"Not so bad, nothing a little rest and a couple of pints of whole blood wouldn't cure."

"Always ready with a wise ass remark. You're incorrigible."

"And I thought that was what first attracted you to me. Are you all packed? It's time to get on the stage."

"All packed."

John pulled the guard's pistol from his belt and jacked a round into the chamber. He decocked it and flicked the safety off. "Take this. The safety's off, just squeeze to fire."

"All right."

She took the extra magazines and tucked them into her belt.

John opened the door slowly and listened. No sounds.

He stepped into the hall and silently told Caitlin to follow.

"Is he?"

"Just unconscious."

John was almost to the end of the corridor when he heard the elevator chime. "Oh shit, we've got company. Back the other way, toward the stairwell," John transmitted as he backed away from the corner.

Footsteps pounded in the hall. Lots of footsteps.

As a uniformed guard came into view, John sprayed a three round burst at his legs. The man went down cursing and the second man stumbled over him. The others held back.

"John," Caitlin transmitted and her pistol barked loudly.

"Back in your room."

John fired another burst up the corridor, turned, stepped over the unconscious guard, and fired a burst at the men coming through the stairwell door.

Gunshots came from behind him and he felt two impacts against his back. They drove the breath from his lungs. He dove into the open doorway and Caitlin slammed it behind him.

"Are you hurt?" She asked as she threw the latch.

"No, the vest stopped them. Let's slide the dresser in front of the door."

The dresser was light and moved easily.

"It won't hold them," she said silently.

"Just something to slow them down."

John unlatched and opened the only window in the room. There was no screen, but a thick steel grating covered the opening.

He unwound a length of rope like material from around his waist and started running it around the edge of the grating.

"What's that?"

"Primacord. Get the mattress off the bed and drag it into the corner."

Footsteps pounded to a stop outside the door.

John finished the hurried wrapping and took a fuse from a pocket. He cut off three inches worth, stowed the rest, and took out his Zippo.

"Get ready, it's going to be loud," he transmitted as he struck the Zippo and held the flame to the fuse. The fuse flared. John dove for the corner and Caitlin pulled the mattress atop them.

The Primacord exploded. It filled the confined space with a roar and a shower of flying glass. From the hallway came shouts of surprise.

John kicked off the mattress and ran to the window with Caitlin right behind him. The grating had vanished. He looked down. It was about a twelve-foot drop to a snow covered boxwood hedge.

"You first. Take my hands, I'll lower you."

Caitlin jammed the gun in her belt and climbed onto the windowsill. Turning, she clasped John's wrists and then stepped back as he lowered her. Their coordination was as smooth as if they done it a thousand times.

At the end of John's reach, Caitlin put her feet against the wall and pushed off as they simultaneous released. She dropped the last distance to the ground, slipped in the snow, but came up an instant later with the gun in her hand.

John climbed onto the windowsill as the door burst open. He turned, firing as he stepped off the sill into space.

Someone else was firing. John saw the man with the M-16 flung backwards as John's burst caught him in the chest.

A burning pain shot through John's gut.

He hit the ground, rolled to his feet, stumbled, and fell.

Caitlin was at his side in an instant. She gripped his arm and helped to his feet, gasping as she felt his pain.

"John!"

"No time. I left my bags at the corner," he transmitted their location and contents in a wordless image.

"Can you walk?"

"Hell, I can run. You get the bags. I'll distract them."

She released his arm and ran toward the front of the building, not seeing him stumble and fall as she did.

John rolled onto his back and raised the Uzi. Snow blocked the end of its barrel, it would melt in a few seconds, but he couldn't wait. He slapped the barrel against his boot, aimed upwards, and fired a long burst at the faces already appearing in the open window.

John forced himself to stand. He fired another burst, shorter this time to conserve his ammunition, and limped toward the nearest trees.

A troubling warmth was spreading outwards from his abdomen.

He reached the first tree, braced himself against it, and fired toward the windows. This time his fire was answered by at least two guns. He rolled around the tree until it was between him and the window. "Caitlin, hurry it up dear. They're getting persistent."

"On my way."

John could see movement at both ends of the building. Caitlin ran toward him from the front and three black suited men did a rapid advance and cover toward him from the rear. They saw Caitlin at the same time she saw them.

Before they could bring their weapons to bear, John opened up, dropping one in his tracks and causing the other two to dive for cover.

Caitlin ran on without pause.

"Go! Keep moving, I'll be right behind you."

John slipped his night goggles back over his eyes while waiting for Caitlin to get a lead on him. He waited until she was nearly to the street. He fired a couple of bursts towards the two men at the rear of the building, another one toward the new group that had appeared at the front corner, and then ran after her.

Automatic fire shattered the branches behind him, sending splinters flying in every direction.

Gunfire sounded in front of him.

"Guards, in a vehicle, coming from the gate area," Caitlin transmitted.

"Stay low, I'll be there in a minute."

Caitlin's handgun quieted and John realized she must be switching weapons. If she just had enough sense to keep her head down.

He transmitted a wordless command for her to stay under cover until he reached her.

There was more gunfire as he approached her position, but a quick check told him it was her firing and only her.

"They're not shooting back because they want you alive," John transmitted.

"And not you?"

"Apparently they feel they can get whatever they need from just you."

"Fat chance." Her weapon sounded again.

"Take out their tires so they can't follow us. It's going to be hard enough to get out of here without having them chase us down these mountain roads."

"What do you think I'm trying to do? They won't stick their heads up long enough for me to hit them."

John reached her and stopped to lean against a tree trunk just to one side. His side hurt. It reminded him of the stitch he'd sometimes get from those ten-mile forced marches back in the Marines, except it had never hurt with such an intensity.

He gazed across the twenty yards that separated their position from the cover of the trees on the other side of the water tower. "They're just stalling us until the others can move up from behind. We have to get across this street in a hurry."

"Any suggestions?"

"I have a diversion set up. When I trigger it, start running. Be sure to stay to the right of the tower."

"All right."

She held her hand toward him.

If she touched him, she'd know how weak he was. It would distract her when she needed to concentrate on her own safety.

He forced himself to ignore her hand, to pretend he hadn't seen.

Pulling the detonator from his coat pocket, John fumbled with the controls until he had it set in the correct position.

"All right, here we go, on three. One."

He flicked the safety off.

"Two."

John lurched from behind the tree and ran toward the street.

"Three."

He depressed the switch.

There was a bright flash at the base of the water tower and a loud boom.

It was followed instantly by a deep throated roar as the ruptured water pipe sent a two foot wide horizontal column of water spraying toward the gate house and the parked Humvee.

Grown men screamed in panic as the jet of water threw the five thousand-pound Humvee out of its way. The men who had been crouched behind the vehicle were crushed before they could even rise to their feet.

"Wow! What a trick. How'd you know someone would be parked there?"

"I didn't. I placed the explosives to wet down the road and maybe knock the main gate off its tracks. I thought it would buy us some time."

He reached the opposite side of the street as Caitlin passed him without slowing. At the base of the water tower, John stopped to lean against the steel columns and cover her retreat.

Headlights were coming up the street.

"John? What did you stop for?"

"I have to work up one more diversion, then I'll be with you. The arroyo is just ahead. Keep going."

"I'll wait for you."

"Don't be silly, you know I can outrun you easily. I'll beat you to the fence."

"Why are you lying? John, how bad are you hurt?"

Hell, the longer they used the Eggs the more information they could glean from the other's transmissions. When they'd started, she hadn't been able to tell if he was lying unless they were actually touching. Now she could do it from a hundred feet away.

"Not that bad. I'll make it. I just want to make sure they don't follow too quickly."

He turned toward her and was shocked to see that she had turned and was coming back.

"What are you doing?" he asked.

"I'm not leaving you."

"You stubborn fool ... Have I told you I love you?"

"Yes, now set off your damn explosives and let's get the hell out of here."

He turned back toward the approaching lights. It was another Humvee. John changed the setting on the detonator and waited. When the Humvee was ten feet from the intersection John depressed the switch and a pound of C4 shattered the rock he'd set on it and sprayed the Humvee with shrapnel. The driver was killed instantly. The vehicle swerved off the road and into the trees.

"Shall we go?" John asked as he turned toward Caitlin.

Twenty feet from him she passed through the shadow of the small pump house and part of the shadow detached itself from the rest.

Although the snow blurred his night goggles, he recognized the shadow's broken nose.

"Caitlin!" His silent transmission told her everything. She spun away from the moving hand. Her gun rose.

The hand slapped away her gun. The automatic discharged a bright line of fire into the snow. Holdren's other hand closed on her coat and yanked her to him before John could bring his own weapon to bear.

"Drop the gun, Blalock, or I'll kill her."

The Uzi was a fine weapon, but it wasn't meant for single shot kills. He needed his Colt and he needed to see Holdren clearer.

"You won't kill her. You've ordered your men to take her alive," John said aloud.

Then silently he transmitted, "I'm going to go for a head shot on him. Wait until I give the signal, then drop. The sudden shift of your weight should give me a shot."

"All right, John. It's your play. Just kill the bastard for me."

"I'll be happy to."

"None of that silent shit!" Holdren said, his voice tight with anger. "I know that you're trying to cook something up and you'd better believe me when I say I'll kill her before I let her escape."

"I believe you, Holdren. You're just the type of sore loser that would stoop so low," John taunted as he shifted the Uzi to his left hand and slipped his right inside his coat.

"Fuck you, Blalock."

Holdren shifted his aim and fired.

John tried to leap to one side, but he was already too weak for that sort of movement. The bullet shattered his left knee and it collapsed under him.

"John!"

The intense pain blacked him out for a moment. When he got his eyes open again, Caitlin was kneeling over him. Holdren stood behind her.

John went for his holstered gun, but it was gone.

"All right, get your ass up. Unless you want me to cap your other knee."

"Leave him alone, you bastard."

"Shut up, bitch. I may want you alive, but you don't have to be unblemished. One more remark out of you and I'll pop one of your knees."

John could feel Caitlin's anger growing hot. She was going to try something that would get her hurt. He tried to calm her, but it did no good.

"Caitlin, help me up. If you're going to go after him, you'll need me on my feet."

"John, you can't walk on that leg."

"No, but I can at least take his aim off of you for a second. Now help me up."

She stood and pulled on his arm.

John thought the pain was going to kill him.

It took all of their combined strength to get him onto his good leg.

As John rose, he drew the Ashley Hunter from its boot scabbard.

They coordinated their movements with Caitlin going left as John went right. Holdren's gun wavered. He aimed at Caitlin's leg, but then recognized the real danger and turned in time to block John's thrust.

Unable to put weight on his left leg, John clutched at Holdren's arm, both to prevent him from firing and to keep himself upright. They struggled, John slipping about on one leg, Holdren having to support part of John's weight and still keep the long blade away from his rib cage.

"I'll get his gun," Caitlin transmitted.

"No, get another one. If you try for his it might discharge."

John should have been able to crush Holdren. The other man was more of an assassin than a real fighter, but John was weak, so weak. It was all he could do to keep the man's gun pointed away from him. He couldn't hold him for long. If Caitlin didn't get a weapon soon, he would die.

"I have one," Caitlin transmitted. "Just another second and I'll shoot the bastard."

"Don't take too long. This dance is tiring me out."

There was a gunshot.

Holdren didn't flinch.

"Drop the weapon if you please, Ms. Maxwell."

It was Romax. Holdren had delayed them long enough for the pursuing guards to catch up.

"John?" Caitlin transmitted.

"They still don't want to shoot you. Leave me. Run for the arroyo."

"No!"

"Do it, damn it!"

John put everything he had left into a twisting motion that broke Holdren's grasp on his knife hand. He slashed upwards. Holdren stepped toward him rather than away and the thrust sliced a gash along the man's ribs.

He danced back out of John's reach, cursing. "So, you want to play with knives, eh Marine? Well, let's see how well you dance."

Caitlin raised her weapon to shoot, but Romax reached her before she could fire. The automatic discharged into the sky as he forced her back.

Holdren holstered his handgun and a second later a Bali Song, butterfly knife, flipped open in his right hand.

"Christ, Holdren, let it go. We have them."

"Shut up, Romax. This man tried to carve up my liver. No one lives to brag about that with me."

John hopped back a couple of feet to get the little pump house at his back. "Come ahead, Holdren. What's the matter? Do you have to shoot me again to feel man enough to dance?"

"I'll show you a man," Holdren said moving unhurriedly after John.

"They say the Roman priests foretold the future by examining the entrails of sheep. You look like a sheep to me Holdren. Tell me, were you raised on a farm?" John taunted.

"What are you doing?" Caitlin transmitted. "Drop the knife John, Romax won't let him kill an unarmed man."

"You really think so, Caitlin? Somehow, I doubt it. I'm sorry I screwed this up for you. Don't let them get to you. Eventually they'll free you."

John took a second to transmit everything he'd set up with the Gunny. "Gunny Zim is already spreading the blueprints. By the time they're dispersed to the four winds there will be no reason for them to hold you. Keep your wits about you and hold on. Zim will get you free. Just don't let the bastards break you."

"No, John. Please, drop the knife. Please."

"Sorry, Caitlin. I can't do that."

As Holdren neared John, Caitlin turned to Romax. "Please, you can't let him do this. It's murder."

Romax shook his head. "I don't have any control over him, Ms. Maxwell."

Holdren moved in.

John parried his initial thrust and slashed back, trying to sever the tendons along the back of Holdren's hand. He missed and his movement caused him to teeter. John stretched a hand toward the building to steady himself as Holdren moved in again.

This time he moved toward John's weak side.

John turned to meet the attack, but knew he'd never make it in time. In a second, Holdren was inside his guard and then behind him. His left arm tightened against John's throat, pulling him back.

John felt a shocking impact between his shoulder blades. Raw pain burned anew in his chest. His legs numbed and the strength left his arms. The knife fell from his fingers.

Holdren drew his knife from John's back and loosened his grip.

Unable to hold himself, John dropped to his knees, tottered a moment, then collapsed face down in the snow as Caitlin's scream shattered his mind.

"John!"

Romax released her and she ran to John's side.

As she made contact, John saw himself lying face down in the snow. Blood seeped from a wound just to one side of his spine. As he breathed, he saw bubbles form around the wound. It was odd that his wounds no longer bothered him. He could barely feel the gunshot to either his leg or abdomen. Amazing.

Caitlin rolled him over and cradled his head in her lap. He looked up into her eyes at the same time he stared down into his own.

"God, dear God. Don't die John."

He coughed and tasted blood on his lips.

She was sobbing. John felt like crying himself.

Over the sound of Caitlin's sobs, he could hear Holdren talking to Romax.

"Call for an ambulance. We still want him alive," Holdren said.

A flash of insight reached John. If they wanted him alive, it was only so they would have two people with the translators. You couldn't very well experiment on just one person, how would you learn anything without the feedback between two users. They would keep him alive as long as they needed him, and they'd never let Caitlin go as long as he was alive.

Although she continued to sob loudly, Caitlin followed his thoughts and his idea. "No, you can't ask that of me. I can't do it."

"Yes, you can. You must. Do you want them to experiment on me forever? They will, you know. Only you can stop them."

As she realized what she had to do, John felt closer to her than ever. How could he have ever let her go the first time? It wasn't fair. They deserved to be together.

Caitlin's fingers no longer stroked John's cheek. They moved down to rest against the pulse that beat weakly through his carotids.

She clutched him tightly to her buxom as her fingers pressed into his neck.

John felt her love filling him. It swirled around him and cradled him in warmth that spread through his mind like the spring sun driving the frost from a meadow.

"What was it that Dewatre said?" John transmitted.

She knew the quote he was referring before he even thought the question. From her mind, he heard Dewatre speaking in memory. "We die but once, and it is for such a long time."

John almost didn't notice when his heart stopped beating.

CHAPTER 28

Caitlin felt John's pulse die beneath the pressure from her fingers. She choked on the wave of grief that washed over her. It wasn't right. He had done nothing to deserve his fate. He had only tried to save her and now he was dead. Caitlin still sensed his mind wrapped around hers and knew he felt no fear at death. She continued to press on his carotids, giving time for his body to go beyond aid. So these bastards couldn't revive him.

His love assuaged the grief in her heart, but still she sobbed. Whatever fate life held for her it would be without the one man who had loved her without limits. It was too much to bear.

* * *

John felt the blackness overwhelm him and he gave into it. He drifted in limbo, directionless and weightless. His pain had gone; even the little pain that had remained after Holdren had partially paralyzed him with a single thrust between his sixth and seventh cervical vertebra. But Holdren hadn't been as good as he thought. His thrust had been off-center and had only cut the nerves along one side of the spine rather than completely severing them. Strange how John knew that now. His trainers had said to severe the spinal cord between the skull and the first vertebra. That insured a quick and silent death. It seemed odd that someone would want to know how to paralyze an opponent.

It also seemed odd that he could still think about it at all.

Was this death? Stuck in blackness with no sensations. It seemed more like hell than mere death. Strange, he'd never given hell much thought. It had always seemed rather medieval to John. Or perhaps something borrowed from the Greek and Roman myths of an underworld ruled by some pagan god. It hardly seemed like the creation of a loving God.

Well, it looked like he would find out sooner rather than later.

Something moved him.

At first, it was as if he was a compass, being turned toward one of Earth's poles. Suspended in nothingness, John saw a tiny light in the distance.

Was that the light referred to so often by people experiencing near-death? It hardly seemed important. But then it was the only thing he could sense.

Or was it?

If the light was like a magnetic pole, lining him up with it, drawing him closer, then where was its analog?

John tried to rotate, to see behind him. Although he didn't sense any movement, the light left the center of his vision and moved off to the side.

The dark split away from him.

In the distance a great light appeared and swelled toward him.

In an instance John knew that this was the light described by so many. It pulled at him with a force that seemed both irresistible and compelling.

But if that was where he should be going, then what was this little light? He forced his awareness to rotate again.

It was still there, a little pinpoint of light. The pull it had on him was small and he could resist it without conscious will, but it begged for investigation, for his attention. Curiosity held him.

Concentrating, he found he could move toward it.

He reached his disembodied hand toward it.

His fingers cupped around the light and John was amazed by its warmth. By its love.

* * *

Caitlin could hear the siren of an ambulance.

They would be too late.

There was nothing they could do to save John now.

She didn't want to let these people take her either. John's knife lay a few feet away, its blade shone in the light of the vehicles surrounding her. Perhaps she should end it here. If she could reach it before they could stop her she could plunge it into her heart and free herself.

Like she had freed John.

Did she have the courage to end her own life when there was no hope left?

John had wanted her to live. He thought that eventually she would be freed, possibly with the help of his friend. Had he been just trying to give her some hope to keep her from total surrender?

What was left when all hope fled?

She reached toward the knife.

Warmth flowed through her.

It was like liquid love.

What? What was this? It was like the first time she and John had made love. They had shared every sensation through the translators until their identities had merged into a single individual. It was a sensation that was unsurpassed by anything she had ever known.

But then what was this? John was dead. She was alone with his cooling body. Why was she feeling him? She put her fingers back on his throat. No pulse. He was still dead.

She must be going mad.

"No Caitlin. I'm here."

"John?" If her emotions hadn't already tightened the muscles of her throat, she would have screamed. "How can this be? I felt you die."

"I know, but something is letting me hold on to you. It's some trait of the translator. I don't know why, but it's giving me an anchor I can hold to."

"Oh, God, John. I don't want to stay here without you."

"I know. I feel everything you feel. But the knife isn't the answer. There's another way."

"Another way? What?"

"Slip the translator off my neck and put it on. Then we'll give these people a surprise."

Caitlin looked up. Tears still blurred her vision, but she could see Romax and Holdren talking a few feet away. Neither faced her. A half dozen or so guards milled around in groups of twos and threes. They talked among themselves in hushed voices and moved from foot to foot as though the cold was getting to them.

Caitlin could no longer feel the cold.

She continued to sob, maintaining the ruse, as she slipped one hand under John's coat and shirt until her fingers closed about the oval shape of the translator. It was sticky with blood.

Pulling it out, she lifted his head gently from her lap to free the chain and then used both hands to drape it over her head.

Her movement drew Romax's attention. He watched her curiously, staring even, but made no move to stop her.

She unzipped her coat and dropped the oval inside her blouse against her bare skin. As the translator settled next to hers she felt the contact with John strengthened past all limits.

"That's good. Very good. I can feel everything you feel. It's almost as if we were sharing your body."

"I know. Bodies and minds. It's an incredible sensation. Now what?"

"The detonator, take it out of my pocket, then let me take control. Perhaps we can get you out of this yet."

"Even if we can't, just make sure they don't take me alive."

"I don't want you to die too, Caitlin."

"And I don't want to live without you."

"You have me now," he said.

"But if they take me they are sure to separate us. Would you stay here without me?"

"You know I wouldn't," John said.

"And I don't want to stay here without you. So either get me free, or let me die too."

John could feel her resolve. It was what she wanted and he could find no reason or will to talk her out of it. "All right, I'll keep us together, one way or another."

Without another word, John felt Caitlin sliding back, releasing control.

S/he felt the snow blow against his face and gazed up into Romax's eyes.

Romax's face darkened with sudden alarm, as if he had seen something he couldn't believe.

John kept their eyes on Romax's as he put their hand inside the corpse's pocket and closed their fingers on the detonator. With their thumb s/he toggled the selector to the "all" position and pressed the switch.

The night erupted with fire and thunder from a dozen locations.

The guards staggered under multiple crashing shock waves.

Holdren dove into the snow.

Only Romax kept his feet as he reached for a holstered weapon.

John snatched up the Ashley knife and lunged to their feet.

S/he closed on Romax as the man's hand emerged with a Berretta. John pounded the hilt of the knife into Romax's temple while grasping the gun with their other hand.

Romax's knees buckled.

John switched the knife to their left hand while transferring the gun to their right. S/he thumbed the safety and turned on the nearest guard as he rose, gun in hand.

S/he fired twice. The first bullet tore open the man's throat. Blood gushed from the wound. The second bullet dissolving the man's right eye in a spray of liquid. His body fell forward onto the snow as the stream of blood from his severed carotid artery changed into a slow seepage as his heart stopped beating.

Holdren was rising from the snow. John took two steps toward him and snap-kicked him in the jaw. The impact hurt more than it should have. Caitlin's body just didn't have the mass of John's and couldn't take the same level of contact. S/he shifted their aim to the next guard; the woman was kneeling at the front of the farther Humvee. John got off two more rounds while the woman fired once. Her shot missed. Their's didn't.

A man lunged at them from the side of the nearer Humvee. John spun on their left foot as the man passed like a bull passing the matador. As he passed, John drove their knife into the side of the man's throat. Twisting the blade, s/he yanked it clear, ripping open both carotid and jugular.

Clutching at his throat, the man fell to his knees.

Someone else fired from behind the farther Humvee. John dropped to the ground, rolled, and fired three rounds under the vehicle.

A woman went down screaming, her left leg spurting blood.

The last two guards were rising behind them. John raised the gun and fired, catching the nearer man high on the thigh and dropping him back to the ground.

The Berretta's slide locked open.

It should have had at least four more rounds. Romax must have fired it earlier.

Before s/he could stand, the last guard reached them. A burley fist closed on her knife hand and another closed around her throat.

S/he was jerked from the ground.

"You bitch! If they didn't insist on getting you alive I'd snap your neck."

John wrinkled their nose and dropped the empty Berretta. "You need to work on your manners and on your breath. Have you been eating horse shit or what?"

The guards eyes flared and his fingers tightened around John's throat.

John made a spear of their right hand and jabbed it into the man's abdomen.

The man's Kevlar vest blocked the thrust.

The man's grip tightened and John could see little glimmers of stars.

"Not again asshole," s/he said.

Locking the thumb knuckles of their right hand, John jabbed it into the man's left eye with all their strength.

It ruptured, spraying John with fluid.

The man screamed and staggered back, clutching at his destroyed eye.

John kicked him in the right knee. With a loud crunch the kneecap shattered and the man fell to the earth screaming even louder.

Something moved in the corner of John's vision and they ducked as a gleaming blade sliced through the air above them.

John scampered back a couple of feet to give them time to respond to the new threat.

It was Holdren.

He held his slender knife in his right hand and smiled.

"Well, well. The little bitch has grown teeth. Well, we'll see how you like the treatment I gave your boy friend. I can't wait to see the two of you strapped down, facing each other for the rest of your lives and never able to touch, to walk, to move."

As he spoke, Holdren moved closer. John backed slowly trying to reach a spot where s/he wouldn't have to worry about tripping over a body.

"You think you're such a man. You were great against me when I was already crippled. Let's see how you do against me now," John said.

Holdren's face wrinkled in confusion, but he lunged forward.

John sidestepped and sliced downward, opening a deep gash in the man's wrist.

"Damn you, bitch!"

"Watch your mouth, asshole. You should have let her go. She didn't want this trouble, this killing. Me, I'm going to enjoy carving you up for what you did to me and to her."

Holdren yanked a handkerchief from his back pocket and wrapped it around his wrist while maintaining distance from John's advance.

"You've gone crazy, woman. What the hell are you talking about?"

"I've been called a lot on things, but a woman is something new. What's the matter Holdren? Didn't you know the translators would let us merge?"

"Merge? What are you gibbering about, Maxwell?"

Holdren lunged again. John blocked the thrust with their knife and as they parted, s/he snapped a backhanded slash at Holdren's eyes.

It almost missed.

The back edge of the Ashley cut a gash just above Holdren's eyebrows. Bone shone in the gash until the welling blood darkened the wound.

Holdren screamed, more in anger than in pain.

"The name is Blalock. John Blalock. And I've come back to kill you Holdren."

"That's not possible. You're not even dead. How could you come back?"

Holdren wiped at the blood flowing into eyes with the back of his sleeve.

"Never under estimate a desperate woman, Holdren. She killed me while you were still gloating over your victory. Now it's my turn to gloat."

"No, it's not possible. You're crazy."

Half blind from the torrent of blood filling his eyes, Holdren launched himself at them.

John stepped easily out of the way and then backhanded the Ashley into Holdren's back, exactly between the sixth and seventh vertebra.

Holdren was limp even before he hit the ground.

Breathing heavily, John knelt and wiped the blood from the knife with the cuff of Holdren's pants.

The bright red and white lights of an approaching ambulance were flashing eerily through the snow. It was almost there.

John gazed around and found no immediate threats. The wounded guards were more concerned about their own fate than that of Caitlin's.

"I think you can handle it from here," he said as he relinquished control.

Caitlin flexed her blood soaked arms and stared about her as she consciously took control of her body. "You are amazing, John. What now?"

"You could probably use a couple of weapons." He indicated which would be the best ones. "And the bags I brought. There are a few items in there that you might still find useful."

"We, we might find useful."

"I stand corrected. Now lets get moving before someone else shows up. I've had enough killing."

"Me too."

She gathered the weapons John wanted and slung one of his bags over each of her shoulders. As she turned, she saw movement in the snow. Caitlin lowered the sights on the Uzi to cover Romax.

The man sat up, gazed past the barrel, and into her eyes. Then he turned his head and slowly surveyed the scene. "Holdren?"

"Dead or dying. Paralyzed definitely," Caitlin answered.

"Death was probably more than the bastard deserved. Go on, I won't try to stop you."

"But will you try to find us again?"

"Us?" he asked, but then he shook his head. "No, not me. Someone else maybe, but not me. I've lost my taste for working with men like Holdren."

"I understand." Caitlin stopped next to John's body, she gazed down at his calm face, finally peaceful in death.

"It seems wrong to leave your body here for them."

"It's just a body now, Caitlin. It's not something I can ever go back to. Dust to dust."

"Ashes to ashes. Yeah."

She bent down and closed his eyes. Her fingers stroked his still warm cheek before she stood.

Anger welled in her. It wasn't fair. It just wasn't fair.

Lights flashing, the ambulance pulled to a stop next to the water tower where the massive column of water was down to a slow flow.

Her teeth grated together as she brought up one of the Uzi. "No way, there's no fucking way I'm giving you up without a fight."

"It's useless. Forget it."

"No! Romax!" She moved the Uzi back to cover him. "Tell those men to get a litter over here and load John in the ambulance."

Romax briefly met her gaze, then rose and waved toward the approaching men.

"You two, bring the litter. This man needs assistance."

One medic went back to the ambulance and the other hurried to where Caitlin stood over John's body. He knelt down and made a cursory examination. A few seconds later he looked up. "There's no pulse."

The medic glanced around where at least three other people were moaning, screaming, and cursing in the night.

"Screw that," Caitlin said as she put the barrel of the Uzi in the man's face. "What's your name soldier?"

His face paled, "Spec Five Murphy, ma'am."

"Well, Murphy. You have a defibrillator. Use it!"

He nodded and shouted toward the ambulance, "Jerry, get the defib. Stat!"

Jerry was just pulling the litter from the back. He leaned it against the rear door and reached back inside. Removing a heavy metal case, he trotted through the snow toward them.

Spec Five Murphy opened John's jacket, pulled loose the Velcro closures on his vest, and then tugged it off him.

When Jerry dropped the case in the snow beside him, Murphy popped open the top and hit the programming button.

The defib's screen lit immediately and instructions appeared. Without stopping to read them, Murphy attached the sensors to John's chest and readied the paddles.

A moment passed before the defib completed its analysis and ordered shock treatment to begin. Murphy was ready. He placed the paddles against John's chest and yelled, "Clear!"

He triggered the unit and John's body lurched.

Murphy turned to study the defib's screen.

"It's not working. Tell him to give it up. You shouldn't be sticking around here," John transmitted.

"No, it will work. Hit him again!"

"It'll take just a moment ma'am. The unit recharges while it determines how much voltage to use for the next attempt."

"Just hurry it up, damn it!"

She turned to the second medic who was watching. "You, Jerry, he's going to need blood. Get what you need from the ambulance and get back here on the double. Move!"

Jerry lurched back as the Uzi rose.

Caitlin watched him for a second then knelt next to Murphy. "Come on, come on."

"It's ready. Clear."

Murphy held the paddles against John's chest and triggered them.

Again his torso lurched as the current coursed through him.

Murphy read the defib's screen and turned to Caitlin. She could she the answer to her unasked question in his eyes.

"No, charge it again."

"It doesn't recommend another attempt."

"I don't give a rat's ass what it recommends. Recharge it and shock him again."

Murphy bent over the defib and switched it to manual. "It'll take just a moment to recharge. I've set it at the maximum voltage."

"Caitlin, you're wasting time. We should go," John transmitted.

"No, not until everything has been tried."

"Caitlin, I don't mind. Really, I found you again. You even love me. That's enough. I can go."

"No you won't you son of a bitch! You aren't going anywhere until I'm sure."

"Clear," Murphy said.

"Wait!" Caitlin screamed.

He lurched back and stared up at her.

Caitlin tugged the chain to John's translator over her head.

"What are you doing?" John asked.

"What do you think? If this thing could help you stay here to join with me then it should be able to help you get back into your own body."

"But Caitlin. The shock from the defib could destroy it."

"Yeah, I suppose it could. But I'm willing to risk it. Are you?"

For a moment, John was silent. "To risk everything to be able to hold you in my arms again? Yes, I'd risk it."

Caitlin raised John's head and slipped the chain over his neck. She lowered his head back to the snow and quickly kissed his lips for luck.

"Are you still there John?"

"I'm still here, still inside you."

To Murphy Caitlin said, "Hit it!"

Murphy placed the paddles and triggered the discharge.

John's body convulsed.

Caitlin felt a great wind blow through her mind. In an instance, it was gone. It left behind an emptiness that chilled her soul.

What had she done? Had she lost him completely?

"John?"

No response.

She dropped to her knees in the snow beside him and started to cry. Reaching out she cradled his face in her hands.

A jolt went through her.

His body convulsed again and he coughed.

The defib beeped a steady pulse.

"My God. John, you're alive."

His eyes opened. "Damn, I'd have to be to hurt this bad. Sweet Jesus, I hurt."

She hugged him, then kissed his face tenderly. "But you're alive."

"Yeah, thanks, love. Look, I don't want to put a damper on my resurrection, but we still need to get out of here."

"Yes, you're right."

She released him and stood quickly.

Jerry was back with a liter of blood substitute and an IV.

"Jerry, you get him hooked up. Murphy, he has a gun shot to the knee and another in his lower side. Bandage them and then put him in the ambulance."

Murphy nodded and the two men stripped John's coat off him.

Caitlin turned. Romax was standing alone a few feet away. He'd been silent for the entire process.

"Did you mean what you said, about coming after us?"

He nodded weakly.

"If you go back on your word I'll kill you myself. Whatever you wanted out of us, it's too late. John released the files before he came here tonight. It's too late to stop them."

Romax glanced at John and found that he was looking up at him. "I suspected as much. He didn't seem the type to surrender."

"He's not."

"You better be going. Other's will be coming, I can delay them for awhile, but not forever."

"I understand."

When Murphy had the bandages in place, the medics put John onto the litter and lifted it between them.

Caitlin followed close behind until they reached the ambulance. "Put him in the back, then take whatever you need to help those others. I'm taking the ambulance."

"But ma'am, that's government property," Murphy said.

"This is still a democracy, isn't it? Well, I'm one of the government's employers. They'll get it back when I'm through with it."

Murphy eyed the Uzi, then motioned toward Jerry. Together they set the litter in the ambulance and secured it. Then Murphy removed two emergency kits and closed the back door.

"Ma'am, he's going to need a doctor," Murphy said.

"I know. I'll take care of it."

Without waiting for another response, Caitlin hurried around the side and got behind the wheel. The engine still idled smoothly and she shifted the transmission into gear.

As the ambulance started to roll, the massive gates to the compound slid back. For a moment, she thought they had taken too long. Then Romax stepped out of the guardhouse.

Caitlin lowered her window as she neared him.

"For what it's worth, I'm sorry about my part in all this. All this," he indicated the ruined landscape around them. "Wasn't suppose to happen. We thought we were doing the right thing."

"Yeah? Well heaven protect us from right-minded fools," Caitlin said and gunned the engine.

She turned right, toward the Navigator John had hidden.

"We'll have to ditch the ambulance," John transmitted.

"I know. Are you going to be able to walk?"

"No, but I have partial use of my right side. I can probably hop along if you support me."

"How bad are you? Will you make it without immediate surgery?"

"I think so. Just get us away from here and then we'll worry about my injuries." He coughed and broke into a strained laugh.

"What the hell are you laughing about?"

"I was just thinking of what I'm going to say to Gunny when I see him."

"What's that?"

"I'm going to tell him he was right that 'even heroes die.' But he's got to know that sometimes they have to die more than once."

EPILOGUE

The black Labrador splashed through the cold waters of Victoria Strait north of Vancouver until he reached the floating Frisbee. He gripped it gingerly in his teeth, then froze as a tall dorsal fin broke the water less than a hundred feet from him. He growled, deep and guttural as a second, larger fin joined the first.

"Bruno, leave the whales alone and bring me the Frisbee."

Bruno cocked his ears and turned to face Caitlin. His tail shook water droplets as it wagged furiously.

"Come on, Bruno. Fetch."

Bruno paused to cast one more growl over his shoulder as one dorsal disappeared and another took its place, then he raced back to shore.

Caitlin wore a cream-colored sundress of filmy cotton over her two piece swimsuit. She waited at the edge of the water, letting the water swirl around her bare feet until the dog reached her. Then she backed away, as he appeared ready to leap against her.

"No, Bruno. Down!"

Bruno sat on the rocky beach, and dropped the Frisbee at her feet. An expression of breathless anticipation lit his face.

John laughed as she bent for the Frisbee.

"What's so funny?"

"I think he's teasing you. He had no intention of jumping on you," John said.

John sat in a beach chair just above the high tide line.

"Yeah? Well I think you're just being anthropomorphic. Dogs don't have human reactions."

"Really? I don't think you've had enough experience with them to make that statement.

Caitlin flipped the Frisbee toward John and Bruno raced after it.

"Wait. Stop. Stay, Bruno, damnit," John cursed as Bruno leapt for the Frisbee just as it reached John.

The dog crashed into him, knocking him backwards, out of the chair and into the sand. John sputtered, cursed again, and spit sand out of his mouth.

"Ah man, now I smell like wet dog."

Caitlin laughed as she walked toward him.

John sat up and gave her a grimace. She ignored his attempted scorn and offered him a hand.

Their emotions mingled as they touched and she knew he wasn't angry.

"Hump, how is anyone ever going to stay sore at someone while they wear these things?"

She pulled him to his feet and then bent to pick up his walking stick. "They can't, or at least they can't fake it."

Bruno trotted back and dropped the Frisbee at Caitlin's feet. She scooped it up.

"That's what I mean. How can I ever go back to being the strong silent type when anytime I touch someone they know how I really feel," John took the cane and put some weight on it. He leaned down and brushed the mixture of sand and dirt from his faded jeans.

Bruno growled and his hackles rose. As John came to his feet, he followed Bruno's stare. Someone was walking up the beach toward them.

"Hey, isn't that Gunny?" John asked.

Caitlin focused on the man. "Can't tell. He's too far off."

"It's him. I'd recognize that walk anywhere. Bruno, relax!"

Bruno gave one more short growl, then accepted the command, and went back to staring at the toy.

Caitlin waved a hand toward Zim and then sailed the Frisbee down the beach. Bruno chased it and caught it on the fly twenty feet from Zim. Rather than returning to Caitlin, he trotted to Gunny and circled around him.

"Hey, Gunny. You're early. We weren't expecting you until next week," Caitlin yelled.

"Thought I'd surprise you," Zim's words sounded clear and soft in her head.

"Well, I'll be. You have a neuralphone."

"It's an early model from Intel. I pulled a few strings with an old friend to get one before they hit the market. They're trying to beat Sony to the Christmas rush."

Caitlin walked to meet him, taking her time so John could keep up. "I'm impressed. I thought no one could get a prototype out in eight months."

"It's amazing what can be done by throwing money at a target. Every electronic firm on the planet has been rushing to be the first to develop this technology. The government is still attempting to claim the patents, but three congressmen have introduced legislation to make the technology public domain."

Caitlin reached him and stopped. She'd been about to hug him. What was it going to be like? The only person she'd ever had full contact with was John. She didn't want to share that kind of intimacy with Zim. She had told him what it was like between the two of them. Would he be insulted if she didn't hug him now that he wore a translator?

"What's the matter?" Zim asked.

"I'm not sure what to expect. The translators can make a hug awfully intimate."

"So you've told me. Well, we can just shake. I've done that with a few of the guys from Intel and while it was a new experience, I wouldn't call it intimate." He held out a hand.

"No way I'm letting you off with just a handshake." Caitlin brushed his hand aside and wrapped her arms around his chest in a hug.

Their emotions mingled, telling them that their feelings toward the other was returned in kind.

"Wow," Zim transmitted.

"We both love you, Gunny. If you hadn't helped us we'd still have the government on our backs."

"Ah, you're not fooling me with that, Caitlin. I know you could have spread the blueprints over the Web just as well as I."

"Has anyone been sniffing around our trail?" John asked.

"No, not for about three months now. The last one was a reporter."

"Oh? Was he legitimate or a deep cover?"

"Hard to tell. He could have been legitimate. Lord knows his ugly face is on the box often enough."

Bruno stood against John, bracing his forelegs against John's chest and chomping the Frisbee in his teeth. He had to push Bruno down to keep from falling over.

"John, how's the therapy coming?" Zim asked.

"They finished the injections. The doc tells me that the nerve regeneration should be complete in another month or so. It'll be nice to be able to walk unassisted again."

"It's going to take a long time to build the muscles back, but the feeling has returned to my leg, and it burns like mad."

Caitlin put an arm around John and shook him lightly. "He's just being a baby about it. The doctors told him the nerves would activate slowly and that it would feel like when your foot has fallen asleep."

"Hey, who's telling this story?" John asked in mock anger.

Bruno dropped the Frisbee at Caitlin's feet, leapt back a ways, then barked.

"He's getting impatient. Throw it for him," John said.

"Throw it yourself. I'm talking with Gunny."

John leaned hard on his cane to pick up the Frisbee. Standing, he flipped the disc toward the water. Bruno burst after it.

"Gunny, could you bring another neuralphone and the encoder with you next trip?" John asked.

"Sure, but who's it for?"

John watched Bruno catch the Frisbee in a splash of sea foam. As Bruno ran back through the surf, Zim and Caitlin felt his intentions.

"You can't be serious," Zim said.

"I don't know. It would be interesting," Caitlin said.

THE END

About the Author

Richard Bamberg grew up in a small town in the heart of Alabama during the 60s. He started work as a logger and truck driver, entered the Air Force as a radio operator and did a little duty as a forward air control operator in a small Southeast Asian nation. After graduating from Texas Tech University, he returned to the Air Force as an electrical engineer where he spent most of his time at the Air Force Weapon's Lab and at the Tactical Air Warfare Center.

He currently lives with life partner, wife, and best friend - Joy in Huntsville, AL, where he works on the national missile defense system.

His writing leans toward thrillers with a touch of science fiction and horror. The Phoenix Egg is his fourth novel.

Also Available from The Invisible College Press:

City of Pillars, by Dominic Peloso
Tattoo of a Naked Lady, by Randy Everhard
Weiland, by Charles Brockden Brown
The Third Day, by Mark Graham
Leeward, by D. Edward Bradley
Cold in the Light, by Charles Gramlich
The Practical Surveyor, by Samuel Wyld
UFO Politics and the White House, by Larry W. Bryant
Utopian Reality, by Cathrine Simone
Phase Two, by C. Scott Littleton
Marsface, by R.M. Pala
Treatise on Mathematical Instruments, by John Robertson
The Rosicrucian Manuscripts, by Benedict J. Williamson
Proof of the Illuminati, by Seth Payson
Evilution, by Shaun Jeffrey
Axis Mundi Sum, by D.A. Smith
Diverse Druids, by Robert Baird

If you liked this novel, pick up some more ICP books online at:

http://www.invispress.com/

Printed in the United States
16699LVS00002B/319-321

9 781931 468152